West Winds
of Wyoming

Also by Caroline Fyffe

Where the Wind Blows
Before the Larkspur Blooms

West Winds of Wyoming

A Prairie Hearts Novel

Caroline
Fyffe

Montlake
Romance

Published by Montlake Romance, Seattle

www.apub.com

Amazon, the Amazon logo, and Montlake Romance are trademarks of Amazon, Inc., or its affiliates.

ISBN-13: 9781477825204
ISBN-10: 1477825207

Cover design by Anna Curtis

Library of Congress Control Number: 2014907539

Printed in the United States of America

*Dedicated to my wonderful husband, Michael,
whose love, support, encouragement (and brainstorming)
mean everything to me. Thank you from the bottom of my heart.*

PROLOGUE

Logan Meadows, Wyoming Territory, April 1882

$\mathscr{N}$ell Page tugged at the collar of her shirt, feeling her moist, prickly skin underneath. The mercantile was stuffy. Too warm for this blustery spring day. Meandering down the wide aisle, she marveled at the items on display. Everything from butter stamps to cherry pitters. *Who dreams up all these gadgets? And who would want to spend their hard-earned money on them?*

"Aren't you a sight for sore eyes." Maude Miller rounded the long pine counter and stopped at Nell's side. Maude had owned the mercantile for as long as Nell could remember. The woman resembled the apple-faced dolls Nell had seen once as a girl. A traveling Mexican merchant had shown her how he carved a face into a peeled apple, then left it in the sun for several months to dry. The finished product, leathery-soft brown and deeply wrinkled, had seemed so real. Nobody quite knew Maude's age, and she wasn't saying, but every time the two of them spoke, Nell couldn't help remembering those dolls.

The store owner slipped her feather duster into her apron pocket, handle first, so the plumes stuck out like the tail of a rooster. "Something special I can help you find?" Her eyes brightened. "That color would look pretty in your hair."

"Oh." Nell pulled her hand away from where it had strayed to touch a bolt of silky yellow ribbon. "I'm just browsing while I wait for Seth. He's over at the sheriff's office talking with Albert and Thom."

Maude's eyes widened. "There's no trouble out at your place, is there?"

"No." Things at the ranch were good. Least, good as could be expected. "I think my brother just gets lonely for male companionship. It's only been him and me since Ben passed."

Maude's face softened.

Nell glanced away, wishing she hadn't mentioned Ben. Maude probably remembered the funeral, and the spectacle Nell'd made of herself.

Uncomfortable, Nell picked up a twisted copper tube that looked like a knot. "What is this, anyway?"

"The newest innovation to—"

A menacing rumble of thunder cut off her answer.

Nell stepped closer to the window. Down the street, dark clouds swirled in the sky. "Storm's brewing and won't hold off for long. Seth better hurry. I don't fancy riding home through a downpour. I've seen too many trees charred by lightning."

The sun completely disappeared then and the room darkened even more, as did the whole of Main Street, casting an ominous premonition over Nell's soul. She pushed the feeling away and tried to smile. "Won't be long before the sky lets go."

"You're right," Maude said, joining her at the window. "Sure is deserted out there. Maybe you and Seth should stay in town and wait it out."

Nell waved off her disquiet, sorry she'd worried the old woman. "We'll be fine—fine and wet is all." She made a funny face and shrugged.

The timeworn wooden floorboards shook as the Wells Fargo stage rolled past the mercantile's plate-glass window toward the El Dorado Hotel.

Maude clapped her hands together. "Oh good. Here's the stage." She untied her apron, revealing an azure-blue prairie-style dress that was a mite too small for her portly frame. "Mind if I leave you alone for a moment while I fetch the merchandise I ordered?"

Nell didn't mind being alone in the store or out on a deserted prairie. As a matter of fact, she preferred solitude. No one yammering in her ear. No one telling her what to do. "I don't mind at all. But how about if I go with you, Mrs. Miller? Help you carry in your things."

Acutely aware of the men's denims, plaid shirt, and leather jacket she wore, Nell followed Maude out the door, pondering what dressing like a lady would feel like. A gust of wind whipped the hat hanging down her back, held secure by a twisted-leather stampede string. She didn't have time to wonder about silly things like that, not with chores to do and horses to be worked. Besides, she liked her life just fine.

By the time the stagecoach had settled and the horses stood quietly in their harnesses, the shotgun messenger was up top with the freight and the driver stood in front of the opened coach door. Maude and Nell crossed the street, a loud clap of thunder making them both duck. The strength of the wind practically pushed them back one step for every two forward.

Several other merchants had braved the wind to see what the stagecoach brought, and they formed a loose circle around the driver. Seth, along with Albert and Thom, watched from several doors down in front of the jail.

"Come out, sweetie," the driver coaxed. He put out his hands in supplication to someone inside the stage and smiled from behind a shaggy beard come alive by the wind. "No one here is gonna hurt ya." After several seconds, he dropped his hands and turned to the crowd. "Ain't no use. I can't get her out for the life of me."

"What's this? What's going on?" Maude asked. Nell followed close behind and rose up on tiptoe to peek into the window of the coach.

A young girl sat alone on the bench, a darling little ragamuffin no more than six or seven years old. Even in her disheveled state, she was a beauty. Her legs were tucked up underneath a calico dress and she gripped a crocheted doll in her hands.

Maude pushed past the driver. "Aw, she looks frightened to tears, Mr. Martin." Her voice softened to barely a whisper. "Where'd you get her?"

The child's eyes followed a pattern. They studied the door, moved to one window, then the other, before pausing on her doll, then back to the door. From there, she started all over again. She reminded Nell of a skittish weanling just taken from her mama.

Mr. Martin shook his head. "She boarded with an ol' woman in Denver. Coulda been her grandma."

Maude straightened up, alarmed. "What do you mean? Where is this woman?"

Mr. Martin waved his hand, put a finger to his lips. "Shush, ma'am." Maude pulled back, red-faced.

"She went to meet her maker yesterday." Mr. Martin spoke as quietly as he could over the growing storm. "The tyke won't say a thing 'cept her first name. *And* she's blind."

Maude placed her hand over her mouth. "Oh, my. That's horrible."

Nell stepped closer to the door. "Do you know anything about her?"

Mr. Martin hoisted a tan carpetbag that had been lowered from the roof and handed it over. "This was the woman's. Had a note pinned inside." He slid a folded scrap of paper from the pocket of his denims.

"May I see it?" Nell asked. By now, the prolonged activity at the stage had drawn Albert, Thom, and Seth down the street. One by one, they glanced inside the coach as Nell read the note aloud.

"Please deliver Maddie to Brenna Lane in Logan Meadows. The child is blind, so I appreciate you looking out for her. Thank you, Cora Baxter." Nell looked from face to face. "To Brenna Lane?" The widow already had three children of her own, plus a boy she'd taken in last year. *Is Brenna kin?*

"Do you know why she died?" Albert Preston asked. The lines on the sheriff's forehead bespoke his concern.

Mr. Martin shrugged. "She felt weak when she went to bed, didn't wake up the next day. Her grave's back at the Gold Bug stage stop."

Albert nodded as he took the note and carpetbag.

"Has the child eaten anything lately?" Nell asked. "She looks hungry. And more than a bit scared."

"Breakfast. I done the best I could for the scared little rabbit," the driver said. When Maude prepared to climb in for the child, Nell stopped her with a touch to her arm. "I'd like to try, Mrs. Miller. Do you mind?"

At first, she thought the shop owner would object, but then Maude drew back to make room. The child's dirty face, messy hair, and frightened eyes reminded Nell of her own childhood. Just her and Seth, no parents in sight. "Hello, Maddie," she said softly. "You've arrived in Logan Meadows. This is where Brenna Lane lives. Is she your aunt?" Another bolt of lightning ripped through the sky, lighting the dark interior of the coach.

The little girl—Maddie—swallowed and fear skittered across her face. She clutched her doll tight to her chest.

"Never you mind about that right now. I bet you're worn out from this rickety old coach." Worried about the growing storm, Nell inched in a little farther and stopped. "That sure is a pretty doll you have." She smiled even though the child couldn't see her. "I used to have one just like her when I was your age."

Are dreaming and owning two different things?

"Let's you and me go over to the Silky Hen and have a cup of hot cocoa. Then Hannah will fry you up some fat chicken drumsticks. Afterwards we'll march right over to Brenna Lane's house."

The child appeared uncertain. After a moment she nodded, lowering her legs to the floor, and reached out. When their fingers touched, another flash of unease moved through Nell, a warning of a coming storm that had nothing to do with the weather.

CHAPTER ONE

About six months later, September 1882

Tristan Charles Axelrose guided his mare under the wooden sign spanning the width of the narrow, wagon-tracked road. COTTON RANCH. This was the place. The outfit the sheriff of Logan Meadows had informed him was looking to hire. A good twenty-minute ride from town, across some of the prettiest country he'd seen in a while. The land was sparse of humans but thick with wildlife, foliage and trees.

He studied the homestead as he covered the distance, letting go a sigh at finally reaching his destination after all these months. The heaviness of his six-shooter pressed reassuringly on his thigh, but the guilt that was never far from his mind pricked his conscience. He rode into the deserted ranch yard, scattering a handful of chickens, and dismounted, hunger and anxiety twisting his gut. He gave his horse one short drink from the watering trough, walked a slow circle, then stopped.

A large barn dwarfed the rustic-looking ranch house. A sturdy, well-used round pen, as well as several good-sized corrals, filled a half acre of land, and several more outbuildings dotted the area. A few green plants in the back, halfway hidden by the house, must be a vegetable garden. Far beyond, in a pasture on the hill, a herd of horses grazed on blowing brown grass.

"Hello?" he hollered. "Anyone home?"

The creaking of the barn's loft door as it swung wide in the wind was the only answer.

"Hello," he called again, then waited. He didn't want to get shot for trespassing.

In its day, this ranch must have been a beautiful sight. He'd hoped to find employment closer to town, but he was fortunate to have heard about this possibility before someone else did. With any luck, the ranch hand job would still be open. What kind of people were Seth Cotton and his sister, Nell Page? Would they tolerate him bedding his tired mount down in their barn without permission? Or would they shoot first and ask questions later?

Five minutes ticked by. A tumbleweed half as tall as himself skittered across the dirt yard and wedged itself against the windmill between the porch and the barn.

Hell. He couldn't let his mare stand out here any longer. He'd ridden eight hours straight on this last leg and Georgia needed tending. The sight of her drooped head made his decision for him. He gave her one more short drink from the long, wooden water trough and started for the barn.

After pulling one of the double doors open, he stepped in cautiously and looked around. Stalls had been mucked recently and were bedded with clean straw. Three horses, interested in the newcomers, watched with pricked ears.

He flipped his reins through a hitching ring and had lifted his stirrup over his saddle when the low metallic click of a gun being cocked stopped him short.

"Drop your gun and turn around."

Habit kept him rooted. He didn't give up his gun to anyone.

"You deaf, mister?"

Indecision warred inside.

"Your choice. Prepare to meet your maker."

It was a woman's voice, but the hard, no-nonsense tone made him reconsider. Without turning, he unbuckled his gun belt and lowered it to the ground.

"Now turn around."

Palms up and forward, he turned. He didn't know what he'd been expecting, but it sure wasn't *her*. Just outside the doorway of the barn stood a woman dressed in men's clothing. With the sun to her back he couldn't see her face, but her tall, assertive stance told him she knew how to handle the gun she held, and would, without blinking an eye.

"What're you doing in my barn?" she asked.

"Waiting on you."

"Why?"

"Sheriff Preston sent me out. Said you were looking to hire. When I rode in, no one was home and my horse is worn out. Didn't think you'd mind me tending to her."

"Why should I believe you? You could have made that up, easy enough."

"I guess I could—but I didn't. In town there was a large, wolf-like dog sleeping in front of the sheriff's office when I arrived. I had to step over him to get inside. The building had a few charcoaled boards from a fire."

She shifted, her right side now obscure in the shadow of the barn door, her gun trained at his chest. Her face, what he could see of it, was red from the wind. That mess of curly blond hair and her lanky body were a lot to take in.

"That would be Thom Donovan's dog, Ivan." Her eyes darted to his horse and her features softened. She pulled a deep breath, then let the air out slowly. "What's your name?"

He'd already made his decision and he couldn't go back now.

"Well?"

If he wasn't going to be looking over his shoulder every day of his life, he'd best stick to his plan. Give the name he'd provided to the sheriff of Logan Meadows, the one he'd used to join the Union Army when he was just a kid so his pa couldn't find him and drag him home. "Charlie Rose."

"Rose?" Her brows arched. "You must get some teasing over that."

His pa had taught him rising to the bait was like sprinkling whiskey on flames, so he ignored her comment and gestured to his horse. "Do you mind?"

"Go on." She motioned with the barrel of her gun. Then she stepped closer and picked up his gun belt off the ground. Her actions said one thing, her eyes revealed another. She was frightened of him, but her gaze never wavered.

He unbuckled the back cinch and let it swing. Next, he undid the breast collar and drew the supple leather through Georgia's front legs, hooking the equipment over the saddle horn. Unlacing the front cinch, he glanced back at the woman to find her watching him. As he tucked the long leather cinch strap into the keep on the pommel he said, "You can relax, Mrs. Page. You have my gun."

He lifted the saddle and pad together from Georgia's sweaty back. Collecting the far stirrup and gear with his free hand, he draped them over the seat. Facing Nell Page, he waited for her to tell him where to put it.

"In there." She pointed. "You have any experience with cattle?" she asked as he strode toward the dark room.

"Yeah," he called as he set his rig on the saddle rack.

"How about young horses?"

Returning, he rested his hand on Georgia's hip. "Some. More than most."

She eased over to the sidewall. "How's Sheriff Preston doing?" *Another test.*

"Said Logan Meadows is a quiet place when I asked about settling. His deputy came in, an Irishman. Both were helpful in directing me out here. Said you had a brother named Seth."

That seemed to satisfy her. She slowly holstered her gun and came forward. She ran her hand down Georgia's left front leg. The mare was a replacement mount he'd bartered for en route here.

"Your mare's been used hard." Her tone was accusing.

It was a truth that didn't sit well with him, either. He'd been impatient to reach Logan Meadows, being months overdue.

She stepped back a few feet. "Well, go ahead and use anything you need in the tack room, then bed her down in a stall and feed her." "I appreciate that. Will your brother be back soon?" Her eyes narrowed instantly. "Maybe. Maybe not."

Not sure what to make of Nell Page's strange answer or suspicious nature, Charlie—it was simpler if he thought of himself that way— went back in the tack room and found a soft cloth. In a slow, circular motion, he rubbed Georgia's coat firmly as the woman watched. "Why do you want to know?" she asked finally. "It's important to me that I get the job." *More than you know.* "Well, relax. You're hired." "Just like that?" "Just like that."

A slight smile played around the corners of her mouth for the first time since he'd arrived, as if under different circumstances perhaps she might be used to teasing. He wouldn't have believed it after the cold reception she'd just given him.

She turned, then stopped and looked back. "When you're finished, you can throw your things in the bunkhouse and come inside. I'll rustle something up for supper."

At the mention of food, a small pain jabbed his empty stomach. His brief time in town hadn't given him a chance to eat a real meal, just a strip of jerky and a biscuit in the bar where he'd washed away the trail dust. A job was what he'd needed most, to enable him to settle in Logan Meadows. And now he had it. "Where's the bunkhouse?"

She tossed him a dry laugh as she strode out the door. "You're in it, Charlie Rose. Pick any stall that's empty."

Nell kicked the dirt and straw from the bottom of her boots before crossing the threshold. After lighting several lanterns in the shadowy interior, she rattled around the cluttered kitchen, now a bit puzzled about what to fix for supper since the new hand would be partaking. She clunked a skillet down on the top of the stove before opening the heavy iron door. Wadding up some old newspaper, she shoved it in and went in search of a match.

The image of the stranger in the barn brought a surge of anxiety to Nell's stomach, strong enough to slow her steps. Last week there'd been another stranger, another night, another inquiry. Up until *that* day she'd never been fearful of anything. Never worried about staying out at the ranch alone. Never had to check her back trail. She'd never feared anything—*or any person.* Her gun, and her fighting skills, made her as confident as any man.

Maybe not so true anymore.

If she were honest, she hadn't had a good night's sleep since the stranger with the hollow eyes had ridden into her yard. She'd heard him coming and went to the window, hoping it was Seth. The man dismounted but stayed by his horse, looking around.

Nell's feet had suddenly felt like boulders, and her mouth felt full of sand. She'd never had a visceral reaction to anyone like she'd had to that man. If the stranger hadn't already seen her, she might have pretended she wasn't home and hope he'd just ride on. But he had seen her in the window, and she'd been forced to go out to the porch. She'd dried her hands and quickly buckled her gun belt around her hips before stepping outside.

The height of the veranda had given her a small advantage. But even ten feet away she could see the obscurity lurking in the back of the stranger's eyes. Something odd. Something deadly. She shivered now, remembering how her heart had thumped painfully in her breast.

"Howdy," *he drawled, his voice deep and slow . . . and something else.* "Can you spare a meal?"

"Nope. The pantry's bare." *The lie slipped out easily, confidently, even though her insides were quaking.*

His nondescript face couldn't cover his displeasure. "You here alone?"

*"Others will be back shortly," she lied again, knowing she'd spill
a bushel of lies to get him off her land. "But I don't see how that's
any business of yours."*

*She felt, more than saw, a whispery shadow, like a gossamer drape
fluttering about him, making fear surge in her mouth, her heart.*

Death.

*He shrugged. "That's too bad about the food. It's been days
since I've had a good meal." He patted his stomach and smiled, but
his action did little to quell her suspicions. His gaze strayed to the
open door behind her.*

"Got nothing here for you."

He mounted and rode out without saying another word.

Nell snapped her thoughts back to the present, her breathing
rasping in her ears. She'd pondered on him for days, wondering
why he'd affected her so. She didn't understand.

Charlie Rose was nothing like that man. At first, when she'd
spotted him coming, she'd thought he was the stranger returning. Determined not to be caught unprepared this time, she'd
grabbed her gun and ducked behind the house, intending to take
him by surprise. She'd stayed hidden until she'd detected him
going into the barn, then snuck up behind. A hot flood of relief
had descended when he'd turned around and his vivid blue eyes
held only caution.

Hiring Charlie Rose had been a quick decision, one based on
intuition more than fact. His presence had actually drawn her in,
made her feel safer than before he'd arrived. *We had to hire someone. Seth is working himself to exhaustion. The two of us can only
do so much.*

But now, she'd better think of something decent to fix or their
new hand just might ride right back out. She pushed away several
strands of hair that had dropped over her eyes. Supper didn't have
to be fancy. Just because he was a handsome cuss, with eyes blue
as a cloudless sky, didn't mean she should care what he thought
about her cooking skills.

Biscuits, eggs, potatoes, and green beans fresh picked this morning. Tonight they'd have breakfast for supper. Food was food. Just something to keep you going. She dumped several large potatoes into the sink and pumped in water to wash them. Adding more water into another pot to steam the beans, she placed the pot on the stove.

The sound of horse hooves in the yard and Dog's familiar bark jolted her.

Seth.

A minute later, the kitchen door opened and her brother came in, looking worn-out and old for his twenty-five years. He tossed his hat on the sideboard and kicked off his boots into a pile of old ones.

Nell dried her hands and hurried over. She slipped into Seth's waiting arms. "Welcome home."

"It's darn good to be here, Nellie girl," he uttered against the side of her head. After several good squeezes, he stepped away.

"You see the new man?"

"Yeah. He came out and took my horse. Imagine that. I think I could get used to treatment like that."

"Well, you're gonna get used to it. I don't want to hear a word about us not being able to afford him."

Seth, older by five years, stretched his back with a grimace. A hard, racking cough made him take a handkerchief out of his pocket and cover his mouth. He'd been coughing for months. She'd mentioned his condition several times to Doc Thorn, but the physician had said he couldn't do a thing for her brother unless Seth actually came in to see him.

"I was hoping that cough would be long gone by the time you got home."

He nodded. "It's just hanging on to beleaguer me."

She assessed her brother with critical eyes. The army contract for horses was the only thing keeping the ranch alive. The compensation wasn't much, especially since a new recession seemed to be looming. Just three years past, the country had climbed out of the last depression, and the outlook had been brighter—for a while. But not now. The army money made the mortgage payment, on which they were a month behind.

The place was too much for just the two of them, and they didn't have the funds to hire the hands needed to get the ranch up and running the way they'd like—the way they had before Ben had died. Charlie Rose was the first help they'd had in almost a year.

"Were you gimping when you came in?" She took in her brother's appearance. He'd lost a few pounds since riding out over a month ago with twenty-five head of horses. His face, partially covered by a week-old beard, was darkly tanned and weathered. His mouth, a grim hard line. Hair in desperate need of cutting, tangled in sandy-brown knots.

"No. Just tired and movin' slow."

She went around and took hold of his shoulders, massaging firmly. "Remind me to cut this scraggly hair." He grunted, but then her efforts drew a long, appreciative sigh from him. Ever since she was a little girl, she'd been tagging along after Seth, her big brother and guardian. She liked rubbing his shoulders. It was something she could do for him. "What did Captain Lewis think of the horses?" she asked.

"Liked every single one."

"You're overdue getting home, which means the captain was late meeting up again. He must think this ranch runs itself. I swear." Bitterness pooled inside. Several months ago, when Seth had delivered a string of mounts for Fort McKinney, Captain Lewis didn't show up to the agreed meeting spot for a month. Irked her to no end. As if Seth had nothing better to do but hang around twiddling his thumbs.

She worked his shoulders hard, then his back and neck. "All those extra days sleeping on the ground couldn't have been good for you."

"Hush, Nell, you worry too much. How were things here? You manage all right?"

At the simple questions, her hands stilled. She'd been wondering if she should tell Seth about the visitor, about how he'd made her feel. If she did, her brother wouldn't feel comfortable leaving her alone. Digging for her resolve, she said, "Same as always. Horses and cattle. Coyotes and hawks—and of course my beloved books."

Seth turned around and pointed her back to the sink with a gentle nudge. Knowing he must be hungry after the long ride, she hurried back and took up where she'd left off.

"Everything went as planned. They want fifteen more in three months."

"What?" She spun to face him, knife in one hand and potato in the other. She ignored the water dripping onto the floor. "We don't have that many."

"I know. We'll have to see if Chase has a few to sell."

"Chase Logan? We can't afford to buy any of his stock just to resell them to the army." At this point, they were clear of any debt besides the mortgage. She didn't plan to take on more.

"I told you to hush. You wear me out. I'll figure it out when the time comes." A string of coughing made him turn away.

A rapping on wood interrupted the conversation.

"Come in," Seth called.

The new man pulled open the door. He wiped his boots on the tattered doormat, glanced at the pile of old boots behind the door, and then to Seth's stockinged feet. "You want me to take these off?"

His voice, deep and all too sensual, sent a ripple of awareness through Nell. She hadn't noticed that before. He'd removed his hat and held the black Stetson in his hands. He must have washed in the trough because the hair around his face was damp.

Nell laughed ruefully. "Just take a peek at the rest of the room. That should answer your question." Heat flushed her face when she realized just how cluttered she'd let the place become. It seemed the kitchen was a catchall for everything. *The livestock are what matter. The horses and cattle. Everything else is just extra.* "I think I'd keep 'em on if I were you. Never know what might bite you."

"Nell," Seth chided. "You can put your hat there, Charlie." He gestured to the sideboard, where several hats rested, rims up. "Haven't had time to put the hat rack back up after the blasted thing came loose and fell off the wall."

Charlie put his hat down with an easy, graceful movement that made Nell jerk her gaze away.

"Come and set yourself down." Seth gestured for the new man to follow. Nell listened as the two went into the living room, knowing her brother would plop down in his favorite leather chair by the window and be asleep in minutes. "Nell will have something for us to eat—in, ah, a bit. I hope before midnight. Don't know what it might be, but I don't ask questions if I want her to keep cooking for me."

"It'll be before midnight, Seth," she called back. "Won't be fancy, but it'll be hot. There's a newspaper from last week. The additions on the schoolhouse are finished and they're having an open house this Saturday before the term starts. And to meet Mr. Hutton, the new schoolteacher. There's also a raffle fundraiser. Be sure to read the article."

The sound of Seth's amused chuckle warmed her insides. The days had been long and lonely without him here.

"Now, why would I need to read the story, Nell, since you just told me the whole thing?" She overheard him mumble something to the new hand, then cough for several long seconds.

"What a fine collection of books," Charlie Rose said to her brother. Her mind's eye envisioned him roaming over the bookcase and all her beloved covers, the pages worn thin from constant use. Stories and worlds to get lost in. His exclamations over them made her think he was also a lover of the written word.

She cracked the last of nine eggs into a mixing bowl. She added two cupped palmfuls of water and whipped them with a fork. "What brings you to Logan Meadows, Mr. Rose?" she called over her shoulder.

"Just looked like a nice place to grow some roots."

She jerked, almost dropping the bowl. His deep voice came from close behind her. Mr. Rose leaped forward and caught the eggs before they spilled.

"Not so tough without your gun?" Amusement flickered in his eyes when they met hers. "Thought as much." She could tell he was older than Seth by a handful of years, but his boyish demeanor made him seem younger.

Embarrassed that he had indeed startled her, she gritted out through a tight jaw, "You didn't *spook* me." Swallowing, she wet her suddenly dry throat. Without his hat, and close up, Charlie Rose was handsome. His nut-brown hair—in need of a trim—was thick and inviting. A scar below his left eye and above his cheekbone was relatively new, with traces still visible where he'd gotten the injury stitched. He had a straight nose and strong jaw. She would have stepped away if the kitchen counter wasn't already biting into her back.

Realizing she'd been staring, she jerked her gaze from his. "The bowl just slipped. Now give me some room or this knife might find itself stuck in your belly."

That brought him up short. His smile vanished and he took a healthy step back. "Mind if I help myself to a glass of water?"

He still held the ceramic bowl in his large hands, as if cooking was second nature to him. She snatched it back, making the eggs slosh dangerously close to the rim. "Not at all."

Cautiously, as if he was afraid he'd spook her again, he took a glass from the open shelf and pumped some water. "Thank you."

His tone, gentle now, lacked the earlier playfulness. She berated herself for the stupid comment about the knife. The blunder had just slipped out when she found herself pinned back against the counter.

That's not the only reason, Nell. Admit it. You're attracted to him.

Charlie Rose was the first man to turn her head since Ben had died. The timbre of his voice was pure comfort and safety. The honesty, deep in his eyes, true. But more, something about him reached out to the woman in her. Made her breath catch in the back of her throat. *That* made her feel like a traitor to Ben. For two long years since her husband's death, she'd felt empty and void—even a little lost.

Agitated, she quickly filled another glass with water and handed it to Charlie Rose. She pushed every notion from her mind except what she was making for dinner. "Please take this to Seth while I set the table. Supper will be ready shortly."

CHAPTER TWO

*A*lone in the shadowy barn, Charlie glanced in on his sorrel mare as she munched the hay he'd tossed her before going in for supper. Georgia raised her head and looked at him. "No, girl, not tonight. You've earned some time off. A lot of time, as a matter of fact." Uninterested in his words, the horse blew hay dust from her nostrils before returning to the sweet-smelling alfalfa at her feet.

Restless, Charlie crossed over to the stalls on the far side of the barn. One stout mare was recuperating from an injury on her pastern. A chestnut-and-white paint horse and a black gelding occupied the other stalls.

Concentrating on his work duties would be difficult now that he was actually here in Logan Meadows. All he wanted to do was ride back into town and retrieve Maddie. Hold her in his arms. Kiss her sweet face.

"When will you get to Logan Meadows, Pa?" she asked as he put her on the stage. *"I don't want to go without you. I'm scared."*

"Don't be frightened, little darlin'," he replied. "Miss Baxter will take good care of you. This town's not safe for you anymore."

Today in Logan Meadows he'd gotten a glimpse of her from down the street. Just a quick look, but that one vision was like a lifeline to a dying man. It had taken every ounce of his willpower not to bolt across the dusty street where she walked holding an older girl's hand and swoop her into a hug. She and her friend had been chatting and laughing, and although the scene brought him peace that his daughter was indeed safe, a part of him, a selfish part, hurt because she seemed to be doing so well without him.

"Taking Maddie to Logan Meadows is for the best, Mr. Axelrose," Miss Baxter assured him. *"I'll get her there safe and then she can live with my niece, Brenna Lane, and me until you arrive. Then if you're willing, you and Brenna can start courting. She's kind and smart—and pretty. A man would be hard pressed to find a wife as good as her. And you know how much Maddie wants a new ma, and sisters and brothers. I can't think of a more perfect solution to both your problems."*

When he didn't say anything she took hold of his arm and gave it a good shake. "You listen to me. This town ain't fit for cockroaches anymore, let alone decent folks like you and me. And now this trouble between you and Grover Galante. He'll not let you be until he kills you. Then where will that leave your little girl? With an old woman, living in a den of thieves? There's no one else here to care for a blind child after I die, and you know it. I've already sold anything I had of value that won't fit in a carpetbag. I'm ready anytime you want us to go."

The old woman's idea had been his only choice. His only way to get Maddie out of town quickly. After Miss Baxter and Maddie had departed on the stage—boarding in the neighboring town to throw off Galante's suspicions—he'd breathed a sigh of relief. With his daughter out of harm's way, he'd been able to concentrate on selling the gunsmith shop. But finding a buyer had taken longer than expected, and so had planning his departure without leaving any traces or information about where he'd gone—all while staying out of Galante's way. He fingered the healing scar on his cheek, remembering the fight the one time when he hadn't.

Once he departed Wilsonville he'd spent a month heading in the opposite direction of Logan Meadows, and then doubled back over difficult terrain, just in case Galante trailed him. The man's vengeance ran deep, though in some ways, Charlie didn't blame him.

Now he was here, about to start a new life, one where he wouldn't have to be worried for his daughter's well-being.

A job had been his first concern, since the money he'd gotten for the sale of the shop was going to be spread thin between finding a suitable place for them to live and having the means to hire a tutor, a woman he'd corresponded with who could teach Maddie to read Braille. And there was Miss Baxter. She'd fulfilled her promise by delivering his daughter safely to Logan Meadows. He'd reward her well for taking care of his little one.

Tired, he pulled up an old stool and sat. He needed to go slowly before barging into his daughter's life without warning. Make sure he hadn't been followed. Make sure he wasn't bringing danger down upon her—or anyone else. He'd not pull the rug from beneath Maddie's feet again. He'd not disrupt her life until he was confident that coming back into her life was best for her, and safe.

The barn door rattled as someone knocked.

He stood. "Come in."

Nell pulled the door open and approached with full arms. The handle of a lantern was draped across one forearm, the golden light enveloping her as she came forward. "I meant to give you these before you retired tonight." She set the blankets on the bench.

A peace offering. An amends for the knife comment.

He smiled. "Thank you, but you needn't have bothered. I have my bedroll."

She hung the lantern from a nail on the wall and went over to check her horses. "The temperature's been dropping pretty good. You may need the extra bedding. The barn can be drafty if the wind picks up."

"In that case, I appreciate the gesture. Oh, and thanks for supper. It was good."

She nodded and turned to go, but he found himself wanting her to stay. He didn't know why. "You planning on going into town for the school open house?"

The lamplight reflected the questions in Nell's eyes, stirring him in a way he hadn't felt since the snowy day he'd met Annie outside the Wilsonville mercantile. Walking ahead of him with another woman, Annie had slipped on the ice and he caught her before she fell. When she'd looked up into his face and smiled, his whole world tilted. Since that day until the accident, it was Annie who'd filled his life with happiness and love.

"In Logan Meadows?"

He nodded when her question pulled him out of his reverie. He supposed it was an odd thing for a stranger about town to ask. "Yeah. Earlier, just seemed you were interested in the article in the paper. Thought you might actually go."

She nodded. "We may live out of town but we're still part of the community. If we get the work done, we should. You willing?"

He shrugged. "Sure. You're the boss." He'd use it as a way to check on Maddie again. See how she was faring. Maddie, his little ragamuffin, who'd been hounding him for a ma for the past year. *"I'll be good, Pa. Even though I can't see doesn't mean I'm helpless. I'll make a new ma love me."* She'd put her hand on his cheek. *"I want a ma more than anything else in the world."*

Nell went to the stall of the injured horse and opened the gate. The mare took a wary step back, but Nell placed her hand on the horse's forehead, between her eyes. The animal relaxed. Moving to her shoulder, Nell slid her hand down the mare's leg and picked it up. The horse stood completely still, even without a halter. Charlie was impressed.

"What happened to her?"

"Caught her foot in the fence." She probed the inside sole of the horse's hoof with her fingers, then pushed firmly with her thumbs. The horse didn't seem to notice. "She nearly bled to death before we found her. It's been a long recovery. She'll never be a saddle horse again, but she'll make a good broodmare."

Nell held her hand over the convex-shaped hoof, probably checking for undue heat. Presumably satisfied, she set the mare's leg back down, the hoof disappearing in the thick bedding of straw. Nell came out and secured the stall, then started for the barn door.

"We rise at four-thirty. I'll have porridge, eggs, and coffee in the house after that. You're welcome to come in and make yourself at home. We ride out around five."

He followed her out into the yard. "What will we be doing tomorrow, Mrs. Page?"

"Ranching," she tossed over her shoulder as she walked. "There's a group of three-year-olds running in the north country we need to bring in. Then start breaking them to sell to the army. You can use the black gelding while your horse rests."

She stopped and turned around. The sun was completely gone and the moon had yet to rise. The temperature had dropped since he'd walked back from supper.

"Nell," she said then.

A warm feeling took him by surprise. He'd been looking over his shoulder for so long, it'd been a while since he'd felt a connection with anyone. "Thank you. And you just call me Charlie—or big dumb ox, if you'd like." That got a small chuckle out of her. "I'll answer to just about anything."

She ambled away without another word, but he thought he heard a softly spoken, "Good night, Charlie," come drifting back.

Back in the house, Seth had already turned in. Nell could hear him coughing all the way from his upstairs bedroom. Antsy, she went about cleaning the kitchen in the dim light. She washed the supper plates, dried them, and put them away.

The disarray closed in on her.

She glanced around. Nothing in the room gave her peace. When she went to the window, Dog, their russet-colored, mixed-breed pal, looked up in question from his spot by the front door. Up until two years ago she'd taken pride in the house. The place was old, and furnished with ramshackle furniture, but it was theirs. Hers, Seth's and Ben's.

They'd had such dreams back then. Dreams to breed hundreds of horses and cattle. Make a mark in Wyoming. Ben had been ranching here for Clarkston Jones, the original owner, when the rancher hired her and Seth. Nell had been only a girl, so her jobs were collecting eggs, keeping the garden, and sweeping the barn. Paid her two bits a week. A year later, Jones got sick. He was a kindly man, and with no kin to his name, he'd sold the rundown ranch to Ben and Seth lock, stock, and barrel before he died, for ten dollars, enough to pay for a proper burial at the cemetery in town. All they had to do was make the monthly mortgage.

Could a decade really have passed? Seemed like yesterday that she'd been ten, running wild and free across the lands, answering only to her brother, and once in a while to his friend and partner, Ben Page.

At first, she was just a pest to Ben, who was a year older than Seth. But the years passed and she grew up. They were best friends for a while and finally they'd fallen in love and gotten married, much to Seth's shock. To her, their love was a natural progression, and one that felt right.

And then Ben took ill. They hadn't thought it serious until his fever spiked, but by that time it was too late. After his death, the Cotton Ranch had gone from a dream to an endless cycle of exertion with no end. She treasured the horses and cattle, but the work involved was driving Seth to an early grave. Nothing was worth losing him, too. But now, with the payment from the last delivery of horses, they could afford to pay Charlie Rose—for a while, at least.

Ben's grave was down by the river, in the exact spot they'd first kissed. The thought of him lying cold in that grave always gave her the need to move, do something, keep her hands busy.

She usually hurried out and jumped on the back of a horse—night or day—and galloped out to see him, be near him. Now, since the evil-looking stranger had showed up at her door, the thought of darkness caused a niggle of fear to skitter down her spine.

No. Whoever that stranger was, he wouldn't come back here. Not after the reception she'd given him. Still, there was something about his eyes, and the way they'd studied her, that made her feel uncomfortable even now.

But Charlie Rose was in the barn. And Seth was home. Her heart slowed and she took a deep breath. Charlie had seemed to appear out of nowhere, just when they needed him most. It might be crazy to feel this way about someone she'd just met, but whenever he was near everything felt calm, at peace. As if the endless days of toil just might be well worth the effort after all.

Taking the broom from behind the door, she began corralling the day's dust that had been tracked in.

"Thought I heard some stirrings down here." Seth came into the room, wearing his denims and the top to his long johns. He took the broom from her hands. "Go to bed, Nell. I'll help you with this in the morning."

Bothered with thoughts of Ben, and now Charlie and her conflicting feelings toward the new hand, she knew it would be hours before she could fall asleep. "What'd ya think of him?"

"Who? Charlie Rose?"

"Who else?"

"Seems honest," Seth said. "Looks like a hard worker. We'll know in a day or two. On a ranch like this you can't hide lazy."

She laughed, took the broom back and swept the dust carefully into a small pile, then went for the dustpan. "No, you sure can't." Bending, she held the dustpan to the floor as Seth swept the grime in. "I just hope he pays for the food he'll eat. That fella last year cost us more than we gained."

"There you go again, worrying over things that haven't happened yet. We'll cross that bridge when—and *if*—we get there."

Nell smiled, appreciating Seth's optimism. Her brother only saw the good in people—which was nice, but not realistic. "If you say so." Letting her expectations of Charlie grow so large was dangerous. Then the only way to go was down. To be disappointed. His face appeared in her thoughts and her face heated. Perhaps it was already too late for caution.

CHAPTER THREE

$\mathcal{B}$renna Lane hurried down the narrow road from her modest home on Oak Street, her basket of mending swinging on her arm. Penny, her eldest, was watching the children, who were now dressed and fed and ready to enjoy one of their last free days before the school started.

Brenna crossed the wooden bridge over Shady Creek, then smiled and waved at Albert Preston and Thom Donovan sitting inside the sheriff's office drinking coffee. As she passed the Bright Nugget Saloon, she held her hand over her nose to ward off the offensive smell that wafted through the open doors, then stopped in front of the bank to straighten her bonnet and smooth her dress.

Bolstering her nerves, she cautiously stepped inside, not wanting to draw attention to herself. Frank Lloyd, the owner of the bank, was a kind man; she just wasn't accustomed to fraternizing with the upper crust of Logan Meadows's society.

Inside the foyer—blessedly empty of customers—long green drapes decorated the windows, and the walls were enclosed in shiny oak siding. Brenna took a minute to check her reflection in the gold-leaf mirror that hung on one sidewall, then studied a lovely painting of an eight-point stag surrounded by several does in a field of snow. She'd overheard others talking how, over the years, Mr. Lloyd had improved the bank, adding this item or that. Last year, when the Union Pacific had requested the businesses spruce themselves up in competition for the new railway, he'd brought in the small but impressive chandelier all the way from Boston. The crystal orbs reflected the light that streamed through the spotless glass windows, making the whole lobby shine so beautifully that it resembled a lovely hotel or restaurant. But Mr. Lloyd hadn't stopped there. He'd also added three handcrafted maple chairs that now sat along the front window.

The bank had been the talk of the town, but Brenna'd been too shy to come in without a valid reason. Today, though, she had the best reason of all. Business with the owner.

She'd entered so quietly the teller had yet to notice her. Head buried in a ledger, he worked away, mumbling unintelligible words beneath his breath.

Approaching the counter, she stopped and waited.

He looked up. "Hello, ma'am. May I help you?"

"Good day," Brenna said, trying not to sound nervous. This was not only her first visit inside the bank; it was also her first mending job for Mr. Lloyd. If things went well, who knew where his business might lead. "Is Mr. Lloyd available?"

He stood. "Let me go see." With that, the young man was gone.

Brenna went to the window. She waved at Maude, who was on her way to the mercantile on the opposite side of the street. A wagon rolled past.

Brenna took another quick glance around, marveling that she was finally standing in the bank, a place she'd wanted to see for a long time. Last week, Mr. Lloyd had spotted her on the boardwalk and asked her to do some mending for him. She'd been surprised, but pleased beyond measure.

Footsteps sounded. "Mrs. Lane. This is an unexpected pleasure."

The exuberant voice almost made her drop her basket. Surprised, she looked into the banker's cheerful face. The teller went back to his stool and picked up his pencil.

"Hello, Mr. Lloyd. I have your things ready."

"Already? You work quickly. I wasn't expecting them until next week."

The unanticipated compliment brought heat into her face. Another kind citizen of Logan Meadows looking out for her family's good. It was truly heartwarming. She took his shirts and trousers from her basket and carefully transferred the neatly folded items to his hands. "Here you are. Please let me know if they are done to your specifications."

Well, that was a silly thing to say. All he'd asked her to do was stitch up a loose seam or two, tighten some buttons, and mend a couple of moth holes.

"Yes, I will. I'm sure they're fine." He set the garments on the counter. "Now, how much do I owe you for your fine and prompt work?"

She swallowed. "Twenty-five cents."

"That's a steal." He fished in his pocket and produced the money. He counted the coins into her hand, their heaviness almost making her giddy with happiness. Her business had steadily picked up since the building of the train depot. A true blessing, to be sure. She now had several regular sewing and stitching customers, and when the laundry shop got too busy, Tap Ling hired her to do the mending that he couldn't get to in a timely fashion. And, of course, Hannah still had her baking for the restaurant. That alone brought in two whole dollars a week. She was finally making ends meet on her own without handouts—and the reality of that felt good.

"There you are," Mr. Lloyd said. "I can't thank you enough. And, since I talked to you last, I've found several more things that I could wear if I'd just have them fixed. Waste not, want not, my mother used to tell me." The tall, middle-aged banker grinned. His dark-blond hair was neatly parted and carefully combed as any proper gentleman's should be. "Us bankers like to keep the money we have. Would you mind if I dropped the items by your house tomorrow after I close up here?"

Pleasure warmed her insides. The drizzle of business had turned into a rainstorm, all in a good way, of course. "That will be fine, Mr. Lloyd. If no one is there to receive them, just leave them on the small table I have on my porch. They'll be perfectly safe."

"That I will. Now I'll let you get back to work."

After Mr. Lloyd had returned to his office, and before the teller noticed, Brenna fished in her basket for the three fresh oatmeal cookies she'd wrapped up before leaving home. She set them on the front windowsill where they wouldn't be discovered right away. Since her circumstances had taken a turn for the better, she felt a need to do something nice for others. Repay the kindly citizens who'd so generously taken care of her and her brood when they couldn't on their own.

One kind deed a day. For anyone. Could be a close friend, a total stranger—sometimes even an animal. Or, on some occasions, when the day was drawing to a close and she hadn't been able to get to town, her kind deed went to a tree or a flower—which were also living entities—by watering or clearing away debris so they could breathe easy. She was up to kind deed forty-nine and the little clandestine actions were often the topic of whispered conversations as people tried to figure out who was behind them. She kept a small notebook tucked away under her mattress in which she listed her deeds. When she was feeling discouraged or overwhelmed, she'd pull out the journal and read a few pages. The words had the power to lift her heart every time.

Happy she'd once again been successful at not being caught, she turned in an exuberant half circle, left the bank—so joyful inside she felt as if she were walking on air—and bumped straight into another person with a loud *woomph.*

"Easy there."

Strong arms reached out to steady her and her basket as she struggled to regain her balance. She caught sight of a brown satchel tumbling to the ground and papers flying everywhere.

Mr. Hutton! The new schoolteacher. Realizing she was gaping into his startled hazel eyes, she snapped her mouth closed.

They'd met last week in the mercantile. He was new and single—but stern and perhaps a bit unapproachable. She recalled being impressed by his grammar and manners. Having been raised by a dirt-poor, illiterate father, Brenna held book learning in the highest esteem. She preached to her children every chance she got that a sound education would open doors and enable them to achieve anything they set their sights on. The well-educated Mr. Hutton had come to Logan Meadows highly recommended, and the town was thrilled, though a bit baffled, that he'd accepted their modest offer.

"Mr. Hutton. I'm so sorry." No sooner had she gotten the last word out than he leaped into action, collecting the white sheets that flittered about on the boardwalk.

Following suit, she bent quickly and gathered the papers within her reach. The breeze, not helping at all, kicked up, and papers fluttered here and there, down the boardwalk faster than she could move. Chuckles and laughter reached her ears as the scene gathered the attention of a few townsfolk.

Embarrassment burned Brenna's cheeks. Finally all the papers—excluding one—were back in their rightful place inside Mr. Hutton's brown satchel. The one exception, a cream-colored, official-looking document, had sailed out into the street on a puff of wind and landed squarely on a pile of fresh horse manure. A large green stain quickly seeped through.

With a grimace, the none-too-tall teacher stepped down into the road and carefully plucked the paper from the pile of horse droppings, holding it between his thumb and forefinger.

Brenna covered her mouth with one hand. "Oh, no."

Mr. Hutton blew a tawny-brown hunk of hair out of his eyes, but it flopped back into his vision. "No harm done, Mrs. Lane." His tone said otherwise.

Brenna was shocked he remembered her name. Everything about his disheveled state resembled a lost little boy, except his white-knuckled grasp on the handle of his satchel, and in the other hand, the soiled paper.

Something had to be done. Before he had a chance to step back, Brenna reached up and brushed his hair back so he could see. "There." She smiled. "Does that help?"

A burst of laughter made her snatch back her hand and pivot.

Dwight Hoskins sat astride his roan horse, his hat pushed up on his forehead as if to get a better view. Huskier than he'd been when he'd moved out of Logan Meadows in disgrace last year, he still carried a bullying light in his eyes. "That's the sweetest picture I've ever seen, if I do say so myself."

Brenna stiffened. "Be quiet, Dwight Hoskins. Nobody asked you."

Mr. Hutton's face blanched, then a stain of red slowly crept up his neck and onto his face.

How could she have done something so stupid? Why hadn't she watched where she was going? School was getting ready to start and Penny was already in a dither about the new teacher from Pennsylvania. The rumor was, he was strict. And hard. Penny wanted to be a teacher herself, and took her studies seriously. She'd be mortified if she knew what her mother had just done.

With a malevolent laugh, Dwight urged his horse forward, leaving her feeling conspicuous and wondering if there was a way of making this better—for her children's sake.

Brenna cleared her throat. "I'm so sorry, Mr. Hutton. I can't believe I just did that. Can I make it up to you?" She gestured to the yucky paper. "I'd be so grateful if you'd let me take that sheet and try to remove the, er, ah—soiled parts." She couldn't make herself say *manure* in front of such a sophisticated gentleman. "I'm a seamstress and have experience removing stains." That was stretching the truth just a tiny bit, but she was sure she'd be able to clean his paper at least better than the mucked-up thing was now. "I'll be sure to be careful and not damage it further."

"No, thank you, ma'am. That won't be necessary."

Ma'am!

Now she was a ma'am. Just somebody's clumsy mother who'd affected his day in the worst sort of way. All three of her children, plus Prichard, the boy she'd taken in last year, would be this man's pupils come Monday. Everyone but Maddie, her mystery child. Surely, he'd think of this event each time he looked at one her brood. "If you won't let me clean your document, at least let me cook you supper some night soon. That's the very least I can do for the new teacher in town."

He took a step back as if the thought could be dangerous. "I assure you there was no harm done. I couldn't put you out in such a manner."

"B-but," she sputtered, "I want to cook. I *love* to cook."

"No. Thank you. Mrs. Lane." His words came out stilted. "You have a nice day." And as her hopes for an entire school year shattered before her, he passed her by and headed for the schoolhouse.

CHAPTER FOUR

*P*enny? Jane?" Brenna set her white wicker delivery basket on the floor by the door and removed her light sweater. *Where are the children?* She stepped into her small living room and shut the front door behind her. Humiliation still simmered inside her breast. *What's done is done*, she told herself. "Stevie? Prichard? Where are you? Maddie?"

Excited voices came from the back door that led to the vegetable garden and small toolshed that served as a coop for their three cuddly chickens. She was just about to hang her sweater on a hook when eight-year-old Stevie burst into the room, skipped the short distance to her and snatched her arm down. His cheeks, two spots of red, needed a good washing. His eyes were alight with excitement.

"Guess what?" he shouted.

By now, the others had caught up and were gathered around. Penny had a tight hold of Maddie's small hand. The blind girl had adjusted nicely to their makeshift family—and they were happy to have her. Brenna still didn't know any more about the child's past than she'd learned on the day Nell and Sheriff Preston had delivered the frightened darling to her door along with poor Aunt Cora's things. But the child was sweet and eager to please. Whenever questioned about her past, Maddie's only response was that she didn't remember. Brenna didn't believe that for a second. But she'd not push her. The child would tell her when she was ready.

"What? Tell me quick." She walked into the kitchen with the children following behind like a row of ducklings. Taking the coffee can that served as her bank off the second shelf, she dropped the handful of coins inside, liking the sound the money created. *My earnings are getting heavier by the day.* That fact brought her peace of mind. Finished with her deposit, she gave the children her full attention. "Well? I'm waiting."

Where Stevie and Prichard's faces were bright with anticipation, Penny stood rigid. Jane was Jane, just happy to be included. She was eleven, only a year younger than Penny, and was the peacekeeper of the group. If a terse word sounded from anyone, Jane moved into action, soothing and placating.

"What's this about, children?" Brenna asked, laughing. "I'm about to die from curiosity."

Penny stepped forward. "Follow me, Mama." She crossed the room to the front door. She pulled it open. "What do you see?"

Mystified, Brenna looked out on her tiny front yard, the wooden fence rimmed with yellow, white, and orange flowers, all of different types and sizes. It was a beautiful sight, a result of many hours of love. "Some pretty flowers that would make any garden gnome a cheerful home?"

Penny groaned. "Keep looking."

Brenna stepped out onto the porch. Nothing seemed out of place. She glanced across the narrow dirt road to the small rental house belonging to Maude Miller, the owner of the mercantile. The well-kept yellow home had been vacant for almost seven months. Today several crates were stacked on the porch.

"Someone's moving in." *How exciting.* "This is wonderful news. Do we know who our new neighbors are yet? I hope it's a family with lots of children. That would be nice. With a woman my age, who likes to knit and bake. Or perhaps . . ."

She glanced back at the children. Penny's and Jane's faces, frozen in an expression between panic and fear, stopped her short. "Who?"

"The new teacher," Stevie shouted, piercing her eardrums. "Deputy Donovan was out this morning to deliver his trunks."

Dread rippled through Brenna. *How? Why?* She wished doubly hard now that she could start her day over and not visit the bank until the afternoon. Or at least pay attention to where she was walking—see Mr. Hutton and have a polite but brief conversation when he passed by. Yes, that's how the exchange should have gone. Anything but what actually happened. When she'd invited him to dinner, he probably thought she already knew about them being neighbors and couldn't wait to sink her widow's claws into him. Humiliated, she wanted to slink into her bedroom and never come out.

"What are you talking about? His house is across town."

Stevie jumped up and down. "Skunks got inside. When they went to get 'em out, they let loose. Won't be fit to live in for some time."

Penny must have picked up her agitated feelings, because she touched her arm. "What's wrong, Mama? I'm not ashamed to say I wasn't glad our teacher moved in across the street, but I thought you would be. Last week when you met him, you said he was nice."

Her daughter had a point. Brenna pasted a smile onto her face, and then patted each child on the head, ending with Maddie, who stood patiently waiting for the problem to be resolved. "Of course I'm thrilled to have Mr. Hutton as a neighbor. Who better when one of you is stuck and needs help with your homework? Lord knows I'm not much good at math, or English, or anything else." Penny, not used to negativity from her, furrowed her brow.

Even though Brenna might have fears and insecurities, she didn't want to instill them in her children. "I think it's absolutely the best news I've heard all week. It's just a surprise, is all. Mrs. Miller's home will be perfect for him. Notice how nice and tidy his trunks are even with him just getting settled. He'll be a good neighbor to have."

"Shall we bake him an apple cake, Mama?" Jane asked. "To welcome him to the neighborhood." Jane's eyes looked up while she thought. "If Penny and Maddie and me get started now, we can give it to him tonight."

Brenna's stomach tightened up with knots. If she knocked on his door, her brood of children all around like chicks and a mother hen, he'd probably laugh—or slam the door in her face before she did him any more harm. But there was no avoiding it. She'd taught the children to be kind and polite. An apple cake would be a nice gesture indeed.

"That's a perfect idea, Jane. I'm so proud of you for suggesting it."

Jane's face brightened like a newly lit lamp, making Brenna glad she hadn't squelched Jane's thoughtfulness to cover her own anxieties. Mr. Hutton would just have to get used to the idea of living next door to them. Who knew? Maybe he'd grow to like them.

Jane started for the kitchen. "I'll take Maddie and go pick the apples while you get the oven heated, Penny. You're the only one allowed to use matches."

"We'll help you pick," Stevie said. He grasped his foster brother by the arm and headed for the door. "I was first to find out about Mr. Hutton. I bet he likes to whittle. He might even want me to show him how to make a super-duper slingshot."

Prichard nodded. "I bet he will, Stevie. We both can ask him."

Brenna stood back and watched the scene unfold. Mr. Hutton wouldn't know what hit him. She could see the whole thing in her mind's eye, and would have giggled if she weren't so worried. Well, that was just too bad. If he wanted to be grumpy, so be it.

In the kitchen, she tied her apron around her waist, and then gathered the ingredients for the pastries she owed Hannah at the Silky Hen. She set up her space, leaving ample room for the children and their teacher-welcoming project, thinking how much her life had changed since Hannah had employed her as a baker. She had persevered through the tough times and now God had rained his blessings on her. With her baking and sewing, she'd learned she was capable indeed. Others depended on her, even if only for a few pies for the Silky Hen. She was making a difference, and that fact made a difference to her.

Penny loaded wood into the belly of the oven and stuffed wadded-up newspaper underneath. It seemed the idea of her teacher living across the street had lost its sting. With the other children outside, now was the perfect time for a mother-daughter talk.

"You're ready for school on Monday?" School was always foremost in Penny's mind. Learning came easy to her. "It'll be here before you know it."

Finished with the stove, Penny washed her hands and picked up the towel. "I think so, Mama. I just have my new skirt to hem."

Penny was growing up. Her tight bodices attested to that fact. Sometimes the blueness of her eyes and the expression they held reminded Brenna so much of Carl, it could render her speechless. They'd been happy, Carl working for Win at the livery and her with a new baby practically every year. They'd had little money but a lot of love. Then, six years ago, he'd been kicked in the chest by a horse and killed instantly. His loss still made her ache.

She'd been lucky to have friends who looked out for her and her children. Just last week, they'd received several items of clothing from Hannah Donovan and Jessie Logan. She and Penny had worked feverishly to alter them to fit. Now both girls would have a new dress and one new skirt and blouse each for the school year.

Brenna took the sack of flour from the drawer and reached for her well-used measuring cups. "That's wonderful. I appreciate your help with Jane's skirt."

Altering the boys' clothes was her job. She'd worked late each evening stitching the pants and shirts. They were a bit more difficult since the hand-me-downs came from Gabe Garrison, the young man who lived with Chase and Jessie Logan and was almost grown. The dress Jessie had sent for Maddie appeared brand new, and by the size of it, must still fit Sarah, Jessie's daughter. When Brenna had objected, Jessie had insisted that she take it, saying Sarah hadn't cottoned to it, and it had hung unused in her daughter's wardrobe for far too long. The garment was perfect for Maddie. How could anyone argue with that?

The front door slammed. The boys bounded through the kitchen door, their arms overflowing with apples. Jane and Maddie, hand in hand, were not far behind.

"What have I told you about using the front door after being out in the garden?" Brenna scolded. "Stevie, take the broom and clean up the trail of dirt I'm sure followed you into the house."

"We couldn't help it, Ma. When we turned the corner we noticed the teacher. He stopped at his gate like he was gonna go home, but then he crossed the street. He's on the front porch now and wants to talk to you."

CHAPTER FIVE

*T*he sound of gunshots brought Charlie fully awake. Adrenaline pushed him from his bedroll and he leaped to his feet. As he strapped on his loaded six-gun, another shot sounded from behind the house.

Had someone followed him from Wilsonville?

Charlie moved silently through the barn to the tall doors. With his back to the wall, he felt for the handle. He carefully inched it open.

All was quiet.

Nothing looked amiss.

Anxiety for Nell sizzled inside him, contracting the muscles in his abdomen. The last thing he wanted was for an innocent woman to be hurt in his war.

He listened. And watched. The silence wrapped around the barn made the predawn darkness seem all the more dangerous.

He pulled the door open just enough to accommodate his size, flinching at the loud squeak. Darting out, he took cover alongside the barn wall, facing the house.

The dog came around the far side of the house, then trotted up the steps. When Charlie recognized Nell's tall, slender shape ambling along after him as if nothing were wrong, he let go a breath of relief.

Holstering his gun, he stepped out of the shadows. "Nell," he called quietly.

She stopped just short of the porch steps.

Striding over, he halted a few feet away. "Is everything all right? Gunshots woke me." He could see that she wore her pants under her nightshirt. The dog flopped down by the front door.

"Dog cornered a rattlesnake against the house. Probably drawn to the warmth of the foundation." Her hand slipped down and caressed the gun nestled in its holster around her hips. "I wouldn't have killed the poor thing if it had been anywhere else. But so close to Dog, plus the horses and cattle, I had no choice."

"And us?" Charlie asked. The sound of her voice stirred his blood. He let his gaze slip over her face. Four years was a long time to be alone—in the real sense of the word. Startled at the direction of his thoughts, he took a step back. "You could have been bitten," he said tersely, wanting to feel anything except the attraction pulling him toward her. "You should have woken Seth or me."

Her stance straightened as if she were looking for an argument. The dog climbed to his haunches and whined. "I don't think I like your tone, Charlie Rose." He thought she was serious until she glanced up at him from beneath her lashes. "You forget who's boss around here?"

"Maybe I have and maybe not."

When she reached out and plucked a piece of straw from his hair, a wave of fire crashed through his body.

"If you stay on, you best get used to me doing for myself." Her tone shifted then from teasing to somber. "Sometimes I have problems sleeping." She pulled her mass of curly hair over her shoulder and her hand trembled. "If I do, I go out." A coyote yipped, mercifully drawing her gaze toward the horse pasture. "Fresh air helps."

He understood that, all right. He hadn't had a good night's sleep since the accident that had killed Annie. When he did drift off, visions of her body crushed beneath the overturned wagon, or of his three-year-old daughter crying for her mama, troubled his dreams. He should have been driving that day. If he had, Annie would be alive and Maddie would still have her sight. A bitter price to pay for putting his work before his family. Annie had driven the route a thousand times, but this time there'd been a runaway horse and wagon coming in the opposite direction.

The front door opened and Seth stepped out, a double-barrel shotgun held firm in his right hand. "Everything all right out here?" His gaze traveled from Charlie's face to Nell's and then back.

"Just a rattlesnake Dog was teasing."

"Kill it?"

She nodded.

"Then I'm going back to bed." He hesitated as if he had something else on his mind, then turned back into the house and was gone.

"Must be near four." Nell pulled her hair over her shoulder again, making him think she was nervous. "Almost time to get up. If you want, I'll put the coffee on early."

"No, thanks," he replied. He'd best keep a tight rein on his thoughts. With nothing remaining to talk about, he turned. "I'll see you later."

After Nell went inside and closed the door, Charlie headed for the barn. The early-morning air prickled the skin on his face. He gulped several deep breaths, feeling the chill in his throat. It felt good, cleared his mind. He needed to stay focused on Maddie. Couldn't let himself be distracted. He had enough problems already.

CHAPTER SIX

$\mathcal{C}$harlie ate the last of the scrambled eggs on his plate, then crunched a slice of crispy bacon as he wondered about Nell's absence. He'd stepped inside without knocking, as she'd instructed, and found a quiet kitchen. Food had been prepared and place settings were out on the table. A bit self-conscious, he'd served himself and eased into a chair to eat.

"Morning," Seth greeted Charlie as he came down the stairs, working the last button on his shirt. He'd shaved his whiskers and combed his hair. "Getting up the day after a long trip is always hard." He yawned and stretched. "That bed sure felt good last night."

"Wish I could say the same." When he'd returned to his bedroll after the encounter with Nell, he'd remained wide awake. He rubbed his gritty, tired eyes.

"I've been thinking." Seth took a cup off the shelf, poured himself coffee, then set it on the table. "Why don't you take the small room downstairs? It's around back and was originally a mudroom. But there's a door, so you can come and go as you please. The bed isn't more than a cot."

"What about Nell?"

Seth's brow furrowed. "Nell?" He glanced around and shrugged.

"How'd she feel about having a man in the house?"

Seth filled a plate, leaving some eggs and bacon for his sister. "Guess you don't know Nell yet. She can take care of herself.

Besides, she's a grown woman and a widow to boot. You being here won't bother her at all." He pulled out a chair and sat across from Charlie.

"Thank you. I appreciate that. A cot sounds darn good over the lumpy floor of a stall."

"And a bit less aromatic."

Charlie wiped his mouth with his napkin. "I woke up this morning with a chicken staring me down from atop the stall door. It was a mite unnerving." He took a drink of his coffee. "By the way, what's Logan Meadows like?" Something vital inside him was shriveling and dying without information about Maddie. Being so close to her without being able to pick her up, kiss her soft little cheek, was killing him. He needed to know where she'd been living and what her life had been like since leaving him. Anything was better than nothing. It sounded like a nice town, but you never knew until you'd lived somewhere awhile.

"Resembles pretty much any place, I'd say."

Charlie glanced down at the outdated newspaper on the table. He pointed to the article about the schoolhouse potluck. "Looks like good, down-home fun."

"Should be. I'm sure we'll be going since Nell feels strongly about community and especially the children. She likes the roots we've sunk here in Wyoming. Guess that stems from us moving around so much when she was just a girl." He shrugged.

Relief mingled with excitement. All he had to do was get through these next three days. Maddie was sure to be at the potluck.

"It's been some time since I've done any roping." Charlie rubbed his palms together. "I haven't thrown a rope or dallied since before my wife . . ." He clamped his mouth closed. The less anyone knew about his past, the better.

Seth's brow shot up. "You're married?"

Pain ripped through Charlie's heart, burning him from the inside out. The worst day of his life was written there in black just waiting to trip him up. Annie dead. Maddie injured, but recovering, only to find she was slowly losing her sight. He scrubbed his hand across his face. "Not anymore. She died in an accident. After I got married, I stopped saddle tramping and bought a store in town. A gun shop. Became respectable to please her." The thought made him smile. "I'll need a few tosses to get my timing back."

Seth's expression said he understood—but how could he? It wasn't possible for anyone to understand the grief that gripped his heart day after day. "I'm sure you'll do fine," Seth said. He glanced up the stairs. "Wonder what's keeping Nell. She can be demanding, but don't let her ride herd over you too much."

"That'll be hard to do, being she's one of the bosses."

The soles of Nell's boots tromped on the wooden staircase as she descended. She crossed the room swiftly and emptied the fry pan onto the last plate. "Sorry to keep you boys waiting." She glanced at him, then smiled at her brother. "Just one of those mornings, I guess."

If Charlie had to choose a word to describe Nell, it would be *conflicted*. Her slender body moved like a snowflake on the wind and seemed more suited for one of those flimsy tea dresses he'd seen in the window of an upscale store in Denver. Instead, she was encased in rugged denim jeans, a shirt that must have come from her brother's closet, and boots older than time itself. A beat-up cowboy hat hung down her back, held secure by a braided-leather stampede string around her neck.

"Something funny?" she asked, chewing on a bacon strip.

Taking her brother's advice about not letting her walk all over him from the start, he gestured to the boots piled by the door. "With all those over there, I couldn't help notice your boots are, well—just 'bout worn through. I wouldn't want to do much walking in 'em."

"Well, it's no matter to you because you aren't going to be walking in them, now are you?" She pulled out a chair and sat.

"And neither am I. I'm going to be riding. The two are different, if you hadn't noticed."

"Nell," Seth warned in a tone Charlie was starting to recognize. "You get up on the wrong side of the bed?"

"No. Did you?"

Seth's expression said Charlie better walk softly. Seth stood, then started for the door. "I'll go saddle the horses."

"I did that before I came in. Also filled all the water troughs."

Seth stopped and one corner of his lips tipped up. "Sure is nice having a hired hand that thinks ahead and don't wait to be told what needs doing. I guess we're ready to head out."

Nell's eyebrows lifted. "I need to put the injured mare out in the small pasture where she'll be able to graze while we're gone."

"You should have mentioned that last night. I could have done it."

Nell stood and dipped her empty plate into the tub of water. "Never you mind, Charlie Rose. We don't expect you to do everything around here."

The morning passed quickly. The trip out to where the group of three-year-olds grazed took less than an hour. Charlie and Seth kept a string of conversation going, discussing politics, the state of the economy, just about any subject under the sun. Nell hadn't seen her brother take to anyone like he had Charlie since Ben had come into their lives. She was taking to him, too—the way his hands and legs were soft as he rode, asking his mount instead of demanding or being a bit cruel, like too many other ranch hands they'd tossed out on their backsides.

Soon the birch-pole corral that she'd helped Seth and Ben construct five years ago came into view at the end of the box canyon. The enclosure connected to a narrow chute, which came in handy for working with a particularly difficult animal. Once the horse or steer had run inside and the gates were closed at head and tail, it was possible to halter, doctor, or even brand the animal through the slats.

The three stopped only long enough to prop open the gates so the corral would be ready to receive the horses.

The roundup didn't take long with the help of Charlie and Dog. Nell flapped her coiled rope against her leather chaps to urge the last horse into the enclosure, then slid Coyote to a halt on her side of the gate. Charlie, a smile splitting his face like he'd just won a thousand dollars, pulled up on the other side and Seth swung the gate closed. Between the pounding hooves, Dog's loud, excited bark, and the wind in the tall trees, excitement fairly hummed in the air.

"I haven't had this much fun since, well, I can't remember when," Charlie hollered above the din.

His blue eyes glinted, which set off a strange sensation inside Nell. The flurries in her stomach grew as she took in his grin and windblown face. Yes, no doubt about it, their new hand was all too disarming for her good.

"Glad you liked it," Seth responded. "Much easier this time with the three of us."

Dog barked and wagged his tail.

"Four," Seth corrected with a crooked smile.

"Those horses are fast." The sides of Charlie's black gelding heaved, and sweat trickled from under his saddle pad, dripping to the ground. "A couple of times there, I thought we lost 'em, Nell."

She stacked the palms of her hands on her saddle horn, stretching up in the stirrups to get a better view of the horses and one less filled with Charlie. Caught up in the excitement, Dog scooted under the fence, barking wildly. One of the geldings kicked out viciously, missing him by inches.

"Dog," Seth shouted. "Get out here before you get your brains kicked clear to kingdom come." A horse charged and Dog scooted back under the fence, then ran over to Seth.

Nell dismounted and tied her horse to a nearby branch. She climbed the corral fence.

The chestnut stud colt with three white socks—the one Seth had such high hopes for—pawed the ground, showing just how angry he was about being brought in off the range. He flipped his head, then galloped the perimeter of the rails.

"Look at 'em, Seth." Nell couldn't keep her appreciation for the beautiful animals from her voice. "They've grown strong. That colt must have gained a good three hundred pounds in the last four months. He's maturing."

"Are they broke?" Charlie strode over to where she perched on the rail and stood alongside. He reached up and grasped the rail.

Nell shook her head. "Just green broke. Most have worn a saddle a time or two. Like Sitting Bull and Geronimo." She pointed to a chestnut in the middle. "Cochise is one of my favorites, but he has a mind of his own."

Charlie shot her a look. "What's with the names?"

"The soldiers who they're assigned to will rename them at the fort," Seth answered. "So for the ones we plan to sell, we just drop a temporary name on 'em so between us we know which we're talking about. Indian chief names are sort of an amusing thing to do."

"But you'd be amazed how some of them actually live up to their names. Like that one over there." Nell pointed to a muscular bay with a zigzag blaze running down his face. The animal stared at them keenly. "That's Crazy Horse and boy, he's one I never turn my back on." She laughed, loving every second of what she did for a living. "We like to start them slow to give them a small taste of what's to come, and then turn them back out. Let them develop and grow up. Also makes them smart. These horses haven't been coddled. They'll go the distance and then some when we're through with them."

Charlie pointed to the chestnut that stood out from the others like a diamond among coal. "He also going to the army?"

Seth grunted and removed his hat to wipe his brow, then replaced it, leaning his arms on the rail and peering into the corral. A long rattling cough made him turn away. "No. We've been waiting for a colt like him for years," he finally said, leaning on the fence again. "He's worth a lot more than an army mount. We'll keep him for breeding. His name's Drag Anchor."

The only stud colt in the group of geldings was full of himself. He flattened his ears and rushed at one of the smaller horses, biting him viciously on the side. The horse squealed and lunged away.

Charlie shook his head. "Looks bad tempered to me."

"He's just scared," Nell said. "In a few hours he'll settle down. He remembers us and knows what's coming, and is none too pleased about it, either."

Snorting and the sound of horses' hooves scuffling in the barren corral filled the air. "They're used to running from predators, and to them, that's what we are. We're not here to steal their lives, but their freedom. That's just as bad."

Sweat dripped from the horses' bellies and down their faces. The lovely scent of warm, wet horseflesh reached her nose even sitting on the top rail. Nell yearned to calm their fears, but that was not advisable quite yet.

Drag Anchor galloped toward the rail again, stubbornly looking for a way out. He slid to a halt on the enclosure's far side, which extended twenty feet along the bottom of a sheer cliff.

"You've ridden him?" Charlie eyed her, impressed. "He looks pretty rank to me."

"I have." Pride filled her. She lived for her horses. All of them. Drag Anchor was special, but all of them were to her.

"I told her to wait," Seth said. "Until he had some ground manners and had carried a saddle a few more times, but, as you now know, Nell can be tenacious as all get-out. She seems to have a special sense of things. I've never seen anything like it before. She knows when they're ready, or when they aren't. It's pretty amazing."

Seth's tone had taken on a soft, curious, amazed quality. Nell glanced down at her brother and a swell of love lifted her heart. Always her champion.

"Sounds like you think she talks to them, Seth."

Seth shrugged. "She does. Not with words exactly. I can't explain it." He repositioned his hat. "Don't matter how she does it; I'm just glad she can."

Turning back to the horses, Nell let go her breath and flexed her stiff shoulders. All they had to do now was set up camp and begin work tomorrow. Anticipation thrummed inside her chest, not only because of the horses but because of Charlie and the way she felt him looking at her right now. With a light in his eyes that said he was more than a little curious about what she'd reveal next.

CHAPTER SEVEN

$\mathcal{S}$aturday dawned with a clear blue sky. As chairwoman of the school council, Brenna had agonized over every aspect of the day, spending all too many hours to count organizing the event. Everything needed to be perfect. The whole town was interested in seeing the new, improved and enlarged schoolhouse. And in the spirit of community, each person had pledged to bring a dish to share for an early dinner after the tours of the remodeled structure were complete.

The Broken Horn ranch, owned by Chase and Jessie Logan, had generously supplied firewood enough to heat the school for the entire term. The school now had two stoves to keep the children toasty on long winter days, one at each end of the enlarged room. Gabe and Jake, the Logans' young cowhands, had delivered several wagon loads throughout the week and stacked them by the door.

Positioned in the schoolhouse doorway, Brenna glanced at Maddie sitting at the table under the tree. The little girl's blindness made it difficult for her to get around easily in new places without help, so Brenna had asked her to be the official greeter. Markus Donovan would join her at the sign-in table as soon as he arrived, to help sell raffle tickets for the quilt Mrs. Hollyhock and a handful of others had donated. The sampler was a sight to behold, each woman having sewn a square with a design of her choice.

Maddie's sunny disposition was always a curiosity to Brenna. Sometimes, in the dead of night, she'd hear Maddie whimpering in her sleep and would go and comfort her. She was hiding something about her family, and her past. Other than her first name, the child refused to give any details at all, even to reveal why she had been traveling with Aunt Cora.

"Good day, Brenna," a voice called out.

Snapped out of her musings, Brenna smiled when Hannah Donovan headed her way. In her arms was a wooden crate too large for her to be carrying alone.

Brenna rushed down the slight incline to help her. "Let me take that for you. Did you carry that all the way from the restaurant? Your arms must be ready to fall off."

"No, no, I'm fine, really. This is all very light. Thom and Markus should be along shortly with the heavier stuff. I wanted to get started setting up the dessert table. How are you? Is everything ready?"

"As ready as it'll ever be," she replied as they walked.

A list of things to be accomplished zipped through Brenna's head. Organize potluck food, place cloth bookmarks on each child's desk as a welcome gift, have the children sign the welcome card for Mr. Hutton. At the thought of the teacher, a bubble of agitation rolled around in Brenna's stomach.

Hannah set the box down. "Hello, Maddie," she called out when she spotted the girl seated under the cottonwood tree.

Maddie twisted around and waved, a bright smile on her face. "Hi, Mrs. Donovan."

"Markus will be along shortly," Hannah called back. "He's looking forward to working with you today. You excited for the picnic?"

Maddie nodded.

Hannah glanced back at Brenna, compassion simmering in her eyes. "It's amazing how she can tell our voices apart so well. I just can't get over it."

"I know," Brenna said. "She gets around so easily in my home. Says she wasn't always blind. It breaks my heart all the same."

"You've done well by her. Have you found out anything more about your aunt? It's all so curious."

Brenna's heart filled with a sadness born of not knowing her aunt's intentions, and for the time lost that they could've had together. "I received a letter from Wilsonville in response to the one I wrote to the postmaster. It was short and I could hardly read his chicken scratch, but he said Aunt Cora just disappeared. Said before that day she'd sold a few things here and there. That would explain the thirty-two dollars I found stuffed into a sock." Brenna glanced away from her friend's concerned appraisal. She'd also found a music box, its top inlaid with walnut, and a beautiful, expensive-looking garnet bracelet mixed in with the articles of clothing. Aunt Cora had been her only living relative. She hadn't seen her for over twenty years, and hardly recalled what her mother's sister looked like. She sighed, wondering if Maddie, as impossible as it might sound, could somehow be her child. If not that, her ward. "He didn't know anything about a blind child. Perhaps Maddie was on the stage and my aunt befriended her. I just don't know."

Hannah nodded intently. "How're you holding up? If you need anything I can have some supplies sent over."

Brenna placed her hand on her friend's arm, shushing her. "We're doing fine." Her heart swelled as she thought how far they'd come in the last year. *I like providing for my family on my own.* "But thank you all the same."

"That's wonderful. The sentiment bears repeating: you've done a fine job with everything."

Brenna's face heated. She did her best to stay in the background, not draw attention to herself. Chairwoman of the school council was the first role of importance she'd held in the community and the last thing she wanted to do was make a blunder.

"Well? What about the other situation?" Hannah's eyes brimmed with speculation.

Brenna tried to pretend she didn't know what Hannah meant. "Situation?"

Hannah plopped her hands onto her hips. "Don't play coy with me, Brenna Lane. How are things with Mr. Hutton?"

Brenna felt her shoulders slump and the happiness and excitement of the day drain from her lungs. "You mean ol' grumpy, grouchy Gregory? I can't win him over. He enjoys being sour—just like a crabapple picked too soon to eat."

Hannah blinked. "That bad? He didn't impress me that way."

"Well, I've given up. You should've seen his pleasant expression fizzle when he learned I lived across the street from him. He came over to introduce himself to the new neighbor and all but shot off my porch when he realized it was me. Hardly even smiled when the girls baked him a cake later that same day. I'll not go out of my way again for him. Not after he broke their shiny little hearts."

"I'm astonished. He seemed so nice when I met him . . ."

The sound of a throat being cleared sent panic shooting up Brenna's spine. She knew without turning who was there.

"Mr. Hutton," Hannah said. "We didn't hear you approach."

The dreadful man stood there all spit shined and polished, ready to meet the good citizens of Logan Meadows. His brown corduroy pants hung to his polished, black shoes. His shirt was clean and pressed. His thick hair, although combed, was a bit unkempt in a way Brenna was growing used to. He gripped the handle of the same leather satchel he'd been carrying when she smacked into him outside the bank. *He's not handsome, so just stop thinking that. And when you're finished with not thinking that, you can thank your lucky stars you're a grown woman and not required to go to class. He'd be sure to stand you in the corner every day.*

"Good day, Mrs. Donovan. Mrs. Lane. I thought I'd come early to be sure everything was ready before the townsfolk arrived." He took a pocket watch from his pants pocket and flipped open the lid. "That shouldn't be long now. Is there anything I can help you do?"

"No, thank you," Brenna said. "Everything is under control." Did he still foster a grudge over her clumsiness? He'd practically turned in the opposite direction whenever he'd seen her. Perhaps he hadn't forgiven her for ruining his paper. Or maybe he wasn't happy he lived so close to her. Certainly, it wasn't because her heart picked up speed whenever he looked her way.

Thom and Markus rounded the corner in a wagon and started up the hill. *Good, reinforcements to the rescue.* Brenna waved.

"How do you like Logan Meadows, Mr. Hutton?" Hannah asked. She lifted several plates of assorted cookies from the crate and artfully arranged them on the table. Next came a cinnamon cake and an apple pie.

"Very much. The people I've met have gone overboard to give me a nice welcome. I couldn't ask for a finer schoolhouse, and I was pleasantly surprised with the supplies."

"And your lodging?"

Brenna cringed inwardly. Why did Hannah have to bring that up?

"Mrs. Miller's small house suits me well—and smells nice." He laughed. "A bachelor doesn't need much room. And the location is perfect." His eyes cut to Brenna, then back. "Only a short walk from my door to the school. That'll be handy when the snow starts to fall."

Hannah laughed. "I hope you brought a wool coat."

"It was the first thing I packed. Harsh winters in Pennsylvania are not uncommon."

He seemed so friendly with Hannah. The conversation just flowed. Why did it always stall out when she tried to speak with him?

Thom pulled the buckboard to a halt a few yards away. He greeted everyone, then made a quick job of unloading a few more tables and some chairs, then the rest of the food the Silky Hen had donated. Markus, his hair slicked back and his face glossy clean, bolted down the hill toward Maddie, in typical six-year-old fashion.

"Appears as if things are just about ready to get underway," Thom said. "I need to get back to the sheriff's office and do a few things, then I'll be back when the shindig is in full swing." He gave Hannah a kiss on the lips, lingering a bit too long, and she pushed him away. He laughed and winked at Brenna, who felt her face heat. "I don't want to miss anything important."

Brenna marveled at how much Hannah had blossomed since her childhood sweetheart had come back into her life. A true fairy tale with a happy ending. Thom Donovan had scared the life out of the whole town last year when he'd passed out, only to reveal he had a bullet lodged in his skull. The operation had been difficult and the recovery long, but he'd come out of the ordeal as good as new, promptly marrying Hannah and adopting Markus as his legal son. Hannah had confided that she and Thom were doing their best to have another little one, but it hadn't happened for them yet.

"Don't forget the side of beef, you rapscallion," Hannah teased Thom. "We've had the meat cooking at the restaurant," she explained to Brenna. "Thom's planning on finishing it over the pit Win dug, so it won't get cold."

Thom saluted his wife. "I wouldn't dream of forgetting."

Brenna chanced a peek at Mr. Hutton to find him watching the interchange with interest. When he caught her eye, he gestured to the school. "I'll just be inside." Brenna nodded, wishing he'd hurry up and be gone. "Mrs. Lane," he added, "thank you for all the work you've done to pull this day together. If the open house goes the way I believe it will, the event will be a huge success. The thanks are all to you."

The generous compliment caught Brenna off her mark and the pleasant curve of Mr. Hutton's mouth chased every coherent thought from her mind. "N-no, Mr. Hutton. The thanks go to the good people of Logan Meadows. They've all pitched in to make our school nicer and this day a time of celebration."

His smile dissolved into a straight line. "Well, if you say so, I'm not inclined to argue."

Hannah jabbed her elbow into Brenna's side as Mr. Hutton walked away. "Be nicer. You seem like a grouchy old hen when he's around. Loosen up and smile."

Brenna sighed and turned to her next task. Several riders on horseback headed toward the school, as did a buggy and some ladies on foot. Chase and Jessie's wagon pulled up among them. More than a handful of citizens were already crowded around Markus and Maddie at the sign-in table.

Old Mrs. Hollyhock climbed the slight incline to the school, barely winded for her eighty-six years. She made her way through the crowd to Brenna's side. They hugged and Brenna inhaled her familiar aroma of golden-brown piecrust.

"How ya be, sweetie pie?" the old woman asked, peering at her through the spectacles on the end of her nose. Her long, gray hair was done up in a soft bun on the back of her head and she wore her Sunday dress. "You excited the day is finally here?"

"I am. I can't believe it."

Mrs. Hollyhock's eyes sparkled as she looked around. She smiled when she noticed the big plaid bows Brenna had attached above the schoolhouse windows. "Well, ya done did a fine job. And yer girl looks a beauty."

She tilted her head toward Penny, who approached and handed Brenna her clipboard with several papers attached. The simple green dress her eldest wore had puff sleeves and a ribbon around her small waist. It wouldn't be long before boys flocked to their porch, Brenna thought in a moment of sadness.

"Mr. Hutton asked me to give you these," Penny said. "Thought you might have forgotten them inside on his desk."

Brenna glanced down at the papers, trying to calm her annoyance. *I didn't forget them. I left them there intentionally so they wouldn't get lost in the hustle and bustle out here.* She wrestled her agitation away when Frank Lloyd, the bank owner, headed in her direction. Determined not to let anything ruin the day, she smiled brightly. "Thank you, Penny," she said, then glanced down at her clipboard. "Please relay my thanks to Mr.—"

She gasped at the list, the words she intended to say shocked out of her mind.

CHAPTER EIGHT

*W*hat is it, Mama?" Penny asked. Her eyes grew round. "What's wrong?"

Brenna willed herself to breathe. Her instantly dry mouth felt like a flowerbed in mid-July. She'd overlooked ordering the six copies of *First Lessons in Numbers: Oral and Written* before the term started. *How could I be so careless?* At her request, Maude had corresponded with the publishing company several months back, with plenty of time for them to be ordered and delivered. The supplier had responded that they were out of stock and asked her to write back later. Last week she'd gone into the mercantile with that express intention and must have gotten to talking and forgotten.

Mr. Lloyd was almost upon them. "Nothing is wrong, Penny. Now run inside and tell Mr. Hutton thank you very much for sending out my list and then go down and see that Maddie and Markus don't get overwhelmed at the sign-in table. Hurry now. People are arriving all at once."

Mrs. Hollyhock went up on tippy-toe to see the clipboard. "Ya sure yer all right?" One couldn't pull the wool over Violet's eyes. "Something on that list has yer eyes buggin' out of their sockets. Can I help?"

"No, Mrs. Hollyhock. I'm fine. I just want to be sure everything is perfect today and for the rest of the school term."

"That's a pretty tall order, missy. One thing is certain—and that is nothin' is certain." She patted Brenna's hand and then headed toward Jessie Logan, who was a few feet away chatting with Hannah's mother, Mrs. Brown. "You let me know if ya change yer mind, Brenna," she said over her shoulder.

"Ah, Mrs. Lane, just the woman I wanted to see."

Mr. Lloyd always dressed nice, and today was no exception. He wore one of the shirts she'd mended for him.

"You've done a fine job," he said, glancing around. "Who knows how many more chances we'll have to enjoy a picnic before the weather changes. If you remember last year, winter came early."

Brenna tried to give the banker her full attention, but all she could think about was that aggravating Mr. Hutton and the forgotten math books. Even if she had Maude send a telegram today or tomorrow, the books wouldn't arrive to Logan Meadows before school started.

"Thank you, Mr. Lloyd," she replied, trying to stop the quiver in her hands. "I had plenty of help. All I had to do was show up."

His brow wrinkled skeptically. "I hardly think so. Someone had to be in charge to delegate. The school council is very lucky to have you."

She wished the bank owner would stop singing her praises. She felt like a fool. A failure. The only reason she'd run for the council position was because Penny wanted her to. Her oldest's face had lit up like the sun when she came home from school last year. The former teacher, Miss Thomas, had told the children that names were being considered for the coming year's term. They needed volunteers—new volunteers. Betty Brinkley, who had several grandchildren in the school, had been the chairwoman for the past six years and she was tired.

If Hannah hadn't asked everyone in town to vote for Brenna, she never would have won. At the time, the position sounded exciting. New. A challenge to be won. And an excellent example to set for her children. Now, she'd gone and forgotten to order one of the most important books for the term. The humiliation of her failure would be devastating, but she could handle it. She'd been taking charity up until last year and she had plenty of practice with unpretentiousness. Penny was the one she worried about, as well as the other children. Even Maddie would hear the talk once everyone found out. Dear God, what would Mr. Hutton think of her then?

"Appears we arrived right on time," Charlie said. He and Nell rode down Main Street, him on the black and Nell on her chestnut-paint gelding. She carried a crock filled with hard-boiled eggs that she'd made last night. Her long braid hung down her back almost to her belt. They'd successfully brought in the eight head of horses yesterday without too much problem. Seth, completely tired out, opted to stay home.

Nell nodded. "Seems like the open house is just getting started. We'll ride over by the alders and tie the horses there."

Anticipation hummed though Charlie, making him sit straight in the saddle regardless of his sore hip and pinched back. Getting the three-year-olds home hadn't been easy. He'd been bumped and jostled. He'd actually been jerked from the saddle once when he was slow on the dally and Drag Anchor hadn't obliged to come along nicely. He hadn't fallen off since he was a kid, and had forgotten how badly it hurt to hit the ground like a sack of corn.

But aching muscles couldn't dampen his spirits. Today he'd see Maddie. She was certain to be here among all the townspeople.

His eyes searched the grassy hummock for a small girl with nut-colored hair and sparkling blue eyes. But at the same time, he had to be on guard for Grover Galante, or anyone Galante may have sent. It was too soon to think he was out of the woods just yet.

Children darted here and there. A small group milled around the open door to the schoolhouse, but no Maddie. *Where is she?*

His anticipation was replaced by worry. *Has something happened to her?*

They dismounted, tied their horses and walked over to where folks lined up past a tall tree. They stopped behind the last person.

A train whistle blasted through the air. Everyone swiveled. Nell shaded out the sun with her hand. "Here comes the Union Pacific."

The shiny black engine rounded the bend a quarter mile away, a plume of smoke billowing from the smokestack. The engineer blew the whistle again and the townspeople cheered, sending the children into a round of excited laughter.

Nell smiled. "The newness hasn't worn off. I know I've enjoyed the convenience. Makes travel easy. I took a trip into Cheyenne last year when all the work was finished."

"Business?"

"Of a sort. But I had a nice stay over in a hotel for the first time. Especially liked the soaking tub and soft mattress."

Nell was such an odd mixture. Just when he figured she needed space and privacy, she opened up, sharing some little detail of her life.

The screech of the steel brakes ripped through the air all the way from the depot. Conversations started back up, and the line slowly moved forward.

"What's this about?" Charlie gestured ahead of them. "Selling some sort of raffle tickets?"

"Yes. A quilt." She pointed to the side of the school building where the colorful prize was displayed against the wall. "Ten cents a ticket or four for a quarter. The article in the newspaper told all about it."

Her eyes lovingly adored the quilt, which surprised him. Then she smiled fondly at a group of children that walked by—confirming what Seth had hinted at about her wanting children of her own. She wasn't one for housekeeping, and she didn't seem to care much about what she wore—or what she cooked. But she always smelled sweet, like a just-picked bundle of lavender. He took a whiff now, the corners of his mouth pulling up in a smile.

"What?"

She'd caught him.

"Nothing. Just wondering what they'll be serving for supper." *She's twenty*, he reminded himself. *Much too young to know about motherly things. Maddie needs to learn about girl stuff, not breaking horses.*

"I'll take two tickets," the man at the head of the line said.

The large woman directly in front of them stepped forward, then leaned in close to her companion. "It's such a shame. I wonder how she gets along being blind. Without Markus and Penny, she'd have a hard time finding the paper scraps. I've been watching her."

"Oh, pooh," her friend uttered. "She's doing a fine job. I don't care if the process takes a little longer. What else do we have to do today? I'm happy to see she's settled in after her odd appearance into town."

The line moved forward again. "Come along," the woman said, "we're next."

CHAPTER NINE

*C*harlie stepped forward, though he was pretty sure his heart had dropped to the ground back there. Maddie? Odd appearance into town? What did the woman mean?

They were nearly to the front of the line, and he could see the table. Maddie—his Maddie—sat between a boy about her size and an older girl, the one she'd been with the other day. If he wanted, he could step forward and run his hand down her soft hair. Tears blurred his vision and he rubbed a palm across his face. He'd missed her so much.

She carefully held out pieces of paper for the raffle. The buyer would write their name, then drop the scrap into a pink-glass pickle jar that sat in the middle of the table.

"Charlie?" Nell's voice held a ripple of humor. "What's gotten into you, anyway? Get up here."

The rotund woman and her friend had moved away and Nell had stepped up to the sign-in table. She'd set her bowl of boiled eggs on the tabletop and had already signed her name in a little book. She grasped his sleeve and dragged him forward.

Maddie's pulse thrummed in the side of her neck, making Charlie think of a hummingbird, as the sight always did. Sunshine glistened in her hair and the freckles across the top of her nose had deepened, a sure sign she got outdoors more often than she had in Wilsonville. *Good. She loves the sound of the birds.*

Nell, a curious expression on her face, handed him the pencil so he could sign the book. Swallowing nervously, he fought to keep his hand steady as he listened to Nell buy four raffle tickets. She scribbled out her name. "Aren't you gonna buy any chances, Charlie? It's for a good cause."

The smile on Maddie's face faded. She glanced around uncertainly, as if she sensed his presence. Worry lines furrowed her forehead. The day they'd exchanged their goodbyes rushed into his mind with the force of a plow breaking new earth.

He locked the front door to his gunsmith shop and hurried out the back, jogging the half block to Miss Baxter's rented alley house.

Galante had tried again to get the sheriff to arrest him. Unsuccessful, Galante had vowed to take the matter into his own hands. An eye for an eye, even if his son was the one who'd been in the wrong. Charlie didn't like the sound of that. The time had come to send Maddie away.

He dashed into the house without knocking, making the old woman drop the canister of flour she held in her hands. Puffs of white went everywhere, then settled into drifts around her feet. "Mr. Axelrose. What on earth?"

"Pa?"

"Yeah, Maddie, it's me. Sorry to scare you."

With an outstretched hand, she made her way by feel in his direction and he met her halfway. He wrapped her in his arms and picked her up, memorizing the sensation her closeness created in his soul. Over her head, his gaze sought Miss Baxter's.

Setting Maddie's feet back on the floor, he squatted to her level, the sight of her almost breaking his heart. Her rosebud lips smiled, but he could tell she was frightened. She couldn't hide the worry from her large, sightless eyes.

"It's time, Maddie. I want you to gather your things."

She reached out with her small hand and gripped the fabric of his shirt just above the pocket. "I won't leave you, Pa. I don't want to go. I can stay. I can help."

He turned her toward the bedroom. "Go do as I asked, darlin', while I talk with Miss Baxter. Time is short. Don't forget what we talked about. Not saying anything about who you are or where you're from until I come and get you. I want you to grow up someplace safe. Where good people have a chance. That place isn't here."

"Hey, move along." Behind him in line someone grumbled and gave him a nudge. Charlie snapped back to the present. He nodded and held up two fingers.

Nell laughed. "Is this some sort of strange game? He'll have two tickets, I guess, Maddie. You're as pretty as a picture today. How are you?"

"Fine, Mrs. Page." Maddie's voice reminded him of bells on a Christmas sleigh. They made him long to swoop her into a hug and never let her go. She looked so much like Annie that his heart burned.

Maddie's smile returned. She felt around the paper cigar box and fished out two small pieces of paper. She held them out to him with her delicate hand.

It was the hardest thing Charlie had ever done. Taking the tickets without touching her fingers. He scribbled his name on each and dropped them into the jar. Reaching into his pocket, he set two coins on the tabletop.

"Thank you, sir," the little boy sang out. "Good luck winning!"

Charlie nodded, but still didn't speak. His gaze was riveted on Maddie and the easy way she fit in. She was happy. Healthy. Her face was clean and her hair brushed and kept off her face with a cloth headband. The dress she wore looked new.

"Bye, Mrs. Page," Maddie called as Nell dragged him away from the table, toward the schoolhouse.

"What in God's name was that all about, Charlie?" Nell shook her head. "Is it the money? Because if that's the case, I'll be more than happy to reimburse you." She looked down at her hand on his arm and let it fall to her side. "Well?"

"Of course I wanted the tickets. Winning a quilt is at the top of my list of desires." Agitation made him sharp, but when he saw her frown, he said, "Sorry. It's just my, er, it's just that I'm danged hungry." It was the only thing he could come up with to explain his strange behavior. "Can't think of anything else except my stomach. I got sidetracked by the smell of the beef."

He pointed up the rise to half a steer cooking over a fire. A man with a white apron wrapped around his waist stood beside the rock-rimmed fire pit turning a handle that rolled the steer over the flames.

"Here then, take one of these. I made plenty." She took the cloth off the top of the bowl and offered him the eggs.

The sight of the slippery white orbs didn't sit well. After seeing Maddie, carrying on normally was going to be tough. "No, thanks. I'm fine now. Dinner will be served soon enough, I'm sure. Let's go see the schoolhouse."

Nell looked more confused than ever. She handed her bowl of eggs to a woman who was collecting the food and followed him into the school. Everything in the large room was neat and tidy. The teacher's desk divided the space, with a bookcase next to it and a half wall nailed with pegs for hanging coats. Each half of the room had eight desks, lined up in two rows. Charlie detected scents of new lumber and soap, as well as fresh air wafting in through the open windows.

"This is nice," he heard himself saying. "Much larger than any school I've ever seen."

"Enlarging the school, as well as building a park and festival grounds, and cleaning the town up were all stipulations for the railroad to consider us for a stop."

"Welcome." A man came forward with an outstretched hand. "I'm Mr. Hutton, the new teacher."

Charlie shook it. "Nice to meet you, Mr. Hutton, I'm Charlie Rose and this is Mrs.—"

"Your beautiful wife," Mr. Hutton finished in a flourish, a bit overzealous. A sincere smile stretched his face but his forehead had a noticeable, nervous sheen.

"Which child is yours?" he asked. "Or should I say children? I haven't yet had a chance to visit all the homesteads in the surrounding vicinity." He trailed his finger down a list until he came to the *R*'s. When he got to the end without finding their name, he looked up, confused. "The Rose family, you say?"

CHAPTER TEN

$\mathcal{B}$renna overheard Mr. Hutton's blunder all the way from the front of the schoolroom. She'd been showing the Logans where Sarah would sit once class started.

The pain that flitted across Nell's face made her ache. She and Ben had been a loving couple. Even after all this time, Nell still pined away for the man—and for the baby she'd wanted desperately and now thought she'd never have.

Maybe the handsome stranger was courting her. Brenna hoped so. Nell could use a little happiness in her life. "Excuse me, please," she whispered to Chase and Jessie. "I'll be right back."

"Hello, Nell," she exclaimed loudly, drawing everyone's attention. She stopped at Nell's side. "I'm sorry to interrupt, but I'm so happy you could come today. I never know when you might show up in town, you living way out on the ranch." She drew her friend into a hug and then released her. "Who is this?" she asked, looking at the tall cowboy.

Disconcerted by the interruption, Mr. Hutton took a small step back. Confusion shone from his eyes—then realization at his error.

The man at Nell's side was a good foot and a half taller than Mr. Hutton, broad of chest, and a bit on the rugged side. The scar under his eye told Brenna he could take on just about anything—and had at some point. The look in his eyes seemed familiar. And the color made her look twice, badgering her memory to recall who he reminded her of. "I don't believe we've had the pleasure of meeting."

Nell's expression thanked her. Now they wouldn't have to go into a long explanation to the teacher. "This is our new hand, Charlie Rose. We hired him on a few days ago. Charlie, this is my good friend, Brenna Lane. She's head of the school council this year and organized this whole affair."

Why did she think the cowboy looked surprised at that? If he did, he covered it quickly, but his eyes appraised her intensely. "I'm pleased to make your acquaintance, Mrs. Lane," he said in a deep voice.

Again confusion rocked Brenna. Mr. Rose's mouth—the way his lips curled up at the corners when he spoke—took her aback. They had never met before, she was sure, and yet . . .

Shivers skittered up her legs and she wished she hadn't been so eager to help grumpy Gregory. Still, her curiosity got the better of her. "I must have been mistaken when I thought we hadn't yet met. Where was it, Mr. Rose? You're very familiar to me. I'm certain I know you."

He shifted his weight and fingered the brim of the hat he held, looking for all the world like he'd rather be sitting on the bank of some river with a fishing pole. "No, ma'am. I've never been to this part of the country before. But I'm pleased to find this fine town to settle in."

She nodded, all the while racking her brain. He wouldn't fib to her, would he? It was on the tip of her tongue and yet she couldn't place him. "I better get back to the Logans. I just wanted to say hello to Nell. Enjoy the day." She dared one more quick glance at Mr. Rose.

"I am so sorry for assuming—" Mr. Hutton was saying as Brenna turned and hurried back to Jessie's side. Sarah sat in her front-row desk, her legs swinging back and forth. Chase had departed and taken three-year-old Shane with him. A few other families now milled around inside.

"Did you smooth things over?" Jessie asked.

"I hope. I don't like to see Nell hurting." Brenna looked down at Sarah. "Jane will be sitting next to you, Sarah. She can help if you have questions." She caressed the child's upturned cheek.

Jessie leaned in close. "Who's the man?"

"A new hand they hired out at the ranch."

"Oh, Chase mentioned him to me. Albert told him when he ran into Chase at the livery. News travels quickly. No need for telephones in this town."

Penny came through the door hand in hand with Maddie, then set Maddie in the seat next to Sarah. "There, Maddie. That's what a school desk feels like. Have you ever been to school?"

Brenna exchanged a quick glance with Jessie, sure Penny didn't know she was being cruel.

"No, never," Maddie said. "My—" Brenna held her breath, in hopes Maddie would say more about her past, but she finished with, "I'd like to go. Do you think Mr. Hutton will let me?"

Sarah bounced up and down in her seat. "You and Jane can both sit next to me."

Brenna, not knowing what to say, looked up. From across the room, Mr. Rose's gaze was riveted on them.

"Ma, will Maddie be allowed to come to school with us? She wants to. She can't see but we can help her."

By now, Penny had realized her mistake and tears shimmered in her eyes.

"I don't know, Sarah," Jessie said. "That will be up to Mr. Hutton. We'll have to wait and see."

Sarah stood. She looked to the back of the room. "Let's go ask him now. The teacher is right back there."

Maddie stood, as well. "Can we?"

Oh, her little heart was going to be broken into a million pieces when she learned that wouldn't be possible. Wait. Why couldn't Maddie sit with Penny? Penny loved her like a sister. Took great care of her. Maddie could learn a lot from just listening to Mr. Hutton and the other children.

"We won't ask him right now, children. He's busy and has too many things on his mind. Just be patient. I'll talk to him later." *But what will he say?*

Penny's eyes, full of love and adoration, gave Brenna courage. "Thank you, Mama. I know you'll be able to get him to say yes."

Brenna glanced up again. This time, Nell and Charlie Rose were gone and Mr. Hutton had another family at his desk. His smile seemed genuine. Perhaps she'd judged him unfairly. She needed to amend her thoughts about the man so he wouldn't feel her uncertainties about him when she tried to butter him up. She was sure he'd never allow a blind child in his class. He was much too organized. But if she could convince him—

"Brenna?" Jessie tapped her shoulder.

Brenna was amazed to find the children had gone. She'd been so deep in thought she hadn't noticed.

"Frank Lloyd just rang the bell. We'd best go get in line if we want any dinner tonight."

"You're right." Maybe she could run into Mr. Hutton while they were—*Oh, no.* She remembered the missing textbooks and her anxiety spiked. He'd never do her a favor once he learned about that.

She and Jessie were the last to leave the classroom. They stepped outside only to find Mr. Hutton waiting on the stoop, holding the door for them.

Brenna pulled up short.

"Ladies."

"Thank you, but that was unnecessary, Mr. Hutton," she said.

"I disagree. Your kind gesture saved me from myself today. I was about to dig myself in deeper before you came to my rescue." When he smiled at her, she didn't know how to respond. "And since you *are* the councilwoman in charge this year, we'll be working as a team. The least I can do is partake of dinner with you—if you're willing. There are several things I'd like to go over before class starts."

Brenna smiled and fortified her spine. Maddie first. The forgotten textbooks could wait. She nodded at Mr. Hutton and stepped with him onto the grass.

CHAPTER ELEVEN

$\mathcal{N}$ell moved down the food table alongside Charlie. She liked how his height made her feel small and, even if she didn't need it, protected. His blue eyes were amazingly alive today, and for the first time she'd noticed golden flecks, along with green and blue, around his irises. He'd looked over to ask her a question and their intensity had stopped her hands and made her forget what she was reaching for.

How foolish. She was no child with a schoolgirl crush. She knew what was what. Still, if she let her guard slip, she found herself pretending she and Charlie were a couple, even the couple Mr. Hutton had believed they were—with a homestead and children of their own.

Seemed she wasn't the only one to think him handsome. She hadn't missed the titter of the adolescent girls when she and Charlie walked by. But it was more than handsome. He was kind with the animals, even when they were giving him a hard time—that was a very telling trait. His appreciation of her books endeared him to her more. And she liked the sound of his voice, especially when he was bidding her good night.

The object of her musings leaned down close to speak into her ear. "That Mrs. Lane seemed like a nice woman. Does she live close by?"

Brenna? Had Brenna caught Charlie's eye? Slender, big-hearted, feminine—of course she would. She kept an immaculate home, cooked like a chef, and could sew just about anything. Today she looked especially lovely with her chestnut hair pinned half up and half down, flowing in the breeze. Any man would be captivated. Brenna was everything Nell wasn't.

"She does. Just over the bridge on Oak Street," Nell answered, making sure her voice didn't wobble. She'd been imaging all sorts of things about Charlie Rose. Well, she just had to stop. "There are several houses up that way."

Charlie turned from the food table, a thick slab of beef on his fork, and looked toward the bridge. Appeared to be calculating something in his head. When he caught her watching, two red splotches blossomed on his cheeks and he seemed unduly interested in the food on the table. Plopping the meat onto his plate, he reached for the potato salad spoon a little too quickly.

He didn't have to hide his feelings from her. She had no claim on him just because she'd given him a job.

Charlie pointed with his fork. "Look. Your eggs are all but gone. People must like them."

He was changing the subject. She nodded. "Or they're feeding them to their dogs."

Her usual pants and shirt, although clean and pressed, felt drab next to all the women in dresses and bonnets. Mrs. Brinkley held a fancy little parasol over her head. Nell couldn't imagine why she needed it, with the mild temperature today. *For looks, you dummy*, she shouted to herself. Mrs. Brinkley made an effort to dress attractively for her husband and the rest of the town. Nell glanced at Charlie. Was he given to feminine women? *What's wrong with me that I never want to wear garb like that?*

Reaching the end of the food table, she followed Charlie onto the grass a few feet away and looked for a place to settle so they could eat. Chairs and tables had been set up, but not nearly enough for the whole crowd. Some women had thought ahead and brought a blanket. Those were laid out on the hillside, looking much like the sampler quilt hanging on the side of the schoolhouse.

Glancing toward the quilt, her breath caught. Charlie stopped and looked at her. "What?"

"That child makes my heart hurt." She pointed to where Maddie was standing as she felt the quilt's soft fabric. Penny stuck close by her side. The smile on Maddie's face was one of adoration. "Isn't she sweet? About the cutest little girl I've ever seen, and nice through and through."

When Charlie didn't respond, Nell turned back to find him staring at Maddie. His gaze was one she'd never seen before. Tortured. Sad. She touched his arm. "Charlie?"

"She is," Charlie finally said.

The words were soft and low, and something in his tone gave Nell pause. Had he ever married? Or longed for children of his own, as she did? "She's blind. Came to town one day on the stage. She was all alone and won't tell anyone her last name or where she's from."

"She was all alone?"

His question was gruff, and the golden flecks in his eyes blazed with something akin to horror. Baffled, she just looked at him.

"Yes. The mystery seems to stem from Brenna's aunt. The old woman died on the way here, just passed away in her sleep the night before they arrived. The child had a note in the aunt's handwriting asking that she be taken to Brenna's house. No one knows who she is or where she's from."

They watched while Penny stepped forward and took Maddie by the hand, then led her down toward the food table. The two girls chatted as if they'd been friends for years.

Charlie turned away, pushing the brim of his hat lower on his forehead, his expression unreadable. "So, she lives with Brenna?"

"Yes. And with Brenna's three children, and one orphan boy."

"Do they get along?" He cleared his throat. "I mean moneywise. Do they have enough to eat?"

Nell could see where this was going. But what would be would be. She had no power to stop it, and even if she could, she wouldn't try. Brenna had a heart of gold. With a man like Charlie by her side, she'd be able to accomplish anything.

"Now she does. For a few years, her money was tight but the people of Logan Meadows helped supply her needs. Made sure she had food for their supper, clothes to wear, wood to burn. She does mending and odd jobs. Now that she's presiding over the school council, she's picked up new customers and is doing much better. I guess some people didn't know her before."

"Yoo-hoo, Nell," Mrs. Hollyhock called. "Come sit with us. I saved ya a spot on my blanket."

Nell waved, then turned to Charlie. "Do you mind sitting with some of my friends?"

"Any place is fine, just so I can dig into this plate."

Nell led the way. "Thank you, Mrs. Hollyhock. "We'd be delighted to join you." She sank onto the lemon-yellow blanket spread across the grass. "This is Charlie Rose, our new ranch hand. I thought I'd bring him into town today so he could meet some people.

"Charlie, this is Chase and Jessie Logan, ranchers and friends. They have the spread next to ours." Chase smiled at Nell. He'd been a good neighbor. Helping out when times got difficult. "And this is Mrs. Hollyhock. Four years ago she sold her store in Valley Springs and followed the Logans here and bought the Red Rooster Inn. And that's Shane," Nell finished, smiling at the robust toddler Chase corralled on their blanket. Shane was tall for his age, and he knew it. Messy dark-blond hair stuck out from his head and his overalls already had grass stains on both knees. The child stomped his foot. "Want t' pway wif Sarah an' Mark," he cried, tugging on Chase's shirt sleeve. His watery eyes tore at Nell's heart.

Chase picked Shane up and bounced him in his arms. "Just as soon as you eat something, son." He took a previously cut chunk of meat from his plate and handed the food to the child. "And *not* a second before."

Shane blinked the tears away and stuffed the food into his mouth, chewing vigorously.

Tantrum averted, Mrs. Hollyhock took stock of Charlie as only she could do. One had to be made of strong stuff to stand up to her squinty-eyed scrutiny. Jessie caught Nell's eye and winked. Charlie was oblivious, having lashed into his potatoes. Guess he really had been starving.

Soon everyone was eating.

Mrs. Hollyhock wiped her mouth. "That secret do-gooder struck the inn last week. I found a purty handful of wildflowers tied up with a blue ribbon stuck behind the handle of my chicken coop where I'd be sure to find it." All eyes focused on Violet. "The sight sure made a nice feeling in my heart. I wonder who the perpetrator could be."

She stared at Jessie for so long Chase's wife finally had to speak up. "It's *not* me, Mrs. Hollyhock—I've told you that before. When do I have time to get off the ranch and come to town?"

Jessie laughed and her husband smiled at the sound, love shining in his eyes. The picture created a deep longing inside of Nell. She wanted a love like that. True and enduring. Something that would last through any hardship.

"I wish I could claim responsibility," Jessie went on. "Because whoever is accountable is making a lot of people happy. But surely the person must live close by. Maude told me on my last visit that the back porch of the mercantile had been swept clean after an afternoon windstorm. You know how the draft pulls down behind her store. She said one minute the porch was a mighty mess and then an hour later, clean as a whistle. She never heard a thing."

Nell caught Charlie's puzzled expression. "Someone in Logan Meadows is doing helpful or nice things for no reason at all. It's really very sweet. Sort of like Christmas every day." When she finished she found Mrs. Hollyhock watching her. "Surely, you don't think it's me."

Violet shook her finger. "I don't know what I think, missy. Could be you."

"No, no, it's not. I promise."

"Well, I'm going to keep going until I find out who's responsible. So I can thank 'em for all the good they's doin'. Fer now, I'll jist have to be satisfied with enjoying this fine supper." Mrs. Hollyhock graced them all with her elderly, well-used smile, and Nell couldn't stop a surge of affection. Violet was the closest thing to a grandma she'd ever had—the sort of grandma who would scold you if your parents were looking, then wink at you when their backs were turned. More than anyone, she'd given Nell a feel for what it might have been like to grow up with parents. Just like now, inviting her and Charlie to eat on her blanket as if they were family.

"I heard tell of a bit of news," Violet went on. "And it ain't gossip because the juicy tidbit came straight from the billy goat's mouth." With that statement, Mrs. Hollyhock had everyone's attention. Seemed she liked the audience she had and wasn't going to waste it. "Won't be but a short spell before the old Donovan farm is plunked back on the market."

"Really?" Chase asked, interested.

"I jist said it, didn't I." The old woman rolled her eyes. "I don't know why he always feels the need to question me. You think I'm makin' it up?"

Irritation rippled across Chase's face. Fond irritation, Jessie liked to say.

"Wilson Nelson and the missus is going back where they come from," Mrs. Hollyhock said. "Seems she's never taken to living so far away from her family. Being she's jist got in the family way, she's puttin' her wifely foot down to go home. Didn't think those city slickers would stay for long."

"That's a nice piece of land," Nell said on a breath, wishing she had the money to buy the place herself. "Nice house, as well." Real estate like that wouldn't last long. She could see Chase Logan over there tossing ideas around like a juggler at the fair. He had the means to buy it tomorrow if he wanted. "What about Thom?" she asked. "Does he want to buy back his family home? Take up ranching and farming again?" Though with acting as the sheriff's deputy and all that he did helping out Hannah at the Silky Hen, that might be tough.

Mrs. Hollyhock shook her head. "Nope. That chapter of his life is over and he's on to the next—at least that's what he told me when I asked. The place is fair game t'anyone int—"

Mrs. Hollyhock stopped speaking—an occurrence so rare that for several moments everyone just stared at her. Then the old woman sucked in a breath so hard she started coughing.

"Mrs. Hollyhock?" Alarmed, Jessie reached out a hand. "Are you all right?"

"Yes, yes," she wheezed. "Gist got the stuffin' surprised out of me." Her crooked, hawk-like talon of a finger pointed toward the road leading to the train station. "Take a gander at who's coming."

Approaching on the boardwalk was a tall, thin woman who looked as if she'd seen better days. One ragged carpetbag was all she carried, and she switched the bag back and forth as if the thing were heavy.

"Who is it?" Nell asked. "She must have come in on the train and walked the quarter mile from the depot. She looks tired."

"No." The word came out of Jessie slow and shaky. "It can't be."

CHAPTER TWELVE

*O*h, yes siree, it can be. And it is," Mrs. Hollyhock said in a conspiratorial tone from her spot on the picnic blanket. Nell leaned in to be able to hear. "That's Beth Fairington, all right. For those of you who don't know her, she was my clerk back in Valley Springs, in the mercantile—that was afore she run off with some smooth talker passing through town." The old woman's face hardened, then the firm line of her mouth faded away into sadness. "Didn't even have the mind to tell me afore. Near broke my heart at the time. I didn't even know if she was still alive. I've sent many a prayer to heaven on her account." Mrs. Hollyhock's tone held censure and affection at the same time.

"Seems she found you, Violet," Jessie said under her breath. "I wonder what she's doing here."

Jessie's face had all but gone white. Chase scowled.

"What's she doing here?"

"Can't say as I know, but it won't be long afore we find out."

Mrs. Hollyhock was right. The woman had spotted them on the hill. Her dress, made of some sort of heavy fabric adorned with fancy stitching around the sleeves and plentiful brown buttons up the front, appeared stifling. The cream-colored ribbons of her bonnet fluttered in the warm September breeze. A strawberry splotch on each of her cheeks told Nell she wasn't as composed as she tried to appear.

"What's wrong with her?" Nell asked quietly. "I mean, from the sound of it, there isn't any love lost between you two."

"Malicious mule of a woman, why—" Chase rumbled.

Jessie and Mrs. Hollyhock gasped. Jessie lunged and pressed her hand against his mouth, successfully shushing him. Charlie started to laugh.

Jessie leaned forward. "She's a horrible gossip, and didn't think twice before saying unspeakably mean things about people in Valley Springs. But, I guess we should at least give her a chance. It's the Christian thing to do. Maybe she's changed her ways and wants to start over. And Violet likes her well enough, isn't that right?"

Mrs. Hollyhock's brows couldn't go any higher.

Jessie's head tilted in question. "Violet?"

"That's right, dearie. Now hush up. We don't want Beth ta think we're gossiping about her."

"Violet?" Beth Fairington stopped a few feet away. Her eyes darted around the group before returning to Mrs. Hollyhock. "Is that you? I can't believe we've run into each other after all these years."

Mrs. Hollyhock, unable to do anything but, climbed to her feet with some help from Charlie. The two women embraced. Nell overheard a few whispered words exchanged.

Charlie leaned down and tapped Nell's shoulder. "What do you say we take a walk?"

She set down her plate. "That's a good idea."

He held out his hand to help her up. When she placed her palm in his large one, a tickle as soft as a snowflake danced in her belly. She could daydream all she wanted about Charlie, but his asking about Brenna told her everything she needed to know.

Relief rippled through Brenna when Mr. Lloyd approached the side of the schoolhouse where the quilt hung. Wouldn't be too much longer and this day would be over. She sat beside Mr. Hutton on some brown chairs, and was ashamed to say she'd not dredged up the courage to ask him about Maddie going to school. She hadn't confessed about the math books, either.

"May I have your attention, please?" Mr. Lloyd called through cupped hands. When he motioned to Brenna expectantly, her insides frosted over. "Mrs. Lane? Would you like to say a word or two before we select the winner of this beautifully stitched sampler quilt?"

Did he expect her to make a speech? This was the first she'd heard of it. She smiled graciously, gathered her skirt and stood. *Oh my.* She wasn't a practiced speaker. Her children were the largest group she'd ever addressed. Making her way toward Mr. Lloyd she spotted Penny with Maddie, Jane and Markus. The pride on their faces gave her courage. How could she let them down? *Please, oh Lord, put some words in my mouth.*

She smiled, then swallowed once. "Th-thank you so much, Mr. Lloyd. On behalf . . . of this year's . . . school council, as well as our new teacher, Mr. Hutton, I'd like to thank everyone . . . for coming out today to make the open house and fundraiser a success." She took a deep breath and let the air out slowly, stunned she'd had something to say. Two whole sentences to be exact. Everyone watched her expectantly, maybe even a bit—approvingly. "There are so many people to thank; I really don't know where to begin. Mrs. Brown and Mrs. Brinkley, for the beautiful new curtains for the school, Hannah and Thom Donovan for the side of beef and desserts for our meal today. Gabe Garrison and Jake for chopping and delivering the wood Mr. and Mrs. Logan donated from their ranch."

She took another breath. "Mr. Frank Lloyd for his generous gift of two new blackboards and chalk, as well as the desks that were needed this year for new students."

She paused again. She hadn't made a list and was going off memory. "Oh, I don't want to forget Albert and Winthrop Preston for their contribution of a second wood-burning stove so our children will be toasty when the temperatures start to drop. We wouldn't want them to get frostbite."

Laughter actually rippled through the crowd. She spotted Hannah in the audience, smiling. Happiness filled her.

She glanced around again, not wanting to leave anyone out. She noticed Mrs. Hollyhock in conversation with a woman she'd never seen before at the back of the crowd. She'd almost forgotten one of the most important people. "And especially to our dear Mrs. Hollyhock and her circle of lovely quilting fairies who spent hours creating the beautiful Logan Meadows quilt for today's raffle. They alone raised twenty-three dollars and seventy-five cents. A good amount that will be used this coming year for books and supplies." A round of applause went up and Brenna waved her arm behind her to direct the attention to the quilt.

"A final thanks to everyone who came to support the school and brought a dish to share for the potluck. Everything was delicious. I hope I didn't forget to mention anyone. Please forgive me if I did."

There. I can't believe it. I'm finished and I didn't stumble, sputter, or go blank. Brenna hid her smile, unable to stay her temptation to sneak a peek at Mr. Hutton. Their eyes met. He gave an imperceptible nod, and then started to clap, and another round of applause went up. Penny's face glowed brighter than the sun on a cloudless day.

"Now, for those of you who haven't had the opportunity yet to meet Logan Meadows's new teacher, who comes to us on the highest recommendation all the way from Pennsylvania, I'd like to introduce him and ask him to say a few words." She held out her hand and their gaze met and held again. "Mr. Hutton."

Mr. Hutton smiled and nodded as he came forward. "Thank you for your gracious introduction, Mrs. Lane."

She felt the intensity of his eyes. She couldn't decide if they were browner than they were green. Certainly, whichever, they made a flutter in her tummy akin to butterflies racing in the wind. She was relieved when he finally turned to the crowd.

"Thank you so much for the hearty welcome your town has shown me. I'm eager to teach your children. I hope to make a mark in their lives. If any of you have questions anytime throughout the school term, I encourage you to come and see me. The door is always open." *Short and sweet.* He stepped away and glanced back at Brenna and Mr. Lloyd as a round of applause filled the air.

Frank Lloyd motioned for the pickle jar. He stuck his hand in and swished the papers around for several seconds, then shook the whole jar up and down. "Mrs. Lane, will you do the honor of selecting our winner?"

This was the best day of her life. "Of course."

He held the glass container high enough that she wouldn't be able to see which paper she selected. Stretching up, she reached inside and let her fingers walk around on the papers for a few seconds, smiling at the anticipation written on the children's faces. She pulled out the winner and looked at the name.

"And the beautiful sampler quilt goes to our new man in town, Mr. Rose."

Charlie stood behind Nell, watching the proceeding from the back of the crowd. He only had eyes for his little girl. The trip here must have been awful for Maddie. He cursed himself for putting her in that frightening position and grieved, as he knew she must have grieved in silence, the loss of Miss Baxter. He swallowed down a lump of regret, wondering if the trip had proved too much for his old friend, or if it had just been her time to go. Either way, he wished he could save Maddie the heartbreak he knew his child had suffered, and perhaps still did.

Beside the quilt, Brenna Lane laughed and held up the winning ticket. Miss Baxter, God rest her soul, hadn't exaggerated when she said her niece was pretty. More than that, she was an angel. She'd taken in his little girl, protected her. There wasn't enough money in the world to repay her for what her kindness to Maddie meant to him.

At his side, Nell gasped with excitement, and Charlie heard the tail end of his name. Guess he'd won. Nell was practically jumping up and down, reminding him of a surprised little girl. He couldn't resist and chucked her under the chin. "And there you go. Who would have known?"

"Me, Charlie Rose." Nell grinned. "I had a feeling you were going to win. Down in the pit of my stomach."

Her face was alive—*really alive*—for the first time since he'd met her. Her smile went all the way up to her eyes. Astonished at her beauty, he dragged his gaze away. "That was just the under-baked potatoes in the salad," he said in a low tone not to be overheard. He chuckled. "My stomach is also a mite queasy."

She shushed him. "Go on, now. Get up there and claim your prize."

Behind the twinkle in her eyes he saw something else. A hot lance of awareness jabbed his heart. He liked Nell a whole lot more than he should. Besides, Galante was out there somewhere, wanting blood for blood, and would stop at nothing to get it. Charlie'd do well to remember that when yearnings tried to distract him.

Brenna went up on tiptoe, scanning the crowd. "Mr. Rose? Are you out there somewhere?"

Nell shoved his shoulder. "Get going, Mr. Slowpoke, before they pick another name."

Charlie threaded his way through the townspeople. Men watched with a pinch of caution—he didn't blame them a bit—and the ladies with welcoming smiles. Almost there, he caught a glimpse of Maddie in the front row. How his heart broke every time he had to pretend she wasn't his. She kneeled in the grass, her hands clasped in front of her. Her head was tipped just so, the way she used for seeing by listening intently. With a jolt of fear, he realized Brenna was quite close to where the children sat. What if Maddie recognized his voice?

"Right up here, Mr. Rose," Brenna called. Mr. Lloyd walked over and handed the bulky armful of quilt to Charlie. "Congratulations. This is a nice welcome to our quiet little town."

When Charlie eked out a high-pitched thank-you to disguise his voice, both Brenna and the banker blinked in astonishment. The boys and girls giggled. All except Maddie. Her smile faded and she took on an expression of deep concentration.

Flustered, he glanced back at Nell, in need of support, but she was frowning at him. The last thing he wanted to do was confuse his daughter, or cause her pain. He'd told her he'd come for her in a month—and the process had taken much longer. He needed to ease back into her life, not shatter it again. Above all, he needed to make sure they were safe first. Although not saying another word made him seem ungrateful, there was no help for it. Nothing mattered but Maddie.

Resolved, he tipped his hat and tried to wrangle a smile, although the way his mouth felt, the sight just might scare some people off. Instead of starting back toward Nell, he turned on his heel and made straight for his horse.

CHAPTER THIRTEEN

With the empty egg crock under her arm, Nell mounted up and reined around with no intention of trying to catch Charlie or find out what was eating at him. It was as if all the blood had drained from his face up there. He'd been speechless.

Thunderstruck with Brenna's charm, more like. Nell tried to shove away her hurt. But what about the expression on his face as he'd pushed his way through the townspeople, then made short work of getting to his horse and leaving? That had her stumped.

She rode up the street at a jog. Everyone was still back at the school, gathering their things to go home. As she crossed the bridge on Main Street, the two bison Win Preston owned at the livery watched her curiously through the sturdy boards of their corral. She passed the WELCOME TO LOGAN MEADOWS sign.

Once across, Nell clucked softly, sending Coyote into a lope. She let the sensation ease away her questions about Charlie and concentrated on the rocking-chair motion of her horse's gait, one of the many things she loved about her mount. As a working horse, they didn't come much better. As a friend, none more loyal. The road under his hoofs sped past. His breathing settled into a cadence that had the power to heal. This was where Nell belonged. Here was where she felt at home. Alone in the saddle where she could never be hurt again. Not by Charlie, not by the eerie stranger that still dogged the edges of her mind—and especially not by *her father*.

Shocked, she slid her horse to a halt. He danced around excitedly and pulled on the bit, not ready yet to stop. She brushed her hand over the silky, soft coat of his shoulder, then asked for a walk by sitting deep in the saddle and giving him his head.

Her father? Where had the thought come from? She had no memories of any life prior to the one alone with her brother. No recollections of either of her parents. For as long as she could remember, Seth had been totally closemouthed about them. He'd changed the subject whenever she asked. She wondered why she should have that thought now.

Nell hooked her reins around the saddle horn. She reached back to her saddlebag, unbuckled the keep to draw out her holster and gun, and stuffed her empty crock inside. Buckling the leather gun belt around her waist, she stood in her stirrups, letting the Colt 45 settle into place on her thigh.

There.

That felt better.

One never knew what might jump out at you once beyond the security of town. But wild animals didn't shake her calm; this unsettled feeling was different—due to something else . . . *or someone else.* Her confidence rattled, she glanced again over her shoulder at the trail she'd just ridden. *Yes. The stranger.* The one in her yard who'd turned her blood to ice. She reached down and touched the handle of her gun, determined to never let herself feel threatened like that again.

Seth was seated comfortably on the porch when Nell rode into the yard. He was hatless and his feet were propped on the rail and crossed at the ankles. Dog slept by his side.

He stood and came down the steps to meet her. "Where's Charlie?"

Her gaze cut to the barn. *He didn't come home.* "Don't know. Maybe he decided Logan Meadows wasn't for him and rode out."

Seth's brow lowered. "What're you babbling about? Did you have angry words or something?"

She swung her leg over the saddle and stepped to the ground, disappointment over Charlie hurting more than it should. He was a drifter. Rode in one day, would ride out the next. He'd never promised to stay for any length of time—although he'd sounded like he was planning to settle. Funny, she'd pegged him as one of the long hires, and actually he was the shortest. "No. Are his things still in the house? Or his horse gone? He rode the black today."

"Don't know. I got home a short while ago and didn't notice. Been here just long enough to turn my horse out to pasture and plop down in a chair. Nell, you must know more. Didn't you leave town together?"

"Nope. It was strange. He was getting along fine, meeting everyone in town, until he won the raffle. When he went forward to collect, something happened. Like blowing out the lamp." *Yeah, like being so close to Brenna rendered him brainless.*

Dog came down the steps and sniffed at Nell's boots.

"Did someone say something to him? Insult him?"

How the heck was she supposed to know what Charlie Rose was thinking? Agitated, she slapped the reins across her palm. "I said I don't know what transpired, and I don't. After he won the quilt he—"

"Quilt?"

"The raffle prize. He won the quilt and went forward to collect his winnin's, made a strange sound out of his mouth that was supposed to be *thank you*, then turned and stalked off. Mounted up without saying a thing to me and was gone. Everyone just watched him go. I had thought"—*no, hoped*—"he was coming back here."

Seth pushed his hand through his hair, then stared out into the distance, as if he could see through space and time. *Too bad.*

Seth had also taken to Charlie. And he'd been a huge help. And would have been an even bigger one when they started breaking the new string.

Oh, well. Easy come, easy go.

"What aren't you saying, Nell? I've raised you since you were a little rascal in piggy-tails. I know that expression. Tell me what's upset you."

"That's *pigtails*," she corrected, and shook her head. She started for the barn, reins in hand and Coyote following behind. Chickens scattered when she walked straight through their flock. "I've told you all that I know. One minute he was enjoying himself, the next—I don't know."

Seth took up step with her. "Did it have something to do with the quilt? I can't imagine an object as benign as a bed covering setting him off, not with his good-naturedness."

Inside the barn, Charlie's chestnut mare poked her head out of her stall and greeted them with a low rumbling nicker. Across the way, Drag Anchor pinned his ears, still angry at being kept inside.

"Georgia's still here. Maybe he'll come back for her." A splash of relief cooled her heart.

"Maybe the quilt reminded him of his wife."

Nell spun around. "Wife?"

"Yeah, didn't he tell you? He lost his wife to a wagon accident some time ago."

Nell blinked several times. She thought about his strange reaction to Maddie, wondering if he'd also lost a child. He certainly was old enough to have had a family of his own. "No. He never mentioned that to me at all."

Seth scratched his shoulder. "I guess it ain't something you go around talking about. He's pretty tight-lipped about his past."

Why hadn't Charlie mentioned he'd lost a spouse, like her? With Seth eyeing her shrewdly she felt like a bug on a pin. "Chances are he just needs more time to get over her death. When you lose a person you love, time can stand still."

She removed Coyote's bridle and slipped his rope halter on, knotting the catch. She ran her hand down between Coyote's eyes, thinking. Perhaps she misjudged Charlie's reaction to Brenna. Maybe the way he clammed up had something to do with his deceased wife. Whatever the reason, her brother stood there expectantly. "I don't know, Seth. Maybe Charlie was hoping to live high on the hog and, now that he's been out here a few days, is making his break before he gets stuck. I guess you just never know a feller until you take him on a picnic." She joked to lighten the mood, all the while her heart shuddering at the possibility.

Seth went over and stroked Charlie's horse on the neck, as if Georgia's being here meant their hired hand would be coming back. That wasn't a sure bet. Men stole horses all the time.

"You stop talking stupid," he said. "You do that when you're scared of something. The crux of the matter is, Charlie means something to you. I've known that since the day he arrived."

She stilled, the back cinch undone and the front cinch strap in her hands. She tossed her brother a flustered smile, noticing the tired lines around his eyes. "Is that so?"

"Yes. It's so."

Finished, she hoisted the heavy saddle from Coyote's back. "Oh, I'm just all aflutter when Charlie is around and you can read me like a book?" She stomped to the tack room.

"As much as you hate the thought, yeah."

She returned with a soft-bristled brush. "That's plain silly." She stroked the tool over the horse's side and muscular hip. "Charlie doesn't mean any more to me than any of the other hands we've employed over the years. I can't believe you think that. Are you teasing to get me back for letting the house go?"

Seth barked out a laugh. "I've been meaning to talk to you about that."

Turning, she aimed the brush at his head and let the bristles fly. He ducked, and the grooming instrument sailed into Georgia's stall and clattered against the back wall, spooking the mare and causing several chickens to fly down from the loft and run out the open door. Georgia snorted and whirled her hip into the gate.

Nell broke into remorseful laughter. "I'm sorry, girl. I didn't mean to scare you. I was trying to silence my big-talking brother. He thinks he knows everything." She hurried over and opened the mare's stall door. "I have no more designs on Charlie than you do on some mystery woman," she called loudly from inside. She picked up the brush from the corner. "Charlie Rose is too much of a ladies' man for my liking. He thinks a lot of himself with his bluer-than-blue eyes and charming smile. I'm sure in his day he's enchanted more women than we have horses."

Nell gave the mare a quick hug and kissed her neck. "Sorry again, Georgia." With a lighthearted chuckle, she stepped through the gate.

And came face-to-face with Charlie.

CHAPTER FOURTEEN

*B*renna took in the scene of the abandoned school grounds, happy and satisfied with her accomplishments. Thom and Albert had just finished loading the last of the boards and barrels and sawhorses that made up the tables, along with the extra chairs, into the buckboard, and they'd taken them away to the livery to be stored in the loft.

Exhausted, she longed to sit on the grass for a few brief moments of solitude, but there were still chores awaiting her at home. She'd go retrieve her belongings from inside the school and be on her way.

Brenna crossed the yard, noting the path that curved between the doctor's office and Lettie's Bakery to Main Street. A mouthwatering aroma floated in the air. Lettie must be frying her confections for the church's standing Sunday order. On the doorstep of the schoolhouse, she reached for the doorknob at the same time the door opened.

Mr. Hutton barreled out full steam ahead, head down and mumbling to himself.

They collided with a *woomph*.

Brenna took an uncontrolled step back, teetered and plopped to the ground on her backside with a cry.

He rushed forward and hoisted her up by the arm. "Mrs. Lane, I'm so sorry. Are you hurt?"

Several moments passed before she could get any words past

her lips. Her bottom felt like a five-foot-wide board had just rendered her a punishment, reminding her of the whuppings her pa used to give her after he'd been drinking. Stars darted around in front of her eyes and she thought she heard the twittering of birds.

"Please, Mrs. Lane, *say* something. I can't believe this has happened again. I should have been more careful, watched where I was going."

"I—*ouch*—" She lifted her foot off the ground quickly as a sharp pain shot up her leg. "And I should do the same."

"Here, sit back on the ground until the pain stops." His expression was panicked as he lowered her carefully down. "What hurts? Your leg? Your foot?"

Brenna leaned forward and fingered her sturdy brown boot. "Actually, I think it's my ankle."

Totally disregarding the damage the grass might do to his lovely corduroy pants, Mr. Hutton sank to his knees and started unlacing her boot. His fingers moved with astounding speed.

"*Please*, Mr. Hutton, you'll ruin your pants. Stand up. I can do that." Leaning forward she tried to push his hands away. *These boots are so old. What must he think?*

"Never you mind," he replied. "I'm almost done." He slipped off her boot to expose her black sock, then pulled that off next.

He tipped his head as he contemplated her ankle. "Do you think it's broken?" He carefully probed around the area. "Can you wiggle your toes?"

"That's a myth," she said, then sucked in a deep breath when he found the tender area.

"Pardon me?"

"That one can't wiggle their toes if their ankle is broken. It's not true."

"Ah." He accepted the correction with grace, then glanced at her face—where their gaze met and held for the third time in one day—before continuing his exploration of her lower leg and foot.

"Ohhh . . ."

"Hurt?"

"No, it didn't—I just thought I'd—"

"Hush."

His hands on her ankle sent a ripple of longing straight to her heart. *A different kind of pain, Mr. Hutton.* She wanted to pull her foot back before she made a bigger fool of herself, but couldn't make herself do it.

"Stay put." He set her foot carefully on the grass. "I'm going for Dr. Thorn."

Flustered, she grasped for his shirtsleeve before he could stand. "That's totally unnecessary. It's just a simple twist. The pain is almost gone." *And I'm enjoying your attention much more than I should.*

"I'm commanding you to stay here, Mrs. Lane. It's for your own good. If you try to walk on a broken ankle you could make the injury much worse." He stood and gazed down at her. "Humor me, please. I've seen a damaged, unattended ankle. I assure you, it's not pretty."

"It's Saturday, Mr. Hutton. Dr. Thorn isn't in his office."

"He might be since he was just here a little while ago. And if he isn't, I'll go to his house." He glanced down the slope toward Main Street, then over at the bridge. "Where does he live? I'm sure he'll come if I ask."

She couldn't stop a soft laugh from slipping through her lips. He appeared so earnest, and she felt so young. It seemed as if the sun had just come out and spring flowers were blooming everywhere. She worked to keep her breathing slow and her eyes trained anywhere but at his face—and lips. "I assure you I'm fine."

Feeling a bit exposed with him towering over her, Brenna slipped on her sock and then her boot, quickly working the laces. "If you'll just give me a hand up, I'll be on my way home."

She extended her arm, holding her palm open.

His eyebrow arched. "This is going against my better judgment, Mrs. Lane." He took her hand and easily drew her to her feet.

Another flash of longing sparked in her heart when his warm palm took hers. He was so close. She wobbled slightly before she set her injured foot on the grass to catch her balance. Her universe shrank until it consisted of Mr. Hutton's hand dwarfing hers. She snapped her gaze to his, but he didn't let go when she attempted to pull away.

"Wait until your color comes back. It won't do any good to get you upright if you tumble back to the grass and perhaps twist your other ankle, or even injure something else." He searched around on the ground. "Where are your things? Were you carrying anything?"

"Inside." She felt small and cared for beside him. She'd been a widow for so long, doing for her children, that having him fuss over her felt strange. "I was just on my way in to collect them when—"

"I came blundering out."

She smiled. "Yes."

"Then we're even. Can you stand on your own if I go get them for you?"

"I'm sure I can. They're on your desk."

Mr. Hutton backed away slowly as if he expected her to topple over any second. He looked so serious; she felt like giggling but knew that would hurt his feelings. When he seemed sure she was stable, he went back inside, only to return a moment later with her clipboard and shawl.

He held her things back when she reached for them.

So, he was going to be stubborn?

"I can walk, Mr. Hutton." She took several halting steps, and although it didn't feel great, she knew her ankle was only twisted and she'd be fine by tomorrow. Her boot, now that she'd laced it more tightly than normal, helped support the offended limb. She could easily make the distance home if she took her time. "It's only five minutes. I'll take those now." Her tone was firm.

Disregarding her statement, he set his leather case on the ground and inserted her clipboard and shawl inside. "If you won't let me fetch the doctor, the least you can do is let me carry your things home. I'm on my way there myself. We *are* neighbors, you know."

The twinkle in his eyes surprised her. He held out his elbow until she took a firm hold.

They'd made peace and the reality felt good. His knocking her down made them even. She didn't have to feel embarrassed anymore. If she was a clumsy oaf, then so was he. Now might be the perfect time to ask him about Maddie. When he seemed open and willing.

"Actually, this may have been a fortuitous but useful meeting," she began, "us bumping into each other again."

"Really?" He regarded her with curiosity as they inched along. "In what way?"

"Well, there's something I've been meaning to ask you, but the timing hasn't been right."

That had his attention. "Go on."

Oh, why had she begun? He'd probably say no, and then they'd argue and ruin this nice truce they'd struck up. Still, she'd do anything for Maddie. They were almost down the gentle slope of the hill and would soon be on Main Street. "I wanted to request—" she blurted out, then stopped.

"Just say it, Mrs. Lane. We are both adults, are we not? You needn't fear my reaction."

Really? I have my doubts. "Fine then. Remember you just said that."

A rueful grin softened his face. "Have I been so stern to give you that impression of me? If yes, I'm sorry. Sometimes I get caught up in my thoughts, memories—ah, but I don't mean to." He patted her hand, the one clutching the crook of his arm. They were now on the boardwalk, heading for the bridge over Shady Creek.

Brenna drew a deep breath and plunged in. "I want to send Maddie to school on Monday with the other children. She's of age and is very bright and—"

"The blind girl?"

Brenna swallowed. "Yes."

"Mrs. Lane, I'm not equipped to handle a child with an infirmity like that." His tone was kind, but fixed. Frank Lloyd came out of the bank across the dusty street. She could see his curious expression.

"What must he think?"

"Pardon me?"

"Mr. Lloyd, the banker. He's watching, well . . ." She squeezed Mr. Hutton's arm and his eyes widened as if just understanding her meaning.

"Oh, yes. I'll explain to him the next time I see him. Now, where were we? In the daily routine of the school day the girl could get hurt, fall, bump her head on the side of a desk, or a number of other dangers. And she'd slow the other children down. I cannot allow it. I'm sorry."

"Maddie gets along fine. She won't be hurt." Exasperation gripped her insides.

"I'm sure you mean well, wanting your daughter to fit in, go to class with the others, but that would just frustrate her. Surely you're aware she is a child with special—"

"Of course I am, Mr. Hutton," she said more forcefully than was polite. "Although Maddie isn't my daughter, I wish she were. Her little heart is going to break into a thousand pieces when I tell her your answer is no. Won't you please reconsider?"

All Brenna's good feelings had flown the coop and been replaced with anger and frustration. How could he say no? It wasn't right.

The man didn't have a heart after all. "I'm sorry to disappoint you, Mrs. Lane. My answer remains the same."

Several hours later, with the younger children fed and tucked away in bed, Brenna and Penny relaxed in the living room with a small fire. Penny reclined on the brown couch, reading a novel. Her legs were drawn up underneath her and a small crocheted blanket covered her lap as she leaned forward toward the lantern resting on a small side table. Brenna sat at the dinner table, a paper laid on the scarred wood, and a pen in hand. The glass-globed lantern in the center gave just enough light for her to work without straining her eyes. So deep in concentration, she didn't realize she'd made a sound of distress until Penny looked her way.

"What is it, Mama?" Penny's concerned tone made Brenna mentally wince. Her daughter had a way of carrying the weight of the world on her shoulders. Penny's waist-length, coffee-colored hair was free, clean after being washed and dried in front of the flames.

Brenna dredged up a smile. "I'm just listing things I don't want to forget." *Like sending a telegram on Monday about the math books.*

Penny glanced under the table to the overturned bucket where Brenna rested her sore ankle. "How's it feel?"

"Much better. By tomorrow I won't even recall I twisted it." Remembering the alarm on the children's faces when Mr. Hutton helped her through the front door brought a small frown. She was still angry with him. He'd been adamant in not changing his mind about Maddie. "Thank you for brewing me a cup of willow bark tea. I'm sure that's why the pain is almost gone."

Penny nibbled at her bottom lip, a nervous habit she had when contemplating a difficult subject. "That was the last of the tea. After church, I'll run over to the Red Rooster and get some more from Mrs. Hollyhock."

Brenna nodded, knowing it wasn't the mention of the soothing tea she used each month to ease her menstrual cramps, and also the other aches and pains of her family, that had Penny pensive. Something else was on her daughter's mind. "Be sure to take three pennies from the can to pay for it."

Her daughter nodded. The moment stretched out.

"Penny?"

"What's he like, Mama?"

"Mr. Hutton?"

Penny nodded again, the light playing off her hair like moonlight on a pond.

Brenna got up, hobbled over and settled next to Penny on the couch. She took her daughter's hand and threaded her fingers through her own. Her eldest was a brooder, so much like her father. "He's nice, sweetheart." *As long as you're not going against the grain. Well, that isn't quite true. He was pleasant until I asked about Maddie.* "I believe the two of you will get along just fine."

Penny's face brightened. "He let me help today in the classroom, me being one of the oldest students and all. I just don't know, though. What if I can't measure up to his standards? I've heard tell he's strict, and English is his hardest subject."

"And it's your best subject. Besides, all that talk about him being strict and unyielding is just speculation and rumor. I felt the same way when I was a girl and Mr. Pender came to our school. He had mean eyes and a sharp face. Nothing ever got past him. We all swore he must have eyes in the back of his head."

Penny giggled.

"Your daddy got stood in the corner every single day for a whole year. It was almost to the point where he'd march there on his own without being asked."

Her eyes were as wide as her smile. "Really?"

"Well, not quite." Brenna laughed. "But close. Nevertheless, Mr. Pender turned out to be the best teacher I ever had. And once I got to know him, he didn't seem mean at all. Strict—but kind in his serious sort of way."

Brenna patted Penny's hand, still captured in her own. "I know you and Mr. Hutton will do just fine."

Penny blinked, her eyelids seemingly unwilling to stay open.

"It's time for bed, my bright, beautiful, girl. You know that's when your body rests and grows tall and strong."

Penny pulled a small frown as she stood and pushed some hair from her eyes. "I don't need to grow any more, Mama. Last year, I was taller than everyone in class, including all the boys."

Brenna stood and followed Penny into the girls' bedroom. She pulled down the cover, being careful not to wake Jane or Maddie, then plumped the pillow. "Sleep tight," she whispered. "No worries tonight, they'll keep till later just fine." With a glance to the small cross on the wall over the children's heads, Brenna thought about taking her own advice. There was nothing she could do about the books, or Maddie, until Monday. Those problems would keep, as well.

CHAPTER FIFTEEN

"Sorry again, Georgia." Standing in the barn doorway, Charlie listened to the sound of Nell laughing like a girl. It brought lightness to his heart.

"Charlie," Nell said in surprise, and took a stumbling step back, spooking the docile Georgia again. Right before his eyes, her cheeks went from their normal rosy hue to an overripe strawberry pink.

He suppressed a smile. "Are you trying to traumatize my poor horse? She's supposed to be resting, not dodging grooming tools and clumsy, frightened women."

Nell straightened. "I'm no frightened woman. I take offense at you calling me that."

Still fighting a chuckle, he shifted his reins to his other hand and repositioned the quilt gripped in his arms. He'd spent the past two hours slowly riding the trails from town to the ranch, trying to get his thoughts straightened out. He'd wanted desperately to ride back to the school and snatch Maddie up into his arms. But he'd be foolish to consider bringing her back into his life before he knew everything was safe, before he even had a home for her. As much as he wanted to, he had to be settled first so she'd have a firm foundation.

On top of that, he had to be patient. The past months of worrying and running would be for nothing if he jumped the gun and led trouble right to her door. He needed to slow down. Stick with his original plan. Maddie was fine for the time being. She was well fed and happy, despite the trauma of losing Miss Baxter. The best place for her to be was right where she was, with Brenna Lane, while he worked out the details of his life. Now that he'd actually met the woman, he felt even better about his daughter's living arrangements.

He glanced over at Nell and found some hurt or sorrow lingering deep in her eyes. What was it about? She did her best to cover it, but now and again her pain slipped out. Maybe while he was here he could help her somehow. At least he could be her friend. "Don't take offense. I'm just having some fun. Anyone can see you enjoy your horses and would do anything for them."

She regarded him through her lashes, the color of her face deepening, "Of course I do—and would. I especially like your mare, Charlie. She has a good sense of humor."

While he wrestled for an answer to her strange statement, she lifted the quilt from his arms and walked over to her brother. A move quite bold for her, he thought.

She held the quilt out to Seth. "Mrs. Hollyhock and the others did a lovely job. Each square is completely different, sort of like telling the story of Logan Meadows." She pointed to the top portion of the folded quilt. "That's Win's livery with Maximus and Clementine in the corral. An extremely good likeness, I must say. Here's the bridge on Main Street and the Red Rooster Inn." Her hand brushed over the top of the fabric almost reverently. "I can't wait to open up the whole thing."

Seth looked at the quilt so long without saying anything that Nell jabbed him in the ribs with her elbow.

"Ouch." He scratched his head, obviously perplexed. "Why on earth would anyone cut up fabric just to sew it back together again?" He chuckled. "Makes no sense at all. But I have to admit, I like this one of the mercantile with the bakery alongside. This quilt must be worth a good amount of money."

Nell pulled back and turned to Charlie. "You're not going to sell it, are you?"

"Nope." Charlie shook his head. "Actually, I'd like you to have it, Nell." He'd planned to give his prize to Maddie when they were together, but that seemed a shame because, being blind, his daughter wouldn't be able to appreciate the craftsmanship to its fullest.

Nell's eyes widened. "Me? I couldn't take this. It's much too nice. Much too valuable. Where would I keep it?"

"What kind of question is that?" He tried to hide the enjoyment that warmed his gut at the surprised pleasure on her face. "Where does anyone put a quilt? On their bed, for one."

Her face turned a bright red right before his eyes, making him realize what he'd just said. He cleared his throat. "Or on a wall?" Feeling conspicuous, he went to the side of the black gelding and started unsaddling him.

He returned from the tack room with a brush and slipped his hand under the leather handle. He groomed the gelding, picked out his hooves, then turned him into a clean stall. Finished, he went over and looked in on Georgia. "So, when are we going to start breaking the horses we brought in yesterday?"

"Monday," Seth answered. Turning, he gripped his side as he let go a long string of body-wracking coughs. When he was finally able to speak again he added, "We take a day of rest on Sunday."

Nell still hugged the quilt to her chest. Her eyes narrowed. "When are you going to the doctor, Seth?"

Seth headed toward the barn doors. "Never you mind. I'm gettin' better. I won't go wasting good money just because I have a lingering cough."

"What's money for if you don't spend it? I say you ride into town on Monday and see Doc Thorn. Charlie and I can handle the horses."

Seth paused at the doorway, raising a brow and looking just like Nell did when she got piqued. "The day I take off work to see a doctor is the day you can push me over a buffalo jump."

Nell watched in consternation as Seth disappeared out the barn door. "A crotchety ol' mule isn't as stubborn as my big brother. And it's smarter, to boot," she yelled, hoping he'd hear her. She went over to the bench and plopped down, dispirited, keeping the folded quilt in her lap. "I've got to get him into town. I know that's why he didn't go along today to Logan Meadows. The scaredy-cat was afraid I'd find the doctor and make him have an examination. He can be so irksome."

Charlie nonchalantly leaned against a post and crossed his boots at the ankle. He took a toothpick from his pocket and stuck it into his mouth. As if by magic, the tiny piece of wood rolled back and forth between his lips without him seeming to do a thing. She tried not to watch, but that was downright impossible.

"You have a buffalo jump around?" he asked.

"Yes. A good portion of our land used to be inhabited by Sioux. We actually have two jumps. A large one not far from where we gathered the horses, and a smaller one somewhat south-west of it."

He made an interested sound in his throat. "I'd like to see them. I've had a fascination for years. Someday when there's time. I don't want going to interfere with my duties here on the ranch."

Nell called Dog over to her side to have something else to concentrate on other than Charlie's probing blue eyes and the interesting tilt to his lips. His bottom lip was just a tad fuller than the top, and they were angled just right, reminding her of—she jerked her thoughts away. And that darn toothpick. Was he doing that on purpose?

"Sure. Any time you'd like." She stroked Dog's scraggly neck. The dog had appeared on the porch a few years ago, all skin and bone. Right now, his wagging tail told her he was happy with the attention she was giving him.

Charlie glanced around the barn's interior. "If everything's done for today, how about right now?"

"It's about an hour's ride." She stood, feeling uncertain. "You sure you want to do that this late in the day?"

"I don't have anything else to do, unless you have some chores for me. Dark doesn't fall until almost nine. We can be back before then."

She shook her head. "No chores."

"And Georgia needs some exercise. I don't want her to get soft."

Coyote certainly wasn't tired from the easy ride into town and back. He might be grumpy being saddled again after being bedded down for the day, but it wouldn't be the first time Nell had done it.

She glanced out the tall barn doors. The afternoon sun had painted the browning stalks of oats in the field golden and the warm Wyoming wind turned the windmill slowly. The house was quiet. They had several hours before the sun dipped behind the mountains. But when that happened darkness would fall and the temperature would drop. The stranger had appeared at dusk. Was he somewhere out there now? When doubt, followed by a pinprick of anxiety, made her mouth go dry, she angrily pushed the feeling away.

"All right." He'd be sorry if he ever came back. He'd not make her a prisoner of fear. "I can show you the cattle along the way, since we haven't had a chance to get out there yet. But first let me go in and fix Seth's supper. He's an able cook, but sometimes he gets lazy. I don't want him skipping any meals."

She should be more frightened of her growing attraction to Charlie than of some stranger who was likely never to appear again. Charlie was a hired hand. Besides, she still wasn't sure about his reaction to Brenna. Whatever the reason, fostering romantic notions about him just because they chased away her loneliness was wrong. She'd not use him in that way. So what if the heartfelt, comfortable feeling that enveloped her whenever he was around was like sunshine to a new crop?

"Sure. While you're inside, I'll get the horses saddled. We'll be ready when you are."

Nell picked up the quilt and fingered the soft, colorful fabric. "You sure about this, Charlie Rose?" Seemed she always tacked on his second name when she was feeling particularly close to him.

She'd never received a gift of such magnitude. There'd been candy canes from Seth at Christmastime, and on her wedding day Ben had given her a bottle of lemon verbena. Other than that, she couldn't remember any other gifts. "You may want to hang on to it for a while. It's all right if you've changed your mind."

He tipped his hat back and his smile reached all the way to his eyes, making the scar on his cheek move toward his ear. "I'm sure, Nell Page. And if I wasn't sure before, I am now. I like the way that thing makes you smile."

Such talk. She could feel the blush creeping up her face—again. Did he know what he was doing to her? She better not forget how Brenna had rendered him speechless. He sure wasn't speechless with her—a plenty good reason not to let her imagination run off into the wild blue yonder. "Fine, then" was all she could muster. "I'll be back in a little while." As enticing as an evening ride with Charlie sounded, she hoped she didn't live to regret it.

CHAPTER SIXTEEN

*C*harlie and Nell eased into a slow lope, crossing the large horse pasture out back and fording a shallow stream. The evening air on his face made his qualms and concerns about Maddie evaporate into thin air.

He glanced over at Nell sitting in her saddle as if she'd been born on the back of a horse. Her hair, the color of the shimmery-gold sky now that the sun was moving toward the mountains, flew out behind in wild abandon, set free of the braid she'd worn at the picnic. As always, she had her gun strapped on her leg like a man.

"What about the horses in the pasture we just crossed?" he called to her. "You don't sell those to the army?" He watched Nell take a deep breath, as if happy to be out in the wide-open space.

"Most are broodmares." She lifted her voice over the sound of hooves pounding the earth. They loped along side by side so close he could reach out and touch her if he'd wanted.

"The ones with good conformation and that have the traits we want them to pass on, like intelligence and a good, willing spirit, stay for breeding. The rest are either injured or just plain not ready to be started. When they're sound again, and broke, they'll go to the . . . good captain for soldier mounts."

He glanced at the trail wondering at the animosity in Nell's tone when she spoke of the army captain. "How do you know when they're ready to be started?"

She reined up to a walk and he followed suit. "For one, they have to be physically ready. Big of bone. Confident." She gave him a smile.

"Confident?" That was the first time Charlie had ever heard that.

"It's just a feeling I get when I'm working them. If they trust they're not going to be hurt, and they're inquisitive, I know they're ready. Getting the first ride right is important. You don't get a second shot at that. And, knowing when to quit."

He mulled that over as they climbed to the top of a small rise and crested the summit. He pulled up when Nell stopped.

"There's part of our herd." Nell pointed at the cattle. It wasn't as many as he'd expected. "We sell some of our steers in town to families who don't raise their own beef, then send the rest to market once a year."

He was surprised. "You drive them to Cheyenne?"

"No, we don't. Our neighbors"—she pointed to her left—"the Broken Horn ranch, take them for us when they drive theirs in the spring. They have a much larger herd than ours. It's neighborly of them to do so."

"That would be the Logans?" he asked, remembering the couple they'd eaten dinner with. The love humming between the two was impossible to miss, as well as their love for their boy.

"That's right. You're catching on fast."

He shrugged. It had been years since he'd ranched for a living, but everything was coming back quicker than he'd thought.

"Spring is when the grass is best, and there's plenty to feed on along the way. We round up the ones we intend to sell and let the strays mother up slowly. Then when we're ready, Chase and his men swing this way to pick them up."

"Mother up?" That was a term he didn't know.

She let a small laugh slip through her lips. She nodded, looking at the cattle. "It never fails that a few heifers and their calves get all mixed up in the roundup. Even as calm as we try to take it, it's impossible not to end up with a calf or two and no mama claiming them. It's a little heartbreaking but if we leave the calf out by itself, bawling its head off, mama and baby will eventually plod back to the last place they nursed. Much like two magnets." She smiled at the cattle and he could tell she was revisiting a memory. "Works every time."

She nudged her horse forward and they rode down the trail and through a thick stand of trees. They rode on for a good three miles in silence before Nell turned in the saddle, watching him over the chestnut-and-white rump of her paint gelding. "Almost there."

"In all these trees?"

"We're coming in from the side. They'll clear in a minute."

When they emerged, open land stretched for as far as the eye could see to the east, and then a hundred feet or so in the other direction, the land fell away sharply. From where they sat, he couldn't see what was over the cliff. The ground was barren, almost worn down to rock.

"Follow me," Nell said.

The drop, with the rugged terrain blending into the mountains way off in the distance, made the sky seem even larger and more spectacular than normal. A feeling of awe filled him.

They rode right up to the edge. At the bottom a sea of buffalo bones littered the land.

Charlie gave a long, low whistle. "How far down?"

"I'd say about two hundred feet."

He looked over his shoulder, back to the trailhead they'd exited, and then far beyond. "It's amazing to think of the Indians running hundreds of animals off at one time."

"The hides and meat kept them alive through a long, cold winter," she replied, looking thoughtful.

"Oh, I'm not criticizing. Not at all. You see any buffalo around anymore?"

"You mean besides in town?" She laughed but the sound wasn't happy. "Rarely. And that makes me sad. At least when the

Indians herded them off the jump, it was to feed themselves and their children. I can't stand what the buffalo hunters have done. It's sickening."

"You're damn right." A hot, unsettled feeling took him by surprise when the image of men shooting the animals by the thousands, just for their skins, flitted through his mind. "So, all this land is yours and Seth's?"

"Just to here. Enough to keep us working hard."

Coyote dropped his head and looked deep into the canyon. Charlie chuckled. "I think your horse is thinking of jumping off," he teased.

She shook her head. "No. He's been here many times. He likes it. I can feel his spirits lift when he gazes out over the distance. Maybe he feels the blood of his ancestors as they galloped down this grade toward the jump wondering if their riders were going to ask them to go over. The paints on our ranch came from the Indians' stock that we caught wild."

Charlie turned and appraised her. This statement, along with the ones about Georgia having a sense of humor and horses being confident, puzzled him. "You're kidding me, right?"

"Partly. But, I do feel a difference in him when I bring him up here. He definitely likes it. It's just something I know. I can't explain, or give you a reason to accept what I'm saying. You'd be amazed to know how much horses really want to serve, to be of use. I'm not just talking about being ridden or pulling a wagon or stage, but to heal what ails you. They have enormous hearts."

Charlie chuckled again, not knowing what to make of Nell's statement. It sounded crazier than a cat in a field of catnip. "And Georgia? You can tell what she's feeling?"

"I can."

He crossed his arms over his chest. "What's she thinking now?"

Nell looked down at his mare as the animal gazed out over the open land below. A light wind moved her reddish-brown mane, and her hind hoof was cocked. Nell reached over and patted Georgia's neck.

"Anyone could tell you she's calm and relaxed by reading her head set, the position of her ears and her cocked hip, and they'd be correct," Nell said. "But actually, she's missing something right now. I'm not sure if her memory is of a previous owner, or perhaps an offspring of hers. I don't know. All I know is she has a powerful longing for something in her past."

Charlie let his defiance go and dropped his crossed arms. He remembered back to the day when he'd finally ridden out of Wilsonville. In an attempt to cover his progress from anyone who might try to follow him, he'd ridden his mount hard. When he'd arrived in Grand Junction, Colorado, he sold his gelding to the first ranch he'd come upon. At first, he'd tried to simply trade animals, but the rancher refused, saying their only saddle horse available, Georgia, belonged to his young daughter, and he didn't have the heart to trade her. That's when Charlie had thrown a bundle of cash into the deal. The owner would have been a fool to refuse. Charlie hadn't given the horse deal much thought at the time with Grover Galante and Maddie on his mind, but now he recalled the rancher saying his daughter had raised and trained Georgia. That she'd be heartbroken when she found out. Could Georgia actually be missing her? The idea of that seemed outlandish, to say the least. Still, the possibility brought a lump to his throat.

"That's, uh, some statement, Nell." He looked over to find her lost in her own contemplations. "I'm not too sure what I should make of it. I mean animals, thinking and feeling, just like people?"

Her smile whispered acknowledgment of being different. Sadness. Perhaps, because of her beliefs, being an outcast of sorts.

"At first, Seth thought my knowing about the animals was a figment of my imagination. I know what I'm saying sounds crazy. It started when I was about six. Instinctively, I knew not to say anything about it. Keep it to myself."

She gazed out over the canyon. "When Dog showed up on our porch, he was half-starved. When I opened the door, he practically vaulted into my arms. A vision of fire, water, smoke and a boat filled my mind. I believe he and his owner were separated by a fire somehow, maybe on a boat while traveling on one of the big rivers. After being lost, he set out cross-country in search of his master. He was exhausted when he arrived. And he's stayed with us ever since."

Charlie let his gaze roam over to the top of Coyote's head and then to Georgia's. Animals with rational feelings and thoughts? That was something he'd have to ponder for more than just a few moments. He could feel Nell's inquisitive gaze. She was waiting for his response. Problem was, he didn't know what to say.

When a minute passed without him responding, she reined around. "We'd better get back. It'll be dark before we reach the horse pasture."

"Sure."

She started off and he fell in alongside. "What are the plans for tomorrow?"

"Like Seth mentioned, we take Sunday off if it's not calving or foaling season. Nothing much to do besides start the new horses, but we'll wait for Monday to do that."

"Well then, if you're sure you won't need me, I think I'll go into town. Spend a few hours getting the feel of the place. Meet a few more people." *Make sure I wasn't followed.* He couldn't stop a smile. *And perhaps catch a glimpse of Maddie while I'm there.*

Her eyes narrowed, and her lips flattened out.

"If you're sure I'm not needed at the ranch, that is."

"No. Not at all."

"I'll take some mending in, just a shirt and—"

"I can mend for you, Charlie. I don't mind. Just because I dress like a man doesn't mean I don't know anything about being a woman."

"I couldn't ask my employer to mend my shirt and darn a few pairs of raggedy ol' socks," he said gently, trying to figure out why she'd offer such a thing. "I'm thankful for this job and plan to keep it. I'll just drop them by Brenna Lane's house. I heard people talking that you could just leave them on her porch with a note." He wanted to make sure Brenna had earnings to keep the children comfortable. Paying for her services was an easy way to do that.

"Suit yourself, Charlie."

Nell looked away, but the rigidness of her posture told him she had a bee in her bonnet, and that was a fact. The only reason he could think of was his ride into town tomorrow, but why would that upset her? He knew better than to mention that the angrier she got, the prettier she looked.

When they came through the kitchen door, Seth called from the front room, "I cooked up a portion of a hindquarter after you left, Nell. Thought you two might be hungry when you got back. I left it on the drain board. I ate your fixings as well, though."

Nell was sure Seth was slouched in his leather chair, with his feet stretched out on the stool.

Charlie preceded her into the front room.

Seth peered up from where he sat. "So, how was the ride, you two?"

The way he said "you two" garnered another glance from her.

Charlie just stood there looking conspicuous.

"A ride's a ride." She wondered if Charlie believed her about the horses. His teasing tone had turned thoughtful, making her believe he did, but he hadn't said much either way. "We checked on the cattle."

"I'm glad you rode out that way." Seth had the same old newspaper from the other day crumpled in his lap. "By the way, have either of you been over by the creek lately? Found some tracks I didn't recognize. Thought they might belong to Charlie's mare."

A black chill crackled through Nell. Tracks? By the creek? She glanced over at Charlie, hoping beyond measure he'd say he'd gone that way at some point. It couldn't have been today on his way home from Logan Meadows, because he was riding their black gelding then, and Seth would easily recognize his tracks.

Charlie's face had lost its little-boy charm as he shook his head. "Not me, Seth. The only creek I crossed was when I rode with Nell out to the buffalo jump."

"Hm." Seth scratched his head. "Wonder who it was and what business they had."

Instantly she thought of the stranger. Was he back? Had he ever left? When her gaze met Charlie's, his eyes hooded before he snapped his gaze away. He pushed an unsteady hand through his hair, making her wonder. *He looks more nervous than I do. Is he hiding something, too?* If he was, she was sure it wasn't in connection with the stranger. She'd never believe that. No, it was something else she couldn't put her finger on—not yet, anyway.

CHAPTER SEVENTEEN

$\mathcal{P}$ounding on the door brought Brenna out of a sound sleep. She dragged her heavy eyelids open to a cold, dark bedroom. Confused, she blinked several times, trying to decide if she'd heard the knocking in her dream, or if the sound had been real. This was Sunday. Service wasn't until ten o'clock. Certainly, the children weren't up yet. Deciding she must have imagined the noise, she rolled over and pulled her covers up to her chin.

Knock knock knock.

This time Brenna sat up, quickly lit her bedside lantern then picked up her watch, working to focus her eyes—five-thirty in the morning?

"One minute, please," she called toward the front of the house. *Who on earth could be at the door? Only dreadful news comes before dawn.*

She fumbled around in the shadowy room. Finding her dress, she pulled the weighty garment over her head and haphazardly adjusted the pleats. She threw her shawl over her shoulders to hide the open buttons in the back. Finger combing her hair as she padded through her bedroom on bare feet, she worried all the way to the front door. Pulling it open, she stopped, stunned into silence.

Mr. Hutton stood between her door and the road, just inside her front gate. He must have knocked on her door, then retreated back ten feet when he'd heard her response. His bare feet protruded from his blanket covering, and he looked as if he'd fall over any moment.

"Mr. Hutton," she gasped. "What's wrong?"

She started toward him but he stopped her with an upheld palm. "Stay back, Mrs. Lane." He swallowed, and swayed. His ghostly white face reflected the light of the moon. *What on earth.* "I'm sick. Came down with something in the middle of the night. I don't want to expose you. I was wondering—"

Brenna hurried down the stairs and pushed past his open palm just as he tilted to the left. Wrapping one arm around his waist, she took a firm hold.

Heat radiated through the blanket. "Come, Mr. Hutton," she said soothingly, alarmed over his high temperature. "Come along with me." When she turned him around and inched slowly toward the gate, he didn't protest. "You need to get back into bed where you belong."

"No . . ." He tried to push her away but she was having none of it.

For a moment his eyes closed and he rocked back on his heels, almost taking Brenna with him. She fought to keep him upright while struggling to keep her dress and shawl on her shoulders. They passed through the narrow gate under a clear sky bursting with stars. They stepped onto the dirt road between the houses and Brenna's bare foot came down on a sharp stone, the pain making her jerk. Mr. Hutton's arm tightened around her waist, and when he turned to see what had happened his concerned gaze was overpowered by the feverish haze within. "Your ankle. You shouldn't be walking on it."

"My ankle feels fine. I just stepped on a small pebble. Keep going. We're almost there."

"Don't want you to get sick," he mumbled. "Only wondered if you'd go fetch the doctor for me—in an hour or two when the sun is up."

"Of course I will. Just as soon as it's light I'll send Penny. But right now the only place for you is in your bed."

They crossed the street and she helped him slowly take the steps to his porch. Pushing into the dark house, she noted the only light was a lantern burning in the bedroom. She stopped in the living room and let him catch his breath.

"Mrs. Lane, I'll never forgive myself if you—"

"Hush."

"—get sick," he finished. "I wish you'd stayed at arm's length, where you'd be safe." He groaned. "And last evening, all that walking together. Surely you were exposed to whatever I have."

"Shush, now, Mr. Hutton," she said firmly. "You can put away your worries. With all the children I have, I've been exposed to almost everything under the sun, and then some. I'll be fine. I nurse them, and I can nurse you as well."

Propriety forbade her admittance to a single man's bedroom, especially since they were alone, but there was no help for it. He must have picked up on her thoughts because as they approached his door he began peeling her arm from his side.

"I can take it from here, Mrs. Lane," he croaked out. "Thank you. I'll just—"

He coughed and wiped his forehead with his palm. Without warning, he went down on one knee, taking Brenna with him. Pain sliced up her leg when her kneecap connected with the wooden floor, pushed all the harder by his weight.

"Oh!" she cried out, but she instantly wanted to recall the word. She struggled, trying to stand and pull him up with her. Somehow, pushing, pulling and praying, she got him into the postage-stamp-size room, and helped him sit on the edge of his bed. She took his shoulders and guided him back. He pulled his feet up on his own and she covered him with the top sheet.

Taking the matches on the bedside table, Brenna went into the living room and lit several oil lamps, turning the wicks low. In the kitchen, she lit the lamp on the counter, and another on a small kitchen table. Now that there was light, she reached around and buttoned up her dress. Having found several folded dishcloths tucked away in a drawer, she worked the indoor kitchen pump until she had a trickle. She soaked a cloth and wrung it out.

When she returned to the bedroom the teacher's eyes were closed. Perspiration shimmered on his forehead and the gray pall to his skin had her worried. Leaning over, she softly wiped the moisture from his forehead and cheeks, then dabbed gently over his lips. Finished, she folded the cloth several times and gently placed it on his forehead.

The house was so quiet. She wondered what illness he had. Worry for her children was never far from her mind. She'd need to stay away until they found out what they were dealing with, and until after she'd changed her clothes and washed.

Uneasy, Brenna left him and went to the front door and looked out. *Is Penny awake yet? She'll be frightened if she finds me gone, my bed empty and me nowhere in the house.* The hour was still early, but the sun had just topped the faraway mountain range and the rosy glow of the sunrise extended out.

Behind her living room curtains, the room lightened. Brenna stepped out onto the porch. "Penny," she called out through cupped hands. Picking up the hem of her dress, she crossed the street and stopped at her gate. "Penny," she called louder.

The front door slowly opened. "Mama, is that you?"

"Yes, honey."

Penny stepped out and started down the steps. "What are you doing out here?" Her voice held alarm, and a bit of surprise.

"Stay where you are, sweetie." Brenna's words stopped her daughter in her tracks. She tried to keep all traces of fear from her voice but by the size of Penny's eyes she knew she'd failed.

"W-why? What's wrong?" Penny replied shakily.

By now, the other children were huddled in the doorway behind her, trying to see who Penny was talking to.

"Nothing too terrible," she answered, nervously clutching her hands in front of her dress. *I pray that's true. Poor Mr. Hutton looks like death warmed over.* "Mr. Hutton is sick. I want you to get dressed and as soon as the sun is up go to town for Dr. Thorn. If you can't find him, go down to the sheriff's office and tell Sheriff Preston and Deputy Donovan, or whomever is there. They'll know what to do. If neither of them is around, tell any adult you can find and then come straight home. Don't dally, or else I'll worry."

When Penny turned to go, Brenna added, "And take Prichard with you." Even though her foster child was younger than Penny, he was almost as tall and was growing strong. "Two heads are better than one." *And safer.*

Penny scuttled back inside and Brenna turned and crossed the street. She climbed the steps and was just pulling the door open when the *clip-clop* of a horse's hooves brought her back around. She strained to see who was coming up their road.

Dwight! Good Lord, of all the people to see me on Mr. Hutton's porch at daybreak. She scooted in quickly and closed the front door, careful not to make a sound. She leaned back against the barrier until she couldn't hear the hoofbeats anymore. *Dwight won't care about the truth, or even if Mr. Hutton is dying. He won't waste a minute before spreading the gossip all over town.*

She firmed her resolve. If the people of Logan Meadows were so hard-hearted that they would fault her for coming to the aid of a person in need, then she didn't care. As she crossed the room, Brenna took note of the furnishing for the first time since coming inside. Most of the things she recognized as Maude's, the owner of the small rental. The brown corduroy couch looked as worn-out as ever. A cushioned chair sat opposite the sofa and next to it was a straight-back wooden chair that was still missing a spindle. The rectangle maple table that divided the two seats held a lantern and a couple of books.

She stopped. Looked around more closely. A smile blossomed. She'd not fancied him a boot wearer until she noticed a beat-up pair of black walking boots by the door. Also, on top of the books on the coffee table was a pair of spectacles. Did he wear them to read? She hadn't known. Now the room seemed to come alive with his presence. A sweater tossed on a sideboard drew her like a magnet. She touched the tightly knit wool.

Her heart trembled softly as she took it all in. Did he come from a large family? Did he say a blessing before his meals? Had he ever been in love?

She snatched her hand away. *Don't go snooping into things that aren't your business. Curiosity only leads to trouble.*

In the bedroom, she placed the back of her hand on one of Mr. Hutton's cheeks. His fever had climbed. He opened his eyes and looked at her groggily.

Not wasting a second, she hurried into the kitchen to rinse the cloth again in cool water. She took a glass from the cupboard, filled it, all the while wishing she had some of the soup Penny had made last night. Thick with chicken meat and carrots, she knew the sustenance had marvelous healing capabilities. She'd have Jane bring out the pot where she could retrieve it.

On her way back into the bedroom, she grabbed a chair so she could sit by his side. "Here you go, Mr. Hutton." She gently replaced the folded cloth on his forehead.

His eyes opened again. They were bleary from his high fever. He studied her face. A ripple of awareness passed between them, and she couldn't stop a small smile.

"Thank you." The words were weak and barely audible. "Thank you, Mrs.—"

"Hush now, Mr. Hutton. You're such a chatty squirrel. Save your strength. You'll be happy to know Penny and Prichard will be on their way to fetch the doctor within minutes. I'll have some nice tepid soup for you soon, as well." *Please, God, let Dr. Thorn be in his office and ready to come right away.*

"I can't eat anything. My throat feels like it's filled with broken glass."

"Still, you need to take some of this cool water to lower your fever. Do you think you can manage?"

He nodded.

She lifted his head and placed the glass to his lips. "Tiny sips," she crooned, holding his head as he struggled to drink. "Just enough to wet your mouth."

When he was finished she laid him back. That's when she noticed the first little red dot on the tip of his nose. Looking more closely, she found a cluster on his neck, and another at the collar of his nightshirt. Taking liberties, she gently pulled the neckline a bit lower and found hundreds of red dots. She didn't need Dr. Thorn to tell her what ailed the teacher. The answer was as clear as the spot on his nose.

CHAPTER EIGHTEEN

$\mathcal{T}$he sun hadn't made an appearance yet when Charlie rolled from the comfort of his small cot in the back of the house and quietly dressed. In the kitchen, he cut several slices of bread from a waxed paper–wrapped loaf, sliced a chunk of beef from the roast Seth had cooked last night and wolfed them down. Being careful with the door so it wouldn't bang, he stepped out into the day. Dog, still on his tattered blanket, eyed him as if wondering why anyone would be up this early on a Sunday morning. Standing, the animal shook his scraggly fur, then followed Charlie to the barn.

Chickens dashed out into the yard when Charlie pulled open the tall, sun-bleached doors, winding their way between and around his feet like a river of poultry. He went to the feed room, scooped some scratch into the rusted can, and tossed the feed into the yard, causing a round of cackles and clucks from the hungry birds. Working quickly, he fed the horses, cleaned the stalls, then bedded them with fresh straw. Making several trips with a large bucket, he watered the vegetable garden behind the house and walked to the end of the far pasture to open the gate so the small herd of steers grazing out back could come up to the barn for some grain. When Georgia had finished her hay, he saddled up, then headed off to town.

He was anxious to see Maddie. It was also time he got a feel, a real feel—not some holiday picnic—for the town. Learn its layout. Get familiar with faces. From what he'd seen on his two prior visits,

Logan Meadows seemed to be a quiet place. Not many drunks shooting off their guns in the streets or other rabble-rousers loitering here or there. Not like Wilsonville.

Didn't take him long to reach the outskirts. Just as he approached the bridge crossing the stream, the double doors of the livery stable swung open and a fella came out leading a horse toward the back of the property. No time like the present to get acquainted. Halting, he dismounted and tossed his reins over the hitching rail.

He paused to admire the pair of shaggy-haired buffalo standing in the corral; they made him think of Nell and her wild ideas about animals. He didn't quite know what to make of them.

The larger of the two meandered over to the fence, looking to see if he had something tasty to offer. The buffalo's large eyeball rolled around as it snuffled though the fence. Charlie reached out and felt the thick, wooly, robe-like fur that covered his neck and head. The gentle giant twitched his ear to remove a fly. Maddie would get a kick from feeling that coarse hair that felt like wire. He wondered if she had.

"His name's Maximus, but we call him Max."

Charlie turned. "He's sure something to see. Seems pretty gentle for such a huge critter."

The man held out his hand. "I'm Winthrop Preston. Owner and operator of the livery and forge, and dubious caretaker of these two cantankerous beasts. Seemed like a fun idea when they were small."

"I'm Charlie Rose. Nice to meet you."

"You won the quilt yesterday."

Charlie nodded, wondering about that little stroke of unwanted luck. He'd intended to remain in the shadows while he got his feel around the place, but the one inopportune moment of winning the raffle had everyone in town aware of his presence.

He stepped back when the smaller buffalo came close and gave the fence where he was standing a nice hard prod with her horns. He looked at Winthrop in surprise.

"That's Clementine. I don't turn my back on her, or she gets me every time. When she was just a calf, controlling her wasn't a problem, but now that she's grown and has a set of horns that I don't want to feel jabbing in my back, I'm more careful. Consider yourself warned." He chuckled. "You're working out at the Cotton Ranch, I hear."

"That's right. Are you any relation to Albert Preston, the sheriff?" Charlie liked Winthrop's friendly face and easy smile.

"Only his little brother." He patted the front of his overalls. "I'll amend that to *younger.*"

Movement caught Charlie's eye. From the direction he'd ridden in, Brenna Lane was hurrying into town. She was lost in thought, her smile pulled flat and her expression pinched. In less than five heartbeats, Mrs. Lane had reached them, then passed the livery.

His first worry was that something had happened to Maddie. "I don't mean to be rude, Winthrop, but I need to be going."

Winthrop's brows rose in question and he glanced at Mrs. Lane's retreating figure. "Well, it was a pleasure to meet you and talk a spell. I can stable your horse for two bits a day if you have the need. Oh, and call me Win."

"Thank you," Charlie called over his shoulder as he hurried to the hitching post and grabbed Georgia's split reins. He jogged after Brenna, his horse trotting behind him to keep up.

"Excuse me, ma'am," he called when he was within hearing distance.

Brenna stopped and turned, then glanced up the way she'd been traveling, as if she didn't have a second to spare. "Yes?"

"I'm Charlie Rose. I met you yesterday at the school fundraiser. I won the quilt?"

"Of course, Mr. Rose. I remember you." Her frown lessened for only a moment. "What brings you out from the Cotton Ranch so early this Sunday morning? Are you a churchgoing man?"

"Er, no. Not really." His face heated. "But, I used to be." Seemed church was always forefront in every woman's mind. How could he find out anything about Maddie without his questions sounding strange? "Just thought today is a good a day as any to meet some of the townsfolk—since it's my day off."

"Still early for most folks." She anxiously looked down Main Street again. "I don't mean to be rude, but I must be on my way."

He smiled as amicably as he could muster. "I'll walk with you, if that's all right."

"I'm walking fast. No leisurely stroll."

"That's good with me."

She gave a sideward glance to his horse, as if trying to figure out what he was about, then nodded. They marched past the sheriff's office and approached the Bright Nugget Saloon. The bar's door was open and sounds of chairs scraping on the floor floated out to meet them in the street. A man stepped through the door and when Brenna noticed, she jerked her gaze away.

"Who's that?" he couldn't stop himself from asking, as they passed the bank, and then the appraiser's office.

"Dwight Hoskins," she mumbled. "A rude troublemaker. He used to live in Logan Meadows but moved to New Meringue last year. Respectable women don't give him the time of day." By then they'd passed most of the businesses and she came to a sudden stop. "Really, Mr. Rose, you needn't bother yourself accompanying me any longer. I'm headed all the way around the corner to the Red Rooster Inn, on the outskirts of town. Surely you have better things to do than tag along with me."

Before he could answer—or figure out how to ask her about Maddie—she'd picked up her brisk pace again.

He started after her. Just a word or two about Maddie. That's all he needed. Just to make sure she was safe and that Mrs. Lane's urgency had nothing to do with her.

He'd just caught up to her again when a rider came down the street, headed in their direction.

Brenna's eyes followed him, and when she noticed Charlie watching, she said, "He must be new to town. I've never seen him before."

"You get a lot of those, do you?"

"Those?"

"I'm sorry, ma'am. I meant drifters. He looks like a drifter to me."

She nodded. "Actually, yes. We used to be a sleepy little town, but not anymore."

Charlie took note of the man's hat pulled low over his eyes. He rode easy, with a Colt 45 strapped to each leg. Charlie didn't recognize him, but that didn't mean he hadn't been hired by Grover Galante.

They rounded the corner of Main Street and Cottonwood Lane to see an old building up ahead. A rooster weathervane topped the moss-covered thatched roof, and a large wraparound porch held several rocking chairs. Pine trees and oaks surrounded the building with shade. A hitching rail out front and a small, shed-like building in the back completed the homey picture. "Ah, the Red Rooster Inn?"

"Exactly. The place for anyone who can't afford a room in the hotel."

At Mrs. Lane's pace it didn't take long to get there. They stopped in front of the long-standing structure. When he started to tie his reins to the hitching rail Brenna's expression turned no-nonsense. "What're you doing?"

"Going in with you." That was the only way he could find out what was going on.

"Mr. Rose, this is where I draw the line."

Her tone said he'd better take note. "Fine. I'll just wait here."

"If you say so." She hurried up the steps and knocked on the door. The door swung open to reveal the newcomer who'd set the other women to whispering and Chase Logan to grousing at yesterday's picnic. A pinched expression graced her long face.

"Oh," Brenna remarked. "I was expecting Violet. Is she here?"

"Yes. Come in."

The door opened wide, and Brenna walked inside. When the woman looked out at him, he nodded an acknowledgment and her expression went from sour to sweet. "Would your husband like to come inside also?"

Brenna's laughter bounced between nervous and disturbed—and much too embarrassed. He cringed at the thought that he was scaring her off. "Mr. Rose is just a friend. And he prefers to wait outside with his horse."

When the door closed, Charlie stroked Georgia's neck, urgency burning in his belly. He hadn't discovered much on the walk here. If the return trip didn't prove better, he'd just have to ask Brenna straight out what had her so edgy. He wouldn't be able to concentrate on anything if he thought Maddie was in some sort of danger.

Unbidden, Seth's words about the riverside tracks came back to him. So did an image of the gun-toting stranger they'd passed in the street. *Blood for blood. An eye for an eye.* Galante wanted vengeance for his son, but Charlie would die before letting Maddie pay the price.

As he waited for Brenna, he turned uneasily in the street.

CHAPTER NINETEEN

*W*arm, spicy scents, like oranges and cinnamon heating on the stove in a pot of hot water, engulfed Brenna. As she followed the woman farther into the room, she took just a moment to allow the inn to soothe her heart. The colorful quilts hanging on the walls, the lacy white curtains, the large stone fireplace at the end of the room. At one point in her life, she'd had thoughts of owning it and filling the rooms with happy customers. However, that was a long time ago, and a nearly forgotten dream.

"Violet," the woman called down the long, narrow hallway. "You have a visitor."

Anxiety tugged at Brenna through the thin wall of peace the inn had given her. She needed to hurry back to Mr. Hutton's. After an examination, Dr. Thorn had confirmed her suspicion: measles. Since she'd had the malady as a child, and all her children had, as well, she was safe to look in on him a few times throughout the day. All except for Maddie. She didn't know if she was at risk.

A shuffling sound preceded the tiny owner of the inn. Soon Violet came down the hall, her arms full to overflowing with bed-sheets and towels. Peeking over the top, her face split into a wide grin.

"Why, Brenna, what brings ya out my way this fine mornin'? Penny, or another of your other little ones, ain't feeling poorly, I hope."

Violet hefted the contents in her arms as they began to slip and Brenna rushed forward, grasping the load. "Give me these, Mrs. Hollyhock. They're much too heavy for you to be carrying."

"I've got them, dearie," Violet protested, taking a step back. "I'm almost to the door."

"You're doing more than you should," Brenna said, holding tight to the linen. "Remember last spring when your back went out."

"She won't let you help her," the unfamiliar woman stated, looking down her thin nose at Brenna. Her know-it-all smirk went right up Brenna's back. Still, Brenna tried to ignore the comment.

"I've known Violet most my life," the woman continued, "and she's always been more stubborn than a grumpy, old mule. You're fighting a losing battle."

With a final tug, Violet won the laundry and proceeded through the kitchen to the back door. She pulled it open and dropped the linen in a pile on the floor of her tiny porch.

"Today's wash day," she called over her shoulder. "I have one paying boarder, plus Beth and me. Won't take me but a few hours."

Brenna counted slowly to three. "You must be the new boarder." Brenna disliked the idle lazybones already. A true friend of Violet's would have at least tried to lend a hand, wouldn't she? Instead, this woman had called her an old mule.

"No. Not me," the woman replied primly. She raised her brows. "He's a lawyer from Colorado."

Violet approached, smoothing her apron. "As soon as we have a visit, I'll light a fire to heat the wash kettle."

"But it's Sunday, Mrs. Hollyhock. Can't the wash wait?"

The woman tipped her head. "Not now that the beds are stripped. My sheets felt stale last night, and there's nothing I hate more. Violet prides herself on her comfortable inn."

Who is this ill-tempered shrew to stand here and tell me any-thing about my dear friend?

As if feeling a smidgen of tension in the air, Violet waved it away. "Brenna, I've yet to introduce the two of ya. This here is my dear friend Beth Fairington. Before I moved ta Logan Meadows, she worked for me in my mercantile in Valley Springs. In her travels all the way from Bozeman, we just happened t' run into each other. Beth, this here is Brenna Lane. She's a seamstress and a baker—and a mother, of course."

Just happened to run into each other? My foot. She's here to leach off you. "How nice," Brenna found herself saying, then she bit down on the inside of her cheek. "How long will you be visiting, Miss Fairington?" *I hope not too long. Violet might not survive your stay.*

Mrs. Hollyhock beamed. "That's just the wonder of it. She's here fer good. I'm sending her into town to speak with Maude, since she has years of experience working in my grand store."

"Your mercantile was just a square box with two windows, Violet. I've told you it's not nice to exaggerate."

Oh. Dear. Lord.

Brenna didn't know what to make of Beth Fairington. Well, actually she did, but didn't like thinking those kinds of thoughts on the Lord's day. "Then let me welcome you to town, Miss Fairington," she said. "Did Mrs. Hollyhock tell you about the long, hard winters? Last year was a doozy. Snow up to the eaves. Most of us were snowbound for a week."

Miss Fairington smirked. "I'm used to Wyoming winters, Mrs. Lane. The idea of a little snow isn't enough to send me running."

Beth's condescending tone felt like biting into a sour apple. "I'm relieved to hear that. Then you won't have any problems when the bears come around looking for something to eat."

"Now, Brenna. You're exaggerating." Violet was shaking her head.

"Mrs. Hollyhock, I think it only fair your friend has ample warning," Brenna said. "Not only bears, but also lots of wolves."

Violet was getting on in years. She didn't need another mouth to feed unless that mouth was going to help out. Do some chores. Pull her own weight. This mouth wasn't the type, Brenna was sure.

Everyone worried about the sweet old woman—including herself, although the feisty eighty-six-year-old seemed to get along just fine.

Beth Fairington pursed her lips and stood a little straighter. "Thank you for all your concern, Mrs. Lane. I'll keep that in mind when walking to town."

"That would be wise. You know, here on the outskirts is where the wild creatures like to dwell. When I'm walking alone I always carry a large stick—just in case."

Violet went over to the kitchen table and pulled out a chair. "If you two are gonna keep up this blather, I'm sittin' down." Mrs. Hollyhock sat with a rustle of fabric.

Brenna held up a finger. "Give me a moment, please." She hurried to the front door and opened it. "Mr. Rose, would you mind terribly going around back and filling up the two large wash kettles with water? The pump is right next to the house. And if it's not too much trouble can you also start the fire underneath? I'd appreciate it a great deal."

She closed the door. "The new teacher has come down with a case of the measles and I'm here to buy more of your willow bark. We ran out of ours last night. He has a headache as well as a sore throat and other aches and pains."

Beth Fairington gasped. She took several large steps back, putting a good six feet between them. "That man outside has the measles? Why, he'll infect us all. Have you been tending him?" She gave Brenna's dress a scathing look, her lip curling in disgust.

"No. Mr. Hutton is home in bed, too sick to do anything, much less walk all the way over here. And I can't be a carrier since I've already had the measles years ago."

Beth Fairington sniffed loudly, wringing her hands. Her eyebrows arched so high Brenna feared they would slip right off the top of her head. Irritated at the woman's reaction, she felt compelled to add, "And I changed my dress before coming out. If you happen to catch anything, it won't be from me."

"The poor man." Violet sprang into action. She scurried for the herb basket she kept on the kitchen shelf. Her fingers walked through the contents. "Here's the willow bark." Mrs. Hollyhock's brow wrinkled. "But there's something else I want to give ya." She carefully took out two squares of waxed paper with several dried flowers resembling daisies pressed between. "This is the last of my purple coneflower. I've been saving them and I'm glad I did. Grind one stem up and add to boiling water. Steep for a good ten minutes, mind ya. The brew will ease his symptoms and fortify his constitution."

"Oh, Mrs. Hollyhock, you're an angel." Brenna couldn't resist kissing her on her furrowed cheek. "Thank you." She took a small cloth bag from her pocket, untied the ribbon and fished out a dime. "Does this cover the cost?"

"Put your coinage away, dearie. I'm donating my services, jist like you."

Brenna wished Beth would just go away. She didn't like the woman's powerful stare taking in every little detail about her conversation with Mrs. Hollyhock. "No, I can't take it for free."

"You will. I don't want ta hear another word."

Gratitude overwhelmed her. "Thank you." Brenna carefully took the willow bark and the dried coneflowers and placed them into her bag. "I need to go." She embraced her old friend, then glanced at Beth.

Beth straightened. "Who's waiting for you outside if it's not the 'good teacher' you're nursing?"

Mrs. Hollyhock seemed interested in her answer as well. Nothing the old woman liked more than matchmaking that led to baby-making.

"Mr. Rose. He's the new man working out at the Cotton Ranch, and I happened to encounter him walking through town."

Mrs. Hollyhock went to the back door and opened it. "Why, it's my new friend Charlie Rose," she called. With the door open Brenna could hear the pop and crackle of a new fire. "Iffin I'd knowed you were out here sooner, young man, I'd made ya come in for a hearty breakfast. You hungry?"

"No, ma'am. I'm fine. But thank you for the offer," he called back in his deep voice.

"Another time then. And I won't take no fer an answer. Thank ya kindly for starting my fire and filling my kettles."

"My pleasure, ma'am."

Why had Mr. Rose walked her out to the inn and now it seemed he was waiting to walk her back? It was strange. She didn't get the impression he was sweet on her, but then, maybe he was shy. At that thought, a vision of Mr. Hutton, Gregory, shadowed any thought of Nell's new hand. Whatever the man's intentions, she needed to get back to her patient. A good, strong cup of willow bark tea, followed by another of the purple coneflower was just what the doctor ordered.

Later, she'd remember to have a long talk with Hannah and Jessie to see about helping Violet more often. Their old friend wasn't getting any younger.

CHAPTER TWENTY

$\mathcal{C}$harlie glanced up as Brenna Lane hurried out the front door carrying her small cloth bag. He noted her high color and the hard line to her mouth. Something had transpired inside that had her blood pumping.

As she descended the steps, he took in her gently curved shape and nicely formed lips. He considered her sunny disposition from the school picnic.

A man could do worse, Charlie, something whispered inside. *Just think how happy it would make Maddie.*

He glanced up at the sky. *Are you putting these thoughts in my head, Miss Baxter? I didn't take your matchmaking seriously before, but maybe I should have.* He took a small step toward Georgia as he waited. *A wife? My wife?*

That's right, the voice encouraged. *She's won your daughter's affections. Why not yours?*

Was he wrong to consider her just for Maddie's sake? Hadn't his own father done just that when he'd married his stepmother, Priscilla? His pa had needed someone to take care of the family of small boys, help in the house, cook meals. Seemed like his pa and Priscilla had been happy enough. He couldn't remember a cross word passing between them. Surely, it wasn't a sin to marry for convenience.

"You needn't have waited, Mr. Rose." Her tone was clipped. "I'm perfectly fine walking back alone. I do it all the time."

She sounded a little bit cross. He needed to lighten her mood. Best way to do that was to get her smiling—then she might tell him what he wanted to know. "Did you get what you needed?"

"Yes, I did."

They turned and started back the way they'd come. Georgia, ambling along behind them, probably thought he'd lost his marbles, what with him walking again instead of riding her.

Wait a second. I'm not sure I believe all that. Horses don't think rational thoughts like people. That's just too farfetched to believe. Nell is lonely. When Seth's gone, she needs something to talk to and she's decided it's the animals.

He glanced back at his mare. The image of Nell riding beside him in the moonlight made his heart pick up tempo. She touched something deep inside him that Brenna didn't—but would that matter in the long run?

"I'm glad to hear you got what you came for," he drawled slowly, trying to capture Brenna's undivided attention, "but actually it's a little hard to believe. You're still empty-handed." He motioned at her hands and the small satchel she carried. "Whatever you came for must be in there? Am I right?"

Her eyes narrowed. "Mr. Rose, did anyone ever tell you that curiosity killed the cat?"

He let go a laugh that spooked a flock of common yellowthroats from a fir tree along the road. They swooped into the sky and Brenna's lips curled up as she watched them fly away. She was softening . . .

"Yes, they have, Mrs. Lane," he said. "They most surely have. But I've also been told that satisfaction brought it back. What about you?"

She arched a brow, surely trying to fight the giggle that finally popped out of her mouth. "So, I see you're a learned man. That is a bit unusual for a cowboy in these parts."

He nodded. "I'd say somewhat learned. Not too much, though. Not enough to be stuffy, or impersonal. I'm hospitable and charming. And you must be learned, if you can recognize my educated state."

She stopped and gaped at him for a moment. "That's quite a statement, Mr. Rose. I'm glad you think so highly of yourself."

His face heated. The devil had placed those words in his mouth.

"And actually, I am—a little educated, that is," Brenna added. "But mostly, I'm self-taught by absorbing my lessons right along with my children as they bring their studies home from school. I do have a small library of books that I read and reread though."

Charlie made a note of that. Maybe he would ask Nell if he could borrow a book or two to share with Brenna. Only on loan, of course. He didn't think Nell would mind.

"That's right clever of you, Mrs. Lane, learning with the young 'uns, I mean. I'm more than just a cowboy, you know. I was a merchant. I used to own a gun shop. My duties included cleaning and gun repair, bookkeeping, ordering parts from back East, and even making nice with the grumpy old man who had the glass shop next to mine. He had a way of turning everything I said back on me. That codger was always stewing for a fight over something." He gave a quick wink to her upturned face, though she didn't appear too impressed. "But—I learned how to get around his grouchy ways, and even make him smile."

He glanced at the pouch clutched in her hands, worry over Maddie never far from his thoughts. "I can't help wonder what brought you out so early on a Sunday morning, to walk all the way across town for something so small it fits in your handbag. Call me curious, or call me a dead cat. Either way, I'd like to know."

She gave another small laugh but kept her vision trained straight ahead. "If you *really* must know, Mr. Rose, I came for some willow bark to make a soothing tea for Mr. Hutton, the schoolteacher, who has taken ill. He recently moved in across the street from me and my family, and the poor man has no one else to fetch it for him. Mrs. Hollyhock keeps a good store of herbs and roots for medicinal purposes, in case you find yourself in need of some."

"Taken ill?" Fear frosted Charlie's inner core. All laughter died. Was Maddie in danger? "I thought Logan Meadows had a doctor. I believe Nell mentioned that to me the other day."

"Oh, yes. Dr. Thorn has just finished examining Mr. Hutton. Unfortunately, he'll be down for some time—just as the new school term is set to begin. That's another situation I need to figure out."

They rounded the corner onto Main Street, where a few more people were out and about. "Did the doctor say what the teacher has? Is it serious?"

"Serious enough. It's a clear case of the measles. I'm sure you're aware that the disease is quite hard on adults."

Charlie breathed a sigh of relief. "Yes, I had them myself when I was in my twenties." He felt like dancing the Texas Two-Step. Three years ago he'd sat by Maddie's side, putting cool compresses on her head to lessen her fever and grabbing her hands when she went to scratch her face. By the time she was well, he'd almost gone hoarse from reading to her constantly. A small scar on the right side of her nose was the only reminder. "My mother's brother succumbed to them but that was before I was born. After that, she always had a healthy fear of the disease."

Brenna nodded. "With good reason, then. Logan Meadows had several cases two years ago, and a few the year before that. My whole brood caught them one after another. Three months passed before my household was back to normal."

"Your children are all well now, then?"

"Yes, they are, at the moment. And that includes my little adopted daughter, Maddie. But I'm worried because I don't know her medical history, or if she's susceptible to coming down with something or not. If she is, she might contract what Mr. Hutton has. She says she's already had the measles, but I'm not sure if a young child really remembers which sicknesses she's had and which she has not."

Charlie let go the breath he'd been holding. No need for Brenna to worry over Maddie needlessly. "The child says she did? Does she show any signs of having them, any pocks or scars?"

Her eyes brightened. "I never thought of that. I'll ask her that exact question when I return home. Measles don't always leave scars, not like chicken pox, but can if scratched deeply. All my children have a mark or two."

Good. Maddie knew exactly where she had a scar thanks to Miss Baxter sulking over it so often. Bemoaning the fact that the tiny spot next to her nose might never fade. *Maddie can't see it, but she'll be able to point it out.*

A large dose of relief loosened Charlie's limbs. And Brenna had called Maddie her daughter. That must mean she loved her. Although he longed to keep the subject going, he didn't dare. The truth would be out soon enough and he didn't want to make matters worse than they were going to be. Feathers would be ruffled. People would feel duped. Anger would flare. He knew that, but he didn't have a choice. If they couldn't understand his reasons for wanting to keep her safe, then they wouldn't understand anything. No one knew Galante like he did.

But what if Maddie is better off with Mrs. Lane and her family than with me? What if Brenna won't consider me? There was that possibility—a good possibility. *What if Maddie doesn't want to leave her?* That was outlandish to think but still he felt his insides heat up. He wiped his free palm against his pants. Of course Maddie would want to come home as soon as she knew he was here. He wouldn't let his uncertainties get the better of him.

"Have you lived in Logan Meadows for some time?"

Brenna gave him a strained look. "I see the curious cat is back, Mr. Rose. Yes, for many years."

"Can't you please call me Charlie? I feel we know each other, at least a little."

She relaxed into a smile. "All right, Charlie. I'd be pleased if you called me Brenna."

He nodded, then said, "Thank you." *Progress.* Several minutes passed in silence. It actually felt good stretching his legs like this. Maybe he should walk more often.

The fact that there was a pretty woman next to him didn't hurt, either. They'd learned quite a bit about each other. *We're becoming friends.* As far as he knew, she wasn't stepping out with anyone else. Surely, she wanted a husband again to help feed her children, didn't she? Wasn't that what all widows desired?

He snuck a quick glance at Brenna when she waved at somebody in the restaurant window. Could he love her? That was the real question. Surely, they could be friends. They'd proven that fact now, by working through several topics of conversation, and ending them with a smile. But was marrying her just to create a mother and home for his daughter right? What about her feelings? And his?

Once in town, Brenna turned to him and stopped. "I've enjoyed our conversation. And thank you for helping Mrs. Hollyhock. She's getting on in age and I do worry about her."

He tipped his hat, well aware he wouldn't be getting any more of Brenna's time today. "I enjoyed the time, as well. And filling those kettles and starting the fire was nothing. I'm glad I could be of some help." He fingered his reins. "Oh, I wonder if I could give you a few of my things that need mending."

Brenna's eyes brightened. "Of course you can, Charlie. Is that why you've been following me all morning talking about everything under the sun?" She laughed. "You shouldn't be shy about asking me about mending. That's what I do. Drop them by anytime you'd like and I'll be happy to put your clothes to rights."

He went to Georgia's side; the horse—seemingly bored to tears—had already fallen asleep in the early sunshine. He unbuckled the keep on his saddlebag and reached inside. "Actually, I have them with me now." He didn't want to go by the house and risk bumping into Maddie.

"Even better. I'm happy to take them."

He handed her the only other shirt he owned, embarrassed now that he'd forgotten the garment was soiled, and two rolled pairs of socks. "Sorry for their condition. Until this minute, I didn't think about washing them first." He wagged his finger through a small hole that was growing in the side seam.

"Not at all. If you'd like, I can wash, mend and then iron them, too."

"Iron the socks?" he asked in shocked innocence.

Brenna laughed. "No, not the socks." She lifted her chin teasingly. "Just the shirt. It's only a nickel more. All total with washing and ironing would be thirty-five cents."

Her smile went all the way up to her eyes and Charlie was mighty happy he'd decided to bring the mending into town. "That's not enough. I'll pay more than that."

"Absolutely not." Her brows drew down and she looked back the way they'd walked.

"What is it?"

"I'm worried about Violet doing all that wash by herself. Wet sheets are weighty. I'd have stayed to help if Mr. Hutton didn't need me."

"You mean Mrs. Hollyhock? Back at the inn?"

She nodded.

He gave Brenna his most charming smile. "Don't you worry about that. I'll take care of everything."

CHAPTER TWENTY-ONE

*A*lthough Sunday was a day of rest and contemplation, Nell knew she couldn't put off the inevitable any longer. The house had to be cleaned. Today. Seth had ridden off with Dog over to the Broken Horn. He mentioned he wanted to talk with Chase Logan about the cattle drive this spring, but that was so far away she believed he just needed a change of scenery. Some men to talk to and play a game of cards with. Charlie was doing who-knew-what in Logan Meadows, and the thought made her grit her teeth for one foolish instant. A jab of longing pierced her heart.

She eased up. Charlie had no obligation to hang around here on his time off. He was a hired hand, nothing more. He was free to come and go.

The absence of both men presented the perfect opportunity for her to give the ranch house a thorough spring cleaning, even if it was mid-September. She smiled at herself. Who was she kidding? If Charlie hadn't shown up, she'd put the all-day chore off until next year.

Glancing around, she admitted to herself she'd let the house go. The poor thing was in a disgusting state of affairs. After Ben died, her desire to do anything except care for her animals just seemed to shrivel up and blow away. From caring for the household to the cooking of meals, she'd been passing off her second best for far too long. Seth, kind brother that he was, hadn't complained a bit. But that wasn't fair to him, or to Charlie now, either. When a ranch hand hired on, room and board were always included. Good food could be the biggest factor in keeping decent help or losing him quick. A clean house and a satisfying meal were things that could easily be remedied today.

Energized at the thought of Seth's and Charlie's reactions, Nell picked up the closest chair at the table and carried it out to the front porch. She followed that with the remaining three. Next, she muscled the beat-up pine sideboard out, which was difficult because of its bulkiness, not its weight. Then the butter churn she hadn't used in a year. The fallen hat rack that leaned in the corner. A milking stool that she set her rinse bucket on. The growing mound of old boots by the door. Piles of old newspapers here and there. A handful of coats that she took up to the bedrooms. Odds and ends.

Soon all that remained was the kitchen table. The piece was too large for her to get through the door alone, but she could easily work around it. Swiping the perspiration from her forehead, and before she lost her enthusiasm, she headed into the living room. Most of the furniture was too large for her to remove. One thing she was able to manage on her own was Seth's upholstered footstool. The lumpy footrest went directly into the yard. She glanced up at the clear sky and stretched her back muscles, liking the way they softly ached.

The interior of the room grew hot. Nell pushed the four large windows open, appreciating the breeze that flowed through. She took down the drapes, intending to give them a good shake. After that, she carefully removed the breakables, like the oil lamps, a mantel clock, and one fragile flower vase that had come with the house. Everything that could be moved needed to go. She'd dust each outside, removing the months of dirt that had accumulated.

Soon items spilled off the porch and into the yard, looking much like the sale Maude had at her mercantile every fall. Beads of sweat gathered on Nell's temples.

The rug was going to be a problem, but she was determined to get the worn floor covering outside where she could beat it clean. Hefting the sofa off one side, and then the chair from the opposite corner, she knelt and began rolling the gray-and-maroon prize. It was the most expensive item that had come with the house and certainly something she'd never have been able to afford if Mr. Clarkston Jones hadn't sold them the place right before he died, furnishings and all.

Finished, she detoured to the kitchen for a cool drink of water. *Charlie is going to get the shock of his life when he gets back. And Seth. Heck, he'll think he's in the wrong house.*

She laughed and water ran down her chin. She felt good. She couldn't remember being this happy in a very long time. Since she was alone, Nell unbuttoned her shirt until the garment gapped open, cooling her heated skin. She took the bandanna from her rear pocket and tied back her hair. After returning to the living room, she eyed the rolled carpet as if the thing were a rival. She'd need every ounce of her strength to get the bulky item outside, but by thunder, she'd do it. This wasn't the first time she'd tackled a man-sized job.

Bending, she took hold and wrestled the closest end around, swinging it toward the door. She rubbed her moist palms down the legs of her pants, then took hold again and heaved backward until the carpet moved a few inches. She heaved again, leveraging her weight back on her haunches, straining and groaning while the muscles in her back tensed. Several more steps and she'd be to the door. Her breath rasped in her throat as she sucked in air.

It'll be worth it. If for nothing else, to see their expressions.

Gripping the carpet again, Nell heaved back across the threshold to the porch. With a final pull, the end popped over the divide, catching for a moment and making her hands slip. She gasped as her fingernail bent back painfully. Tears sprang to her eyes. She angrily shook her hand several times before sticking her throbbing appendage into her mouth. Hot tears spilled from her eyes.

Irritated, Nell marched out into the yard and plopped down onto Seth's footstool. Her finger pulsed. She examined the damaged nail carefully for a moment, then stuck it back in her mouth. It wasn't fair. Although she was strong, the men were so much stronger. Moving the furniture and rug would be nothing to them.

Frustration turned to anger. Who was she fooling? Seth and Charlie might not even notice the effort. Didn't seem like they noticed the disarray, at least they didn't say much about it. Maybe this was all for naught.

Closing her eyes, she sucked in a calming breath and tried to ignore the pulsation. This confusion was all because of Charlie and how he made her feel alive. *Your feelings are all one-sided*, her better sense cautioned. He'd never given her one iota of encouragement or reason to believe he felt the same.

But I want to love again, her heart argued back. *If I don't let him know how I feel, I may miss my chance.*

If nothing else, she'd get the place cleaned up for herself. Get her house in order. That was enough reason. She didn't have to do it for Seth or Charlie. It was time she came back to living her days as she should. She'd best remember she wasn't the only person in the world who had suffered a loss, or was confused over her feelings.

Charlie had lost a wife. That's what Seth had told her. She'd wanted to ask Charlie about her, but held back. Had they been young and in love, like she and Ben had been? Where had they lived? Did they own a ranch . . .

Nell gave herself a mental shake. She needed to mind her own business and get back to the business of cleaning up her life. She'd start with the house, and after that was finished, she'd concentrate on her feelings. No more thinking about the past. No more grieving over the way things had turned out. No more wishing Ben hadn't died. No more hankering for the baby they never had.

The future was here and now—and staring her in the face. She'd not waste it, or she might regret that on top of everything else.

Resolved, Nell opened her eyes. The metal blades of the windmill twirled slowly above her head, the sight familiar and comfortable. Her gaze moved to the horizon as it usually did, then toward the horse pasture up on the hill.

She froze. Looked again, making sure she wasn't mistaken.

A lone rider sat on the ridge, watching her.

CHAPTER TWENTY-TWO

*H*urry up, children. Line up. Let me check you over. I don't want you to be late and interrupt Reverend Wilbrand while he's giving his sermon. That's not polite." Brenna eyed each child, making sure they were dressed correctly for the church service. She sent up a little prayer of thanksgiving when her gaze drifted over the tiny pock on the side of Maddie's nose. Just as Charlie had suggested, the child was able to point out proof of her immunity, putting Brenna's heart at ease. Mr. Hutton, or her nursing him, would not present a problem to her household.

As Stevie tried to hurry past, Brenna stopped him by grasping his arm. His shirt was rumpled, clearly not the one she'd washed and pressed and hung on his peg two days ago. "Where is your Sunday best, Stevie?"

He scuffed his shoe. "Err . . . I thought this one was fine, Ma. I don't want to change."

Brenna opened his top button to find his sleep shirt underneath, tucked into his pants. Alarmed, she peered behind one ear, then the other. "What's this? You haven't taken any time whatsoever for church? I'm shocked, son. Now, go wash—and hurry. Then dress in the shirt I intended you to wear, but only after you don a clean undershirt."

With a sullen slant to his mouth, Stevie pulled his shoulder from her grasp and hurried toward the kitchen and the two rooms beyond.

"He's becoming a handful," Penny said. "He won't listen and he even talks back to me when I ask him to do what you've instructed."

"Is that so? Well, we'll just see about that. The next time he disobeys you, Penny, you let me know." Feeling the need to get the willow bark over to Mr. Hutton, Brenna eyeballed the rest of her clan, making a note to herself to address this situation with Stephen later.

Stevie rushed back into the room and skidded to a halt, almost upsetting the oil lamp on the side table. Clean shirt, face washed, and hair slicked back.

"Thank you. That looks better. Now, like I mentioned, I'm staying home to take care of Mr. Hutton. Everyone best remember that Penny is in charge. You are to mind her no matter what she says." Brenna frowned at Stevie. "Stephen, if I hear of any shenanigans in church or after, you will bear the consequences."

Everyone nodded.

What those consequences were, Brenna didn't know yet. Her children had always been so good and respectful. She hadn't had to deal with a troublemaker and wondered how she would. She didn't believe in the rod, having suffered through many an unfounded whipping when she was a girl. The anger she'd felt afterward was certainly not what the Lord expected her to feel for her father. And certainly not what she wanted Stevie to feel for her. She'd not put her children in a similar situation that caused guilt and hurt. "Is that clear, everyone?"

"Yes, ma'am," Prichard and Jane said in unison.

"Stevie?"

He nodded.

Prichard was the height of prompt obedience, as was Jane. One could almost forget Maddie was even about, the girl was so quiet. And Penny was Penny, her right arm. "Good. I'm glad to hear it. It's time to leave."

Jane reached over and took Maddie by the hand, and the children filed out the door and down the porch steps.

"Careful, Maddie, here we go down," Brenna caught Jane say as they descended the stairs. Her heart swelled. They were good children, sweet and kind. Stevie's actions weren't normal for him. She watched him go, his brown hair reflecting the sunshine. School would be starting, with or without Mr. Hutton. The ranching families depended on the schedule. She would need to find a willing adult to fill in for the teacher in his absence. Someone who wouldn't let the children ruffle their feathers. Who that was at this point was a mystery and she didn't have time to ponder. She had a sick teacher waiting on her return.

Brenna tapped lightly on Mr. Hutton's door. What if he was asleep? Should she just go in quietly and see? With the spots just appearing at dawn, he was going through the worst of his illness and needed his rest.

Brenna opened the door and crossed silently to the kitchen. She filled the kettle she'd brought with her and set the steamer on the already lit stove. Dr. Thorn had started the fire for her before he'd left but after he affirmed her diagnosis. Mr. Hutton suffered from a case of ordinary measles. He should start to feel better in a week and be able to return to teaching a week and a half after that.

Brenna made another trip to her house for the pot of chicken soup, then hurried back and placed the container on the stove to heat. Walking on tiptoe to avoid tapping her heels on the wooden floorboards, she approached his bedroom.

Mr. Hutton was nestled in his bed, his face a warm-looking pink, dotted now with a multitude of tiny, red spots. He breathed deeply, making the sheet that was lying around his face ripple every time he exhaled. His damp chestnut hair stuck to his forehead, telling her his fever was still running hot.

Dr. Thorn had instructed to let the illness run its course—as if they could do otherwise—and see to his comfort. Do her best to keep his temperature down with drinks of cool water. If that didn't work, and Mr. Hutton became agitated, she was to send Penny for Dr. Thorn right away.

Brenna's mind warred with the questions of what the doctor meant by *too hot* and who would teach the class tomorrow. Guilt squeezed inside when she realized she was a bit relieved she'd been granted a reprieve from telling him she'd forgotten to order the math books. In no way was she happy he was sick, but she was relieved she'd have a little more time to rectify her blunder. Perhaps the books would arrive before he made it back to class.

When the teakettle whistled, Brenna hurried to sweep it off the heat. She poured the steaming water into a large mug, then found a knife, finely chopped a sprig of the willow bark, and dropped the bits into the blue-and-white cup. The tidbits floated around the surface like tiny boats. She set the concoction aside to steep. With that done, she tried the soup, making sure it was tepid and not hot.

A hacking cough sounded from the bedroom, followed by a groan, then a gasp. Mr. Hutton was awake.

When Brenna peeked in, his eyes moved to the doorway.

"Hello," she said gently.

"I feel horrible. You should stay away." His voice came out in a garbled, gravelly whisper.

"Yes, I know. I've made you some willow bark tea. It should help the pain in your throat and head. Would you like me to get it?"

He nodded.

Brenna departed and returned with the cup and a cloth. She set them on his bedside table. Grasping his upper arm, she helped him to sit up. When that was accomplished, she propped one of his pillows behind his back. His face scrunched as his Adam's apple bobbed again. Why did a sore throat cause a greater impulse to swallow? She settled back in the chair and picked up the cup, stirring briskly to cool down the liquid. After a second she leaned forward and held out a spoonful of the liquid.

He blew on the tea first, then carefully sipped out of the spoon. They repeated the process several times. When he'd taken about a quarter of the cup, she set the mug aside and refreshed the damp cloth for his forehead.

"You don't have to stay and take care of me, Mrs. Lane. I'm sure you have other things to do. Your children must need you. I can manage now."

Did he think she was overstepping? "They're all off at church."

"Ah, yes. Church."

He had an air of fragility about him. As though what he was saying and what he really wanted were two different things. He gazed at her and when he tried to swallow, his face pinched in pain.

"You let me worry about what I should be doing, Mr. Hutton. There's nothing on my list of things to do that can't wait a day or two." She thought of Mr. Rose's clothes. He'd never mentioned about being in any great hurry to get them. "Can you take the rest of the tea now?"

His eyes darted over to the table, and he winced.

"Your head still hurt?"

"Yes."

"The tea will take a good half hour to get into your system. Until then, just lie back quietly and close your eyes—that is, after you finish the rest of the cup."

Brenna helped him, then adjusted the folded cloth on his forehead. "When you feel better I have some chicken soup on the stove. It's important that you keep up your strength. When your throat feels better, I'll help you eat a little."

He closed his eyes but one second later they popped open full of panic. "School starts tomorrow."

"I know. I haven't been able to think of anything else. What should we do? The children are excited to start back. Shall I tell them school's been postponed for two or three weeks?"

She was aware of his scrutiny as the clock on the dresser marked the seconds. "No. It's important to keep our schedule. You take the class, Mrs. Lane."

Brenna straightened and blinked several times, wondering if she'd heard him correctly. "Me?"

He nodded.

Dread rose inside her. No way in heaven was she able to do this. But also, she didn't want to appear like a frightened child. She'd somehow get him to see the light. "You understand I have no teaching experience whatsoever."

"I do now."

"My expertise is with mending, cooking, and cleaning."

His gaze softened, and a whisper of a smile played around his lips. "You can do it, Mrs. Lane. In the short time I've known you, I've come to see that you can do anything you set your mind to. You're exceptional with the children. And patient. More patient than I, if I dare to say honestly. I'll write up an outline that tells you what to do each day."

She stood. *Tomorrow* was Monday. Her eyes darted around the room, searching for a way to make him understand. "Anyone is more qualified than I am, Mr. Hutton. I don't want this responsibility." Her mind raced through the townspeople hoping to sway him away from this harebrained idea. "Maude Miller, Jessie Logan, Hannah Donovan come to mind. Or even Betty Brinkley. She was the chairwoman of the school board for years. I can't think of a person better to take over for you."

Holding the cup now, Mr. Hutton swallowed the rest of his willow bark tea and set the empty container back on the side table. "I don't know any of those women beyond hello." His voice sounded like a sick frog's. "But I've observed you long enough to know you'll do fine. And I'll give you the pay that I'd be receiving for that time."

He waved his hand, stopping her protestations, then cupped the front of his throat, pain shadowing his eyes. "I need to rest the inside of my pharynx, Mrs. Lane." He punctuated his sentence with a scrunched-up face as he once again swallowed. "As far as I'm concerned, the subject is closed."

When she didn't respond he smiled, his face resembling one of Mrs. Hollyhock's speckled hens, only red and not black. "Please? The children need you. I need you. And it won't last forever."

She was in over her head for sure. She should have known better—much better—than to volunteer for the board position. What had she been thinking? That led to this, and who knew what else could be next. She was just the daughter of a dirt-poor, illiterate miner, with no aspirations beyond putting food on the table and a roof over their heads.

She stifled a nervous shiver. If it were anyone besides Mr. Hutton doing the asking, she'd tell him no. Did he know how charming he looked, even sick as a trampled gopher, when he looked at her like that? His concerned hazel gaze seemed to reach deep into her heart. *Yes, he must. That's why he's doing it. Has probably charmed more than his fair share of women back East and I'm easy game. There, that expression—where he looks like a gloomy little pup—he knows he has me right where he wants me, and I have no power to tell him no. I may as well admit the truth. I'll help him in whatever he needs, anytime he asks.*

CHAPTER TWENTY-THREE

With aching shoulders and a damp shirt, Charlie rode Georgia under the COTTON RANCH sign and asked his mare for an easy lope by squeezing his legs. At a leisurely pace, they made for the ranch house a quarter mile away. The sky had darkened earlier today and now several weighty gray clouds filled the horizon, promising a good dose of rain before long.

Even with him doing most of the work, Mrs. Hollyhock's wash had taken two hours. He would have been able to get the chore done more quickly if the old woman hadn't insisted on helping—while talking his head off. The yards of linen were awkward and tough to work with. He'd never imagined it took such strength to stir them in the boiling water with the wooden paddle. Then they had to hang them out. No wonder Brenna worried about her old friend doing such strenuous work.

Finally finished, he'd taken on her woodpile, split some logs and stacked them close to the back door. Once, feeling like he was being watched, he discovered Miss Beth Fairington peeking from behind the curtain in her bedroom. Then, with a few more odds and ends around the inn, the day had passed quickly.

As he drew closer to the house a prickle of alarm started in his belly. Chairs and tables were scattered about. He recognized Seth's footstool. Nell's bookcase. What was going on? Had they been raided? He didn't see Nell, Seth, or Dog anywhere.

He urged Georgia faster, galloping into the yard. He dismounted in one motion and tossed his reins over the hitching rail. Fearful, he took the stairs two at a time and went inside. "Nell?" he shouted. The gutted kitchen—what had happened? His heart picked up at the thought of trouble. "Seth? Anyone here?"

Nell stepped out from behind the stairs, her gun strapped to her hip, her face sweaty and red, and her shirt unbuttoned and exposing her chemise. None of that meant a whit to Charlie. Her frightened eyes were what scared him. He covered the distance between them and gripped her by the shoulders. "What's going on?" he demanded.

She straightened. Relief washed over her face. "Nothing."

"I don't believe you. Spit it out."

"When I heard your horse, I had a strange feeling and went inside. That's all."

Nell? Afraid of a rider? That doesn't make any sense at all. "Why didn't you just wait to see who was coming? You would've been able to see me soon enough." Aware he was still holding her by her shoulders, he gave a gentle shake. "Nell? What's going on?"

She stepped back and his hands fell away. Embarrassment replaced the relief in her eyes.

"Nell?"

"Earlier today a rider was on the ridge watching me. I didn't see him until I sat down in the yard."

"Sat in the yard?"

She held out a red-tipped finger. The action reminded him of Maddie and he had to stifle the urge to kiss it and make it better.

"I bent my fingernail and the pain was unbearable. I sat down until most of the pain had passed."

"You didn't recognize him? You sure he wasn't someone you know?"

The curls that had broken free from her braid bounced when she shook her head. "No. He was too far away."

"And Dog? Did he put up a racket?" Charlie glanced around and out the door. "Where is the mutt, anyway?"

"Gone with Seth this morning."

Her soulful amber eyes took him in from head to toe, almost making him blush. "You're sure he was watching you?"

"Gosh, Charlie. Pretty sure." She crossed her arms over her chest. "What other business would he have up there?"

Charlie walked over to the counter in the empty kitchen and leaned back, studying her. The rider could've been anyone. A drifter. A rancher taking a short cut. But maybe it was his past catching up to him. Had Galante found him? He didn't want to think that. He wanted to get his life back in order again with Maddie and start living—the sooner the better.

Nell's fear was unusual, though. Strange, really, that she would be so shaken. "That's your land up there?"

"Yes."

"It's clear to me you were fearful of him. Why, Nell? I have to admit I'm surprised. Seems you've stayed out here by yourself before with no problem. You obviously weren't scared of being alone then. What's changed?"

Nell turned away, pretending, he was sure, to glance out the window. Her hand went down and caressed the handle of her gun. "Nothin', Charlie. The rider just gave me the creeps because once I spotted him I didn't know how long he'd been watching me. Would you like someone peeping in on you?" Her tone was defensive. She glanced down and quickly buttoned her shirt. "I'm sure you wouldn't."

When she turned back, a shadow of insecurity crossed her eyes. In actuality, she was young. At most times, her toughness seemed to mask that fact, but she was having a hard time of it now. He wanted to close the distance between them again and this time wrap Nell into his embrace. "What did you do?"

"What could I do? Not much. On my next trip into the house, I strapped on my gun, making my job of lugging furniture around twice as difficult. When I looked up the hill again, he was gone."

Something didn't quite add up, but questioning her more now wasn't going to get him anywhere. She'd also been skittish the day he'd arrived, when he'd met her in the barn at the end of her gun. That wasn't the reception he'd been anticipating after talking with Sheriff Preston. He'd keep his wits about him and try to figure this out.

She took a deep breath and the smile returned to her face. "But you're home now and I'm glad."

The warmth in her smile charmed him. "And it's this special thing you have with animals that tells you I'm a good guy, not like the stranger on the hill?"

"No. It's your clean teeth and the nice way you take care of Georgia."

Her impish smile zipped through his heart like a bolt of lightning, down his legs all the way to his feet, scorching the ground where he stood. "You're teasing me?"

She shook her head. "I never tease, Charlie Rose. I thought you knew that by now."

"I guess I do." He shooed away the crazy notions trotting around his head about how pretty she looked in her disheveled state and asked, "So then why don't you tell me why all the furniture is outside. I can't imagine. Did a snake crawl in the kitchen door and you're on the hunt to chase him out?"

An embarrassed flush rose up in her normally creamy cheeks. She lifted a shoulder. "I got the urge to clean the house."

He stifled his compulsion to scoff. "By taking everything outside? That must have been one big urge." He glanced about. "How on earth did you get the large rug out the door?"

"Persistence."

"And a lot of elbow grease." The already dim kitchen darkened even more. Time was short before the summer storm let go several inches of desperately needed rain. "You do know a rainstorm is moving in?"

Nell started for the door. "When I began this crazy notion there wasn't a cloud in the sky. I best get everything back inside so the—"

"Not before we get the place the way you want it." He grabbed a scrub brush from the drain board and tossed her a cloth. "I'll start in here on the countertops, then sweep the floor. You can take the living room and do the windows."

Her face lit up. "You'll help?"

"I'm your hired hand, aren't I?"

"For ranching. Not housekeeping."

"Job's a job."

She wrinkled her face. "It's Sunday."

"Yeah, that's what I keep hearing, but that hasn't stopped me yet." He gave her a little push. "Let's go."

She hurried toward the other room. "Thanks, Charlie Rose."

"You're welcome, Nell. Get moving. I don't know how long we have before the rain hits."

The weather held for a good hour. When he had the kitchen as clean as he could get it, he swept the stairs, the back rooms, and then ventured into the living room where Nell still toiled.

"The wind's picking up." He looked out the front door. "We need to get the furniture inside if you want to have anything left."

Georgia still stood at the front hitching post. She pawed impatiently and her tail and mane whipped around in the wind. Nell and Charlie lumbered back and forth, bringing the furniture back inside. Just as he took the mare's reins, a few large splashes of water landed on his head.

"I'll get that rug as soon as I get back. Don't do it without me," he called over his shoulder as Georgia trotted at his heels. "I'll feed the horses as well."

Charlie dashed inside the barn. The worries he'd suppressed for the last hour rose up full force. Who was Nell's stranger on the hill? What did he want with the Cotton Ranch? Or was the man really after Tristan Axelrose? Had Galante hired a gunman to track and kill him? Would he hurt anyone—man, woman, or child—who got in his way?

A loud boom of thunder snapped Charlie out of his musing. He unsaddled Georgia and put her in her stall. Once in the loft he went to the loft door. Rain spattered onto his face as he took a good look around. Nothing unusual out there except the storm. The windmill twirled violently in the wind. He'd feel better if Seth were home already.

Who'd been watching Nell? The question badgered his mind. If anything happened to her because of him, he'd never forgive himself. He could see her as she paced up and back on the front porch, waiting on his return. All of a sudden the Cotton Ranch felt miles too far from any civilization.

CHAPTER TWENTY-FOUR

*N*ell marched up and down the now cleared porch, wondering what was taking Charlie so dang long in the barn. She wrung her hands in an attempt to still her nerves. The instant she'd noticed the rider, her irrational fear had come rushing in. She'd held back today from Charlie, just as she had with Seth. Why was it so hard to share? Since the stranger's visit, she'd slept with her gun at her side. She didn't like it, or appreciate it. Her independence was important to her and she didn't want anyone taking that from her, ever.

And where was Seth, anyway? The wind had turned cold, which would surely worsen his cough. As she paced she told herself not to let her imagination run off. Seth was fine, probably at the Logans' until the storm passed. Wyoming was known for fast-changing weather, especially in the summer and fall.

She glanced down all the way to their sign and the road that led to Logan Meadows. Dark, low-hanging clouds made seeing anything difficult.

"All right, let's get this done," Charlie said, taking the steps two at a time.

Nell whirled around. "What took you so long?"

"The barn was too drafty to light a match, so I had to move a little slower in the dark. Didn't want to fall from the loft and break my neck." He motioned to the rug where it hung over the porch rail. "Did you get a chance to beat it yet, or should I do that now?"

"That's what I was doing when I spotted you coming—although I didn't know it was you." *And my squirrely heart sent me scampering for cover.* She winced, not liking what she'd turned into. "It's as clean as it's gonna get."

Charlie grasped one end and waved Nell away when she went to take the other end. "I can get this." He pulled a portion off the porch rail, rolled it, and repeated the process until he could hoist the whole thing to his shoulder, frustrating Nell even more. As strong as she was, she still couldn't hold a candle to Charlie.

As he started for the door, Nell ducked under his arms and preceded him. She guided the front of the rug away from glass lantern chimneys and the mantel clock. Once on the narrow side of the rectangular room, Charlie bent over and dropped the heavy roll with a *woomph* on the old but now-clean hardwood floor.

Charlie moved back. With a push from his boot, he unrolled the rug.

The colors, though worn, brought life to the place. Spots of interest to brighten the drab off-white walls. The black cast-iron clock that sat on the fire mantel picked up the dark hues, while the greens and maroon just added appeal, something the room was dearly lacking.

"I'll light the lamps," he said. "We still need to arrange the furniture." In their hurry to get everything in before the rain, they'd just brought the items in and set them anywhere.

She nodded. "While you do that, I'll light a fire in the kitchen stove and get some supper going."

She turned around to find Charlie watching her. "What?"

"Nothing."

"Thanks, Charlie." She admired their work. "Actually, the house looks pretty darn good already, even with everything out of place. I like it clean."

"You're welcome. Now, what about that supper? I have a powerful hunger. Anything hot sounds good."

In the shadowy room it was impossible to see his eyes, much less anything else about him. Regardless, she was darn happy he'd returned when he did, and helped her with the house. *And calmed my runaway fears.*

She went into the kitchen while he lit the three oil lamps in the living room. Before she knew it, Charlie was finished and stood in the doorway.

"One last thing," he said. "Do you have a hammer and some nails in the house?"

"Why?" She cocked her head.

"You'll see" was all he said, and Nell went into the hallway and returned with what he'd asked for. "What're you doing?"

"May as well finish what we started. Where'd you put that hat rack that used to be in the corner? I'll hang it up."

Nell couldn't stop her smile. She hurried to the back porch, where she'd stored the rustic rectangle of wood after bringing everything in from the front yard. Back in the kitchen, she handed it to Charlie, who positioned the contraption on the wall.

"Is this where you want it?"

"Absolutely."

Nell held it in place and Charlie sank the nails with ease. The chore that never seemed to get done was finished in two minutes. From the sideboard he picked up her hat first, and then his, and hung them side by side. He turned. "Supper?"

Nell went to her pantry shelf and retrieved the two large cans of pork and beans Maude had given to her to try. Something quick and easy. She worked the can opener around the lid and dumped the contents into a pot, scraping every bean from the can with a knife. She repeated the process with the second can, then placed the pot on the stove. Hurrying down to the root cellar for the smoked flank steak she had stored away, her mouth watered thinking about the food. After returning to the kitchen, she cut the beef up into small pieces, then added them to the pork and beans. *This should be interesting.*

With the supper simmering on the stove, Nell went up to her bedroom, stripped off her dirty clothes, and dropped them into her hamper. At her washstand, she filled her porcelain bowl as far as the crack in the side allowed and splashed her face several times, soaped it, scrubbed for several moments, rinsed, and dried. Taking her jar of Pond's Extract she'd purchased on her trip to Cheyenne, she dabbed on two dollops and worked it around her face. She'd originally bought the extravagant luxury for days she'd stayed too long in the sun, but after finding how soft it made her skin, she started using it often, though sparingly.

Next she bathed the rest of her body, then donned a clean corset, chemise, and soft, white blouse. She didn't know why but she felt compelled to wear a pretty blue skirt Ben had purchased for her from a small band of traveling *comancheros*. Finished dressing, she unbraided her hair and brushed her soft curls, examining her reflection. She was taller than most women, slender, her face browned by the sun. What did Charlie see when he looked at her? Another cowhand? A silly bother? Or, a desirable woman yearning to be kissed?

Yearning to be kissed! Where had that notion come from?

Agitated, Nell withdrew from her room, closing the door with a soft click, but she stopped on the hallway runner. She listened to the patter of rain on the roof and wondered what Charlie was doing downstairs. Her heart stilled. A rumble of thunder far off made her wish Seth were already home.

Reentering her bedroom, she picked up Ben's old guitar and a bottle of red wine she'd been saving for a special occasion. If she weren't careful, her whole life would go by without any day feeling special. Now was as good a time as any to appreciate a roof over her head and a friend who made her smile.

She found Charlie in the front room. He'd arranged the furniture pieces back where they belonged and had started the fire in the fireplace. Relaxed in Seth's chair, his feet were propped on the ottoman as he stared into the flames. When she entered he glanced up. His eyes widened and he stood.

"Thank you for starting a fire." She set the guitar on the sofa and went back into the kitchen where she'd left the bottle. Once she found the corkscrew in the back of a cabinet drawer, she opened the bottle and poured two glasses of the dark-red wine into the best glasses she could find, then walked back into the living room.

She handed a glass to Charlie without asking, seeing he'd picked up the guitar.

"Thank you. It's been some time since I've had a glass of wine."

She backed up to the fire and took a sip, letting the liquid ease down her throat.

"Me, too. The old owner of this place left two dozen crates in the root cellar when he died. Can you imagine? Why would anyone want that much?" She drank again, liking the taste. "We didn't find it for a while because the small door leading to the chamber was hidden by several broken crates and a stack of halved barrels." Sipping again, the wine hit her empty stomach with a weighty goodness. "I'm no expert, but I think it's good. It came all the way from France."

He nodded, then drank from his glass.

"Besides this one, Seth and I've only consumed two bottles in all the years we've been here." She felt a bit lightheaded from the wine, the fire crackling behind her and the sight of Charlie sitting on the couch holding the guitar. "One bottle in a rash moment of celebration on the day we found them, and the second on the day Seth and I buried Ben."

She walked over to the window and stared into the night. "The guests had gone and the house was quiet. So Seth and I gathered three glasses and walked down to the river where Ben is buried on the bank by a large oak tree. The grass had just sprouted and was soft. I remember how it tickled my toes when I took off my boots and I laughed until I cried. Seth cried, too. We poured a glass for Ben and set it on his grave. We knew he'd like that."

She turned around and smiled. "Ben Page was a good person, Charlie. You would've liked him. Always looking on the bright side of things. Always looking out for me." She took another sip and held the savory liquid in her mouth, enjoying the richness of flavor. "I sure miss that man. And the little one we never had." She was probably making him feel uncomfortable but once she opened up it was hard to stop. "I'd love to have a child of my own, Charlie. How about you?"

He shifted, and glanced away. "Sure. Who wouldn't."

She nodded. "As it is, I don't feel complete. It's like I'm missing a great big piece of my heart and the pain never quite goes away no matter what I do." A low rumble of thunder drew her attention back outside to the storm, then a flash of light. As powerful as the tempest roared, the storm couldn't compare to the razor-sharp feelings flashing around inside her.

CHAPTER TWENTY-FIVE

$\mathcal{C}$harlie took another sip from the long-stemmed glass, wondering on Nell's peculiar mood. He hadn't liked dodging her question, but he'd been caught off guard. And with the stranger on the hill, the less he said, the better . . . for now. He held up the crystal goblet and studied it. "Pretty fancy."

"Another particular that came with the place. At one time Clarkston Jones was a big name in these parts. Seemed he had an eye for all things expensive."

Charlie shifted his attention to the flames. Nell had gussied up. Looked beautiful, wild, and enchanting in the soft, snowy blouse embroidered with soft-looking thread. The garment hugged her body in a way the shirts she usually wore never could. She stood before him at the hearth, her wine glass in one hand and the other reaching toward the flames, enjoying the warmth. She sipped her wine, likely unaware that her cheeks were an alluring warm pink.

"So," he replied, feeling a bit nervous at the shift in her disposition. "Do you play the guitar?"

"No. Ben did, though. It's his. I was hoping you knew how to play?"

"I do, a little. Been years, though. I'll probably break your eardrums if I try."

Her lips twitched, then curled up. "Will you humor me by playing a song or two?"

A memory of Annie asking him the same thing slipped into his mind. "Anything in particular you'd like to hear?"

She shook her head, golden curls moving like the wind through a field of ready-to-harvest oats. "Not really. It's been too long since we heard music in this house."

Charlie set his glass on the floor and turned the instrument in his hands. He strummed a few cords with his thumb, testing the sound. He twisted the D, B, and E turners and strummed the strings again. He picked, then plucked, then strummed again. "I'm pretty rusty. You sure you want me to do this?"

She nodded. The savory scent of whatever was cooking on the stove floated in. He reached for his glass, took another sip, then set it back down.

He strummed some more, thinking about what to play. He began but after two sour notes in a row he started over. Annie used to like to sit on the floor next to him with one arm draped over his knee. She'd been a good listener, a good wife. She knew how to make him feel special.

Nell tipped her head. "That's pretty. I recognize the melody but can't put my finger on the title."

She retreated back into her silence as he played through to the song's end. Finished, he set the guitar aside. "Did you ever figure it out?"

She shook her head.

"'Somebody's Coming to See Me Tonight.'" *One of Annie's favorites.*

"I liked it. Thank you."

The shadow that flickered in her eyes must be due to her melancholy for Ben. He stood, walked to the window, and gazed out at the rain that showed no signs of stopping. "I think Seth must have stayed over at the Logans'," he said. "No one in his right mind would ride home in a storm when a dry roof is available."

"He never stays out." Her voice was small.

"Well, he may have tonight. Thrown in with the bunkhouse hands."

Charlie turned from the window and went to the bookcase. He traced his finger over the row of books, spotting several Annie used to love. They'd been young when they married, and he'd had a handful of wonderful years with her. He wondered about Nell and Ben. Seemed Nell's grief was different than his, tied up more with loneliness and longing, where his need was now about doing right by Maddie. He wished he could make sense of things. Confused, he pushed his thoughts to Brenna. Why couldn't she bring out this soulful mood that Nell did? Brenna was much more like Annie. A womanly type of woman. One who needed a man. One who wanted to be cared for. Genteel, guarded. Skirt-wearing, butter-churning, hearty-meal-cookin'. Things that would make a good mother for Maddie. He glanced at Nell from the corner of his eye as he drew out a copy of *The Adventures of Tom Sawyer* and opened the novel to the middle. She was so young. He kept forgetting that but it was true.

"That's one of my favorites," she said, nodding toward the book. "I've read it twenty times, if once."

He remembered his plan to borrow one or two of Nell's books to lend Brenna. The notion didn't feel quite so appealing right about now.

"How was Brenna today?" she asked. "Did you drop off your mending?"

A rush of heat smacked him. He closed the book, slid the volume back, and pulled out another. "As a matter of fact, I did." He flipped the pages. "Seems Mr. Hutton has come down with the measles. I ran into her on her way to the inn Mrs. Hollyhock owns."

Concern flashed across Nell's face. "Measles?" She set her empty wine glass on the mantel and closed the space between them, close enough for him to see the gold flecks in her amazing amber eyes. He had to stem these irrational thoughts. His awareness of her was the wine talking, and the fire, the cozy room. It had nothing to do with how close Nell stood or the enticing scent of her hair. "I hope he isn't too sick," she said. "What did Brenna need at Violet's?"

"Some willow bark for tea. I walked with her from the middle of town and back. After that, I returned to the inn and helped Mrs. Hollyhock with some chores. Split some wood, did her laundry."

Nell's brows rose. "That was awfully kind, Charlie."

"Actually, Brenna was worried over the old woman trying to do too much. I didn't have anything pressing to do back here at the ranch, so I decided to lend a hand."

She gave him a smile. "Maybe you're right and Seth is staying over at the Logans'. I wouldn't have believed it. But I say it's time to eat."

That sounded good to Charlie. Seemed Nell's pensive mood had passed. He was glad. He didn't like all the unsettling feelings growing in his heart. At the stove, he took a potholder and lifted the lid of the cast-iron pot, taking a whiff of the contents cooking inside. "Beans? They smell different from what I'm used to."

"Right again." Nell brought two plates to the table and placed them across from each other. She went back for utensils, and then the bread and butter. "Some newfangled canned beans with pork. I wouldn't have spent the money on such, but Maude gave them to me for free so I'd sing their praises all over town after I tried them."

"Sure smells good."

Nell retrieved his wine glass from the living room and set it at his spot, refilling the goblet halfway, then lit the candle. "I do admit to doctoring them up a little. We had some beef in the root cellar. I cut it up and also added some fresh snow peas from the garden, which still may be a little crunchy. So this isn't a true test of the item. When I poured them from the can and into the pot, the pork seemed a bit skimpy for two hungry men, thus I improvised."

"And a hungry cowgirl," he added with a chuckle. "Whatever you did, they smell mighty good. I'm sure my stomach will thank you."

Across the table and overtop the small candle flame, Nell watched Charlie eat. She ate, too, moving her fork from the bowl to her mouth, but the action was one of reflex, not desire. The wine she'd consumed had not only mollified her appetite, but had her head a little fuzzy and her emotions close to her heart.

Charlie is the handsomest man I've ever seen. He stopped shoveling for a minute to wipe his mouth with his napkin and then take a sip from his almost-empty glass. The patter of rain on the roof sounded like music, and the heated air from the living room fireplace, as well as the cook stove, had her skin prickly.

"I like these. There're good." His gaze dipped to her lips.

She wasn't good at this. She'd met Ben when she was just a girl, and then grew up talking honestly with him. This was different. An imperceptible dance between two people, led by instinct and desire. She glanced away. "I'm glad."

"You're not eating much."

Her lips trembled. "I'm not as hungry as I thought I was."

He seemed to accept that and went back to his supper.

Finished, Nell stood and picked up both their plates and took them to the sink. Anticipation zinged within her, as well as a little fear of the unknown. Charlie came up behind her with the two empty glasses and set them on the drain board. He stayed close. "The kitchen looks nice."

"Yes," she breathed. "I'm going to do the dishes right now. So Seth can see it when he gets home. If I don't, one item draws another just like a magnet. Before you know it, you have a sink full. I don't want to fall back into my old ways." She glanced around the room. "This feels good."

He tied an apron around his waist. "I'll wash if you dry." He started pumping water into the basin.

"*I'm* washing," she replied, and tried to push him out of the way.

No luck. He'd already beaten her to it. With three quick swipes, he finished the first wine glass and handed it to her to dry. "You have to be faster than that if you want to best me."

Taking the glass, she wiped it dry and set it back on the shelf. Finished with the two bowls, Charlie scrubbed the bean pot and set it upside down on a towel.

"You're good at that."

"I've done my share." He dried his hands and removed the apron. "Can't say as when I've enjoyed an evening more. As thanks, can I have this dance?"

He held out his arms expectantly, waiting as she grappled with her feelings. She gazed up into his eyes. One heartbeat later she slipped into his arms and he pulled her close. Her palm against his was heady, sending all sorts of tingles coursing up and down her arm. His other hand, on the small of her back, kept her close.

They were awkward at first, but kept at it. He hummed as they moved around in a circle, her skirt swishing against her legs and sometimes tangling between his. A slow burn started on her neck. When they finished he let her go and took a small step back.

"Charlie, I . . ."

"Stop talking, Nell."

His eyes closed and his lips covered hers. The kiss was gentle as he pulled her tighter against him, driving all thought from her mind. His hands moved down and bracketed her waist and he tilted his head, deepening the kiss.

CHAPTER TWENTY-SIX

*C*harlie rolled to his side and pulled his blanket up over his bare shoulder, wondering what had awakened him from his deep, wine-induced sleep. Even with his eyes closed, the thumping in his temples reverberated painfully.

He could never be a drunk. Didn't like the way alcohol made him feel the next day. Nell's red wine indulgence had proven too much for this cowboy. By the time they'd consumed the pork and beans and bread, leaving a generous portion for Seth just in case he came home hungry, the rain had stopped. The lone candle had burned down to the cactus-shaped, carved-wood candleholder and they'd finished the whole bottle of wine. She'd sat across from him, her blue, soulful eyes playing havoc with his mind and heart, while Annie's memory sat in Seth's chair, keeping watch.

He grimaced and rubbed his forehead. Had he really asked Nell to dance? Talk about adding fuel to an already confusing situation. Her pretty skirt and soft-looking blouse must have been his inspiration.

After the question had rolled off his lips, as if dancing without music in a kitchen was the most natural thing in the world, he'd waited. She'd stood there so long with the towel in her hands that he'd thought she was going to decline. But she hadn't. She'd slipped into his arms. His fluttering heart had made him feel like a traitor to Annie, but not enough to let go of Nell's sweetness.

They'd waltzed slowly around the kitchen as he hummed. Then afterwards he'd gone and kissed her.

Well, there was no hope for it now. Couldn't go back. Releasing a breath, he reached for his pocket watch on the side table next to his cot. He pressed the catch until it popped open, then tried to make out the time. Unable to read it in the dark, he glanced out the window. From the inky-black sky opposite him, he'd guess the hour was around three in the morning.

He snapped the watch closed, thinking of his father and brothers, and of his stepmother, Priscilla, and how she'd made their lives so much better. As the middle child he'd been, at times, invisible to his pa—until Lance got into some trouble and shifted the blame to him. But it was the memory of Charlie's younger brother, Langdon, that grappled with his heart. The happy-go-lucky boy had been young enough to be spared any haunting memories of their real ma. Like the day she'd taken ill, her funeral at the country church outside town, and her newly dug grave. The remembered image never failed to send a shiver into Charlie's young soul whenever he thought of her buried underneath the cold, packed earth.

"Tristan, you're such a sweet child. I don't know why God has blessed me so," she'd say often, and kiss the top of his head while squeezing him in her arms. She always smelled of vanilla and cinnamon, and a day didn't go by she didn't cook something sweet to entice them. His pa, a hard-working Iowa farmer, worshiped the ground she walked on. Treated her with respect and love, and during the summer brought her a handful of wildflowers every day when he came in from the fields.

After her death it was three long, struggling years before his pa met and married Priscilla, a widow from the South. She'd embraced her stepchildren as if they were her own and was a light in their lives until she passed away from influenza. By then he'd been a grown man of thirteen. The war was on and he wanted to enlist. After his pa forbade him until he was older, he snuck away in the night to join up. Charlie still carried guilt over that choice. Perhaps if he'd stayed home, his pa would still be alive and the family intact. Years later he'd gotten word his pa had died and his brothers had sold the farm, wanting an adventure of their own. Now the family was split up and he didn't know where Langdon or Lance lived. Or even if they were still alive.

Charlie rolled to his back, now fully awake. If he got up and started the fire in the stove, he might wake Nell. He slung an arm over his eyes, again pushing away the desire that she evoked in him. She was twelve years younger—he'd best remember that. He needed someone like Brenna, someone established, with children of her own. That was best for Maddie.

A scuffling sound caught his attention, chasing away his thoughts. Then a small scrape—was that a boot heel? No. He was letting his imagination run away with him. He turned his head. Listened to the early-morning sounds. Wilsonville and Grover Galante were never far from his thoughts. His heart swooshed in his ears as his heartbeat picked up when he thought about Nell asleep upstairs, an easy target.

Could have been a gopher, or squirrel, foraging for food on the porch. But when the kitchen door creaked open, Charlie bolted upright in the bed and knew the intruder was inside.

Nell came awake when the hinge on the kitchen door squeaked before stopping abruptly. Staring up into the darkness, she wondered if she'd conjured the sound out of thin air. Intuition told her the noise had been real.

She'd been dreaming about Charlie, the two of them swimming in the river on a hot summer day. He'd dived under the water and she'd watched with excitement to see where he would surface.

Pushing through the chest-high water, she spun in a circle, then back the other way, laughter bubbling up from inside. Charlie surged out of the water and burst into the air, the sun glistening off the droplets gushing off his head and chest. Their laughter mingled and filled the air of the wide-open grasslands. Her heart nearly burst with the rush of love she felt.

Now, her skin tingled. Someone was downstairs. Had Charlie gone out for some fresh air? He mentioned he did that every now and then. Or perhaps Seth had finally come home and was trying to sneak in without disturbing anyone.

Or—a shiver skittered up her back—was the stranger back? If yes, he could kill Charlie in his bed; kill him before he even knew what happened. The memory of the coldness in the stranger's eyes again frightened her breathless. Her heart thumped painfully against her breastbone. She needed to get down there before anything bad happened.

When Nell swung her legs over the bed and reached for her pants, her head exploded in pain as if she'd just been smacked between the eyes with a horseshoe. She grasped the dresser to steady herself and gasped for air until the pain ebbed and her stomach decided not to empty itself on her bedroom floor. What in tarnation had prompted her to open that bottle of wine? And why had they felt inclined to finish the whole thing? Her stomach rolled and the walls tilted.

Breathing deeply, she pulled on her pants, strapped on her revolver, then silently opened her door. She crept down the hallway toward the stairs, avoiding the boards she knew were loose. Her head throbbed. At the top of the staircase she stopped and listened. Didn't hear anything else. Took the first step, then another and another until she was at the kitchen.

She found Charlie waiting at the bottom, shirtless and bootless, but armed and ready. He stood in a beam of moonlight that slipped through the window and splashed across the kitchen floor.

Her heart beat wildly in her chest and without thinking she stepped into his arms.

"Don't be scared," he whispered against her hair, sending a bevy of chills rippling up her spine. An image of them kissing on the river's edge flashed in her mind and she realized the memory was from her dream, buried in her subconscious until now. "It's gone."

"It?" She could feel the thump of his heart against her own. His skin under her fingertips was intoxicating.

"A raccoon. Must have jimmied the door, somehow. You know how resourceful those critters can be when they're hungry."

She held him tighter.

He hesitated. "He'd made it up onto the counter but I got here before he made a mess. Maybe smelled those pork and beans set aside for Seth," Charlie said. "Scared him away before he got a chance to mess up our clean house."

Does he feel anything for me? Is he aware my heart is about to burst? She rested her head on his shoulder, absorbing his musky scent, remembering the kiss from a few hours ago. Anxious to commit to mind this moment, she closed her eyes, memorizing his feel. Her pulse galloped off in excitement, her breath swished in her lungs.

To her amazement, he didn't step away, but held her in that magical, silver-golden line of moonlight. Like in the fairy tales she used to read when she was a girl.

"How's your head feel?" he asked, his mouth close to her ear.

She tried to laugh, but pain in her temple stopped her. "It's felt better. I guess the wine wasn't such a good idea."

"Go back up to your room and try to sleep it off. I'll take care of the animals in the morning. Don't get up until you're ready."

A light breeze drifted in the half-open window, bringing scents of rain-dampened earth, hay in the fields, reminding her of the horses and the schedule they were on. "But today we're starting the horses."

"You sure you're feeling up to that? What will one more day hurt?"

"Feeling up to it or not doesn't matter. We have a contract with the army with a delivery date fast approaching and don't even have the number of horses they're asking for. If we don't provide, the army may go elsewhere. There're plenty of outfits from here to Miles City who'd jump at a chance to take our place."

She heard him grunt, then he stepped back and she instantly missed his warmth.

"Coming here, I rode cross country. I—"

"You were coming here?" she asked. She remembered the tracks at the stream and how sure she was they didn't have anything to do with him. Had she been wrong? "I was under the impression you'd just happened to stop and liked Logan Meadows."

"Yeah. Anyway, I happened upon a herd of horses tucked away up in the mountains. I was surprised to see them up that far because no rancher would risk injury to the animals in such high country. I didn't see any brands. Lots of paints. Makes me think they were wild, descendants of the horses set free when the Indians were forced onto the reservations. Like some of yours."

He had her full attention. "How far away?"

"Not exactly sure. A couple of days maybe."

"How many horses?"

"That I don't rightly know. If I had to guess, I'd say around sixty or more. Rounding up wild horses will be a heck of a lot harder than gathering your bunch you'd turned out."

Her smile was his answer.

"Fine then, boss." His voice held a modicum of humor. "Now that we have a possible solution to that problem, you go get some sleep. I'll see you when I see you. I'll keep busy until then." Taking her by her shoulders, he turned her around and gave her a gentle nudge toward the stairs.

CHAPTER TWENTY-SEVEN

*A*pprehension zinged through Brenna like a runaway loco-motive on ice-covered rails. Monday morning dawned early. Mr. Hutton, as she'd predicted, was too sick to do anything except lay flat on his back and stare at the ceiling, leaving everything up to her. She stood in the middle of the empty classroom—just moments before her day was scheduled to begin—whispering a heartfelt prayer to heaven for help and guidance.

Last night Mr. Hutton—with his mottled face and blood-shot eyes, and between his bouts of sleepiness—had scribbled out a teaching plan of sorts, nothing more than a brief outline on a piece of paper with suggestions on what to do and when. "You'll do fine," he'd croaked out, the cool cloth still molded to his fore-head like a helmet. He handed her the paper. "Penny can help you if you get stuck on anything."

That hurt. He held her thirteen-year-old daughter in higher esteem than her. Not that she disagreed with him, for Penny was well read and each year her grades improved. She was bright. She would make a wonderful teacher, one day—when she grew up. *I'm grown up now and ashamed to say that Mr. Hutton's opinion of me means more than it should. How have I let myself get so carried away?*

She glanced at the paper and the Roman numerals marking the left-hand side of the page. The instructions felt like a lifeline as children's laughter in the play yard reverberated through her heart. *In minutes it will be time to ring the bell, calling the day to begin. I've landed myself in a real mess this time.*

Footsteps heralded someone coming up the steps. The door opened and a whoosh of cold air burst into the toasty-warm room.

"Hannah." The name gushed from Brenna's mouth when her dear friend entered. "What am I going to do? I feel faint. And I need some water to wet my parched throat. What if I go blank and can't think of anything to say?"

Hannah marched over until they were face-to-face. "You're as white as a store-bought hankie, Brenna. Get a hold of yourself." She patted Brenna's cheeks several times. "There. That's better. Get that blood flowing. You're going to do just fine. No, better than fine. You know how the children love you."

Brenna shrugged. Even though she didn't entirely believe Hannah, she was thankful her friend was here to bolster her courage.

"How is Mr. Hutton feeling?" Hannah asked before Brenna could respond, her eyes sparkling with mischief. "Is he being a good patient for you?"

At the mention of Mr. Hutton, Brenna felt a rush of heat surge to her face. She hoped Hannah wouldn't notice. She'd spent last evening at his place, tidying up and cooking a bland meal. "Just depends on how he's feeling at the moment. When he's rested and his calamine-lotioned face isn't itching too much, he's kind, and even quite pleasant. He also has a quirky sense of humor, which is nice to be around."

Hannah tipped her head thoughtfully. "Is that so?"

"Yes—that's so. But don't go putting the plow before the ox, you hear? He can also be a horrible handful. If he's hungry, or he wants the fussing to stop, he gets crankier than a hobbled billy goat. That man has a scowl on him that can singe the hair right off your head."

Hannah let go a hearty laugh as if that were the funniest thing she'd ever heard. "I can just picture that in my mind. I'm sure you're killing him with kindness and he doesn't know how to respond."

"Well, I don't know about that."

Hannah's eyes hooded. "I hope you don't mind that I got you into this mess in the first place, with the school council, I mean. I feel totally responsible."

"You didn't know *this* would happen, Hannah. And I'm grateful for all the doors the school council position has opened up for me. Most of all, I'm appreciative the children are getting a dose of how to be civically minded. And see that hard work and perseverance do pay off. Elbow grease and determination go a long way— even without much money to back it."

"Amen to that, Brenna. You've done a fine job raising your family alone."

"Well, I do try. Hannah, I have a favor to ask of you."

"Anything."

She hurried to her desk and opened the top drawer, withdrawing a folded piece of paper. "On your way to the restaurant this morning, can you stop into the mercantile and give this to Maude for me, please? She'll know what to do. It's really important so please don't forget."

Hannah looked at the note curiously. "I'd be happy to."

There was a long pause, and Brenna knew she'd have to tell Hannah about her oversight or else hurt her feelings. "When I first tried to place the order for the math books, the publisher replied that they were out of stock and to contact them in a couple of months. But I completely forgot until the day of the picnic. Mr. Hutton doesn't know. And I don't really want him to. I don't want him to know how stupid I can be."

"Brenna. Stop that. We all make mistakes."

"I hope Maude will consider sending a telegram and asking the publisher to send the books as quickly as possible. Perhaps, since Mr. Hutton is sick, the books will arrive before he recovers and returns to class." She smiled just thinking about it. "Then he'll never even know."

Hannah took the note and tucked it away in the deep pocket of her skirt. "Don't worry about a thing. I'll take care of it."

The door opened again and Jessie Logan came in holding Shane with one arm and Sarah's hand in the other. Both Brenna and Hannah hurried over to greet them.

"Good morning, Sarah." This was the child's first day of school and Brenna knew she had been anticipating it for a whole year. "Good morning, Shane," she added, and patted the tot on the head. "Sarah, are you excited?"

Sarah's little head nodded up and down enthusiastically, making her pigtails wobble. "Yes, ma'am."

Brenna gave Jessie a quick wink before addressing Sarah again. "Well, I just have to say you're as pretty as a little primrose in your purple dress."

"I got to wear it since we came in the buggy," Sarah chirped, and she twirled around to show off the dress. "But most days I'll ride Cricket, my mommy's horse. Then I'll have to wear my old split skirt."

All three ladies laughed.

Shane strained to get out of Jessie's arms, but she held him fast. His gaze darted here and there, taking in the schoolroom. "I wan down, Ma," he cried.

Sarah's faced squished up. "No, Shane. Babies can't come to school. You'll wreck everything."

"Sh now, sweetie." Jessie cupped Sarah's cheek. "He doesn't understand why he can't stay with you and the children." She bounced him a few times. "Shane, remember we're going to bake cookies when we get home."

At that, his bottom lip pulled in and he managed a smile. "Cookies."

Jessie rubbed the top of his head but winked at Brenna. "I just heard the news about Mr. Hutton last night, Brenna. How's he feeling?"

"Still running a fever and is tomato red from all his spots when he's not covered with calamine lotion. Dr. Thorn said from the timing of the outbreak, he must have come in contact with the disease in his travels before reaching Logan Meadows."

Hannah tipped her head. "Maybe on the train."

Concern flitted across Jessie's face. "Are you sure you'll be able to handle the children?" She bounced Shane harder. "I'd stay and help but with this little cowboy around, not much learning would get done."

"Of course I'll be fine," Brenna assured her. "Don't forget I have Penny and even Jane. They'll be a big help."

Relief passed over Jessie's face, and she nodded. "Of course. With those two you won't have any trouble at all."

Even without the ringing of the bell, children started to file into the room between bursts of laughter and bits of conversation. Shane stretched up in Jessie's arms to get a good view. Eager students set their lunch pails along the wall underneath the coat rack and milled about.

"Your names are on your desks," Brenna called to them.

"I'd stay and help if I didn't have to go to the restaurant today," Hannah said, looking guilty. "Monday is usually my day off, but Mother woke up with a headache and needs to stay home. She's watching Markus, so I'm taking her place."

Sarah gave a little squeal of excitement when she spotted Maddie sitting, hands folded, on the desk adjacent to the teacher's. Quiet and compliant as usual, the sweet child hadn't drawn anyone's attention until now. "Look, Mommy. Maddie's here. Just like we prayed."

At the mention of her name, Maddie turned to the group and smiled.

Brenna reached out and caressed the top of Sarah's head. "She sure is, Sarah. At least for now, because I don't have any place to leave her." *And I have no idea what Mr. Hutton will say when he finds out I disobeyed his wishes.*

"It's time," Hannah announced. "I need to be going. Should I ring the bell on my way out the door?"

The room was filling up right before Brenna's eyes. Penny came in, followed by Jane, Prichard, and several other children. Stevie was nowhere to be seen. Ringing the bell wasn't going to be necessary, but it was a town tradition that on the first day of school, when the first bell of the school term was rung, everyone who heard the pealing came outside and clapped.

Jessie shook her head and started for the door. "The teacher should be the one to ring the bell, Hannah," she said, and she gestured for Brenna to come along outside. "I'm so proud of you, Brenna. What an accomplishment."

"You're right, Jessie," Hannah said, nodding approvingly. "I couldn't agree more."

The three women walked to the door and then out onto the porch stoop. As Brenna reached for the rope hanging down from the bell tower, Shane lurched up in Jessie's arms and grasped the thickness in his hands, pulling down with gusto.

The bell rang out loudly, announcing the term had begun for another year. The sound of cheering and clapping from Main Street made the women laugh. Brenna couldn't resist Shane's proud expression and leaned over and kissed him on the cheek. "Thank you, Shane Logan. You're a handful for your mama already. I can't wait to see you in a few years."

"And that's an understatement," Jessie said, shifting Shane to her other hip. "I'll see you when school lets out."

Brenna took a deep breath, turned, and walked to the front of the class. Her heart tripped seeing all the faces waiting patiently for her to say something. Anything. Brenna reached deep inside, remembering the tiny, tattered memory of her mother. "There's not a single thing in this world you can't accomplish, sweetness, with hard work, fortitude, and love. Just set your mind to it and march ahead. Never let anyone rob you of your dreams."

Brenna swallowed nervously and rubbed her moist palms together. "Good morning, class. I want to welcome you to another school year."

CHAPTER TWENTY-EIGHT

Charlie hauled down on the wrench until the bolt he was tightening wouldn't go any farther. He looked up through the crisscrossed boards of the windmill, through the slowly turning metal blades, to the sky, dotted with clouds and a V-formation of geese flying south. The sight brought a smile to his face. He'd been tinkering on the wind-power device for a good hour, musing the time away thinking about Maddie, Brenna, and, of course, Nell and the mess he'd made of the situation last night.

He'd already cleared the leaves from the crystal-clear water in the holding tank. The land in the aftermath of the storm was fresh. The scent invigorating. Moist earth gave easily beneath his boots, but the patch of grass under the windmill kept the ground from being muddy. The cool breeze felt good and he took a long draw, filling his lungs. He picked up the can of grease and took hold of the boards, climbing up. He set the small container in the crook of two boards.

This was hardy land, good land, land that could heal anything that ailed you, even a broken heart. Especially a broken heart. He thought of dancing with Nell and at the same time he thought of Annie. What would she expect of him? What did he expect of himself? Things had gotten muddled in his mind and the reason didn't have anything to do with the bottle of wine they'd consumed. His thoughts came back around to Nell, and who might have been on that ridge. He had his suspicions but couldn't be sure. That rider could've been anyone.

Too many unknowns to know anything. Last night when he'd heard the noise in the kitchen, he'd been sure Galante, or one of his men, had found him. Truth be told, he'd been sick with worry for Nell. The advice the Wilsonville sheriff had given him popped into his mind. *"If I were you, son, I wouldn't wait around for Galante to make good on his promise. He's mean and he's driven. I know you have every right to stay in Wilsonville, but for your little girl's sake, maybe you should clear out."*

Although the sound turned out to be made by a raccoon, the incident reminded him to get to town and deposit his money in the bank, where his life savings couldn't be stolen. Everything he'd worked for was in those saddlebags. The means to get Maddie settled and hire a tutor. A saddlebag under his cot was not secure.

Just as Charlie reached up to tighten the last bolt within his reach, Nell came out the kitchen door.

If he hadn't known she'd been in a world of hurt just hours before, he'd never be able to tell as she crossed the yard toward the barn. Her face was alight in thought. Her hair was pulled behind in a ponytail and her hat hung down her back. The skirt she'd worn last night was replaced with her usual denims and leather chaps, and a leather vest he'd never seen before hugged her upper body in a fascinating way. A lead rope, gathered in neat loops, hung over one shoulder. The memory of her standing in his arms distracted him and his hand slipped, causing his knuckles to grate across a metal joint painfully.

He bit back a curse, then pressed the tops of his fingers against his pants. Angrily, he shoved the agitating memories of Nell out of his mind. If he daydreamed about a woman, it should be Brenna, not Nell.

Nell was just about to pass by the windmill when he called out to her.

She stopped abruptly. Searched around. When she found him perched in the legs of the windmill, she smiled brightly. "Morning," she called up.

He was in more trouble than he realized.

Looking up through the blades again, he gauged the sun's straight-up position in the sky. It must be about noon. "I'd say you just made it." He returned her smile, tired of all the pondering he'd been doing on his problems. All he wanted now was a nice, uncomplicated day.

"What the heck are you doing up there?" She placed a hand on her hip.

"What do you think? Ranching chores."

She laughed and the sound made his breath catch. "You sure? Looks like you're hiding from somebody."

"Not the last time I checked. How're you feeling?"

She shrugged. "Better. Now it's time to get moving on those sassy-pants colts." She gazed at the one he'd roped earlier and moved to the round pen. "You want to start with Cochise?" Her brows rose. "He's one of the greenest of the bunch. Why him?"

The leggy chestnut gelding with the small, white star still wore the rope halter with its three-foot length of rope attached, which was meant to make catching him somewhat easy. The short tether was frayed and dirty. The horse had his head down, uneasily sniffing the dirt and manure scattered about.

"Because he's the one my loop happened to land on. Didn't think you'd mind." He'd been aiming for a smaller, calm-looking colt, but this was what he'd gotten.

"I don't mind at all, but I think you might." She glanced around. "Seth ever come home?"

"He did. Around seven this morning. He got a bite to eat and now he's ridden out to check the cattle."

"Did he say where he'd spent the night? The Logans'? How's his cough?"

Charlie laughed. "That's a lot of questions, boss. You *must* be feeling better. I didn't ask where he spent the night because men don't do that—and he didn't offer." He gave her a long look. "Anything else you'd like to know?"

"Did you tell him what you told me about the horses?"

That's why Nell was in such a good mood. She'd been thinking about the horses and how it could help the ranch if they were able to round them up and get them back. It was a good idea, though a difficult job to accomplish. "I did."

"What did he say?"

"He's interested. Wants to head out tomorrow or the next day."

Nell plunked her hands on her hips. "I've been thinking about that. I think it best he stays behind. He's worn thin from his last trip and needs some rest. Besides, someone has to get these geldings started. The job won't get done on its own."

"Rounding up those horses will be impossible for the two of us. We need Seth."

"You're right about that. Instead of Seth, I'm gonna see if Chase Logan will lend us a couple of his hands. Most of the ranch work is done with branding and sorting by now, and most of their hay should be brought in. I'm sure he has some men we can use."

"You have the whole thing all planned out, don't you."

"Pretty much. This could be the break we've been waiting for and I'm not letting it slip through our fingers." She started for the round pen. Cochise picked his head up and trotted to the far side of the corral, where he watched her approach with suspicion. She looked over her shoulder at him and smiled. "You coming, Charlie?"

The boulder in his stomach told him he'd met his match with Nell. And now, to make last night's blunder worse, he'd be working side by side with her for the whole day. "Yes, ma'am. Right on your heels."

CHAPTER TWENTY-NINE

*A*n army of lightning bugs had hatched in Nell's stomach, flashing here and there as if proclaiming, *She's in love, she's in love.* She jerked her gaze away and started for the corral before Charlie noticed her stare. One second of his blue-eyed gaze, the amused tip of his lips, and the humorous note in his voice sent her imagination running wild like the horses they'd brought in just days before. *How pathetic!*

The crunch of his footsteps made her think of last night and the kiss they'd shared. How they'd danced slowly around the kitchen by the light of the single candle. She'd never forget the way he'd made her feel. Cherished. Desired. And then later, standing in his arms after the raccoon had woken them, protected.

At the corral fence she studied their pupil as Charlie caught up. Cochise seemed relaxed, having gotten used to the barn and house area over the last few days. The gelding knew something was up, though. He watched her warily from across the twenty-foot enclosure.

Charlie grasped one of the poles in front of him, the light wind tossing his hatless hair. "So, what's your plan? You want me to go fetch your saddle?"

She hid her smile. "Your saddle? Yes, I do."

His eyes narrowed. "Why my saddle?"

"Because you're going to ride him." When his Adam's apple bobbed, she asked, "Anything wrong?"

"Not a thing. As a matter of fact, when I roped him I hoped I'd get the first go." Charlie gave the animal another quick glance. "He's a fine-looking horse."

She laughed. "You were not."

"You don't know everything about me, boss."

"You're right about that. But I do know you're not a bronc buster—but there's no time like the present to rectify that shortcoming."

He turned and sauntered over to where Georgia stood at the hitching rail in the barn's shade. Within moments he had the heavy western saddle off and carried it toward the round pen as if the burden weighed nothing at all. Slinging his rig over the top rail, he turned to her and held out his hand. "The rope."

Nell shrugged the lead rope off her shoulder and tossed it to him. He caught it midair and slipped it through the bottom two poles. On the other side of the round pen, the gelding instantly turned his hip to Charlie and flattened his ears.

She was teasing him, but she couldn't help it. She felt like singing today. Surely Charlie wouldn't have kissed her if he wasn't attracted to her, would he?

"Whoa, boy," Charlie crooned as he slowly walked toward the horse. He held the rope behind his back in one hand and the other he stretched forward, open palmed. The gelding swung back around to face him, and Nell could see his muscles gather. When Charlie was halfway across, the horse dropped his head and bolted, loping the rails in a circle.

Nell pursed her lips to keep back her smile.

Charlie looked around at her, his brow furrowed. The young horse, full of spunk, bucked a couple of times before picking up speed. In an effort to stop him, Charlie took one step toward the rail, not in front of the charging horse but enough that the animal did a handy roll back on the fence and started in the opposite direction.

Nell let out a chortle. "You two going to do that all day?"

Charlie didn't appear so amused anymore. "You have a suggestion?"

"Yes. First off, climb on out here and let him run the bugs out. Then we'll start again."

Charlie stomped back, clearly annoyed, again cutting the gelding off. The colt slid to a stop and snorted loudly, drawing Georgia's glance from the hitching rail. When Charlie was back outside the corral with Nell, she leaned onto the fence. Feeling saucy, she lifted her leg and hooked her heel on the first rail.

Charlie slapped the lead against his legs. "Go ahead and say what you're dying to. I can see you have more than one suggestion for me."

"You're right. First, think about the horses out on the range. Picture them grazing and moving around. Then, act like them."

He crossed his arms over his chest. "Act like a horse." His tone was pure skepticism.

"Well, yes. What I mean is, never approach a skittish horse straight on, and never look him directly in the eye."

"I just did that."

"I know."

"Why didn't you tell me?"

"I had fun watching."

He harrumphed. "Good of you. What else?"

"Approach from the side. When you get close enough, angle your position so your head is sort of close to the horse's shoulder, as if you mean to smell his scent."

"You *can't* be serious."

"That's how horses get acquainted with each other. Next, move closer to his face so he can smell you." She grinned. "Even though he's acting pretty full of himself now, he is halter broke. I'm not saying you always have to do this—not with a horse that already knows you, just the edgy ones. Shows you're not going to hurt them. However, I wouldn't try it with Cochise until you've gotten a hold of the short lead. Make sure he can't turn around and kick you."

"You're making this up to make me appear a fool. Like sending me out to buy striped paint."

The chestnut had stopped circling the corral and stood on the other side of the pen, watching them debate.

Her fingers itched to push back the hank of hair that had fallen over Charlie's forehead. Feel the texture on her fingertips. Soothe away all the injustices he may have suffered as a youth. "Striped paint?" She softly laughed. "Sounds like you're speaking from experience, Charlie Rose. Care to elaborate?"

"No. I'll just say I had an older brother whose day wasn't complete until he had a good laugh—usually on me."

Nell shrugged. "I'm not making this up. You can ask Seth when he gets home."

He handed her the rope. "Why don't you demonstrate for me, then." Why not? She took the challenge and ducked between the rails. "And no using any of your ooglie-booglie mind-reading ability right now. Just pretend you're me."

The gelding was still breathing harder than normal from his exertion. Keeping the rope behind her back, Nell approached the side of the horse, keeping her face turned away. Cochise lowered his head for a moment before it came up like a flag, and yet he didn't bolt off. She stopped for a few seconds. This could easily go either way since the horse was already tense.

"Whoa, big boy," she all but whispered. She felt his energy bunch, but the gelding stayed where he was. He put his head down and sniffed the dirt.

"Whoa, boy," she said again. "Whoa, now." As soon as the horse turned his attention on Charlie, Nell slowly reached for the frayed lead. When she took hold he shied, but Nell stayed calmly by his shoulder and stepped forward with him. She let him settle. She stayed there a good three minutes without moving. Then, still not looking him in the eye, she clipped on the longer lead she held in her hands. She let her arm and hand linger while he got her scent. Moving slowly, she reached up and put her hand on his neck. She stroked him once, then moved her hand up toward his jawbone, where she pressed firmly with one finger until he took one step away. Satisfied, she started for the pole sunk deep in the center of the pen and secured him there.

"Well, I'll be." Disbelief was written all over Charlie's face. "Honestly, I didn't think you could do it." As she walked toward him she took off her hat and wiped her forehead with the back of her shirt sleeve. "You do this with all the army horses?"

"I wish we could, but no. Only when we have the time. Like I mentioned earlier, he was started a few months ago, before being turned out. He's been haltered, tied, and had a saddle on his back at least twice. He just needs to be reminded what we want from him. We'll leave him to stand now for a while and go catch up a few more."

There it was again. The concern in his eyes that did strange things to her insides. Had someone upstairs sent him her way, knowing how desperately lonely she'd been this past year? The notion was nice to think about, possibilities of a greater power watching over her and Seth. She didn't much believe in things she didn't understand and yet she didn't not believe, either.

Charlie stared at her for so long she began to feel uncomfortable. "You got something on your mind?"

"Yeah, about last night, Nell. I wanted to explain that—"

Afraid of what he might say, she shushed him. "These things happen." *Where did that come from? Not really. At least not to me.*

"Yeah?"

"Yeah."

He let go a big sigh. "Good. Didn't want my hasty actions to ruin our friendship."

Friendship. Her stomach tightened.

"Was also hoping to ride into town this afternoon."

This time a stone dropped inside. *Brenna.* His face was turning red. If there was ever a guilty party, it was him.

"I have business that needs doing that I couldn't do yesterday because it was Sunday."

"Sure. You could go right now, if you have a mind."

He scoffed. "No. We're working the horses. I just need to get there before the bank closes."

Bank? Hope blossomed. Maybe Brenna wasn't his reason. "That's no problem."

"I appreciate that."

Charlie paused and watched Cochise testing the lead. Next, the youngster pawed at the dirt with his front hoof. Seemed as if Charlie was struggling with a decision. "You have something else you want to say, Charlie?"

"You know me pretty good, Nell. Was also wondering if I might borrow a book from you."

"A book? Of course." *What book of mine could he want?*

"Well, it's not for me."

A hint of pink darkened his cheeks again. His uncertainty made for an attractive mixture with his long, lean body and strong chest and arms. Nell felt desire well up within, as the sun warmed them from above. "No? Who then?"

"Brenna. She mentioned she enjoyed reading but she doesn't have many books of her own. With your bookshelf full to overflowing, I just thought you might not mind lending her one."

The wind was knocked from Nell's sails and she struggled not to let his comment register on her face. The sunshine dimmed and the air lifting her hair didn't smell quite as sweet as it had a moment ago. He stood a mere arm's length away, thinking of another woman while Nell had been daydreaming of him. *What a fool you are, Nell. Don't you ever learn?* "That's thoughtful of you, Charlie. I don't mind in the least. Take as many as you like."

He stepped forward, indecision written in his eyes. "I only want one."

One was enough to break her heart.

CHAPTER THIRTY

*W*ith a copy of *Jane Eyre* tucked under his arm, Charlie reined up in front of the bank in Logan Meadows, sadness holding his heart quiet. As soon as he'd mentioned the book for Brenna, Nell's happy mood had evaporated in the hot sun, leaving him confused and regretful. The instant the words were out of his mouth and the hurt she'd tried so hard to hide crossed her eyes, nothing had felt right. They'd worked the horses in edgy silence until time came for him to set out.

He dismounted, wrapping Georgia's reins around the hitching rail next to a palomino and a broken-down bay. Yanking his brim lower against the setting sun, he unbuckled his soft leather saddlebags from the back of his saddle, all the while making sure Nell's book didn't fall into the dirt.

Across the street, the door to the mercantile opened and a woman stepped out, a broom in her hand. She glanced left and then right then started sweeping. It wasn't until she noticed him and waved that he recalled her from the picnic and then again from the Red Rooster Inn as the long-faced woman who'd opened the door to Brenna. The apron around her waist and pencil tucked behind her ear told him she'd gotten the job she was after.

"Charlie Rose," a man's voice called out.

He turned. Sheriff Preston and his deputy, Thom Donovan, strode down the boardwalk in his direction, the big wolflike dog following dutifully behind.

"Sheriff," he said when they stopped in front of his horse. "Deputy." He flopped his saddlebag over his shoulder, then joined them on the wooden walkway.

"Albert and Thom work fine for us." Thom stuck out his hand and Charlie took it, then did the same with the sheriff.

"Seems pretty quiet." Charlie looked around. "Is Logan Meadows always like this?"

The dog, old by the gray and white hairs around his muzzle, lay down on the boards. "Pretty much so," Albert replied. "By now everyone's on their way home to get some supper."

"That's where I'll be headed in a moment," Thom said. "Hannah will bring something home from the restaurant. Comes in handy."

Albert smiled. "Anything going on out at the ranch?"

Charlie hadn't planned on saying anything, but now that the sheriff and deputy were here, he thought better of it. The farther he got away from Wilsonville, the less the threat became. Nell alone at the ranch was his main concern. "Actually, there is. Had a visitor of sorts."

"Oh?"

"Nell was out at the ranch yesterday alone. When I came back from town, she told me there'd been a rider up on the bluff. He was too far away for her to make out who he was. I figure, he would have come in and said hello if she'd known him."

Thom scratched his chin. "Could have been someone passing through giving his horse a rest."

"Maybe," Charlie agreed. "But that's Cotton Ranch land." He struggled with whether to tell them everything about his past but wasn't quite ready for that just yet. "Seems to have spooked her pretty bad. And Seth found prints he didn't recognize by one of their streams."

Thom looked at Albert. "Logan Meadows isn't so small anymore that we know each and every person, at least not when they first arrive."

"I'm glad you spoke up, Charlie," Albert said. "Nell seems to think she's invincible. She's a very private person. We'll ride out your way from time to time."

"Thank you. I appreciate that. We're going up into the high country in a day or two to round up some stock. We'll be gone for at least a week. I'm not sure, but Seth may be staying at the ranch." All three men doffed their hats when two ladies passed by, one carrying a baby in her arms and the other a basket covered with a cloth.

"Nell's made it perfectly clear that she can take care of herself," Albert said. "She and her brother have been living on their own most their life. Anytime anyone tries to coddle her, she gets cranky. Just thought I'd warn you."

As if I didn't already know that. "She may talk big and for all I know she's telling the truth. Still, she's a woman, Sheriff. I don't like the thought of some unknown person out there watching her—for whatever reason. Who knows what he had on his mind."

The sheriff's comment rankled. They stood eye to eye and Charlie had the urge to knock some sense into him. Nell was a woman who needed protection whether she thought so or not.

"I agree with you, Charlie. I didn't mean to ruffle your feathers."

Charlie tamped back on his temper. "I'm glad we agree on that at least." He hefted his saddlebag. "I need to get this into the bank before it closes."

He took a few steps, then stopped and turned back. "I'm sort of in a hurry to get back to the ranch. Could you drop this by to Mrs. Lane?" He held out the book. If they were waiting for some sort of explanation, they'd have a long delay.

"Not at all," Thom said. "We're walking down that way right now."

The bank lobby was vacant, but Charlie heard voices in the back. He sat in a chair and opened his saddlebag. Going through his things, he pulled out the final post from the tutor he'd corresponded with before the trouble in Wilsonville had started. She'd come highly recommended from Perkins School for the Blind in Boston and wasn't averse to a new town—as long as she wasn't stuck too far out from civilization. That might be a problem out at the Cotton Ranch. He opened the folded note and skimmed down the page, stopping at the part that had him worried.

. . . that is why, Mr. Axelrose, I must insist that wherever I will be staying is within a town proper—or close by. I am getting on in age and my knees are not what they used to be. I do not desire to live where I cannot go to church or buy something in the mercantile. That is my only stipulation. I believe close proximity to others is also best for the child. I will wait to hear from you. At that time, I will book my passage and bring all the necessary tools for teaching Braille to your child. I look forward to this new challenge of opening up your little girl's world.

Charlie folded the letter and slipped the correspondence back into the envelope. He stared at the wall, thinking about Maddie.

The voices in the back office became heated. A door opened.

"And I say again"—it was a deep male voice—"if they miss another payment my client will put in an offer not even you can refuse, Mr. Lloyd."

"This is *my* bank and I won't be bullied, Mr. Simpson. I don't care who your clients are. Oil barons, as you say, or pig farmers, everyone is treated the same. You won't change my mind."

"Progress won't be put off, Lloyd. This whole territory is rich in oil. Finding it is only a matter of time." Footsteps sounded as the men approached the lobby. "I'll be on my way now, but don't think I've forgotten about the Cotton Ranch. That is some of the most promising land we've seen in a long time. You can't tell me you wouldn't like to have a piece of that yourself."

Could that be the rider on the hill? Scouting the land for oil? A rush of relief flowed through Charlie at the explanation—*not Galante*—but his elation was short lived. Who was trying to buy

Nell and Seth's land out from under them before they knew what happened? Charlie stood.

Mr. Lloyd pulled up short when he found Charlie standing in the lobby.

"I'm sorry, I didn't hear you come in. Benson went home early today. I hope you haven't waited long."

"Not long."

The two men walked outside together, still talking. Charlie watched through the window as the wealthy fellow, Mr. Simpson, with his expensive pants and topcoat, gathered the palomino's reins. Charlie took note of his wide-set eyes and thick nose. One bushy eyebrow spanned his forehead. The two men shook hands, then the banker turned and started for the door.

"Good to see you again, Mr. Rose," Mr. Lloyd said. "Congratulations on winning the quilt. Now, how can I help you?"

Annoying the banker with a demand to know what business Mr. Simpson had with the Cotton Ranch wouldn't do anyone any good. Angry men didn't spill the beans. "I'd like to make a deposit."

The banker's face lit up. "Well, then. You've come to the right place. Come right over here."

Charlie followed and hefted his saddlebags onto the counter. He withdrew the manila envelope that contained his life savings and handed the package to Mr. Lloyd. The banker counted out the stack of one-hundred-dollar bills and made note of the amount on a deposit slip. At the total, his eyebrows raised. Not a fortune, but more than most people had.

Charlie signed the slip and handed it to the banker. On another slip he scribbled out a message and folded the paper so what he wrote couldn't be seen. Mr. Lloyd tipped his head in question.

Charlie set the note on top of his stack of money. "In case something happens to me."

"I understand."

Charlie nodded. "I couldn't help but overhear part of your conversation earlier. I also want you to know I'm fully prepared to make that payment for Seth Cotton in case he and his sister default on their loan. You know I have the money."

Mr. Lloyd's eyes narrowed as if trying to figure him out. "That I do."

"Do you need me to sign something? I don't want their land bought out from under them."

Mr. Lloyd shook his head. "First, your handshake will suffice. Second, I have no intention of allowing a third party to come in and make trouble for Nell and Seth."

Charlie straightened and picked up his saddlebag. "That man sounded quite determined."

At that, the banker smiled. "Indeed. And so do you."

CHAPTER THIRTY-ONE

Charlie departed the bank with every intention of heading straight back to the ranch. He'd done what he came to do. *And more.* He wasn't sure how much Nell and Seth's mortgage was, but he'd all but promised the bank owner that he'd make sure they didn't miss their next payment, even if the solution meant using the funds he'd been paid for his gun shop. Not a goldmine, but a good-sized nest egg he was building upon to pay for Maddie's schooling.

The thought of losing that hurt. An unsettled sensation swirled around in the pit of his stomach.

Charlie flopped his now empty saddlebag over the back of his saddle and buckled the keeps. As he did, a flash of blue calico print caught the corner of his eye. Mrs. Logan, with her son in her arms and a small girl child by the hand, headed for the mercantile across the street. He remembered her from the picnic. And from Nell mentioning how Jessie Logan had helped Brenna Lane throughout the years and now shared her own daughter's dresses with Maddie. He felt a strong urge to go in and thank her. Not straight out, of course, not for caring for his daughter when he couldn't, but he'd be able in some way to make her day a little nicer.

He crossed the street and stepped into the store. *I'll think of something I need to buy.*

"Dwight Hoskins saw Brenna Lane at Mr. Hutton's house in the wee hours of the morning—while it was still dark. Just the two of them," Beth Fairington was saying. She seemed to have Mrs. Logan trapped up against the mail counter in the back of the store. The one-sided conversation had kept them from noticing his arrival. "It's not hard at all to imagine what tomfoolery they were up to," Beth went on. "Her being a widow and all."

Mrs. Logan's chin came up. "Hush your mouth, Beth. I'm sure you've heard Mr. Hutton has taken ill. Brenna was only doing her Christian duty by nursing him, nothing more." From her arms, little Shane Logan scowled up at the store clerk, resembling his pa.

"Still. It's unseemly for her to be alone with him in the middle of the night. Seems you're just brushing that fact under the rug, Jessie. But then, you always did turn a blind eye to propriety— I recall your shenanigans back in Valley Springs. You and Mr. Logan living out at your cabin without a chaperone."

Mrs. Logan's chin went even higher. "Keep your voice down," she commanded under her breath. "Everything that spews from your mouth is tainted by your unkind heart. Violet told me Maude had hired you, so I came in today to say hello and welcome you to town, all the while praying you'd changed. It didn't take more than two minutes to see that you haven't." She shook her head and Shane followed suit. "Where is Maude?"

"Taking the day off since I'm here now. Said it's her first in years. She'll be back tomorrow."

"Fine." Mrs. Logan pushed away, stepping over to a shelf that held several bolts of colorful textiles. "I'll look these over now and place an order with *Maude* tomorrow. As far as we're concerned, I won't share another word with you."

Charlie opened the door until the bell tinkled, then let it close on its own, not daring to listen in any longer. They'd have his hide if they knew how much he'd heard already.

They both glanced up.

Miss Fairington hustled away, while Mrs. Logan seemed to be struggling to contain her anger.

He smiled, holding his hat. "Mrs. Logan. Nice to see you again." Her daughter was playing near the window. She resembled Maddie so much his heart thwacked painfully against his ribs.

Memories of Maddie came flooding back. A sweet babe in his arms the day she was born. At six months, colicky and cranky as he walked her around and around the room. The rough feel of her gums as her first tooth poked through. Dressed in pink, a perfect bow tied at her back. Her crying in his arms when she learned her mommy wasn't coming back. Her frightened face the day her eyesight started to fail. Swallowing, he pushed back his sentiments. Then, like a cub to a honeycomb, he couldn't stop his feet from taking him closer to the child. "Hello there, little one."

The child searched out her mother to see if speaking with him, a stranger, was all right. "That's Sarah, my daughter," Mrs. Logan said from across the room. She seemed to have regained her composure. "You didn't get a chance to meet her at the picnic on Saturday." She cut her gaze to Beth, who had gone behind the counter. The clerk's bright-red ears almost made him laugh.

"I'm sorry I didn't." He glanced back at Sarah. "What've you got there?" Charlie asked her.

The child held up two three-inch-long oak twigs someone had put into an old shoebox along with some buttons, a few scraps of fabric, and an old shoehorn. "Stick people," she said. "This is Skinny Ma and this is Skinny Pa." She held them out for his inspection, then marched one along the top edge of the box.

"Is that so? Good to meet you, Skinny Ma and Skinny Pa. Are you finding what you need in the store today?"

Sarah's eyes lit up with delight at having found an adult to play along with her make-believe. "No, I am not," she responded crossly. "I need some flour to bake a birthday cake for my little girl. You must be out 'cause I can't find any."

Sarah stood and went toward the aisle. "See." She pointed the stick to a container of lamp oil. "No flour there." She continued down the aisle and then stopped and waited for him to follow her. When he didn't move fast enough, Sarah hurried back and took his hand to pull him along.

"Don't let her wear you out, Mr. Rose," Mrs. Logan cautioned, holding back a laugh. "Now that she has you, she'll not give you up easily."

"I'm sure he has better things to do than play with Sarah," Beth Fairington said in a sour tone, her gaze trained down on the store ledger.

"I don't mind at all, Mrs. Logan." Charlie glanced at the little hand wrapped around his. He'd better change the subject before he embarrassed himself in front of the two women. "How is that boisterous lad of yours?" he asked as he was dragged down the aisle by Sarah.

"Growing like a weed—and all too quickly for my liking." She gave the child a hug, adoration shining from her face. "I love the feel of him in my arms but can see the day coming when he'll think himself too grown for such silly indulgences from his mother. I'm not looking forward to that. Before I know it he'll be in school, just like Sarah."

He nodded, remembering Maddie at that age snuggled in his arms. "They do grow faster than we'd like."

Beth harrumphed but kept silent.

Sarah pulled on his hand. "School is fun. Even Maddie gets to come and she's blind."

Maddie in school? A swell of pride threatened to block his throat.

"Here's the flour." Sarah enthusiastically opened the lid to a large, wooden barrel and reached inside for the scoop.

Before she could touch anything Beth swooped down and snapped the top closed just as Charlie pulled Sarah back, her eyes wide. "Stay out," Beth screeched.

"No need for that," Charlie said, giving the shopkeeper a reproving look. He picked up Sarah, who was still startled by the clerk's action.

Mrs. Logan hurried over. Charlie set the whimpering girl down and Mrs. Logan took her by the hand. "As much as I hate to admit it, Miss Fairington is correct, Sarah. You know you're not allowed to play in the flour. Now put the stick people back so we can go. Good day to you, Mr. Rose."

"Goodbye," Charlie replied as she went out the door. Sarah ran to catch up. A pinch of loneliness threatened his mood.

He went to the counter and looked at the candies behind on the shelf, thinking he'd like to buy a dozen of each for his little girl. Instead he said, "I'll take two scoops of peppermints, please."

Miss Fairington filled his request and set the small white bag on the counter.

"Can I open an account? I'm new to town but I plan on staying."

"I'm sorry. I don't have the authority to approve that."

He fished a dime out of his pocket. "Is this enough?"

She traced her finger down a list of items, stopping near the bottom. "Yes. One moment, you have two pennies coming back." She punched a couple of keys on the cash register and the drawer at the bottom popped open. She gathered the coins and handed them to him. "I'll tell Maude that you're interested in an account. She'll take care of the rest."

"Thank you."

Beth Fairington smiled, reminding him of a viper. "Hope to see you again, Mr. Rose."

Charlie settled his hat on his head and went out the door. He took one of the peppermints from the bag and popped it into his mouth, thinking about Maddie being in school. Her first day and he'd missed it. Oh well. As long as she was happy, so was he. He'd make their lives right, somehow. If it was the last thing he did.

CHAPTER THIRTY-TWO

$\mathcal{W}$orn to a frazzle, Brenna took the stairs at Mr. Hutton's house quietly, carrying a get-well card the children had made and a jar of her strawberry jam, her none-too-secret good deed of the day, to further sweeten him up. She was exhausted. Felt like a twelve-team wagon had used her as a road. A room filled with excited children was a dangerous place, she now knew all too well.

Heat warmed her face remembering all the times they had stumped her—her response was that she'd have the answer by the next day. Writing them all down was a job in itself. She hoped Mr. Hutton felt well enough to read the questions over and give her the answers. If he didn't, she didn't know what she would do.

She stopped at the front door. She gave a gentle knock, just in case Mr. Hutton might be asleep.

"Come in." Mr. Hutton's voice sounded stronger.

She pulled up short when she entered and found him settled in the chair instead of in his bed. An oil lamp burned on the table beside him. A book was open in his lap and a cup of tea on the table. She hadn't realized how much she'd been anticipating this meeting until a surge of happiness jostled her heart. "You feel better. I didn't expect to find you up."

He nodded. "Don't know how much better I feel, but I needed to get out of that bed for a little while."

He'd donned a shirt and pants. Pinky-white calamine lotion

covered his face and his hair needed a good scrubbing. The two days' growth of whiskers hid his strong, attractive chin.

He smiled. "How did your day go, Mrs. Lane?"

Was he eager to see her?

She glanced about, taking in the tidied up living room. Through the doorway to the kitchen, she spied the drain board stacked with dishes that had already been washed. In his bedroom the bed looked neat and things put away. She lifted an eyebrow.

"Mrs. Hollyhock," he said in explanation to her silent question. "I *finally* got her to go home. Please, if she inquires about me, tell her I'm better."

Brenna laughed, sinking into the chair opposite him. The horsehair cushion welcomed her aching back, tired after standing for the whole day.

"She forced me to gargle with warm water laced with cayenne pepper to draw out the infection. I tried to tell her I had the measles, not strep throat, but she wouldn't listen."

"Once Violet gets an idea into her head, there's no way to stop her. I don't think anything I say will persuade her away—but I'll try."

"Thank you. That's all I ask."

Mr. Hutton's eager face lifted Brenna's mood. She wasn't quite sure how the day had passed, except that it had in a blink of an eye. She handed him the get-well card.

His mouth crooked up when he unfolded the paper. Dry calamine flakes floated down into his lap. He brushed them away as he read the card. "This is nice. Thank you."

Even in his infirmity, he was a handsome man. Broad of shoulder and thick of arm. On top of all that, he was educated, intellectual, and mannered. She glanced away to gather her nerves.

"Please, don't keep me in suspense any longer," he said.

"The day went well—I think. We read from the readers in the morning, practiced writing words and simple sentences after that, and played a game of Duck Duck Goose."

"Duck Duck Goose?" His smile faded and his eyes went dark.

"Yes. We had a good twenty minutes until lunchtime with nothing to do. When Penny suggested the game, all the students agreed that's what they wanted to do." *And I was wholeheartedly relieved.*

Mr. Hutton glanced away, his mouth firm. Her idea of the perfect solution to the problem did not please him at all. "Games should be saved for recess on rainy days."

Brenna's emotions welled up. She'd done her best for hours to be cheerful and use the time well. She'd struggled to answer every question tossed her way. Twenty minutes of a game wasn't worth a dressing down. "I didn't think one game would hurt."

He waited so long to respond she knew he thought otherwise. "It won't. But if you add that time to other wasted moments, a child's education could be squandered away. We don't want that to happen. Now . . . tell me more."

She didn't want to. Surely he'd find more things to criticize. Even the watercolor portrait hanging on the wall, of the staunch-looking woman with the narrow face and close-set eyes, looked more disapproving than ever. "Are you sure you're feeling up to it? You look a little peaked. Maybe you better get back into bed."

"That's the calamine lotion. What did you do after the lunch break?"

All Brenna wanted to do was go home and relax, where no one would ask her questions she couldn't answer. She still had an hour's worth of mending and some baking before she could go to bed. And since she hadn't had an opportunity to do a secret good deed today—she decided that the strawberry jam didn't count, not when she now begrudged it—she vowed to do two tomorrow. "We read aloud some more, this time from the history book."

"Did you work in the math books like my schedule instructed?"

Brenna swallowed and her heart beat double time. *What can I say that won't be a lie?*

"Mrs. Lane?" He sat forward. "Are you feeling all right?"

"Yes. And actually, no. I mean, I'm fine, but we didn't use the books. I thought some review on the blackboard would be good. The children worked in pairs to solve addition problems. As long as they got the correct answers, they were allowed to do another problem. The older students helped the younger and the session ending up being quite fun."

Mr. Hutton's mouth pulled down at the dreaded word. "School is not supposed to be *fun*."

The frown on his face reminded her of Mr. Pender, the teacher from her childhood who had been so frightening. Grouchy ol' Mr. Pender re-embodied as a young man—who would have thought.

"Mrs. Lane," he said slowly, as if struggling for the right words to make her understand. "For this to work, you need to follow my instructions. It's important. School isn't just a time for play. No need to entertain. The students don't even have to like you."

"But I like them."

He held up a hand to shush her. "The children need to be challenged. If not, their minds grow stagnant. They may as well stay home on the farm and clean a stall."

What? Brenna's ire lifted its head. She was tired, cranky, and hungry. Penny was seeing to supper and she needed to get back to her own home to help. What did he expect of her? She was doing her best. She'd told him she didn't want the responsibility and that she didn't have any experience. Heck, she'd struggled to get through school herself. The interesting eyes that had intrigued her from the very first day they'd met now sent a ripple of anger shooting through her heart.

"Please don't get upset." His eyes searched her face. "I can see you're taking this personally. I'm not criticizing you."

The heck you're not!

"If the students think every day is a play day, they're never going to want to be serious when you ask them to buckle down."

"It's the first day, Mr. Hutton."

He held his hand to his forehead and closed his eyes. "Still, Mrs. Lane."

Compassion cooled her anger. He was still a very sick man. She needed to remember that. He'd waited up for her, to hear how her day went. That should count for something. She should not be angry. "You're feeling weak. Let me help you back to your room."

He smiled, loosening more flakes of dried lotion from his face. "No, no. I'm fine. Just a little shooting pain. Now, where were we?"

You were holding my feet to the fire and watching me squirm.

"Did you have any problems? Or troublemakers?"

One. Stevie had decided to play hooky on the first day—darn that boy of hers—but she wouldn't tell Mr. Hutton that. No use looking for trouble when enough was sure to find the lad on its own. "No problems." *Three trout pulled fresh from the stream is not an excuse to miss school.*

She leaned forward and handed him the list of questions from that day. "If you could, please, I'll need these answered before tomorrow morning. I'd appreciate it."

He glanced at the list. "Of course."

"Fine then. If there isn't anything else you need, I'll be going." She glanced about, noting again his papers on the table, books and a cup. Her stomach growled softly, reminding her that she was famished. "Your supper?"

"I had some of the soup you brought over not long ago. Thank you again for that." He sounded contrite. Like he wanted to make up. She wasn't quite ready for that.

"Penny made it."

"Please tell Penny it's very good and I appreciate her sharing such a fine dish with me."

"I will." The jar of strawberry jam still clutched in her hands felt like an albatross around her neck. "Oh, I almost forgot. I brought you over some jam I put up last month."

"That was kind of you."

She shrugged, still feeling hurt over the unfair interrogation. "It's good on toast."

She stood and headed into the kitchen. As she opened the cabinet door, the corner of a paper stuck halfway out of the drawer below caught her attention. The creased paper looked important, like an official document. Surely, Mr. Hutton hadn't meant to squash it in there like that. Perhaps Mrs. Hollyhock was accidently at fault, as she'd tidied up. Intent on righting the wrong, Brenna opened the drawer, her hand halting midair.

The manure-stained paper! The unlucky relationship-wrecker that had started the whole mess with Mr. Hutton in the first place. The large, bold type was impossible not to read: OFFICIAL MARRIAGE CERTIFICATE OF THE STATE OF PENNSYLVANIA.

Of their own volition, her eyes skimmed down the page and stopped on the date. November 20, 1879—three years ago. Brenna stifled a gasp. Mr. Hutton, with his lovely hazel eyes, tempting broad shoulders and strong, manly chin, was married! To a Miss Helen Boyd. She noted the September birthday listed, year eighteen fifty-one. The same one she'd read on Mr. Hutton's application. She'd remembered because hers was the same month, only a year earlier.

A surge of sadness filled her. A large dark-green stain covered a good portion of the upper left-hand corner, but the names were mostly visible, leaving no doubt in Brenna's mind who the document belonged to.

Wife? But where was she?

With a shaky hand, she pulled the drawer open a tad bit farther but stopped when she noticed a stack of letters, the post on top addressed to Gregory Hutton, Logan Meadows, Wyoming Territory. The sender was listed as H. Hutton, Poppyville, Pennsylvania.

Well, that answers my question quite nicely. Poppyville, Pennsylvania.

"Mrs. Lane?"

"Yes. I'll be right there."

Her voice sounded clogged. She pushed her emotions aside and set the jar of jam on the shelf, closing the cabinet door with a shaky hand. Careful not to make any noise, she quickly tucked away the document and slid the drawer closed. Returning to the front room, she took in Mr. Hutton's feverish eyes and struggled against the crushing weight of disappointment that pushed in on her from all sides. *He doesn't mean anything to me.* "I'll check back with you in a couple of hours before I go to bed."

"I assure you, there's no need for that, Mrs. Lane."

"I assure you *there is*, Mr. Hutton, and I won't hear another word about it. I want you to get well as soon as you can—so you can take back your class and I can go back to my mending."

She hadn't meant to sound so cross, but cross she was. Hood-winked, although he hadn't done one single thing to encourage her, and if she were truthful, he'd done the exact opposite. "And I assure *you*, I need that list of questions answered before class tomorrow. I hope you'll be able to return them to me this evening so I won't worry."

Brenna said goodbye. She hurried across to her own house and was met by the familiar scents of bread baking, the clove-studded apple Jane had made and hung in the living room, and the boys' clothes after a hard day of play. All the things that would have brought her comfort yesterday left her cold. Loneliness gripped her heart and pain stabbed behind her eyes.

She smiled at the children sprinkled through the rooms but headed for her bedroom. Stevie sat on the couch, book in hand, as if she wouldn't even notice he'd missed school today. She didn't have the energy to address the situation now. "I'll be out in a moment, dears." Her hand rested on the glass doorknob. "I just have to slip off my boots and freshen up. Is supper ready?"

"Yes, Mama," Jane and Penny called back in unison. "And the table is set," Jane added.

Such good girls. "Wonderful. I can't wait to hear what you thought of the day." Brenna closed the door to her bedroom with a soft click, then leaned against the wood for support. *I've been pinning my hopes on Mr. Hutton. What a silly nilly I've been. What would he want with a dumb peasant like me?*

The hated, ugly nickname had the power to drop her to her knees. Her pa's angry, red face rushed into Brenna's mind. *"You'll never amount to a half-bent clover, girl. Yer useless to me. Use your head. Why didn't God send me a son to hilp me work in the mine. Least then, he'd be worth something."*

Mr. Hutton's disapproving expression. The forgotten math books. Her years of struggle, heartbreak, and loneliness all welled up within her heart until she thought it would burst. Sliding down the door to the floor, Brenna covered her ears with her hands, trying to block out her father's mocking laughter. Why had she taken on such responsibility? She should have known she couldn't do it. That she'd mess it up. And she had.

There was a soft knock on the door. "Mother, is anything wrong?"

Brenna quickly wiped her eyes with the hem of her dress and made sure her voice wasn't shaky before she responded. "I'm fine, sweetheart. I'll be right out." She worked to make her voice sound cheerful. "We have so much to talk about."

"We sure do, Mama." Jane had joined her older sister on the opposite side of the door. "School was fun. I liked everything you did."

Fun. Don't let Mr. Hutton hear that word.

After she climbed to her feet, Brenna squared her shoulders. This was just one tiny, little setback in the bumpy road of life. She'd faced bigger problems than this. Mr. Hutton had a wife in Pennsylvania to nurse him. Brenna would do what she could, but that was all. She'd not worry about his health, his supper, his soaring temperature. She'd put that man across the road where he belonged—at the bottom of her priority list.

CHAPTER THIRTY-THREE

$\mathcal{M}$orning," Nell called to Gabe and Jake. The hands on loan from the Broken Horn rode toward the ranch yard. It had been four days since she and Seth had made the decision to round up the wild horses, and each day the sun peeking over the far mountain range filled her with hope. "I see you have everything you need," she said, gesturing to their bedrolls on the backs of their saddles, stock whips lashed to the pommels and faces full of excitement. Dog trotted off the porch and out to meet them, barking, whining, and wagging his tail.

She lifted her coffee cup and took a drink. This wild herd just might be the thing to get the ranch back on track. Surely there would be some three- and four-year-olds in the group, which they could use for the army order that hung over their heads. But more than that, there would be broodmares and fillies they could add to their breeding stock. The thought was heady and boosted her mood even more.

At the hitching rail Gabe and Jake swung their legs over the backs of their saddles and stepped off their horses. Each had a long rifle in a leather scabbard on the saddle and a six-gun strapped to his leg.

"Thanks for coming. We couldn't do this without your help."

"We ain't done nothin' yet, Nell," Jake drawled. "I'd wait to see what happens before you go singing our praises. That's a lot of country up there. Finding that herd will be like finding a penny at the bottom of Grant's quarry."

She'd not let him spoil her good mood. "You may be right. Charlie only has a vague recollection where he spotted them. But from here on out, we're thinking positive. We'll find those horses and bring 'em in."

Jake nodded. "Point taken. Besides, both Gabe and me are mighty pleased with your terms. Four mares each to start our own herds. I'd say that's a pretty generous offer. We find and gather the herd—hopefully in the first week—then camp at the box canyon and sack 'em out enough to get 'em down to your ranch. I'd say three weeks, tops. That's good pay." He glanced around and smiled at Gabe standing a few feet away. "Hey, you better wake up." He buffed Gabe on the shoulder, then came up the porch steps. "You got any coffee left inside?"

"You bet. Help yourself to anything you'd like."

As Jake went through the door, Nell recalled the days when she'd enjoyed teasing him, and even Gabe sometimes. She was younger then and they'd never really seen a woman work the cattle and horses like the men. She'd been an anomaly to them, something strange—probably still was.

From inside she heard Seth greeting Jake. The next moment Seth joined her on the porch, a coffee cup in his hand.

"Howdy, Gabe," Seth said. "Seems you grow an inch every time I see you. How tall are you now?" A round of hacking stopped Seth, and he turned away.

Gabe waited to respond. "Not sure. Last time Jessie measured me I was six feet one." He took in Seth, then glanced around. "You're not going along on the roundup?"

"Not this time. But don't be thinking I'm getting off scot-free. I'm driving the buckboard up to the mountain corral with a load of hay. Feed for the horses while we sack 'em out enough to be ponied back to the ranch."

Gabe nodded, then followed Jake's trail up the steps and headed inside.

Charlie came from the barn leading the black gelding, Nell's chestnut paint, and a packhorse. His leather chaps swung easily as he walked. A giddy, happy feeling made her tremble and she gripped her coffee cup tighter. Even though he'd tried to explain away the kiss and the dance there, was no denying what she'd felt deep in her soul and the emotion she'd sensed coming from him. Perhaps he was holding back because of his wife. Like she'd said to Seth, maybe his grief ran deep. That he was still healing. And the book lent to Brenna didn't mean anything tangible was going on. He hadn't been back to town since. Who knew what this trip might bring.

The packhorse was laden down with camping tools and food-stuffs that would keep them happy for a week, or two if they stretched things. Interested in the newcomers tied at the hitching rail, the horses nickered. Seemed people and animals alike were ready for this adventure.

Charlie stopped a few feet from the porch. "You ready?"

She nodded, ignoring what his gaze did to her insides. She turned to Seth. "Be careful while we're gone." Her eyes searched his. She didn't know why she felt so sentimental all of a sudden. "And if you get to town, go see Doc Thorn. I told him you'd be coming in."

"You shouldn't have done that. He'll be waiting for no reason."

"And if you get tired working the horses here, leave 'em till we get back. The army won't care if we're a few days late."

"Nell, you told me all this last night. Stop your henpeckin'."

She held back a retort and willed her eyes to stay dry. Even the sunshine that streamed in under the porch overhang couldn't lift her spirits over Seth's health.

"On the ride out," she continued like she hadn't heard him, "we'll stop at the corral and prop open the gates so it's ready when we bring the herd in."

"You said that before, too."

"Am I forgetting anything?"

"No. Now mount up before all these men change their minds about riding with a sentimental girl."

"If we find 'em, we'll do our best to cut out the stud and a few head, and leave 'em behind. With Drag Anchor, we have no use for him."

Seth shook his head. "You'd think you was my ma, not my baby sister. Don't go doing anything foolish. A few horses ain't worth risking your neck for."

"And I know that, brother."

Unable to stop herself, Nell gathered Seth into a big hug. "I'm not leaving without a kiss and hug. I don't care if you're shy." She gripped his body tightly to hers. "I love you, Seth."

He stepped back and put his hand on her forehead, drawing a chuckle from the two boys who'd just come out of the house. She avoided looking at Charlie. In return, Seth laughed. He gave her a quick kiss on the cheek and sent a look full of meaning to Charlie, who had just finished giving his cinch one last slow pull before mounting up.

"I'll watch over her, Cotton. You don't have to worry about that."

"And us," Jake added. Gabe nodded agreement.

Nell, feeling more grateful than any woman had a right to, stifled her usual smart-alecky comeback and took in the group, her heart filled with love. Her gaze stopped on Charlie. What was going to happen after they had the horses? Something, she felt sure. Change was in the air, but she didn't know what that change was.

CHAPTER THIRTY-FOUR

$\mathcal{B}$eing in the wilderness always had the power to move Charlie's soul. He leaned forward, giving the black plenty of rein as the gelding carefully picked his way up the narrow path strewn with pebbles and rocks that skirted the side of the mountain. Charlie took his bearings. Up ahead on the path, Dog stopped and waited.

Charlie hadn't come this way on his route to Logan Meadows. He'd tried to find the exact trail, but this wasn't it. Since they'd crossed a fair amount of land today and made good time, he didn't feel like backtracking just yet. Maybe if they went a bit farther, he'd find a way inland.

The view pushed out as far as the eye could see, until the rolling land joined the base of the Bitterroot Mountains. Several good-sized lakes dotted the hills before them, and dense forest stretched forward until it thinned into miles of open range. The rise in elevation was evident by the drop in temperature. A puff of cold air crossed his face and the possibility of not finding the horses crept into his mind.

Where the path widened out, he reined up and waited for the others, listening to the scrape and clip of the horses as they grew closer. Nell was the first to arrive. She leaned forward, stretching her shoulders, and looked at the view. "You recognize this?"

She was going to be disappointed. "No."

"We've just started, Charlie. None of us thought this would be easy."

Jake was next, leading the packhorse, then came Gabe bringing up the rear. Jake reached back into his saddlebag for his jacket and Nell did the same. "This is mighty steep," Jake said. "You're not thinking about driving the horses back this way, are you?"

Anxiety gnawed at Charlie's insides. So much rested on his shoulders. Nell's desperate attempt to save the ranch depended on his recollecting a trail he'd traveled once, in a place he didn't know, and finding horses that could be anywhere by now. What Nell expected of him was a pretty tall order. "No. Once we get over these mountains and locate the horses, I'll need to find the path I originally traveled when I came to Logan Meadows. We won't attempt to gather anything until we have a way down."

"Least we got the corral fortified and the gates propped open. I hope no one comes along and closes them," Jake said, now buttoned up all the way to his chin. Red splotches from the cold marked his cheeks, as well as Gabe's and Nell's.

Charlie reached in his pocket and tossed everyone a peppermint. "Can't worry over something we have little control over. Now, let's get off this mountainside so we can set up camp before nightfall catches us unprepared."

"Sounds good to me." Gabe nodded. "I'm hungry."

Jake laughed. "You're always hungry. I don't know where you put it." Jake shook his head as Charlie squeezed the black with his legs, moving him up the trail. The boys bantered back and forth but Nell remained quiet. Could she read his feelings? Did she know they were doomed to fail? In the moonlit kitchen, with Nell standing in his arms, this had sounded like a good idea. He hadn't known then that the ranch was actually at stake. If Seth hadn't told her about the missed mortgage payment, maybe Nell didn't know, either. But now he did. And that was the problem because it made him feel all the worse for it.

Once they'd climbed the steepest part of the mountain, Nell gave a sigh of relief. They descended and the footing gradually became less rocky. Shale and granite gave way to soil and sparse, finely sprouted grass that colored the ground jade. Trees became more abundant and Nell's mood lifted. Jake tossed the packhorse's lead rope to Nell and loped off ahead, as if impatient to see what was over the next foothill. "Wait up," Gabe called, galloping off after him, followed by Dog.

"You feeling deserted?" Charlie asked. The sun had disappeared. The quiet time between day and evening, when the sky turned pink and a hush covered the land, descended. Besides the horses' breathing, the random chirp of a faraway cricket was the only sound.

She smiled. The Charlie she knew was back. For a while he'd been so quiet she'd been worried about him. "Yeah, I am. I hope those two don't find any trouble they can't get themselves out of."

He stacked his hands one atop the other on the saddle horn and stretched up, the black moving along nicely with a ground-eating stride. "When I came this way I never thought I'd be back so soon. Pretty, isn't it?"

"Oh, yeah. Very."

"You've been here before?"

She nodded. "With Ben. He liked to go bear hunting now and again. I have a few memories." A colorful-feathered pheasant darted out from under the grass a few feet away. He took flight and was gone.

"A missed opportunity," Charlie lamented with a laugh as he watched the bird disappear under the brush. He turned in her direction. "Bear, you say?"

She laughed. "Be serious, Charlie, I'm sure you're aware there're lots of bears in these mountains."

"Guess I did, now that I think about it. Stands to reason. Did you ever kill any?"

She glanced over, taking in Charlie's expressive blue eyes. It was hard to tell where the sky quit and his gaze began. Seemed Ben's eyes were fading from her memories, replaced with Charlie's. She guessed that was natural. One couldn't pine forever. "No. We never did. Didn't even find any scat."

He twisted in the saddle and studied their back trail. "I'm glad to hear that. Still, we need to be cautious with the food in camp."

"Always."

Up ahead, Gabe and Jake came loping back in their direction.

"We found a good spot to set up camp," Gabe said. "There's water and a stand of trees gives a bit of shelter."

"Good work." Charlie glanced around again, taking in his surroundings, then gave her a secretive wink. That was when she realized he'd been kidding her about the bears. He couldn't have traveled all this way on his own without knowing how to take care of himself. She smiled, liking everything about him. His gentleness, his ability to make her smile. The way she felt safe whenever he was around.

Gabe and Jake crossed around back behind them, then rode up on both outside positions until they were riding four across. Charlie pointed at Jake's stock whip, then fingered the one on his saddle.

"I was never very good with these."

"Just like casting a fishing rod. Let it drag by your side as you ride along, then, when you want to pop it, throw your wrist forward and pull it back fast. Ain't supposed to touch the animal, of course. Gets 'em moving real good."

"You make it sound easy. But I know different."

Jake held up his hand and wiggled it around. "The secret is all in the wrist."

The horses, sensing that quitting time was near, strode ahead willingly in the fading light, ears pricked forward. The scent of water wafted by, tickling Nell's nose. She was anxious to get out of the saddle. Get some supper rustled up. Stretch her aching muscles and wash her face.

"Right over yonder," Jake said. He pointed to a level area between some trees and a small stream with plenty of grass for the horses. "Farther out is a good-sized stream we'll have to cross tomorrow if we continue in our current direction. Those hills will act as a windbreak when the mountain breeze stirs up tonight."

They halted a few feet away. "Looks good," Nell agreed. "And I'm saddle weary anyway."

Charlie nodded. "Since we'll be moving on early, we won't unpack much. Just our bedrolls and a pot to heat some beans. The coffeepot, utensils, and the lanterns. Gabe and Jake, get the supper going. Nell will help me with the horses. I'll gather some wood and dig a fire pit." The North Star had just appeared over the top of the trees and the crickets were in full swing.

Still in the saddle, Jake sat up straight with a jerk. "What? I thought Nell would do the cooking."

"She will. And so will I, and so will the two of you. Out here we'll share the chores—no matter what they are. Cooking and cleanup is a bit of a bugger. Just because she's a girl doesn't mean Nell should shoulder the responsibility of fixing every meal herself."

Gabe and Jake's grumbles faded away when everyone dismounted and loosened their cinches. Charlie went straight to the packhorse and unbuckled the rigging. With a tug, he slipped the heavy load off the animal's back, then muscled it to the ground.

Delighted with Charlie's decision, Nell went to the far side of the large pack and sank to her knees in the tall grass. After working the thin ropes that held the lanterns to the crossed wooden frame, she set them on the ground and fished around for the matches in a side pocket. After she lit the wicks, she was careful to make sure the match was extinguished. The grass was drying out and she didn't want to start a fire. The natural light was fading fast and the boys would need the illumination to be able to sort through the canvas compartments for foodstuffs. By now, a few more stars had made their appearance in the sky. She opened another pocket, withdrew a handful of the jerky they'd brought along to feed Dog, and tossed it to him.

Charlie went from horse to horse, unsaddling and haltering. He had three done before she had finished Coyote. She could hear Gabe and Jake discussing what they should do for food. "Just open a couple of cans of beans for tonight," she called. "They're in the large compartment, and the can opener's in the side. I brought along bread that needs to be eaten tonight and tomorrow, before it's hard as a stone."

Turning with Coyote's lead in her hand, she met Charlie on his way over. "I'll take those," she said, taking the other four leads and splitting them between her two hands. The breeze had turned into a light wind, moving the grass at their feet.

"You sure you can handle them all at once?"

She wasn't sure if he could make out her I-can't-believe-you-just-asked-me-that expression in the dimming light. "Pretty sure, Charlie."

"That's right. You're the horse trainer of the bunch. The animal talker. Why did I doubt?"

She laughed. "You makin' fun?"

"Never," he called over his shoulder. She watched him take one of the lanterns and head for the trees, most likely in search of firewood.

As she headed for the stream, she studied the terrain for the shape of any other large animal quenching its thirst after a long day. Seeing nothing but the quiet landscape, she approached a long, easy-sloped bank and carefully stepped forward, three horses on one side and two on the other. Front feet in the stream, they all drank for a good minute. She let her hand linger on Coyote's withers, taking in his contented attitude.

Foaled on the prairie, her horse always preferred being out in the open spaces. He lifted his head high, water dripping from his muzzle. His nostrils flared when he inhaled the fresh air. He spooked at something and stepped toward her, but she knew his giddiness was caused by the adventure at hand. "Easy, boy," she crooned. "We have a long week ahead. You're gonna get your fill of wild scenery and wide-open spaces. Scents on the air that stir your blood."

A voice came out of the darkness behind her. "What's he saying back to you?"

CHAPTER THIRTY-FIVE

*C*harlie! You devil! Are you trying to frighten the life right out of me?"

What he could see of Nell's face made him bust out in a laugh. Her mouth was a perfect O, her eyes were wide, and she was smashed flush up to Coyote's side for protection. "What'd ya think? That I was a big ol' bear come to cart you off?"

"No. Eat me alive is more like it. Don't do that again, or be ready to face the consequences."

"Yes, ma'am." He chose a steady rock, then went from step to step where the stream appeared deep. He scooped a bucketful of water, then made his way back to the shore.

"Thought you were going for firewood," she said.

"I did. There were several half-decayed oak branches close to camp. Enough for tonight and tomorrow morning. The boys helped drag them over." He patted Coyote on the neck. "Supper's almost ready." He reached over and took two of the horses' leads. "You never answered my question about Coyote. What's he have to say tonight?"

He caught her soft laugh. "For one, I believe he's glad to be off the ranch. The scent of the wild horses has him excited." They both watched the paint as he studied the horizon. Alert, his ears flicked back and forth, then he let go a deep, loud call, rousing the other animals. They danced around nervously.

"I see what you mean. What about the black?"

"I'm not sure if you believe me or you're making fun."

He realized he wasn't making fun of her. Something about her made him want to believe. "Trust me, Nell. Your ability has me thinking harder than I have for some time."

Nell stepped under Coyote's neck and reached up to the top of the black's neck, placing her hand on his coat. After a moment, she turned and started back toward camp with the horses.

"Well? Anything?" he asked, hurrying to catch up. They fell in side by side as they walked.

"He's a bit harder to read. One thing is he's never been up this far in the open country. He seems jittery for different reasons than Coyote. The black is frightened. Mountain lions are just as common as bears up this way. Much more dangerous to horses. He'll need all the confidence you can muster when we start after the herd."

"You sound pretty sure we're going to find them."

"I'm certain we will now. It's just a matter of time."

Something in the air has me skittish, as well, Charlie thought. Maybe it was that their kiss was always on his mind. Every time he tried to tell himself it was Brenna he needed to court for Maddie's sake, Nell popped into his head. Maddie had grown attached to Brenna; Nell lived too far out for the tutor's liking. Agitated with thinking of the two women, he realized he'd given precious little thought to Grover Galante since they'd set out.

Nell stopped about halfway back to camp. "Let's hobble them here, but take one to camp and tie him there. We can switch him out later."

The horses immediately dropped their heads and began cropping the grass. Dog bounded into their group, his tail wagging happily as if he were on a grand adventure. Nell laughed and patted his head. They made fast work of hobbling the horses' front feet, and then they led Jake's horse back toward camp and snubbed him to a tree.

"I'll switch him out with Coyote later tonight," Nell said when Jake came close to see if anything was wrong. "Being they don't know the country, they may be skittish. This way the others won't wander off."

His reply was a grunt. Gabe squatted before the crackling fire. "Supper's on," he finally called. With a large spoon he ladled out generous portions to all and Nell ripped chunks of bread to pass around.

As hungry as Charlie was, the simple fare was satisfying and tasted good. But a slather of fresh butter would make it a whole lot better. Like the sweet, creamy goodness his stepmother used to glob on a crumble-topped apple pie as soon as the sweet was out of the oven. His mouth watered and his taste buds squeezed just dreaming about it. He couldn't think of one thing he wouldn't give to have a nice, big slice in front of his nose right now.

Nell cleared her throat. "Charlie?"

He jerked his gaze up, realizing he'd been mesmerized by the recollection of the tasty boy-taming concoction he missed so much.

He skimmed the faces. "Yeah?"

"Gabe just asked you about the horses. What you remember most about where you found them and numbers and such." Her excitement was palpable from the opposite side of the campfire. The golden light made her hair gleam as the shadow of the flame danced across her face.

"Not too much, since I thought I was just passing through."

"What about a stallion?" Gabe asked. The boy hadn't said more than a few words on the ride here, so Charlie didn't have a measure on his disposition. Nell thought a lot of him, though. If she believed he was a good-enough hand when the pushing started, that was enough verification for him.

"Never saw him," Charlie said. "Probably caught my scent and took off. There was plenty of white in the herd. Paints, grays, roans, lots of solids with tall socks and large blazes. Some pretty nice-looking animals."

Nell took a sip from her cup. "I'd venture to guess the stud is probably a paint himself, with what you're saying about the makeup." Dog lay with his head on Nell's boots as if they were a pillow.

Gabe and Jake exchanged glances. "I wonder why no one else has rounded them up before this," Gabe said. "Sounds too good to be true."

"Maybe they have." Nell tossed the scant remains of her coffee behind her. Dog lifted his head at the sound. "Who knows how large the herd used to be before Charlie's sighting. Staying in the high country keeps them pretty secluded. We could come away with just a handful ourselves."

Again a glance passed between Nell's friends.

"Jake," Nell said. "What's new with you and Daisy?" Jake lifted his cup to his mouth as she added, "You two have weddin' plans yet?"

"Nothin' set in stone."

Gabe perked up. "He's waiting on gettin' a place of his own. So he don't have to live at the ranch afterwards."

Jake sent his younger companion a disparaging look. "You talk a lot."

"Nell asked."

Nell sat forward, clearly interested. "Jake?"

"I've worked out a deal with Chase about buying a small place he owns on Shady Creek. Not much bigger than a chicken coop, but there's room to grow."

"And you'll need stock." Charlie admired these hardworking young men.

"That's right. That's why I pounced on the chance to go with you. A few mares crossed with Chase's stud will be a nice start."

"It sure will," Gabe added.

Dog stood and shook, then settled his head in Nell's lap, making her laugh. "And Daisy?" she asked, scratching behind his ears.

"Don't know if you heard, but Hannah hired her on."

"At the Silky Hen?"

"Yep. In the kitchen. Hannah says when people forget her past, she'll let her start waitressing a day or two." Jake shook his head. "I don't know. People can be cruel."

Although curious, Charlie didn't ask for an explanation. If the fella had wanted to say, he would have. "Well, that was a nice supper." The vastness of the stars expanded as he shrugged down deeper into his coat. Didn't matter that it was still only fall, evenings in the high country got cold at night. "What does everyone say we get to bed? I don't know about the rest of you, but I'm beat and tomorrow'll come early."

Gabe stood and stretched. Jake followed and Nell handed Gabe her bowl and cup along with her utensils. The two started toward the creek with a lantern and Dog at their heels. Charlie heard their grumbles until they were out of earshot. Nell sat on the far side of the fire on a rock, looking pretty small in her sheepskin coat.

Time to set up bedrolls. He was exhausted and was looking forward to stretching out on the ground. He went over to where he'd unloaded the packhorse, hoisted his saddle and Nell's, and brought them close to the fire. "Where would you like yours?"

"I guess that's as good a place as any."

He set hers down, horn to the ground, then placed his beside it. He waited for her to object but she didn't. "I just think it's smart if we all sort of stay close," he said to her unspoken question. "You know—snakes."

"Snakes?" Amusement tinged her voice.

"Yeah. Snakes. Like the one you shot the first night I arrived out at your ranch? You remember that, right? You admitted yourself that the rattler was large."

"I wasn't questioning you, Charlie."

"I think you were, Nell."

Her gaze did funny things to his stomach as he laid out his bedroll and then positioned his saddle for a backrest. He got down on his knees and patted down his blanket and then hers, reaching under for the stones that would be sure to keep them awake if left to chance. The brightness of the fire between them kept him from seeing her eyes but if he was right, she was smiling.

"You do that well."

"Thank you. I'd rather take more time now than be sorry in the morning."

Off in the distance, Dog barked.

Charlie, a little self-conscious, stood and looked around. "Guess I should go swap out a horse."

Nell lunged up. "I meant to do that and forgot. I'll do it, Charlie."

A coyote yipped and the sway of the tops of the trees drew his attention. When he looked back she was halfway across the clearing, her body shimmering in the gloom like something otherworldly. Somehow it felt a whole lot more desolate out here with her, this far away from civilization, than it had even when he was out here himself. It'd be easy to forget that any other life existed. And all too easy to let his desires run away with him.

CHAPTER THIRTY-SIX

*T*hree o'clock couldn't come fast enough. Brenna checked the watch pinned to the bodice of her blue cotton dress as the children worked feverously on the essay, "What I Did over the Summer Break," that Mr. Hutton had asked for.

Eleven whole days had passed since the first day of school and even though she had a schedule that kept her busy, she'd settled into a routine that was no longer fearful or draining—although her feet did ache by the time the children went home. If she was lucky, she caught a glimpse of Jessie now and then bringing Sarah to school or picking her up. It was like living on a deserted island with the children and Mr. Hutton—*married* Mr. Hutton. That knowledge still hurt.

Thankfully, his was the only case of measles to appear in Logan Meadows so far this year. His spots had faded to a light-rose color and he was feeling much better, always up and about when she checked in on him twice a day. He'd try to engage her in conversation, but since learning about the wife back in Pennsylvania that he'd failed to mention, she'd kept her distance. A home wrecker she was not.

"Time's up, class. Please be sure your name is on your paper—and is legible. I'll collect them as you leave the room." She went over and pushed open the door, allowing a rush of fresh air into the room. Conversations twittered as the children gathered their things. "Have a nice weekend. I'll see you on Monday." *Only one more week and I'll have my life back.*

Penny, followed by Jane and Maddie, approached and stopped at the door. The two handed in their assignments. Maddie handed her a drawing of a flower she'd done from memory, not much more than some curved lines, but to Brenna it was a masterpiece. Prichard and Stevie had been the first out the door as they scampered on ahead. "Thank you, thank you," Brenna said, collecting the papers from the children as they passed.

"Do you want us to wait for you, Mama?" Penny asked.

"No, honey. You go on ahead and I'll be right along. I'm going to the mercantile for some flour."

"I can get that for you if you'd like."

"I'd rather you make sure the boys aren't tearing down the house in our absence. I'll be there as soon as I can." *After I check in with Hannah.* The math books were always on Brenna's mind. She'd hoped they would have already arrived. She caressed Maddie's cheek. "You did well today, sweetie. I was so proud when you raised your hand and named the first president of the United States."

A ghost of a smile crossed Maddie's face. "My pa used to tell me."

Brenna's eyes cut to Penny's. This was new. The first time she'd ever mentioned her father. "He did?"

Maddie nodded. "'Cause he was in the war. Said history is important."

Penny and Jane watched with curiosity. "Did he say anything else?" Brenna asked.

Maddie scuffed her foot against the floor. When a teardrop landed with a splash between her small feet, Brenna quickly bundled her into a hug. "Girls, why don't you two run along. I feel like spending some time with Maddie today. I've been so busy with school, I've missed out on more meaningful things—like snuggling her in my lap."

Brenna picked Maddie up and sat on the bench against the wall. Jane and Penny stepped out the door quietly. A good five minutes went by without a word being said. Brenna rocked back and forth, crying inside while she felt the wetness of Maddie's tears on her neck.

Brenna put her hand on Maddie's forehead just to be sure she wasn't coming down with something. As she suspected, the child's head was cool. She was just tired. Probably homesick. Off-kilter with her stepmother's new role as teacher taking time away from seeing to her needs. Maddie never complained. If not cheerful, she was quiet. She was no trouble at all. Brenna prayed this time the child would open up to her.

"Tired, sweetie?" Maddie nodded into the crook of her neck. "Me, too. I'll be glad when Mr. Hutton is able to come back and I—we—can stay home."

Maddie didn't respond.

"You said your pa was in the war. Can you tell me more about him? I'd like to know because I love you and I want what's best for you. If I know a little more, perhaps I can help find him."

A moment ticked by. "Maddie?"

"No." The word was a whisper. It wasn't as if Maddie didn't want to share with her, it was more that she was fearful to.

"That's all right, you don't have to tell me a thing." She kissed her cheek. "Ready to stand?"

Maddie nodded. Brenna set her down and wiped her face with a hankie she had in her pocket. "There. You look prettier than a falling star." That made Maddie smile. "Now let's make a quick trip down the street to the Silky Hen so I can have a word with Hannah, then we'll stop in Miller's Mercantile for some flour and a penny candy."

Brenna peeked her head into the restaurant from the lobby of the El Dorado Hotel, holding on to Maddie's small hand. Several tables were occupied. Susanna, looking as regal as ever in her purple dress and starched white apron, came out with a water pitcher and began refilling glasses. When she noticed them she waggled her fingers. "How're things at school, Brenna? You're a brave woman to take that on."

Brenna laughed. "Brave or knuckleheaded. I'm not sure which. Mr. Hutton's return can't come fast enough to suit me."

"Well, don't just stand there. Come in. Can I get you something? Hot tea?" She smiled at Maddie. "A cookie?"

Brenna glanced down to see a tiny smile on the child's face.

"I think a cookie would be just fine, Susanna. Thank you."

"Fine, then. Follow me." She led the way into the cluttered kitchen where Hannah sat at the table looking over a list and Daisy smiled from the far side of the room where she was mixing something in a large bowl.

"What a nice surprise," Hannah said, laughing happily. "I wasn't expecting to see you for another day when you brought in my pastries. How're you, Maddie?" she added. "How was school today?"

"Fine, ma'am." Maddie's voice wasn't quite back to normal after her crying, causing Brenna's heart to pull up tight. Now standing, Hannah scooted out two chairs for them to join her at the table. Susanna went to the cookie jar and returned with a large oatmeal-raisin cookie that she placed in Maddie's palm.

Maddie's face lit with pleasure. "Thank you."

"Hannah, look what Maddie drew today in class." Brenna handed her the picture from the top of the assignments she held in her arms. "Isn't it the prettiest flower you've ever seen?"

Hannah gasped softly. "It is. You have a nice touch, little one."

"Very pretty," Susanna agreed from over their shoulders.

"It's one of the loveliest flowers I've ever seen, Maddie," Daisy added, admiring the picture.

Maddie was everyone's favorite.

"So, what do I owe this unexpected visit to?" Hannah asked. "I'm glad because I haven't seen you for almost—"

Hannah gasped loudly and Susanna looked over from the stove in surprise. Hannah's eyes grew so round Brenna reached over and touched her hand, but the guilty expression was almost more than she could stand.

"Please, Hannah, tell me it's *not* true. Tell me you didn't forget about the books."

Every day that passed, Brenna had meant to check with her, to be sure the order had been placed. But every day she'd been way-laid with things that needed to be done. She'd counted the days until the books' arrival, making up all sorts of half-lies to keep Mr. Hutton from the truth. Hannah's white face gave her the answer.

"It's true," Hannah whispered. "How could I be so careless?" She reached down into her skirt pocket and pulled out the note Brenna had given her the first day of school. "And it's even still in my pocket. I've worn this skirt three times since and never once put my hand inside. How can I ever make this up to you, Brenna? I feel horrible."

Brenna hadn't heard anything past "It's true." Her stomach turned sour and a prickly heat broke out over her body. What in land's sakes was she going to do? Dr. Thorn had cleared Mr. Hutton to come back sometime next week. He'd made a surprisingly fast recovery.

"Brenna. Please. Say something."

Brenna reached out and ran her hand down Maddie's back. The girl had stopped eating and was listening to the tense conversation, a frown pulling her small lips downward. When she felt the caress, she reached over and clutched Brenna's hand.

Hannah slid the note across the table. "Tell me what I can do to help. Anything, Brenna. I can talk to Mr. Hutton myself, if you want. I'm so sorry."

Brenna tried to smile, but knew she was failing miserably. "I don't think there is anything anyone can do now. Please don't worry overly much. It was—and is—my mistake. I'll have to tell Mr. Hutton tonight."

CHAPTER THIRTY-SEVEN

*T*he disappointment of the last few days had Nell's head hurting. No horses. And hardly any sign of them, either. She reached up and rubbed the two sensitive spots on the side of her skull while she gazed up at the multitude of stars. Or perhaps her head hurt because of the hours she'd lain awake thinking about Charlie and how she would miss him when they got home and he picked up where he'd left off with Brenna.

A rustle of blankets sounded from across the campfire. Gabe rose, grabbed the coffeepot, and headed for the stream. This was their ninth campsite. She closed her eyes and pretended to be asleep for another few moments. They needed these horses. She wasn't giving up. She opened one eye to see Charlie's place empty. Through her lashes she watched him working on the fire. Jake rose, stretched, greeted him quietly.

She rolled to her side and stood.

Charlie glanced over. "Morning."

His tone said he was as frustrated as she was. They'd been going out in pairs. The boys' disappointment had turned them quiet, while she and Charlie had become argumentative. She didn't want another day like yesterday. "Morning," she finally replied, heading to the stream to wash up. She owed it to everyone to stay strong. They were here doing their job. She could at least put away her fear of going home empty handed and make each moment count.

Charlie had just filled his coffee cup when Nell came back into camp. The red, glassy sheen in her eyes pummeled him right in the gut. He'd let her down. That didn't sit well. He'd find those horses today if it was the last thing he did. He filled another cup and handed the coffee to her.

Jake and Gabe sat on a log by the fire. "Biscuits will be done shortly." Gabe extended his leg and pushed the Dutch oven with his toe. "I can smell 'em already. We running the same drill today?"

"Yeah," Charlie replied. "Go out in pairs. If you find the herd, return to camp and wait for the others. Check in every two hours. If we find nothing, we keep moving south."

Nell nodded. "Sounds good."

Charlie sipped, then said, "We have provisions for a few more days unless we want to hunt."

Nell reached over and scratched Dog on the head. "I don't want to stay out longer than we agreed. Chase won't like it and I don't want to leave Seth alone any longer than I have to. If we can't find the herd in a few more days, we'll have to give up for now."

Charlie nodded. "Guess that means we'll have to find them today. Which direction is the corral from here?"

"Southeast," Jake said.

Gabe, just finishing a sip of coffee, nodded. "I'd say the same. I was studying the stars last night." He got up and went over to a long branch placed on a large, flat rock. "I marked the North Star so we can be sure of our direction today."

That sounded good to Charlie. "Fine then." A warm, heady aroma filled the air. "Do I smell biscuits?" Gabe ran back and with two thick potholders dragged the heavy cast-iron pot from the flames.

"And I've got the honey," Nell added. "Let's eat and get out there. Those Cotton Ranch horses are just waiting to be caught."

Charlie popped his hands together. "I think we should mix it up today. I'll ride with Gabe, Jake can go with Nell." Time apart would do them both some good.

Gabe removed the lid of the Dutch oven and reached inside, breaking apart the crusty bread blobs. Every few seconds he pulled his fingers back to give them a good shake. "These puppies are hot. Be careful." He tossed one to Nell and another to Charlie.

Jake reached in himself and drew out two. "The advantages of sitting close."

"Well, eat up," Charlie uttered sternly. "I'm sure we're all a little antsy to get back to civilization.

Ten minutes later, he watched Jake and Nell ride out of camp. This had to be the day they found the horses. The dull ache in his heart whenever he thought of Maddie grew, swelling so much at times he couldn't even think. He'd made a decision last night. On their return he'd let Maddie know he was back in town. Even if he couldn't take her yet until he had a place, at least they could spend time together. He didn't want to live any longer without his daughter in his life.

He'd also made another decision. Once he revealed himself to Maddie, he'd start courting Brenna.

"Ready to go?" The reins to both their horses were in Gabe's hands. Lost in thought, Charlie hadn't even heard him approach.

"Sure. Only one way to find those wily animals and that's to get to it."

One hour turned into two. It was time to head back to camp to check in, but Charlie didn't want to just yet. The terrain here was different. Less rocks, more grass. He pulled up and studied the ground. Gabe reined up beside him.

"What?"

"I don't know. I just have a feeling." He rode a little farther. "There." He pointed to an area of trampled grass, much too large to have been made by deer. He spotted a pile of fresh horse manure, not more than a day old, and wanted to shout with joy.

They crossed a shallow creek, then rode for the brush, staying out of sight. Charlie reined up and listened. "Did you hear that?"

"Yeah," Gabe said. "A horse neighing."

A minute crawled by. "There it is again," Charlie breathed. "Unless that's Nell and Jake." He dismounted and tied the black to some scrub brush. Gabe did the same. Crouching, they ran along the side of a bank, then proceeded forward, up the hill. At the top, they dropped to their bellies and crawled to the crest of the rise.

The herd grazed peacefully on the open land below them.

Gabe gave a huge sigh of happiness. "Didn't think we'd ever find 'em. They're sure pretty."

They were. About the prettiest sight Charlie had ever seen. Along with the paints, there were bays, liver chestnuts, a few palominos and duns. "The herd is larger than I thought. How many would you say?"

"Seventy-five, if there's one," Gabe answered. "That's a lot of horseflesh running free. And not a brand in sight."

"They're ours for the taking." Charlie gauged the path of the sun and the landscape. "You have any idea where we are, Gabe? You and Jake mentioned you've been up here before. Do you recognize any of this?" They were low enough in the grass, and upwind, that the horses were none the wiser.

"Yeah. I've seen that outcrop of granite before," he said, pointing. "Beyond should be a trail that hooks over to another. We'll have to check it out. If I'm right, we're not all that far from the holding corral. We've just come in a roundabout way."

"How many miles, if you had to guess?"

"Between twenty and thirty."

"That's doable." Charlie studied the idea. "A lot could happen between here and there." He was thinking of Nell, and also of Gabe and Jake. Nothing was worth losing a life over.

"The corral will be tight for this many horses, but they'll all fit." He felt Gabe nod. He couldn't take his eyes off the horses. When a twig snapped, Charlie turned. Nell and Jake had found them. Nell's beautiful face, alight with anticipation, indicated she already knew what was over the rise.

CHAPTER THIRTY-EIGHT

$\mathcal{C}$harlie gestured for them to stay low. The two came forward cautiously until they were beside him and Gabe. In awed silence, they admired the sight for a good five minutes before starting back to their horses. At the scrub brush where the horses were tied, the three gathered around Charlie. Excitement zinged between them. "Who besides Gabe recognizes this area?" Charlie asked, scanning the land filled with squatty oaks, stunted pines pushed sideways by the wind, and mesquite trees.

"I do," Jake offered. "Gabe and me were up this way a year ago with Albert and Win hunting deer. The land's rough and at some places little more than a game trail, but I know there's a way back toward the corral."

Nell nodded. "If it's the trail I'm thinking of, the horses can travel two or three across over most of it, if they choose to. It'll be easy driving, as long as we can keep them together."

"Fine then." *There are still a lot of hurdles to overcome. And won't be easy no matter what anyone thinks.* "Since it's still early, we have time to get prepared for tomorrow."

"You have a plan?" Nell asked.

"Yeah. We'll drive them in relay. That way our horses can keep up with them even with the extra weight they have to carry. Rider number one, that's me, circles behind and pushes west. They'll be fresh, and that leg will be the most difficult to keep the horses from splitting off. That row of dense trees over there will help."

When no one offered a different idea, he went on. "If it's approximately twenty miles back to the corral, I'll drive them five miles to Nell. By then, they'll barely be winded. The key is to keep them running. By the time they reach Jake, they'll be tired. Trying to slow down to a trot—to catch their breath. Don't let 'em. Push 'em hard and keep 'em running. If they're allowed to catch their wind, they'll be able to outrun our horses. After I turn them over to Nell, I'll cut cross-country to the box canyon where the corral is and be ready to help drive them in. After each one of you finishes, make your way to the corral."

If anyone had an objection, it would be Nell.

Her eyes narrowed. "I think it'll work. Where'd you learn to think like a horse, Charlie?"

Gabe and Jake laughed.

"One of us should go collect the packhorse now. Then we'll all go look for the trail we want to use to drive them to the corral tomorrow, using what terrain we can as a guide for the horses. Gabe, you'll be stationed closest to the corral. Come morning, you'll take the pack-horse and tie him inside the corral in plain sight as bait. The horses will go in easier if they see another of their kind inside. Then get back to your assigned spot and wait for Jake to bring you the herd."

Nell nodded. "That's a good idea. Besides, by then they'll be pretty tuckered out, wanting to stop."

Charlie nodded. "Exactly. Once we know where we're driving them, we'll start back this afternoon and drop each of us off until we're stretched out along the route. That means you boys will go it alone tonight. I'll stay with Nell, then bring them down first thing in the morning."

Nell straightened. "No, you won't. I've camped by myself before. If you have to ride up in the morning, the black won't be as fresh as he could be."

He wouldn't argue with her now in front of Gabe and Jake, but he had no intention of leaving her alone. Not after her reaction to the rider on the hill. "Whatever you say, Nell."

Suspicion burned in her eyes. "You're giving in too easy."

"Seems I'm damned if I do and damned if I don't."

"What about the stallion?" Gabe asked, probably wanting to change the subject before the conversation escalated.

"He'll come along no matter what we do," Nell said. "But once we get them caught in the corral, we'll turn him back out with a good number of mares and any horses we can't use."

They all nodded.

"It's a decent plan." Nell met his gaze. She leaned against her horse, taking them all in.

"You sure you're ready for this, boys?" Charlie asked Gabe and Jake. "It's a lot different than driving cattle. The horses can get away from you pretty fast."

"I'm as sure as I am that I'd already like to be back in Logan Meadows holding Daisy's hand."

Everyone laughed. A little jocularity before the big ride was good.

Charlie went over to his horse. "I'll retrieve the packhorse and be back as soon as I can. Be ready to ride out after that."

He couldn't stop worry from dogging his mind. So many things could go wrong. The last thing he wanted was for someone to get hurt, or worse. He didn't want anything to happen to himself, either. Maddie needed him. If the worst came to pass, Frank Lloyd would read the note that left his money to Maddie and also asked Brenna to adopt her. He hoped she would. "Tomorrow, I don't want anyone trying to be a hero," he said, looking at Nell. "I mean that. Seth wants to see us all riding into the yard."

"I understand, Charlie. I won't be doing anything foolish, I promise you."

"Good. That also goes for the two of you." He sent Gabe and Jake a serious gaze. Abruptly he felt mighty old. And mighty responsible for the good outcome of this task.

CHAPTER THIRTY-NINE

$\mathcal{B}$renna climbed Mr. Hutton's stairs carrying a covered tray of beef stew and cornbread. She knocked on the door. It seemed as if she'd done this a thousand times, if once. But today was different. She swallowed and pushed back the trepidation that burned inside. Instead of him calling for her to enter, like he usually did, he opened the door and greeted her warmly. He'd bathed and shaved. There wasn't a trace of measles to be found. He was dressed as if on his way to class and there was a twinkle in his eye. Perhaps giving him the news about the books wouldn't be so bad.

He held the door open and gestured for her to enter. "Mrs. Lane, so good to see you." His eyes darted to the tray in her hands. "I thought we discussed this yesterday. You don't need to provide meals for me any longer. But I have to say I *will* miss your cooking."

Why had he put emphasis on the word *will*, and why was he giving her such a charming smile? *What is he up to?*

"Your meals are so much better than mine. I'll be sure to savor this last one."

"It's only beef stew and cornbread."

"A feast." He followed behind as she made her way to the kitchen.

"Well, your appetite has certainly returned." She set the tray on the counter.

Now that he seemed well, she felt a little off-kilter. She struggled for something to say.

Mr. Hutton leaned back against the cupboard, the exact place he kept his marriage certificate stashed out of sight, and fingered his chin between his thumb and forefinger. "How was school?" He smiled pleasantly. "Any questions for me today?"

This had been the first day she hadn't been stumped by a single question, and it felt nice. "No, actually. None today."

She didn't know why she felt so prickly toward him. Things just hadn't been right since she'd found that marriage certificate. Even after all these days, the discovery still felt like a shock.

One eyebrow arched up. "That's wonderful." He reached over and lifted a corner of the cloth napkin covering his supper. "Looks delicious. Dr. Thorn was here today. I'm cleared to go back to school on Monday. I'm sure you're happy to hear that."

"I am, indeed. I won't know what to do with all my extra time." She took a step toward the other room. Remembering Maddie, and also the dreaded math books, she whirled back around, well aware he was only a few feet behind her. "There's something I need to tell you," she said quickly before she lost her nerve.

Clearly she'd surprised him, because he froze. Embarrassment registered on his face and he put his foot to the floor and waited. Darn his hazel eyes. They reminded her of butterscotch and mint, two of her favorite candies. She forced her gaze away.

"It's about Maddie," she said. "She's been going to school with me this whole time without any problems at all. Penny and Jane are happy to keep her close. She's even raised her hand a few times to answer a question—and has been correct. Will she be able to continue on come Monday?"

He went over to the sofa and gestured for her to sit in the chair opposite, but she was too keyed up. After Maddie's bout with tears earlier, she dreaded having to tell her she was no longer welcome in school.

"Please, Mrs. Lane, sit down for a moment. I can see you're overwrought. I think the reason may be more than the situation with Maddie. I'd like to get to the bottom of it, if I could. Maybe I can help." His gaze turned serious. "Please."

"All right," she agreed, and settled in the chair. "There is something you need to know. It's about the—"

"Math books?" he finished for her. He picked up a telegram from the side table.

A telegram?

"Dr. Thorn brought it with him today. The math books that you've had such a hard time obtaining will arrive on the Monday stage. I'd say that that's perfect timing, wouldn't you?"

The math books? He knows about the math books? Shaken, Brenna held out her hand. "May I?"

He handed the telegram over.

It was addressed to the schoolmaster in Logan Meadows. Her eyes scanned the short note:

Back-ordered math books will arrive next week Monday barring any weather holdups STOP Sorry for the delay STOP Best regards, Leach, Shewell & Sanborn Publishing

She handed the small yellow paper back. "This is wonderful news." He must have put two and two together after all the times he'd inquired and the half-truths she'd given him.

"Mrs. Lane," he said gently. "You could've told me. I can see this issue has caused much distress over the past two weeks. I'm sorry. I should have arrived earlier and taken care of the situation myself, but you see, even if I had, the results would have been the same. You couldn't print the books yourself." He reached over and patted her hands, clasped in her lap. "This wasn't your fault."

She didn't dare look up. If she did, he would see her shame. How she'd tried to be someone—no, something—that she wasn't. She'd never fit in with the upper-class citizens of Logan Meadows.

"Please." His one word was a silky plea. He scooted off the couch and went down on his knees in front of her so he could see into her face. "Please, Mrs. Lane," he whispered again. "You've done a *fine* job preparing the school, and the children, for this term. I couldn't have done any better myself." With a gentle touch to her chin, he raised her face so he could see into her eyes. "I know how much this all means to you. Thank you for everything you've done."

Brenna struggled against the biscuit-size knot of emotions clogging her throat. She needed some air. Blinking, she locked her gaze on the creamy-white ceiling, wishing she were anywhere but here.

"Please say something."

"I should have told you the moment I realized my mistake—at the picnic. I haven't had a good night's sleep since."

Mr. Hutton stood slowly and pulled her to her feet. He wrapped her in his arms and stroked her hair, a comforting touch she hadn't felt since Carl died.

"Hearing that makes me even sadder," he said. "With all the chores you have weighing on your shoulders, you didn't need something silly like math books robbing you of your rest. I hope you don't get sick yourself."

"I can't. Dr. Thorn said I'm—"

"I don't mean the measles. I mean exhaustion. You're working so hard. I've noticed dark circles under your eyes that weren't there the day you tried to knock me down in front of the whole town."

She pulled out of his arms ready to remind him how *he* had bumped *her* to the ground, when she'd merely knocked his briefcase to the boardwalk. But she stopped, her defense dying in her throat at the sight of his smile and humor-filled eyes.

"Yes?" he asked innocently. "Do you have something to say? Don't hold back on me now."

She let go her agitation and sighed, glancing at the clock. She'd been here over half an hour. "I need to be going." His close proximity, as well as this most affable mood, had her heart doing cartwheels. *He's a married man, Brenna.* A most attractive and congenial married man, to boot. Unless she wanted to feel like a bigger fool when Mrs. Hutton finally decided to show up in town, she'd best remember that.

"And Maddie? What about her?"

"I'm sorry, Mrs. Lane. My answer is still the same."

CHAPTER FORTY

*A*lone at her campsite, Nell absorbed the absolute beauty of the velvety black sky that stretched as far as her eye could see. She took a deep breath and let the chilly night air fill her lungs. Life was good. Once they had this herd corralled and readied for breaking, it would be even better. So many good-looking animals.

Nell tossed another branch overtop her crackling fire and watched the sparks dance into the darkness. Dog was stretched out on the ground, his nose between his paws and his side to the flames. She smiled at how his brows rose and fell as he watched her.

How are Charlie and the boys making out? After scouting the trail, they'd been pleased with the natural obstacles of the landscape that could help direct the horses on the course they wanted them to go. In the few instances where the logical choice would be to go otherwise, they'd stopped and gathered brush and, with the hammer and nails Charlie had thought to bring from the packhorse, they'd constructed barriers. Superficial, but the horses wouldn't know that. They'd see resistance, and turn the other way. Because of the time spent doing that, darkness had fallen by the time Charlie had dropped her off.

"You sure you don't mind staying alone?" he'd asked, standing so close that not thinking about their kiss in the kitchen was impossible. "I can easily stay. I'll just get up a bit earlier and walk the five miles back. Won't take a thing out of the black. I want to, Nell." He'd run his hand down her arm and stopped at the elbow, the touch intimate.

Well, she was having none of it and sent him on his way. She'd spent nights out alone tending the cattle. This wasn't any different. *You sure about that, Nell?* This was ridiculous. That rider, the stranger, was long gone. If he were still around, they would have seen traces of him, or run into him face-to-face. She liked the night. It had always been her friend.

She closed her eyes and concentrated on happy thoughts. Seth, his attempt to bake her a birthday cake going very badly wrong. Seth bringing in a small pine tree on Christmas morning and helping with the decorations. Seth, best man at her and Ben's wedding, smiling ear-to-ear. He'd always been there for her. What would his life have been without her around? Would he have found a woman and married?

That was a disturbing thought. Had she held him back from a life of his own? A wife? Children? Uncomfortable now, Nell stood and meandered out to where Coyote was hobbled a few feet from her camp. Dog got up and followed. She rested her forehead against Coyote's shoulder, letting her troubled thoughts ease away.

The horse took an awkward step, then lowered his muzzle back to the ground to continue cropping the grass. A pang of guilt for the foot-long leather strap of the hobbles pricked her heart. *I'm sorry*, she thought. She slung her arm over his back and ran her hands over his silky coat, loving the feel of it under her fingertips. Relief filled her when a shadowy impression eased through her veins like honey, telling her he didn't mind the hobbles. He was anticipating running with the wild horses.

Nell almost gasped at the desire radiating from him. Dog, who'd buddied up close, let go a lonesome whine, then pushed his nose into her hand, as if not wanting to be left out. Nell fought back the hot prickle of tears behind her eyes and rubbed her cheek against Coyote's side as she contemplated setting him free when the roundup was completed. She loved him, didn't want to part ways. He reached around and nudged her with his muzzle. Her heart slowed down. Seemed he didn't want that, either, and was content where he was. That's when she picked up a crunching sound in the grass beyond the light of her fire. Dog spun around and advanced a few feet and then stopped, his right paw tight to his chest as he pointed. Her gaze cut to the campfire, and her gun sitting on her blanket.

Was it too late? Too late to make a grab for it—and maybe get shot?

"Nell?" More steps in the grass. "Nell? Don't go and blow my head off."

Charlie? Dog bounded out to greet him. "What in Sam Hill are you doing here? I told you I was able and willing to stay out by myself. What do you have in that head of yours? Straw for brains?"

"Just settle down. When we started this venture, no one ever said anything about splitting up. That was my idea and I feel responsible—*for you*. Seth would have my tail in a corn husker if something happened to his sister under my watch."

"Is that the only reason? Seth doing you bodily harm?"

He shook his head. "You know better." His tone sent a ripple of awareness slipping down her back.

She glared, struggling to hold on to her anger. "Where's the black?"

"Just off in the trees. I'll go get him."

Nell watched him and Dog go, then reappear shortly after that. "I guess telling you to cut out now won't do a bit of good. Did you ever leave or have you been waiting in the trees watching me? As for you, Dog, some protector you are."

"Ease up. I didn't watch you from cover—just waited a little while before I showed my hand. As for Dog, he knows my scent. He came to visit me a time or two." Charlie chuckled.

She stomped over to her campsite. "Well, get your mount turned out so he can graze and come set up your bedroll. I know there's no way to talk you out of this." Coyote's head came up as Charlie led the black out to where the paint was hobbled.

She rattled the pot over her fire and scraped a few more beans onto her already dirty plate. "There's some grub left. Not much, though."

"Thanks. I also have mine." He came into camp, tossed his bedroll across the fire from her, and set his saddle nearby. He opened his saddlebag and pulled out his portion of the jerky they'd doled out when they'd split up, the last of some dried fruit, another can of beans. "It's gonna be good to get back and eat some real food. I was thinking about trying out the Silky Hen for supper and the fried chicken I keep hearing about." He ate a strip of his jerky. "What I wouldn't give for some right now. How about you?"

Does he think a little idle conversation will smooth things over? Well, his scheme wasn't going to work. Staying the night here put more strain on the black with the extra miles the gelding would have to travel in the morning, albeit at a walk.

She took a breath, and let it out, thinking about what these horses would do for the ranch. A means to hire more help. Then Seth could get well and maybe, just maybe, take a little time to court a wife. That brought a small smile to her lips as she imagined him gaining weight from being pampered and loved. But that only lasted a second. Her and Charlie's bickering from the past few days popped into her mind and her smile fizzled. Maybe Seth was better off staying a bachelor.

CHAPTER FORTY-ONE

*C*oyote's deep nicker rousted Charlie out of his sleep. He pulled his blanket up over his shoulder and snuggled deeper into his thick leather coat, shivering from the cold. Opening one eye, he glanced at the stars in search of the moon. It wasn't much past two. Still several hours to rest.

"Mm," Nell moaned in her sleep. "Seth . . ."

Charlie opened his eyes. He lifted his head and looked across the amber coals of the campfire to make sure she was all right. Last night, still gruff as all get-out, she'd wrapped up in her blanket and turned her back to him without a good-night.

She rolled to her back. "Get back . . ."

The sob at the end of her last word had him up and at her side in three strides. "Nell," he said. "Wake up. You're dreaming." She seemed so small and vulnerable in her blankets. Not knowing what to do exactly, he took her shoulder, shaking gently. "Nell?"

With a gasp, she bolted into his waiting arms and buried her face against his chest.

"Nell," he whispered against her hair. "You're all right. I'm right here. It's me, Charlie. Wake up."

"Charlie," she said shakily. "I finally remembered my pa. Seth has never spoken of him. Would never tell me anything about our father even if I asked. The memory was awful."

She wrested in a few deep breaths, then calmed in his arms. "Seth took me away from him to keep me safe. I was little, and

I guess I pushed those memories to the back of my mind. After our ma died, we ran away. I assumed that they both had died, but that's not true. We snuck away the night after Pa buried her."

Charlie laid her back on her bed and retrieved his own blankets from across the burned-out campfire, laying them next to hers. He pulled her close and she rested her head on his chest.

"Do you want me to build a fire for some light?" He gently smoothed her hair down her back and she snuggled in closer.

The shake of her head was almost imperceptible. "I just want to lie here with you . . ."

The horses snorted at something and moved around, probably unsettled by Nell's distress.

"Sometimes talking helps."

Several seconds went by in silence and he thought maybe she'd fallen back asleep. "I wish I could remember my mother," she said wistfully. "Or had a picture of her. It's hard going through life not knowing where you came from or the sound of your mama's voice."

He nodded. "Maybe this is just the first of more memories to come."

"I don't want to know about Pa. In my dream he was chasing Seth with a switch." She quivered and he stroked her back. "I was hidden away somewhere small and dark. Seth told me not to come out until he came for me. I had a tiny peephole and watched Seth dart away, and Pa take off after him."

She started to cry again and all Charlie knew how to do was hold her and whisper that she was all right, that he wouldn't leave her, that she was safe with him.

She took a deep breath and let it out. "Sometimes dreaming about a family of my own is all I ever do." Her voice was small, her hand gentle as it slowly traced circles on his chest.

He understood that all too well. Imagining Maddie happy and content, with a mother to love her. Would they ever be settled again? "I had a wife once," he said through a tight jaw. "And even more. We were a happy family, scraping out a living on not much more than love and a prayer. When Annie was taken from me, I didn't think I could go on. Didn't think I'd ever recover. It was like somebody opened me up with a knife and cut out my heart." He swallowed down a lump of grief. "A man is meant to have family around him, though, and I want that again. More children to hold in my lap and watch grow."

He kept his gaze on the stars when she lifted her head to look up into his face. At that moment he realized he'd been wrong about Nell. Even as young as she was, she was the strongest, bravest women he'd ever met. Tenacious. Loyal to a fault. The way she guarded Seth was heartwarming. She might not hold womanly things in high esteem, but that wasn't everything. She had an abundance of love just waiting to be shared. She would make an excellent mother for any child.

"Try to get some sleep," he said into her hair. "Tomorrow's going to be long and dangerous. You need to be alert. Close your eyes and dream about the land in the spring and how everything turns a soft, velvety green."

He felt her nod as he gazed at the Big Dipper still bright in the sky.

Her hand moved higher on his chest. "This feels nice," she whispered.

"You want to roll over so you can see the stars? It's a mighty fine show tonight, if I do say so myself. I'm always amazed how they glitter like water splashing down a creek bed of rocks in the sun."

She shook her head and hung on more firmly. "That's quite poetic, Charlie Rose."

Dog scooted closer and dropped his head onto Charlie's midsection. Charlie reached down and scratched the animal's head. "This is turning into a party."

"He scared me, Charlie. I'm not too proud anymore to say it." Her voice was soft and vulnerable.

"Your father?"

She shook her head again. "No. There was another stranger who came out to the ranch. The week before you showed up. I couldn't put my finger on why he seemed so evil, just a feeling I had inside, like when I can tell what the horses are feeling. All I wanted was for him to ride away. Leave and never come back. Guess it's me thinking about him that's brought back these memories of my pa. That's the only thing that makes any sense."

"Are you talking about the rider on the hill?" Charlie about stopped breathing. The week before he'd arrived? What was she talking about?

"No. A stranger in the ranch yard. Seth was still gone with the army horses and you hadn't arrived yet."

Fear gripped his insides. Tracking him, ahead of him—the stranger on the ridge, the footprints near the river. If whoever it was had been after him, wouldn't they have made a move by now? Or was Galante biding his time for some reason? Would he make a move on Maddie if he couldn't get to Charlie? He wanted to jump on his horse and beat his way back to Logan Meadows right now in the dark. But he couldn't. This job had to be done. "Try to forget about him now. He's long gone." *I hope.* "We'll get our job finished tomorrow, then figure out who's been watching you out at the ranch, and why."

Nell sat up on her elbow and looked down into his face. Through the darkness he could barely make out the curve of her cheek. "What's wrong?" she asked. "I can hear it in your voice. There's something you're not telling me."

"Sh, now," he said. "It's time for sleep. All the rest can wait."

She nodded and snuggled back onto his chest. A hush fell back over the campsite and her breathing evened out. Everything was quiet, except the thudding of Charlie's heart.

CHAPTER FORTY-TWO

*N*ell sat loose and comfortable in her saddle even though her stomach clenched with excitement. Some thirty feet from the trail, behind a stand of trees, she drew in a deep, steadying breath and tried to calm her nerves. What she wouldn't give right now for a strong, hot cup of coffee. All she'd had since rising was a handful of beef jerky.

She went over in her mind all that needed to be checked before taking on an endeavor of such magnitude, knowing full well her cinch was tight, Coyote's hooves divested of even the smallest grit, her supple, split-leather reins knotted, just in case she were to lose one. Her bandanna was tied around her neck in case the dust got bad and she needed to cover her nose. Swallowing down an egg-sized ball of disquiet, she clenched the stock whip that was neatly curled and held in her right gloved hand against her thigh. Her heart beat triple time.

Charlie and the herd should be here any moment.

He'd departed camp around five, saying he should be passing her pickup point around seven or eight. That gave him time to go at an easy pace back to the herd, get around behind the horses, and then start them off. The five miles at a gallop wouldn't take long. "Don't get antsy," he'd told them all yesterday. "We don't know what problems I might encounter. I'll get there when I get there and not a minute before. Just be ready."

Nell's thoughts circled around to the subject she'd been trying to avoid by staying busy. Charlie. And lying in his arms most of the night. He'd been so tender. He must have been a devoted husband, judging by the way he'd treated her. Just his tone had the power to chase away her fears and calm her racing heart. When he'd finally told her about his wife, he'd even said more that she hadn't picked up on in her drowsy state. That he wanted *more* children. That meant he must have had a child, or children, who had perished in the wagon accident. Poor Charlie. A surge of compassion pressed her heart. That fact must have been just too hard for him to share with Seth.

Where did they go from here? Anywhere? He'd alluded to wanting a family again—to mend his broken heart. Brenna had that family built in and ready to go. Was that the thing that kept attracting him to her side? But if that were so and he didn't feel anything for Nell, how could he possibly hold her so gently all night long? Anger threatened to spoil her mood. She'd not speculate things she didn't have the answer for. She cherished last night. And if she read him correctly, trusted the sense she felt from him, he had, as well. That was good enough for her.

Dog whined, unhappy she insisted he stay put by her side. He sat at attention beside Coyote's hip, watching up the trail as if he knew exactly what she was anticipating. Coyote's ears flicked forward, then back. He seemed calm and collected. She'd know when the herd was close because he'd be hard to hold.

She closed her eyes and visualized the section of trail along which she had to drive the horses. For the most part the ground was level, with an easy downhill slant. But toward the end, where Jake would be waiting, there was a section of land that years ago had given way to a small slide. They'd have to go over and down a good twenty feet, and at a very steep angle. She'd taken Coyote over it several times yesterday to give him confidence when the time came, but the obstacle would be different going at a full run. Now she just needed to bolster her own resolve.

All would be fine. She'd been riding as far back as she could remember. She'd just sit tight and let Coyote do the work.

Dog leaped to his feet and barked. Coyote's head snapped up and his body quivered with excitement.

Thundering hooves announced their arrival. Nell reached down and steadied Coyote with her hand to his withers.

The first horse galloped around the bend.

With a blaring neigh, Coyote reared, but she held him steady, talking softly but keeping a firm hold on his mouth. He tossed his head and she spun him in a circle. "Whoa, now," she said deeply. "Whoa, Coyote. Your time's coming, boy. Just hold on. Let some of them pass."

The pounding of hooves to earth was almost deafening. Nell searched for Charlie amid the galloping horses but with everything happening so fast, that was next to impossible. Horses raced by. It was all she could do to keep her horse from grabbing the bit and joining them. Dog was gone. She hoped he had sense enough to stay out from under the mass of horses or he'd be killed.

A loud crack rent the air.

Charlie?

She searched the far side as the horses galloped past. Where was he? Frantic to see him, she scanned from one side to the other. There. Her heart swelled at the sight. His hat was low over his eyes and seeing his bandanna up, she yanked up hers, getting ready.

In a matter of seconds she'd let Coyote go. She counted, held her breath, then leaned forward and yelled, "Hee-yah!" giving Coyote his head.

With a ferocious snap, Coyote bolted away. In seconds they pulled in next to the horses and their ground-eating strides at about the middle of the herd. Nostrils flared. Manes and tails flew everywhere. It was the most exhilarating feeling she'd ever experienced. "Hee-yah! Hee-yah!" she cried.

Fresh, Coyote had no problem keeping pace. Horses surged

behind them, then moved around like a river, drawing Nell in until she and her mount were surrounded. A dark roan veered in and clipped the bay in front of them. Coyote jerked up, trying to keep his hooves from getting entangled. His footing once again strong—and Nell's heart in her throat—she crouched close to his neck, watching between his ears as they galloped. Squinting through the dust, she was surprised when the throng of horses curved right, when they should have gone left. The bush barrier they'd constructed yesterday hadn't held them. She needed to do something, and fast.

Taking hold of Coyote's mouth, she guided him back to the outside of the galloping herd, now urging him on for all she was worth. She squeezed with her legs and he gave her more speed. They passed two horses, then three, then winged ahead of a handful. Coyote's belly expanded as he gulped in huge amounts of air, giving her all the swiftness she asked.

With a frightful jerk, she suddenly recognized the lay of the land. She hadn't put the pieces together yesterday, but the small buffalo jump was approaching about a mile ahead. She needed to get the wild horses turned before they all went over.

"Hee-yah!" she yelled into Coyote's ear, now desperate to get to the front. "Let's go! Let's go!"

Coyote surged forward. She'd never ridden him this fast. She couldn't imagine where he found the energy. His breathing now rasped in her ears but he didn't waver, and he didn't slow down. At this rate she didn't have much time. The trees ahead were thinning. The mustangs labored, some glistened in their own sweat. Still, they didn't have her weight to carry, or that of the saddle. They galloped on with no signs of slowing down.

"Faster, faster, boy," she chanted over and over into Coyote's ears as she moved her hands along his neck, matching his strides, urging him on. Doing whatever it took to help her courageous mount forward. They needed to be in the front of the herd to be able to turn them. Certain death was fast approaching.

Charlie reined up when Nell bolted out of the trees to take command of the herd. He eased back, slowing the black to a lope, then down to the jog. His horse labored for breath but he'd done well. Soon the herd was out of sight, and Charlie veered toward a hill that was dense with trees but would be in a direct line to the corral, cutting off several miles. He let the gelding take the first part slowly, but after he'd caught his breath, Charlie asked for more power to the top, to where the trees became sparse.

He reached for his canteen but was surprised when he caught sight of the herd in the distance running along an elevated plateau. His brows dropped. They must have veered off the path!

His breath caught. Where was Nell? Had she fallen? Suddenly a very ominous feeling filled his heart. He searched the area the horses were heading. The buffalo jump! The other one Nell had told him about was directly ahead.

"No!" he yelled at the top of his lungs. A flash of yellow toward the front of the herd caught his eye. Nell! Standing in her stirrups as she cracked her whip over her head in an effort to turn the mass of horses. He'd been a damned fool to let her take the herd alone. "Turn, turn." His whispered plea lodged in his throat.

His heart thwacked painfully against his rib as he watched in stunned horror.

CHAPTER FORTY-THREE

A light tapping at the door barely registered in Brenna's head as she went about her living room with her duster in hand. Saturday morning was allotted to household chores. After that she'd get to her mending, and then baking. Stevie and Prichard, already finished with their short list of things to do, had gone off to Shady Creek to try to catch something for supper. The girls' giggles, coming from their bedroom where they were making their bed with fresh linen, made Brenna smile.

"Hello? Anyone home?"

Mr. Hutton? Outside?

Brenna crossed the room and stopped at the door. She pushed some wayward bangs from her moist forehead with the back of her wrist and frowned at her soiled apron. What in the world could he want today? He knocked again, giving her no choice but to open up.

"Hello, Mrs. Lane." His face was bright with something. There were no visible signs that he'd been sick, and he looked relatively healthy. *Must be all the meals we've fed him over the past two weeks.*

"Hello, Mr. Hutton. What can I do for you?" *Again.* Ashamed at her unkind thoughts, she plastered a smile on her face.

When he shifted his weight, she noticed he had his hand held behind his back. "First, I just wanted to thank you again for your excellent care over the extent of my illness. I don't know what I would have done without you."

She warmed. He had a way of doing that to her without even trying. "You're welcome." She stepped back, realizing she was being rude. "Would you like to come in? I'm sure you're ready for a change of scenery."

He inclined his head. "Indeed I would. Thank you."

She hadn't thought he'd accept. Didn't he notice she was in her work clothes? As she clicked the door closed, a soft mewing brought her spinning around to face him. She tried to see what he held behind his back. "What on earth do you have there?"

He bent over and placed a tiny tiger-striped kitten on the floor between them. "She was crying outside my window this morning. I thought your girls might want to have her, that is, if no one comes to claim her. She can't be more than a month old."

A cat? She had enough mouths to feed already without adding a pet to the mix. "That's a kind gesture, but we couldn't—"

"A kitty," Jane squealed. "A kitty!" She scampered over and dropped to her knees. As she picked up the animal and snuggled it to her beaming face, Penny and Maddie followed her into the living room, their expressions alight with excitement. People all the way down on Main Street probably heard Jane's enthusiastic announcement. "Thank you, Mr. Hutton," Jane said between nuzzles. "Thank you so much."

Mr. Hutton's bright smile and engaging eyes made Brenna bristle. Now she was going to have to be the big meanie. "We can't possibly keep her, Mr. Hut—" The words died in her throat as her girls stared up at her with pleading eyes. They'd been begging for a kitten for years. Jane placed the rascal back on the floor and the animal instantly hopped onto her daughter's legs, snagging her socks with claws like little fishhooks. Brenna blinked. "A pet is a big responsibility."

"I'll take care of her," Penny begged. "I promise."

"I'll help her." Jane nodded.

"And me, Mama," Maddie said softly.

That about sealed the deal. Breaking her daughters' hearts was the last thing she wanted to do on an early Saturday morning. "I guess you win, Mr. Hutton." She smiled but knew her expression fell short because he gave her a bemused smile that slowly died away.

He extended his hands in a pleading manner. "Girls," he said, watching the three circled around the mewing kitten, "I should have asked your mother before I brought the kitten over."

Oh, sure, *now* he decides to be sensible with Penny, Jane, and Maddie gazing at her like kittens approaching a saucer of milk. That image made her soften up. She stifled a giggle. "As if I could say no now? Of course we'll keep her. The only question is, what are we going to name her?"

Mr. Hutton's smile was back.

The back door flew open and then banged shut as Stevie and Prichard came into the room. The kitten skittered under the sofa as the boys came to a screeching halt in front of their soon-to-be teacher. Brenna could tell they were dying to know what was going on but were afraid to speak in front of Mr. Hutton. Penny reached under the sofa and drew out the fluff ball.

"Oh," Stevie said, his voice full of delight. "Do we get to—"

"Yes," the three girls sang in unison. Jane's sweet smile warmed Brenna's heart. "Mr. Hutton gave her to us."

Mr. Hutton gestured for Brenna to step over by the window. "I'm sorry. I can see I've put you in a difficult position." He chuckled, apparently not very sorry at all. "And since I have, I was wondering if I could treat you to dinner at the Silky Hen as reparation. Perhaps tonight, or tomorrow?"

Brenna felt her eyes go wide. What on earth was he up to? A married man asking her out? "Why?"

"Why?" He rubbed his forehead. "Well, for one, to thank you for your expert care in my time of need."

"I told you, I was happy to be able to assist."

"And for taking such wonderful care of my class."

Brenna swallowed, trying to be discreet. Her heart went pitter patter but she was not at all sure she should say yes. But then, they did work together. Perhaps dinner with a married man wasn't such a horrible thing to do, as long as it was in a public restaurant and was strictly business—

At her long delay his brows drew together and disappointment flared in his eyes.

Glancing over her shoulder to make sure the children were still occupied with the new member of the family, she led him closer to the door so they wouldn't be overheard. "As long as you understand that this is business. We could use the time to talk about the school Christmas pageant and the spring book drive."

He chuckled again and she couldn't imagine what she'd said to make him do so. She struggled to ignore how comfortable he acted standing in her house in a pair of dungarees, his worn boots, and a dark-blue chambray shirt that appeared impossibly soft, just begging to be touched. Her imagination took flight and she had to rein in her thoughts before they got her into trouble.

"Yes, we could discuss those, but I also hoped we could make the occasion a little more personal. You're an adult and so am I. What could it hurt?" He held her gaze so steadily that she was sure he must have plenty of practice hoodwinking unsuspecting females. "I mean, that is—"

Seemed he'd lost his bravado.

When she remained silent, he shrugged. "If you're not interested, just say so, Brenna. May I call you that? I feel we know each other quite well by now."

Scalding heat rushed to her face. She tried to focus on the children playing with the kitten, what they were saying and doing. But no matter what she tried, his soul-searching eyes had everything inside her all jumbled up.

"*Mr.* Hutton."

Surprised, he took a quick step back.

"I'm sorry." She glanced again at the floor to find her cool tone had drawn her children's attention. "May I please speak with you out on the porch?"

"Yes, of course." She went out and he followed. "What have I done that has you so upset? In all our days together I don't think I've ever seen this expression on your face."

She spun around to face him. "You must think me a silly fool, Mr. Hutton."

"Gregory. And why?"

"Do you think me so desperate that I'll fall at the feet of any suitor? Or be a married man's mistress? Thankful for any scrap of attention that is given me?"

Again, the chuckle. She was getting ready to show him how funny a slap across the face would be. She might be poor but she was a proper lady, and a proper lady she would stay.

He took a step back and his eyes dropped from her face to her feet as if he were clearly mixed up and looking for an answer. "Forgive me if I have no idea what you're talking about. Why don't you start at the very beginning so I can make sense of it." He cleared his throat. "If that's not too much to ask."

"All right, I will. While straightening up in your house I found . . ." She glanced away, spotting Dwight riding up her street again. What was with Dwight, anyway? She wished he'd just go back to New Meringue and stay there. "Just a moment. Wait until Dwight goes by."

Mr. Hutton followed her line of vision, nodding back to Dwight when Hoskins acknowledged them. They stood in silence until he was out of hearing distance.

"Just wonderful," she said in a sour tone.

"What?"

"Now he has more gossip ammunition. I can just hear it now. *Brenna Lane has taken to entertaining married men in her home. Has she no shame?* Rumors will fly like bats at sundown."

"Who's married?" His hand came up and touched his chest. "Are you talking about me?"

"Who else?"

Shaking his head, he walked over to the two chairs and table on the far side of the porch. "Sorry. But I need to sit down. I have no idea what you're talking about." He sat and she followed suit, her mind swimming with confusion.

"What gave you the impression I was married? Did I call my wife's name in my delirium? Is there an indentation I'm not aware of?" He pointed to his bare ring finger. "Please, tell me. I'm dying with curiosity."

Either he was slyer than a wily fox, or somehow she'd made a horrible mistake. "I found your marriage certificate when I put the strawberry jam away in your kitchen. The one with the horse manure stains." At the memory of that travesty, a blush crept up her neck. "I'm sorry about that whole incident, by the way."

He waved it away. "An accident. But I assure you, that isn't *my* marriage certificate, but my brother and his wife's."

"But your name was there. Gregory Hutton and Miss Helen Boyd."

He made a sound, the mixture between a chuckle and a sad sigh. "So that's why you've been so sensitive of late. I've pondered the reason for days." He reached over, took her hand, and cocooned it between his. "My brother's name was Greer. Greer Hutton. We were twins."

That explains the birthday.

She dropped her gaze to her hand in his. His touch was gentle and had her totally distracted. "But I read it with my own eyes. I *saw* your name."

When he shook his head a shadow of sadness crossed his face, making him appear years older. "You just thought you saw it. The stain covers most of Greer's first name, but, if I recall correctly, the *g-r-e* is still visible. Your brain filled in what you were expecting to be there. An honest mistake, to be sure."

"But then why do you have it, if it's not yours?"

He blinked, and stared down the road toward town. "Because they're both dead. Killed last year in a ferryboat accident."

How sad. With her free hand Brenna reached over and covered their hands, giving his a squeeze. She could see he was eaten up with grief. Not only a brother but a twin, and his wife. No wonder such a qualified teacher had taken such a low-paying job. He was running from painful memories. Hoping to start fresh. She'd never guessed.

"How on earth then did you receive letters from—"

He crooked a brow.

"I'm sorry. The letters were right there in plain sight. From Helen Hutton? How is that possible?"

His boyish smile told her he wasn't angry with her snooping. "They're from my mother. My mother and father, Harriett and Oglethorpe Hutton. They still live in Poppyville, Pennsylvania, where I grew up."

"Oh, Gregory," she whispered. "I'm so sorry for your loss. I can't imagine the pain you've gone through." She gazed into his eyes.

"I thought a change of scenery would do me good." A wistful smile played around his mouth. "A new town. New friends."

When she nodded, something in his eyes changed, making her feel like the most beautiful, desirable woman in the world. "I'm so glad you did."

CHAPTER FORTY-FOUR

*M*ustering every ounce of strength left in her body, Nell leaned forward and cracked the whip over her head for the fifth time. A loud pop sent the horses next to her veering away. The rest galloped straight for the cliff. For one moment of rest she gripped the saddle horn and just held on. Enough of that; she had to do more.

"You can do it," she shouted to Coyote. Her horse labored with every stride. How could she think of rest for herself even one second when Coyote had been running flat out for so long? "Almost there," she shouted. "Faster, Coyote, get up there!"

By sheer will she propelled him along, but every rasp of his breath was like a lance to her heart. They were almost to the front of the herd. If they could just get to the lead, and stay there, she was sure she'd be able to get most of the horses turned. She didn't want to lose a single one. Not because she wanted them for the ranch but because they were beautiful animals, deserving to live until their natural death.

She hated to do it, but the time had come. All her wiggle room was gone. She had to act now, or lose the horses and perhaps her own life. Stuffing the whip under her thigh, she took the extra length of her split-leather reins that hung down on the right side of Coyote and gathered them. With force, she whipped them over and back on Coyote's flanks as hard as she could, lashing him with a brutal sting. Surprised, the gelding sprang forward and increased his speed. She dug her heels into his sides and lashed him again.

She felt every one of his muscles strain. Dig deep. He lowered his head, flattened out his topline, and passed several horses. She could see the edge of the drop clearly. They would be there soon. Sweat dripped into her eyes and she tried to blink it away. They were on the outside track. Grabbing the whip again, she cracked the long, braided leather above her head. Again and again. Horses began swinging away. They were thinning out, turning as she'd hoped.

"Hee-yah!" she screamed. "Hee-yah, hee-yah!"

Like liquid buffeted with the curved edge of a bowl, the herd swung away from the cliff in a gentle arc. It was a moment she'd never forget. The wind in her face. The scrabble and screeching on the shale torturing her ears. The edge of the cliff just inches away, where the rocky earth, a hundred feet below, waited for its next victim.

They'd done it! The horses were turned! Galloping back toward the correct route to the corral. *Thank you*, she found herself thinking. *Thank you, thank you. Thank you, God, for sparing our lives.*

A pebble kicked up by one of the horses in front flew into Nell's face. She jerked at the pain and wiped at the blood dripping into her eyes, all the while never taking her sight from the direction they galloped. A quick scan of the animals told her that, from what she could tell, all the horses had turned. Now she had to get them back to the trail and into Jake's hands. She pulled up on her brave mount, giving him a few strides to catch his breath. Reaching down, she patted his hot, sweat-soaked neck, feeling the stickiness through her leather glove. "Good boy, Coyote. Good boy."

Charlie loped into the box canyon knowing full well he'd be the only one there. A buckboard filled with hay was parked in the area, delivered several days ago, judging by the age of the tracks. Charlie's heart rippled with fear for Nell. He'd seen her valiant effort. Anyone else would've forsaken the horses and saved themselves. But not Nell. She gave her all and then some. He couldn't believe his eyes as she'd ridden so close to the front and come so darn close to going over. He'd held his breath and prayed for all he was worth.

At the water trough on the outside of the pen, he gave the black a short drink, then went over and checked on the packhorse Gabe had tethered inside at the back of the corral.

With everything in its place, Charlie rode back a quarter mile and waited.

The long, low rumble that preceded the horses came sooner than he'd expected. They arrived still loping, but not very fast. Sweat covered their coats. He cracked his whip and hollered at the top of his lungs. Tired now, they turned quite handily into the box canyon as some slowed to a trot. Their sides heaved and their eyes were dull with exhaustion. He caught sight of Gabe, and then Jake, still pushing from behind. Searching around, he didn't see Nell. The three men drove the horses into the corral. Gabe rode into the fray of excited mustangs and made for the back side of the corral to retrieve the packhorse and bring him out, while Jake and Charlie dismounted and swung the gates closed. When Gabe reached them, they opened up and let him out.

Jake and Gabe grinned from ear to ear.

"Either of you see Nell?"

"I did when I picked up my leg," Jake said. "Why? You think something happened to her?"

Charlie didn't have the energy to explain everything right now. "No. Just wondering." He scanned the entry of the canyon. A whoosh of relief gave way when Nell came up the bottleneck on foot, leading Coyote, with Dog at her heels. "Here she comes." He strode out to meet her. As he got closer he could see a streak of blood on her temple and down her cheek. She took a handkerchief from her pocket and pressed it to her forehead.

When they were within shouting distance, she called out to him. "Charlie?"

She obviously didn't understand why he was walking out to meet her. Questions crossed her eyes like clouds moving over the sun as she searched for answers. There was no way for her to know he had to see her face. Touch her skin. Prove to himself that she was indeed alive and she wasn't a mirage conjured up by the longing in his heart.

"Charlie?" she said again. "What's wrong? The horses are in the corral. What?"

He didn't say a single thing, just pulled her into his arms and crushed his lips to hers. Staked claim to her mouth, her heart. Instantly she responded, surprising him. This was different from their first kiss in the kitchen. That had been soft and inquisitive. This was hard, and perhaps a little angry. The picture of her almost going over the cliff unleashed his passion and terrified him at the same time. Hungry for her, he moved from her lips and kissed her neck, then made his way up to her ear. He loved the way she felt in his arms. "I can't live without you, Nell," he murmured. He could never marry Brenna when it was Nell he loved, when she was the woman who fueled his blood.

She pushed on his chest until he gave her enough room to lean back and see into his face. She reached up and traced his lips with the tips of her fingers. "Charlie," she whispered. "What's gotten into you, cowboy? Did you fall off and thump your head or something?" Her hungry, desire-filled gaze stoked his fire.

"You could've been killed. And after you promised you wouldn't take any unnecessary chances. I should have known better than to trust you with your life."

"How did you know?"

"I saw the whole thing from the top of the ridge. You scared the life out of me." He pulled her into his arms and kissed her again until they both were breathing hard.

Nell finally pushed away and a wobbly smile moved her lips. She reached over and placed her hand on Coyote's drooping neck. "I'd do the same again."

Taking a step back, he laced his fingers through hers, warmth filling him at the picture of their entwined hands. "Yeah, I know you would. That's what terrifies me." He gently pushed the hair from off her forehead so he could see the slice half the size of a dime directly above her left eyebrow.

"It's nothing," she said as she started for the corral, dragging him with her since their hands were still together. He tugged her to a stop far enough away from Gabe and Jake that the two couldn't hear their conversation. Both young men still gaped openmouthed, probably flabbergasted from the kiss and entwined hands.

"I have to go," he said.

Her brow fell. "Why?"

"Something you mentioned last night. It's bothered me ever since and I need to get to town to check on something."

"Check on something?" The light that danced in her eyes went out. "Don't you mean *someone*?"

Does she know about Maddie? He thought about their conversations and realized he'd said more last night than he'd wanted. And the way she sensed so much with animals, it wouldn't be difficult for her to put the puzzle together. That had to be it. "Yes. Then you understand why that someone means everything to me. I'll take the packhorse since he's fresh." He started for the corral again but glanced over his shoulder when she didn't reply, noting the straight hard line of her mouth that only moments before had been soft and kissable.

Was his fatherly protectiveness over Maddie that hard to understand? Was she jealous of a child? Confused, he wondered if he'd made a mistake. He thought she cared for him, but maybe she only wanted something fleeting.

He unsaddled the black and put his rig on the packhorse. Jake and Gabe wandered over, their faces still flushed with color. "What're you doing?" Gabe asked.

"I have some business in town that won't keep. I'll stop by the ranch and let Seth know we've arrived. I'm sure he'll be up as soon as he gathers some grub to bring along."

Jake crossed his arms over his chest, probably perturbed at being abandoned. "Yeah, well tell him to send a lot. We're hungry. Some steaks will fill the bill right fine. Bread, coffee, a pie or two."

"Or three," Gabe pitched in.

Charlie nodded. Finished with saddling, he slipped his boot into the stirrup and swung abroad his new mount. "I'll tell him." Nell still stood where he'd left her, the look on her face saying she never cared if she saw him again.

He didn't understand women at all. No, sir, not one little bit.

CHAPTER FORTY-FIVE

*B*efore going to Brenna's home to put this sham to rest, Charlie stopped by the sheriff's office. If he had to be watching his back trail from this day forward, then he could use some help doing it.

He poked his head through the door. Thom Donovan sat at the desk flipping through some papers. "You have a minute, deputy?"

"Sure. I'm just going through wanted posters. We get so many it's difficult to keep up with them." He gestured to the potbelly stove in the corner of the room. "Help yourself. The pot was fresh about three hours ago." He chuckled. "And don't mind Ivan. He takes up position in front of the stove and stays there all day, if I let him."

Charlie hadn't had a cup of coffee for a day and a half. "Thanks." He stepped over the dog and poured a mug of the thick brew. This would stand the hair on the back of his neck. He took a long guzzle, liking the way the dark liquid heated him all the way down to his belly. He walked behind the desk and gazed at the posters over Donovan's shoulder.

"Tandy Smith," Charlie said under his breath. He took another drink of his coffee. "Not much of a name for a bank robber—but a darn good bounty on his head. Eight hundred dollars."

"Don't let the name fool you." Thom pointed to the small print under the picture. "Says he has an unknown partner. They've successfully pulled off countless robberies and are also wanted for seven counts of murder. Not quite as notorious as that scoundrel Jesse James. Albert and I sure heaved a sigh of relief last April when we read the news." Thom shook his head. "Killed by a member of his own gang."

The deputy pushed the posters aside. "Well, enough of that. What brings you to the office, Charlie? Last I knew you and Nell and the boys were up in the hills rounding up horses. Were you successful?"

The pit of his stomach dropped at the mention of Nell's name. He didn't know what was up with her. "Yeah. Brought the horses in this morning, actually." He could see the wheels turning in the deputy's head, wondering what was so important to bring Charlie all the way into town.

"And?"

"I have a history. Just wanted to let you and Sheriff Preston know in case it shows up here in Logan Meadows."

"Go on."

"I'm from New Mexico. Got into a scuffle there and a boy got hurt. By now he may be dead."

Thom listened intently.

"In the Wilsonville saloon someone shoved me and Dan Galante spilled his whiskey down the front of his shirt. When everyone laughed he got furious. He was drunk. Challenged me to a gunfight. When I couldn't talk him down, I tried to walk out. Galante drew. If the bartender hadn't yelled, he would have shot me in the back. I fired, intent on winging him, but he dove and the bullet caught him in the gut. A seventeen-year-old kid." Charlie gazed at the ceiling for several long moments. "I was cleared by the law, but the boy's father was adamant he'd get even with me. Infection set in, making recovery long and hard. And like I said, he may now be dead. Galante gave me this scar when I tried to talk sense into him." He pointed to his cheek. "I thought it best if I cut my ties and moved on. I'm no killer, and I don't want to become one. But I'll defend myself"—*and what's mine*—"if I have to."

The deputy pushed back his chair and stood, heading for the coffeepot. He refilled his cup. "You have reason to believe you've been trailed?"

"Yes."

"What's the name of this fellow?"

"Grover Galante. But he could've hired someone. He had the means. That rider Nell saw on the ridge at the ranch wasn't the first. I just learned there had been another stranger out there before I showed up. I believe he was looking for me."

Charlie reined up at the end of Brenna's street and dismounted. Now that the time had come, it felt as if boulders had had a landslide in his stomach. He removed his hat and pulled his arm over his brow, thinking how much he needed a bath and a shave. Should he wait? Get cleaned up? As if of their own accord, his feet moved slowly up the street toward Brenna's home.

Standing outside the picket fence, he looped his reins around a spike. Laughter came from within. A multitude of happy voices carrying on at the same time made it sound like a party. Was Maddie better off here in this family? The thought tortured his heart. He didn't have a home. Or a mother for her. And given Nell's reaction, he wasn't likely to find a mother there.

Had Maddie forgotten his promise to come for her and given up on him? How long was a little girl's memory?

A loud squeal, followed by another round of laughter, made his decision for him. He collected his reins and went to mount up when the front door opened. Mr. Hutton stepped out onto the porch, followed by Brenna and all the children. Maddie came last, carrying a tiny gray kitten.

Brenna broke out into a smile when she saw him standing in front of her fence. "Why hello, Mr. Rose. You must be here for your mending. I started to think you'd forgotten."

His mending? He *had* forgotten. "Yes, ma'am."

As she hurried back into the house, Penny took the kitten from Maddie's hands, went over to one of the chairs, and set the little animal on the seat. It mewed loudly, drawing more giggles. Without any trouble at all, the fluff ball scampered up the backside of the chair and teetered on the top, as if putting on a show for the children.

"Let's name her Tracy," the middle girl said, fluffing the kitten's fur. "That's pretty."

One of the boys frowned. "Naw, that's a person's name. I don't like it."

Maddie's face brightened. "Skippy sounds like a kitty," she offered. Actually, the name sounded like a puppy to Charlie, but he was pleased when all the kids nodded to his daughter's suggestion.

Mr. Hutton regarded him with a pleasant smile on his face. He came down the steps and held out his hand. "Good to see you again, Mr. Rose."

Charlie dragged his gaze away from Maddie. "Th-thank you." He wasn't quite sure how to proceed. A plucked chicken couldn't have been more uncomfortable. "I, ah—"

Brenna was back, breezing down the steps with her arms full. "Here you are. Washed, mended, and ironed. That'll be thirty-five cents."

"Thank you. I appreciate you doing this."

"Not at all, Mr. Rose, er—Charlie." She smiled.

He paid her, set his items on the seat of his saddle, and glanced up to find Maddie watching from the veranda. Her head, tipped to the side, alerted him she was listening intently as she tried to hear their conversation. The other children had stopped their chatter, and had turned to see what she was doing. She took an uncertain step forward and one of the boys set his hand on her shoulder, as if to make sure she didn't go too close to the edge.

"Pa?" He saw her mouth the one word as her face lit up with joy and uncertainty.

He pushed past Mr. Hutton and Brenna, crossed the yard, and from the edge of the porch scooped his daughter into his embrace.

"Maddie," he breathed before his throat closed with tears. The feel of her in his arms almost dropped him to his knees.

"Mr. Rose!" Brenna shrieked, running to his side. She gripped his arm with the strength of a bear. "Put the child down this instant!"

CHAPTER FORTY-SIX

*I*rritation over her stupidity sizzled inside her chest. How could she continue to be so senseless day after day? She fell for Charlie's charm every time, forgetting all too quickly that he had some unspoken bond with Brenna. The fact he'd ridden all these miles today, after days in the saddle, even after their encounter last night under the stars and their kisses in the box canyon—probably a goodbye, a what-might-have-been—told her he'd never truly be hers. If she didn't want to go on suffering each time that cowboy did a reversal, she had to put a stop to this one-sided relationship. The best way to do that, and make sure she didn't weaken and go back on her intentions, was to do it in front of both Charlie and Brenna. Clear the way—and the air. Then she could start fresh, a life without a man named Charlie Rose.

But on top of that, a forewarning had hit her the second he'd ridden away. The sensation of an oncoming tempest, like the one she'd had in the mercantile, and then again in the stage when Maddie had arrived. It was urgent, and hot. She didn't know what it meant, but she intended to find out.

Nell arrived in front of Brenna's home, surprised to see that Charlie had only just arrived himself. When he moved she steeled herself, prepared to watch him sweep Brenna into his embrace, but instead he passed her by. It was Maddie he hugged, bundling her into his arms. The little tyke wrapped her small arms around his neck, and held on for dear life as he rocked her back and forth, her face buried in his neck. *What is going on?*

Brenna hurried to Charlie's side and gripped his arm in an effort to get the child back. She turned toward Mr. Hutton. "Gregory, help me! He's gone mad. He may do harm to Maddie."

Maddie pulled back. She laid her hands over Charlie's face for several seconds, feeling its contour and shapes, then a smile brighter than a July sun moved across her expression. Cupping his face between her palms, she kissed his cheeks, forehead, and even the tip of his nose. Nell gasped. On the porch, the other children's mouths gaped open in surprise.

"I knew you'd come, Pa," her little voice shivered. "I just knew you would. I never gave up hoping and praying."

All of a sudden little pieces started fitting into place—the way he'd watched her at the picnic, his interest in Brenna, him talking as if he'd had a child and now here she was conjured up out of thin air. But why had he concealed her? And why had he let Nell make a fool of herself going on and on about wanting children? He should have been truthful with her then.

"Maddie. Maddie," Charlie's tortured reply made Nell wince. "I'm so sorry it took me so long, little darlin'. I'm so sorry."

Maddie was Charlie's daughter. Sent ahead on the stage? How had Brenna's Aunt Cora become involved?

Brenna continued to pull on Charlie's arm, fear marring her pretty face.

Charlie took a step back and turned to face everyone. Nell knew the exact moment he spotted her. Their eyes locked. Against her will a surge of longing took hold of her soul.

Fuming, Brenna stepped back and stomped her foot. "Charlie Rose! Put Maddie down!"

He shook his head. "No, Brenna. Maddie's my daughter. I'll never put her down again."

Nell dismounted and tossed her reins over Brenna's picket fence next to the packhorse. She went into the yard and up to

Charlie. She touched Maddie's slender leg. "Hello, Maddie," she said. The smile on Maddie's face was angelic.

"Hi, Mrs. Page," she replied. She kissed Charlie one more time on his cheek, then laid her face against his whisker-stubbed jaw. That child wasn't going to let Charlie go anytime soon.

"So Charlie Rose is your pa, then?" Nell asked softly. Close beside her, Charlie's gaze caressed her face. She craved to feel his lips on hers again, the way he'd kissed her today in front of Gabe and Jake. She dared a glance up through her lashes and lost herself in his eyes.

Maddie nodded. "But his name's not Charlie Rose. It's Tristan Axelrose. And I'm Maddie Axelrose."

Brenna gasped again. The other children stood silently on the porch. The kitten had long since jumped down and picked her way through the sparse grass. She rubbed back and forth against Charlie's boot, or Tristan's boot, or whatever the man Nell was going to marry called himself.

Nell felt a smile coming on as she gazed into Charlie's eyes. "Tristan Axelrose?"

He shrugged and the color of his face deepened.

When Charlie took a step away, Brenna gripped the sleeve of his shirt. "You can't imagine I'll just let you walk out of here on your word. This goes against everything inside me. I can't let you take her."

"I understand. And it does my heart good to know you've loved my little girl just like she was one of your own. Ask her few questions about where she's from. And her ma's name. I'll be able to corroborate. She brought her crocheted doll with her. The one she calls Beatrix. You still have her, Maddie?"

When Maddie nodded, Jane dashed into the house. She returned with the doll and set her into Maddie's arms.

A fond smile appeared on Charlie's face when he saw the toy. "Miss Baxter, your Aunt Cora cared for Maddie in Wilsonville. She's the one who suggested she bring Maddie to you in Logan Meadows. Until I could get here myself."

Brenna straightened, her eyes softening. "She cared for Maddie?"

Charlie reached over and placed a hand on Brenna's shoulder. "I'm sorry she didn't make it here, Brenna. It's a real shame. She had a heart of gold, for sure. Took wonderful care of Maddie. I didn't learn of her passing until Nell told me at the school picnic. I couldn't be more sorry for your loss—*our* loss—even if she were my own aunt."

Still cradled in Charlie's embrace, Maddie's smile faded.

"Honey, what happened to Miss Baxter?" he asked tenderly. "Can you tell us what occurred?"

"She didn't feel good," Maddie said softly. She blinked several times before saying, "We went to bed, but I woke up later when she called my name. She wanted her bag so she could write a note. I got scared and started to cry, but she told me everything would be all right. That nothing bad would happen." Tears trickled down Maddie's cheeks. "Then in the morning when she didn't wake up, someone came and told me she was dead and they would dig a grave." She buried her face into Charlie's neck and he rocked her back and forth.

Poor child. Nell reached up and rubbed Maddie's back.

"I'm sorry, Brenna," Charlie said, his voice low. "Your aunt wanted to make the trip. She wanted to settle here in Logan Meadows with you. Actually, she wanted me and you to get marr—" Charlie quickly closed his mouth.

Brenna's hand fluttered to her chest.

Charlie looked uncomfortable and cleared his throat. "Things have a way of working themselves out."

When Brenna swayed, Mr. Hutton folded her hand into the crook of his arm. Her ashen face was rife with grief. "Since her things arrived on the stage, I've wondered. I sent a letter to the postmaster in Wilsonville trying to learn why she was coming here and what her connection was to Maddie." She gave a small sob. "I'm sorry she passed on by herself."

"I was with her," Maddie said softly, still nestled next to Charlie's neck. "Holding tight to her hand."

Brenna tried to smile, but her face crumbled. She turned into Mr. Hutton's arms. "Thank you, Maddie," she said between gulps of air. "Thank you for being with her as she passed."

Charlie looked adoringly into Maddie's face. "Can you wait a little longer for me? I need to find a place for us to live before I can take you home."

Brenna sniffed, then used the hankie Mr. Hutton fished from his pocket. "Take as long as you like," Brenna said. "Maddie is always welcome here."

Charlie nodded. "Thank you." Nell thought she saw a shadow of something pass over his eyes.

"But, Pa . . ."

"I know, I know, sweetheart. I'm just as anxious as you are, but some things have to get worked out." He glanced at Nell, a smile tugging at his lips, before he kissed Maddie on the forehead. "And I'll be by to visit as much as I can. Brenna, I've intended from the start to compensate you for your generosity. We'll take care of that later today as well."

"No, I couldn't—"

"You will and I don't want to hear another word." He dug in his pocket for the bag of peppermints. He put it in Maddie's hand, kissed her cheek, and set her on the ground. "There's enough to go around." The children crowded in excitedly.

"Nell and I have some unfinished business to take care of," he said. "I had no idea she'd follow me into town."

"You angry?" Nell asked, understanding now that the premonition that had moved her from the box canyon and the others before wasn't a warning of impending danger, not in the way the stranger had been. Instead it was a message of love, a major change for her life—all for the good. Marrying Charlie and having a daughter of her own.

The twinkle in his eye made Nell's breath catch. "What do you think?"

If Grover Galante showed up now, or had already shown up, at least Charlie knew how he'd been found. The thought of the confrontation that was sure to come was just as troubling as it had been the day he left Wilsonville. Brenna's letters to the postmaster asking about Miss Baxter had been an easy tell. Anyone would put two and two together. Charlie walked toward his horse, Nell's hand in his own. "We need to talk. There's more to this story."

He gathered his reins and looked back to the porch where everyone crowded around his daughter. "Maddie," he called. "I'll be back in about an hour and we'll take a walk into town."

Her face brightened. "All right, Pa."

Charlie gestured to Gabe's horse.

"Yeah, he was the freshest mount left, since you took off with the packhorse. I came straight here, thinking you were coming to see Brenna."

They turned toward town and started down Oak Street, leading the horses. "Brenna?"

"All the signs pointed to her. And if she was the one for you, I wasn't going to stand in the way. Not with Brenna being such a kind soul. I was happy for her."

"Happy?"

"As happy as I could be for the woman who was going to marry the man I loved."

Warmth squeezed his heart. "Is that true? Do you love me, Nell?"

She nodded. "You know I do."

He stopped and ran his thumb down her cheek, surprised so much had been going on in her head that he didn't know about. His happiness evaporated. He still had a heck of a lot of trouble dogging him. Nell just might not want to be involved. "I have a lot more to tell you, Nell," he said, looking deep into her eyes. "After-wards I'm going to ask you something very important. Seems God plunked me down in the exact spot I needed to be. I'm not going to look a gift horse in the mouth."

"Do you have to wait to ask me, Charlie? What if I know my answer already?"

Darn, she made him feel good. Like the luckiest man in the world. "Yes, there's a lot to consider. But first I need to know if you could love Maddie as your own. Being blind, she can't do what most children can. Caring for her will be harder, more time con-suming."

Surprise washed over her face. "Of *course* I can love Maddie—I already do."

At her words, he gave her another quick kiss. By then they'd walked to the livery. "Let's see if Win has some hay for these hun-gry horses while we get a bite to eat ourselves. I don't think I can go a step farther without some food. But I don't want to go to your friend's restaurant. Someplace out of the way where we won't be interrupted."

Ten minutes later, on the quiet side of town, Charlie and Nell took a table along the wall at Nana's Place, thankful the room was nearly empty. They ordered and were waiting on their meal as Charlie filled Nell in with the details of his arrival in Logan Meadows. He couldn't imagine what she thought at this point. He hoped she'd still have him. He couldn't envision his life now with-out her.

"So this man, Galante, may show up here. Then again, he may not. Is that right?"

"That's as much as I know. But when you told me about the stranger who appeared at the ranch the week before I arrived, I got worried. Also the man on the bluff. But if that's the case, I don't know why he hasn't already made his move."

"You can't live your life in fear."

"I know. I finally came to that conclusion. I couldn't go another day without Maddie, either. I miss her something fierce."

"I could see that. Seemed the feeling was mutual." An old woman approached with two plates of food. She placed them on the table and hurried away.

Nell cut her meat and took a bite of her steak, chewed, and swallowed. "Do you want me to call you Tristan Axelrose or Charlie Rose?" Her mouth curled up when she said his given name, setting off a flush of warmth inside. "Because I like 'em both."

"Until I'm sure about Galante, I think it would be wise to stick with Charlie Rose. I took the name to make Galante's finding me more difficult. If I knew for certain he wasn't looking, I'd go back to my real name."

She nodded, as if that made perfect sense. "So, is that the gist of everything? Anything else I need to know besides your secret daughter and the vengeful father who may be on your trail? If yes, I'm waiting on that very important question you said you were going to ask me."

To appease the ache in his stomach, he scooped in several mouthfuls of creamy potatoes slathered in gravy, swallowed, then wiped his mouth with his napkin, worried what she'd say to the fact that he intended to live in or close to town. "There's one more thing, Nell. Something I can't imagine you'll agree to. It's a pretty large hurdle—"

"What, Charlie?" Her gaze lingered on his. Her tone was a bit impatient. "It won't get solved with you sitting over there keeping it to yourself."

How would she react to his decision? What did she love more, him or the ranch? She'd said plainly that . . .

"You know I'm not getting any younger, Charlie."

When he chuckled her eyes narrowed. "You're twenty, Nell. Your life has practically just begun."

"Twenty-one," she corrected. "Well, I will be next month." Hunger winning out over her persistence, she took another bite of her meat and chewed vigorously. She swallowed and said, "Is that what this is all about? Our age difference? Because if that's what's bothering you, I have to say, you may be older but you don't act it."

He reached over and covered her hand. If he knew Nell at all, this would be the deal breaker. His concern wasn't so much about age anymore. It was more that Nell was a rancher and she loved the place she'd built with her brother and Ben. He had no idea how she'd respond to moving into town, leaving her memories and Ben's grave down on the riverbank.

Unexpectedly, Nell flipped the hand he'd been covering to the top of his and gripped it with a vengeance. She squeezed so hard he almost pulled his back. What was she doing?

"Charlie," she wheezed out. "That's him. The stranger at the ranch. He just came through the door."

CHAPTER FORTY-SEVEN

$\mathcal{C}$harlie sat back and disengaged his hand from Nell's. He mentally checked off in his mind that his gun was loaded and in the holster around his hips. That Nell would be in the line of fire if a gunfight broke out. That this could be one of the last breaths he ever took.

Watching Nell's eyes, Charlie could tell exactly where his adversary went. The scrape of a chair against a wooden floorboard in front of the window by the door. Charlie started to turn, to see if it was Galante, but Nell held up a palm.

"Wait," she murmured under her breath. "Someone else just came in. He's looking around. He's joining the bad fellow."

"The bad fellow?"

"He is, Charlie. I felt it at the ranch—I can feel it now." She picked up her water glass with a noticeable tremble.

Charlie leaned forward. "I want you to get up and walk out, Nell. If it's Galante, or someone he's sent, as soon as he sees me, this could go bad. Or maybe he already knows I'm here."

"No. I won't leave you."

"How is everything tasting?" The old woman appeared out of nowhere. "Would you like more gravy, young man?"

"No, thank you," he gritted out. "Just the bill."

Her brows raised in question and she turned and hurried off.

"Nell, stop this foolishness and do what I ask."

Her eyes popped open at his order.

"Get up and walk out now. If anything happens to me—"

"The whole town will take care of Maddie, if that's what you're thinking." Nell's mouth was set in a hard line and her flinty eyes said she didn't appreciate him bossing her around. "Nothin's happening to you because I'm *not* leaving without you."

Charlie pulled a dollar coin out of his pocket and put the money on the table. He turned in his seat and looked over his shoulder fully expecting to see Galante, but both fellows' backs were to him. He stood and looked down at the table. He really hated to leave such a good meal. All those days in the high country had him almost weak with hunger. He glanced at Nell. She stood and he put his hand on her back to escort her out. Just as he reached for the doorknob intuition told him he wasn't going to make it out the door.

"Mister," one of the men called. "You know the time?"

Charlie opened the door and pushed Nell out, then turned to address the question, knowing full well it just might have been a trick to stop him.

Confusion descended. One man was the fellow in the bank who'd been talking with Frank Lloyd. Wasn't he some fancy lawyer? The other man wasn't Galante, either—far from it. He'd seen those black eyes today staring back at him from the wanted poster in Sheriff Preston's office. Tandy Smith, outlaw and murderer, was the man who'd been out at the ranch, interested in Nell.

Charlie drew his gun. "Tandy Smith!" he shouted. "Put up your hands so I can take you in. If you go for your gun, I'll shoot you dead!"

As if in slow motion, the outlaw spun in his chair as he reached for his gun. Charlie pulled his trigger, but not before Smith, the slick outlaw that he was, got a shot off himself. Searing heat almost knocked Charlie's weapon from his hand, but not quite. Smith's eyes went wide when Charlie's bullet sunk deep. He tilted and fell, gripping his chest.

"Don't do it," Charlie warned when indecision flashed in the other man's eyes. Outside the window Charlie recognized the man's fancy palomino tied to the hitching post. Ignoring the blood he felt seeping through the sleeve of his shirt, Charlie went over and kicked away Smith's gun. He pulled the lawyer's from his holster and stuck the heavy weapon in his belt. "Go get the sheriff," Charlie said over his shoulder to whoever might be watching. He dared not take his eyes off the men.

Running footsteps sounded outside. Sheriff Preston, Thom, and then Nell came cautiously through the door, guns drawn and ready.

Albert locked the cell door as Nell looked on, then joined the group over by the coffeepot. Her insides trembled at the thought of almost losing Charlie in the stunning turn of events. One moment they were eating, the next, he was gunning for his life. When she reached out and softly touched him, he looked down at her and smiled. Placing his good arm around her shoulder, he pulled her close. The graze he'd taken to his other had stopped bleeding, leaving a round bloodstain on his sleeve.

"That was sure something," Thom said. "The town's first shootout since I've been deputy, and I missed it. Must be my Irish luck—or lack of it."

Albert tossed the cell keys onto his desk. "The fewer people involved, the better. Thank God you know how to handle a gun, Charlie."

"And that you came in today and saw the new posters," Thom added. "I hate to think about what those two had planned. A lot of innocent townsfolk could've been killed." He shook his head in dismay.

Frank Lloyd strode through the open door. "I can tell you what they were cooking up," he said. He acknowledged Nell with a courteous nod and Charlie pulled her closer. "Well, at least I think

I've put the puzzle together." He nodded to the cell where the outlaw's partner stood with his back to them, staring past the bars on the window. "Mr. Simpson is a lawyer, all right, but his interest in the Cotton Ranch was only to distract me. A ploy to get into my office and case the place. Gain my trust."

Charlie grunted. "He even had his partner, Tandy Smith, out on the ranch leaving tracks to corroborate his story, just in case talk got around."

And spying on me, Nell thought with an inner shiver. Charlie had told her fifteen minutes before about the conversation he'd heard in the bank about her ranch between the man in the cell and the bank owner.

Lloyd nodded. "Yes. We had another appointment this evening. Said the only time he was available was after hours at nine tonight. I'm thinking he planned to show up, along with Tandy Smith. Rob the bank and then be out of town with no one the wiser until the morning."

Thom pointed out the window at the buckboard rolling by. "Well, Smith won't be robbing any more banks—killing any more people—or bank owners." He gave Frank a knowing look. "He has a date with the undertaker."

"What's next, Sheriff?" Nell asked. She had unfinished business with Charlie she wasn't going to let him forget.

"Nothing, really. Paperwork. First thing tomorrow I'll wire Kansas City about the reward. Shouldn't take long to get a reply."

She blinked in surprise. "There's a reward?"

"Quite sizeable, being Tandy Smith was a murdering son-of-a-jackass besides a bank robber," Thom said with a smile. "Eight hundred dollars, to be exact."

Nell gasped. Eight hundred dollars! Charlie would be a rich man. Would that change his feelings for her?

Charlie looked over at the pendulum clock hanging on the wall. "I have a date with Maddie and I don't want to be late."

"Maddie?" Sheriff Preston asked. "The blind child?"

"There's more to my story, Sheriff. But I don't have time to tell it right now. Say, in an hour or two?"

Disappointment squeezed Nell's stomach.

"And Nell and I still have some talking that needs doing." He kissed her on the lips, drawing sounds of surprise from all three men. "Didn't think I'd forgotten, did ya . . . darlin'?"

She just looked at him.

"Nell?"

"I did, Charlie."

"See how little you know me." He took her hand and pulled her out onto the boardwalk.

Nell couldn't contain her excitement and went up on tiptoe. "The answer is yes."

He chuckled. "You're jumping the gun again. Seriously, this is something you're going to want to think about, I'm sure."

Positive he was drawing this out just to torture her, she pulled free from him and planted her hands on her hips. "I'm waiting."

He removed his hat, rolling the brim in his hands. This was the first time she could remember seeing him nervous. Even when they'd danced in the kitchen, he'd been more composed than he was now.

"Because Maddie's blind, she can't live way out on the ranch. If something happened, it would take too long to get into town for the doctor."

Nell swallowed. His reasoning made sense.

"Besides," he went on, looking deep into her eyes. "She needs to be close to town where she can go to school, or where I can have a tutor for her. I have a woman who's agreed to come out and teach her, but she insists on living in a town, or close. Do you understand what I'm trying to say, Nell? If you marry me, your whole life will change. You'll have to leave the ranch."

Happiness swirled within. Nothing was going to stop her from marrying the man she loved. "I understand," she whispered.

"Well?" His soulful question made him look like a little boy. "What about Seth?"

She put her arms around his middle and laid her head against his chest, not caring who might be watching. "All I know is I love you, Charlie. I'll live anywhere I have to. There's no question about that."

When she looked up into his face, Charlie's lips found hers and chased away every question in her mind. Tentative at first, the kiss seemed to ask sweetly for her heart, sending tingles racing everywhere through her body. Then the kiss changed. Now it promised her days, years, a lifetime of love. His strong arms held her closer as she ran her own hands up his chest, looping them around his neck.

"I love you, Nell, God knows I do."

She wanted the kiss to go on and on, but she pulled away and smiled up into Charlie's face. "I just happen to know about a really nice piece of property coming on the market," she whispered against his mouth.

"The Donovan farm?"

She nodded. "I can work the horses for the army from anywhere, and it's only a short walk from town. I'd say the place is perfect."

His eyes twinkled with happiness. "I was thinking the exact same thing. Let's go tell Maddie."

CHAPTER FORTY-EIGHT

*F*ive hours later a bathed and shaved Charlie, looking more handsome than ever, sat by Nell's side on the veranda of the Red Rooster Inn with Maddie on his lap. They watched Brenna and her children, along with Mr. Hutton, walking up the lane. The sheriff, who was going to marry them, was inside with Thom and Hannah, helping Mrs. Hollyhock set up the place for an impromptu party. Nell had tried to lend a hand but they were having none of it.

"If you want to wait, make plans, and have a proper wedding in the church, there's still time to call this off," Charlie said. "I didn't mean to rush you."

Mrs. Hollyhock had lent them separate rooms to get ready. The bath had been luxurious, and Nell soaked until the water was cold. After washing her hair Mrs. Hollyhock had insisted on brushing out her locks while she sat in a chair. She felt like a pampered princess. The moment Brenna had heard that the wedding would be today, at the Inn, she'd sent Penny over with a beautiful white blouse adorned with yellow ribbons. The garment was the frilliest item Nell had ever worn. She was ready. "Wait and plan a wedding? Is that what you want?"

He shook his head.

"Me, neither. You should know by now I'm not one for fancy stuff, Charlie. The simpler the better."

He pulled her close and Maddie giggled. "I'm not sure if I quite believe that," Charlie said. "You looked awfully pretty the other night in your soft white blouse and blue skirt."

Nell's face prickled with heat and she chose to ignore his comment. "Seth should be here anytime." She anxiously searched past the gathering folks. "It was nice of Win to ride out and get him. I hope he caught him before Seth headed up to the corral."

Charlie picked up her hand and brushed a kiss across her knuckles. "Don't you worry. We won't start a thing until he arrives. I know how close the two of you are. Besides, you have a pretty little girl to stand up with you," he added, gesturing to Maddie. "I need a best man."

"I wonder what he'll think when Win tells him. It's sort of out of the blue."

"You may be surprised."

Nell shook her head, the mass of curly blond hair moving with her. "No, you're wrong. He'll be shocked."

Charlie held out his hand. "Two bits says he's not."

Tension mounted in her tummy with each moment that passed. If she only knew how Seth would react, then she could relax. "You're on."

Charlie stood and set Maddie back in the chair when Brenna and the rest reached the porch and started up the steps. Nell also stood.

Brenna marched right over and gave Nell a long hug. "I'm still so surprised," Brenna whispered into her ear. "Delighted beyond measure."

For one moment, Brenna's gaze darted to Maddie and Nell felt her pain. "I'm sorry you're losing her, Brenna."

"You shush. It's right and fitting for Maddie to be back with her pa. I couldn't be happier if I tried. And now she'll even have a mother of her very own to shower her with love. And Gregory, after spending some time with Maddie and seeing how smart she is, wants her to stay in school. He's actually going to order a book of Braille and see if he can figure out a way to help her there. I'm not saying she won't need that tutor Charlie is considering, but it sure can't hurt. I'm so happy I think I could just float away." She laughed and hugged Nell again. "It's the perfect ending to this story."

Penny stepped around her mother and set the gray kitten in Maddie's lap. "For you, Maddie. We all want you to have Skippy." The kitten gave a loud meow.

Maddie beamed. "To come to the new ranch with me?" Maddie reached out and her fingers found Nell's hand. "Can I keep her, Ma? Can Skippy come to our new home?"

Nell blinked back a surge of emotion. The love swimming in Charlie's eyes almost had her in tears. "Yes, sweetheart. The kitty can come with us."

With the happy laughter and everyone talking, Nell missed the hoofbeats galloping up the road until Seth was right in front. He slid to a stop and dismounted, tossing his leather reins over the hitching rail. He made short order of meeting Nell on the veranda. His face, lined with worry, made her stomach drop.

"What's this I hear? You're getting married today?" He had a bottle of wine stuck under his arm, a yellow bandanna around his neck, and wore his best shirt.

Nell had wanted to speak to him in private, but now there was no help for it. "Yes." Her hands trembled. "Charlie and I are in love."

Seth whipped his hat off and waved it around. "Halleluiah!" he sang out at the top of his voice.

Nell couldn't believe her ears. "What're you saying, Seth?"

Charlie laughed and stuck out his hand to her. "Pay up."

Seth winked at Charlie, then broke into a face-splitting grin while stifling his cough behind his hand. "I don't move just any-one into the house on a whim, or miss a town picnic," he said. He leaned in close and whispered just loud enough for the both of them to hear. "Or stay out all night. Or send Nell off to camp under the stars."

Charlie chortled and slapped him on the back. "I knew I liked you for a reason."

"You mean when you went over to the Logans'?" Nell struggled with her brother's statement. Was there no end to today's surprises?

"You just thought I was going over to the Logans', little sister. I was in New Meringue, where I go often. I don't want my sweetheart to find a new fella."

"What?" Nell swayed.

Charlie gripped her by her shoulders. "Steady now, darlin'."

"How come you never told me?"

"Don't know. Shy, I guess."

Nell knew his reasons were more than that. More like he didn't want her to feel like a third wheel. Like she was holding him back. Didn't want to move another woman into the house and usurp her position. Her heart surged with love and she threw her arms around Seth and hugged him.

"Hold on, I don't want you to bust this bottle of wine I brought to toast with." Fumbling, he handed the wine to Charlie.

Mr. Hutton, who'd been silent until now, stepped forward. "May I see that?" He took the bottle from Charlie and read the label. He looked up, surprised. "This is a *very* nice bottle of French wine. I know several restaurants back in Pennsylvania that sell this exact year for a good seven or eight dollars a bottle. Is there more where it came from?"

CHAPTER FORTY-NINE

A month later, Charlie sat in the saddle in his tan, oil-rubbed rain gear and gloved hands, waiting for Nell and Seth to arrive with the first group of horses for their ranch. With his arms crossed over his chest, he surveyed their new spread. He liked the picture it created under the billowy dark clouds that tumbled across the sky. A small flock of birds brave enough to dare the weather were tossed around by the west winds.

"I wish you could see her, Annie," he said as he followed the path of the birds. A glimmer of sunlight popped out from behind a bank of clouds, transforming the light patter of raindrops into diamonds. "Maddie's happy. *Really* happy. And Nell loves her so much. As if she were her very own." Emotion filled his throat but he swallowed it down. He shook his head in disbelief. "Life's strange, Annie, and that's no lie. I never expected to love someone so much again."

Charlie brushed at the wetness on his cheek that wasn't created by the rain. As if in answer to his heart, far off in the distance he spotted a double rainbow arching the expanse of sky. He nodded, then smiled.

It had taken a lot of work to get the old Donovan place up to Nell's liking before she'd bring any horses over from her old ranch. He'd hired Win and a new fellow in town, to help with the construction of two sturdy round pens and several more corrals. Four stalls were added to the already large barn. The fields still had to be prepared for next season to seed with hay, but he'd do that this coming month.

With his chores completed and Maddie dropped off at school, he waited impatiently. Every now and then a thought about Galante and the man's unrelenting vengeance crossed his mind but he wouldn't let it destroy his happiness. Come what may, he had to live his life to the fullest, one day at a time.

He liked the way their new home had turned out so far. A few chores remained to be done inside to make the place safe for Maddie, but the majority of the work was completed. He'd added additional slats to the front porch rails so she couldn't fall through, put up double handrails on both sides of the hallway steps that led to her bedroom, and added a twist lock on the cellar door out of her reach. They didn't want her to accidently open it and fall down the steep flight of steps. With two ropes strung tight, one to the outhouse and another to the barn, Maddie could find her way.

They had few furnishings yet, but Nell insisted on hanging her quilt on the large living room wall as the focal point for everyone to enjoy. Next month, as a surprise, he planned to rig up some kind of bathing room.

Nell's voice drew him out of his musings. She came down the trail leading a line of eight horses. She also wore her slicker and had her hat pulled down low. Dog trotted ahead, wagging his tail. The livestock walked along nicely, having had a handful of miles to work out their rambunctiousness. They looked good. Five were from the mustang herd, but three were the colts he'd collected with Nell and Seth when he'd first come to the ranch. He recognized Sitting Bull, Cochise, and Geronimo. A burst of gratefulness for how things had turned out filled his soul. Yes, indeed. They were going to have their work cut out for them.

Seth came behind Nell, leading another eight head. Riding at his side was a woman who must be Ivy. She was smiling from ear to ear as Seth's mouth moved quickly. Nell's main concern had been leaving her brother alone at the ranch. Now with Seth's not-so-new sweetheart and the supply of wine giving him the means to hire help, that worry had grown wings and taken flight. Mr. Hutton had promised to help Seth market the cases of wine in the cellar to some of the better restaurants in Wyoming, Montana, and even San Francisco.

Eager for a kiss, Charlie galloped forward, splashing through puddles created from last night's storm. Nell's string of geldings skittered around and pulled at the lead when he got close.

"Hey, cowboy," she called. "You should know better than to spook my horses." Some geldings had stopped completely. Others snorted and kicked out.

Sliding to a stop at her side, he gathered her into his arms. "I do know better," he said against her cheek. "But I'm hankering for a kiss. You've cast some sort of love spell over me. Last night was our first night apart and I didn't like it one bit."

It was true, he thought, kissing her. He couldn't get enough. She laughed, kissed him back, and sounded happier then he'd ever heard her. "I love you so much, Nell," he said, as if she didn't already know that. "I missed you."

They drew apart and he waved to Seth, who was a good thirty feet away. He swung Georgia around to ride along with Nell. "I've been thinking."

"Uh-oh. What now? You and that hammer of yours have had a mighty good workout of late. I can't imagine what could be next."

With his outside leg, he pushed Georgia closer to Coyote, drawing a sideward glance from the gelding. Charlie reached out and placed his hand on Nell's thigh. "Not about building. About Georgia."

Nell looked over to his horse, a small, contented smile playing around her lips. "You want to breed her to Drag Anchor. I agree. They'd make a really pretty baby."

"You're right about that, but no. My idea has to do with what you told me about her from your ability to know what the horses are feeling. It's been eating away at me."

She cut her gaze to him. "Eating away at you? Why?"

He rubbed her thigh and their knees banged together as they rode down the road. "Nothing bad. More to the lines that I don't want Georgia to miss that girl who raised her anymore. We have enough horses now. If she's longing for her, I want to send her back."

Nell's brow arched up. "With all due respect, husband, I think she'd make a better-than-fine broodmare. Her conformation is perfect, she's kind and—"

Surprised, he just looked at her.

Laughing, she covered his hand with her gloved one. The twinkle in her eye told him he'd been had.

"I'm just kidding you, Charlie, I think that's an awfully sweet thing to do."

Charlie shifted in the saddle. "I don't know about sweet, but right, maybe. I'd just feel better." He reached down and pulled affectionately on Georgia's mane as they walked along. "Oh, I checked the mail after dropping Maddie at school. We didn't have any letters, but someone had stuck this in our mail slot. Maude was pretty surprised when she found it. Said it must be that secret do-gooder. Said she hadn't seen anything yesterday when she was putting the mail away."

He pulled his slicker back just far enough that she could see something white in his pocket. "I don't want to take it out and get it dirty, but it's a dishcloth stitched with two red hearts." When Nell broke out into a smile, he said, "I thought you'd like it."

"How sweet. I wonder who the softie is? I sure would like to know." She rode through the opening of the first large corral and Charlie swung the gate closed.

From Coyote's back, Nell began releasing the horses one by one. Eager to be free, each horse trotted off through the puddles, sniffing their way around their new enclosure. When Seth arrived Charlie reopened the gate for him and his bright-eyed string.

Finished, Nell approached the gate and waited for Charlie to let her out. "I'm excited for Maddie to see the horses." She pulled her wrapper more securely around her to keep the rain off. "Well, you know what I mean. That's the only thing she's been able to talk about since we bought the place. Won't be long before it's time to ride into Logan Meadows and pick her up."

Charlie greeted Seth's girl when she stopped next to him. "You must be Ivy. I'm Charlie. I'm pleased to make your acquaintance."

Her face pinked up and Charlie liked her instantly. She had long brown hair tied back at the nape of her neck and wore one of Seth's old, bent cowboy hats. She was slender and, by the length of her legs visible when the wind blew back her slicker, must be almost as tall as Seth. From the way Nell talked, he wouldn't be surprised if another wedding was already in the makings.

"I'm pleased to meet you," she said to him, but she winked at Nell.

Charlie felt a tad self-conscious. He wondered what they'd talked about last night. "And I like your new place. Especially your guard cat." She pointed to Maddie's kitten asleep on the front porch on a cushioned chair. The kitten didn't seem to notice the blustery weather.

Charlie nodded. "Every ranch needs a cat."

When Seth finished with his horses, Charlie let him out the gate and fastened the latch. "It's quite wet out here. Can I offer anyone a cup of coffee? Won't take but a minute to brew."

Seth pulled his hat down on his forehead. "No, thanks, Charlie. I'm taking Ivy into town for a meal at the Silky Hen. She's yet to eat there."

"Charlie hasn't been there yet, either," Nell said. "Why don't we all go together."

The wind tugged at their slickers as Charlie said, "That's a darn fine idea. And we'll just be finishing up when school lets out.

I wouldn't be surprised if the place is packed, this weather having run everyone inside."

Nell smiled, her face blossoming into a beautiful sight. "Let's go. I'm sure there's a table for us." She turned and squeezed Coyote into a lope, and the others followed.

Charlie had been right—again—Nell thought as they pressed into the doorway of the Silky Hen, scanning the room for an open table. The floor was messy from customers tracking in mud. Hats and slickers cluttered the rack by the door and a clamor of voices mingled with the clink of utensils against porcelain plates. The air was warm and heavy with the aroma of coffee, and a sweet scent from syrup served over flapjacks mingled with the savory smell of bacon. Seemed breakfast in the afternoon was a popular notion.

Roberta Brown, Hannah's mother, approached them, carrying menus. "Nell, Seth, it's so good to see you," she said. "It's been quite some time." She turned and gave Charlie a good once-over. "And you must be Mr. Rose, the man who risked his life to stop the bank from being robbed. I'd like to say thank you. You may have saved my brother's life. I'm indebted to you."

Nell almost laughed at Charlie's expression. "Mr. Lloyd is Mrs. Brown's brother," she whispered.

"You're welcome, ma'am," Charlie said. "Any man would've done the same."

Roberta shook her head. "Well, I'm not so sure about that."

"This is Miss Ivy Lake." Seth gestured to his girl.

"I'm pleased to meet you, as well, dear." Roberta smiled kindly at Ivy, who nodded. "Please follow me. I have a nice table over here by the kitchen door, out of the draft. Come in and get warm. I hear Beth Fairington at the mercantile has come down with the measles. We don't want you to catch a chill and be susceptible." She led them through the room and placed their menus in the center of a round table large enough for the four of them. "Since there's not room on the coat rack, just give me your slickers and I'll put them in the back room until you're ready to leave."

Just as Roberta hustled away with their coats, Susanna came through the kitchen door. "Well, hello. I'll be right with you all," she offered as she passed by their table. "Would you all like coffee?" she asked over her shoulder.

"Yes," Nell called.

Charlie pulled Nell's chair out, the gesture making her smile. It was a little embarrassing, but it made her feel cherished and loved. As she sat, he scooted her chair closer to the table.

Seth picked up the menus and passed them around. "What does everyone feel like eating?"

"Anything hot," Ivy said, rubbing her hands together. "I'm hungry and a little cold after that long ride from the Cotton Ranch."

Seth smiled and covered her hands with his own. When he started to cough, he withdrew his kerchief and covered his mouth. "Before you say anything, Nell—I'm much better. But just to shut you up, I plan to see Doc Thorn next week."

"Thank heavens for that," Ivy said, gazing into Seth's eyes. "I've been pestering him for months."

Suzanna appeared and poured coffee all around. "Do you know what you'd like?"

Charlie looked to Nell, who said, "I'll have the fried chicken, please."

Ivy nodded. "Same for me."

Seth pointed to the menu. "I'll have beef stew."

Charlie chuckled. "Same. What's that say for the differences between men and women, I wonder?"

"I'll put your order in and be right back with some bread and butter." Susanna stuck her pencil behind her ear and hurried away.

Forty-five minutes later, Susanna cleared away their dirty plates. Nell didn't think she'd had a finer meal in the last year.

"Did you ladies leave any room for dessert?" Seth asked, looking more robust to Nell than he had since before his last trip to the army. Seemed everything was going their way.

"Tristan Axelrose," a deep voice called out.

Nell's cup clattered to the saucer, spilling coffee across the royal-blue tablecloth.

CHAPTER FIFTY

A man stood in the lobby between the restaurant and the El Dorado Hotel. He was older and dressed like a cowboy. His large silver spurs looked as deadly as his cold, gray eyes. A deep pain pierced Nell's heart.

"Charlie," she whispered, feeling completely naked without her Colt 45. She'd left it in her saddlebag under this new false security called happiness. *How could I be so stupid?* Thank God Charlie was wearing his.

The man took a step toward them.

A hush fell over the room, so still Nell heard her blood swishing in her ears. When Charlie started to stand, Nell grasped him by his arm and struggled to keep him in his chair. When he glanced at her, a lifetime of living passed from his heart to hers.

"No! I won't let you go," she cried under her breath, still clinging to his arm. "He won't shoot you in here, it would be murder in cold blood." She glanced around the tables, hoping to see Albert or Thom or someone who could help them. She knew Seth would, but something in this man's eyes said he could take the two of them as easy as pulling trout from the stream.

"Galante." Charlie shook Nell off and stood. "I wondered if you'd ever show up. What took you so long?" Somewhere a baby started crying and his mama worked to quiet him. "Let's take this outside. It's nobody's business but mine."

The man nodded.

"Charlie!"

"Seth, you keep Nell in here."

"You sure you don't want some backup?" Seth asked quickly, worry lining his face. "I'm more than willing."

The corner of Charlie's lips pulled up. "No. I'd feel better knowing I have you to watch over her—and Maddie."

Without a backward glance Charlie walked out onto the boardwalk and into the rain.

When Nell bolted from her chair, Seth rose and gripped her around the middle, hoisting her back, avoiding her wildly kicking feet. "Let me go!" she screeched. "I need to help Charlie! That man is a killer!"

"Charlie wants you to stay here. Have faith in him. Don't count him out just yet."

Nell tried to jerk away but Seth's grip was too strong.

Sick with fear she clenched her eyes closed and did the only thing she was able. *God? God! Are you there? Help Charlie. He's the best man I know. I love him. Just*—She didn't know what else to pray. Too much time had passed. She expected to hear gunshots any second.

Instead, the door opened and Charlie stepped in. Seth relaxed his arms and Nell bolted through the room and launched herself into his arms. A miracle? There'd been no gunshots. When she felt Seth and Ivy behind her, she loosened her grip on her husband and stepped away.

Charlie just stood there.

"So? What happened?"

"Galante's gone." He let go a long sigh, then a smile broke out on his face. "I didn't see that coming at all. Seems Dan Galante is alive but will be in a wheelchair for the rest of his life. Galante acknowledged his son had taken the wrong path a few years back but at the time of the shooting he couldn't admit that ugly fact to himself. Seems because of the time the boy had to think while recuperating, he's turned his life around. His pa thanked me for not killing him. Said a lesser man would've. I don't know if I believe that. Anyway, he swears if I hadn't put him in the chair, he'd be dead by now." Charlie looked from face to face. "And that's all."

Joy surged inside Nell. "He's gone for good?"

Charlie nodded, then cupped Nell's cheek with his warm palm and gazed into her eyes. "Yes, darlin', it's over. Finally over. He came all this way to right his wrong. Didn't want me looking over my shoulder every day of my life."

Charlie gave her a quick kiss and brushed her hair out of her face with a gentle touch. "Now I say we pay our bill and get moving. School's out and I don't want to keep Maddie waiting a single moment. It's time to take our daughter home."

ACKNOWLEDGMENTS

*S*pecial thanks goes to Maria Gomez and the whole Montlake crew for believing in Logan Meadows and the men and women who reside there.

To Caitlin Alexander for making this story shine! I'm amazed at your insight, knowledge, and skill. You make it all seem so easy.

To two renowned horse-trainer friends, Al Dunning and Mike Kevil, for your professional advice on how to round up a herd of mustangs in the mountains. Your suggestions and stories kept me smiling all day.

To Lauren Wingate, animal communicator, for sharing with me your understanding and knowledge of our four-legged friends. If only all of us could do what you do!

To my two critique partners, Leslie Lynch and Sandy Loyd, for going the extra mile.

To my family, Michael, Matthew, Adam, and Misti, for being my rocks. I love you all so much!

To my sisters, Sherry, Shelly, Jenny, Mary, and Lauren, for your help and encouragement. My life is rich because of you.

To my lovely readers, who make what I do possible. I appreciate each and every one of you. Thank you from the bottom of my heart!

And mostly to our awesome God for His many blessings and for giving me the opportunity to do what I love each and every day.

ABOUT THE AUTHOR

Photo by The Family Gallery, 2007

USA Today bestselling author Caroline Fyffe was born in Waco, Texas, the first of many towns she would call home during her father's career with the US Air Force. A horse aficionado from an early age, she earned a bachelor of arts in communications from California State University, Chico, before launching what would become a twenty-year career as an equine photographer. She began writing fiction to pass the time during long days in the show arena, channeling her love of horses and the Old West into a series of Western historicals. Her debut novel, *Where the Wind Blows*, won the Romance Writers of America's prestigious Golden Heart award as well as the Wisconsin RWA's Write Touch Readers' Award. She and her husband have two grown sons and live in the Pacific Northwest. To learn about upcoming novels, visit her website at www.carolinefyffe.com.